**John Michael Doyle (BA Hons. IEng, MIED)**

The author was born in Beaufort Co. Kerry, the son of an Irish father and English mother and lived there until moving to England at the age of 17.
He worked in the engineering industry, mainly in aerospace, and served three years in the British Army.
In 1988, the author graduated from the Open University with a Bachelor of Arts degree and achieved BA (Honours) three years later. He then joined the staff of The Institution of Engineering Designers with responsibility for Continuing Professional Development.

**Published Work:**

**The Last Coachman (2010)**
*Olympia Publishers*
ISBN: 9781848970885

# THIS BITTER LAND

# THIS BITTER LAND

# John Michael Doyle

# THIS BITTER LAND

Olympia Publishers
*London*

A CIP catalogue record for this title is
available from the British Library.

ISBN: 978-1-84897-173-8

This is a work of fiction.
Names, characters, places and incidents originate from the writer's
imagination. Any resemblance to actual persons, living or dead, is purely
coincidental.

First Published in 2011

Olympia Publishers
60 Cannon Street
London
EC4N 6NP

Printed in Great Britain

*I had this thought a while ago, 'My darling cannot understand What I have done, or what would do In this blind bitter land.'*

**(William Butler Yeats: 'Words' from the Green Helmet and other Poems.)**

For Katie *iníon agus cara*

# Preface

*The Last Coachman (Published June 2010 by Olympia Publishers)* tells the story of Michael Quinlan, a coachman at a large estate in Ireland in the early twentieth century. As the First World War is underway, so the fight for an independent Ireland is gaining momentum and the prospect of armed rebellion looms ever closer. Michael's services as a coachman are no longer required and he is forced to seek alternative employment.

With his son, James, he travels to Gretna in Scotland where a gigantic munitions factory is being built to alleviate a shortage of ammunition as the war intensifies. There they inadvertently become involved with an Irish rebel plot devised by the mysterious 'Man from Dublin' to sabotage the factory in conjunction with the Easter Rising in Ireland. The rebel scheme is eventually foiled but Michael dies in tragic circumstances. Because martial law has been declared in Ireland as part of the British response to the Easter Rising his body cannot be taken home for burial, and he is interred in a pauper's grave in Carlisle.

The Man from Dublin escapes, mistakenly believing that that both Michael and James are dead leaving no witnesses to incriminate him for his part in the rebel plot.

*This Bitter Land* now takes up the story.

# Prologue

## Fron-goch, Wales 1916

From his position in the breakfast queue he could look out to the west, where beyond the tall wire fence, the rising sun touched the hills of Snowdonia. They were neither as high nor as rugged as the mountains of his native County Kerry, but they reminded him of home, a home he feared he had little hope of seeing again, at least not for a considerable time. The thought brought back the full horror of his situation, and a deep sorrow replaced the bitter anger in his heart.

He had arrived at the recently established internment camp late last night, having been transported there with a group of other prisoners from the cells at the Royal Irish Constabulary barracks in Killarney. On arrival they had been given a mug of tea, and a cheese sandwich. Under the supervision of a sergeant, and two private soldiers armed with Lee-Enfield rifles, they were marched to a stores building. There they were issued with some rough grey blankets and a mess kit comprising knife fork spoon and enamel mug. All of these items being sullenly handed to them without a word by a sleepy corporal who would obviously have preferred to be back in bed.

"Jesus Christ, we're being conscripted into the bloody British army," commented one of the new internees.

This drew an immediate sharp response from the sergeant: "No talking in the ranks!"

They were assigned bunks in a wooden hut, which already housed a dozen sleeping prisoners. There were mutters of complaint at being woken up, but little further attention was paid to the newcomers. In common with the new arrivals, they were among the hundreds of people arrested by the authorities following the suppression of the Easter Rising – the full scale armed rebellion against British rule in Ireland. Some had taken an active part in the fighting, some were known Nationalist sympathisers, but many were guilty of nothing more than being in the wrong place at the wrong time. All were victims of martial law, which had been declared by the British authorities in Ireland in the aftermath of the Rising.

In spite of being dog-tired from a long train journey to an un-named port, followed by hours on a converted troopship which had pitched and

15

rolled its way across the Irish Sea and made most of its closely confined passengers ill, he did not sleep well in this alien environment. Most of what had happened to him since his arrest was still a blur in his mind.

His only clear memory was of the tall thin man with angular features and dark moustache who had attempted to address the prisoners on the troopship. This man still wore the uniform of a commander in the Irish Volunteers and, unlike the other prisoners, was handcuffed. Even without the uniform and 'cuffs' he would have stood out in a crowd. He had attempted to raise their spirits by telling them that the fight for Irish freedom was far from over, but he was hastily removed by the guards before he could say any more. He had spoken for long enough, however, to make an impression on the new internee from County Kerry, who asked one of his companions if he knew who the man was.

"Don't tell me you don't know him," said the prisoner with a frown. "Sure isn't that De Valera himself. He was sentenced to death for treason, but the Brits must be bringing him over the water to murder him instead of doing it in Dublin where they murdered Pearse and the rest."

These words occupied his mind until he eventually managed to sleep. At six the next morning he was noisily roused by the same sergeant, and told to follow the lead of the other plainly more experienced internees. He washed in cold water but could not shave as he had not yet been issued with a razor. Somewhat refreshed he took his mess kit and joined the complaining disgruntled queue that snaked out of the cookhouse door. When his turn came he collected his breakfast of porridge, bread and tea, and found a bench at one of the bare wooden tables. He gazed morosely at his unappetising breakfast.

"To be sure it's nothing like the stirabout your Ma makes at home, but you'll get used to it soon enough. It's a case of either eat it or starve." The man sitting opposite to him spoke between alternate mouthfuls of bread and porridge. "I see you were one of the fellas that were brought in last night, what part of the old country would you be from?"

It was the first friendly voice he had heard for days, "Killarney in the County Kerry," he replied.

"Good man yourself, sure didn't a good few sound men come up from the south to give us a hand," said his dining companion in an accent that had unmistakably originated in Dublin. "And God knows we were glad to see them. Where did you do your bit, I don't remember you from the GPO?"

He looked mystified. "I don't get you," he said.

"Where did you fight in the Rising?" another man seated across the table explained.

There was silence for a minute. Then the first man said: "Ah sure you *must be one of the Volunteers that fought out there in the country. Jesus I thought all you boys escaped after Pearse surrendered." The last remark was delivered with distinct air of bitterness.*

*He had still not fully come to terms with the events of the last several days but slowly the meaning of what they were getting at seeped into his scrambled consciousness.*

*"Oh sure I had no part at all in the Rising," he said. "I was just picked up off the street with a few other fellas. Some of them were in it all right, but I wasn't."*

*"Jesus," said the first man. "I heard they were doing that, rounding up people whether they took part in the Rising or not. But sure you must have done some devilment to the Brits to get sent over here"*

*"No," he replied. "I did nothing, nothing at all."*

# Part One

## Blood and the Moon

*The purity of the unclouded moon*
*Has hung its arrowy shaft upon the floor.*
*Seven centuries have passed and it is pure,*
*The blood of innocence has left no stain,*
*There on blood-saturated ground, have stood*
*Soldier, assassin, executioner,*

**(W.B. Yeats – from 'Blood and the Moon')**

# Chapter 1

William Quinlan eased off the pressure on the line and let the salmon run. He followed it along the riverbank for some thirty yards before cautiously raising the tip of the rod to gently slow it down. Having reasserted his authority he began to reel in the fish. The battle had been going on for about twenty minutes and he sensed that the fish was beginning to tire, but experience told him that it was still a long way from being beaten. One false move on his part would result in him losing his prize. He knew that he had to proceed carefully, because the salmon still had sufficient strength left to break his flimsy tackle and escape. The fish leaped to show its defiance and William let it run once more.

The river Laune was not the longest river in Ireland, it ran for a mere fifteen miles from the Lakes of Killarney to enter Dingle Bay just below Killorglin. But it was renowned for the quality of its salmon. Under normal circumstances - if anything could have been described as 'normal' in the Ireland of May 1916 – William would have been exhilarated by the struggle to land the salmon. The fact that he was in effect illegally poaching the fish from the stretch of the river Laune belonging to Beaufort House would only have added to his enjoyment. Even though the house had been closed for the duration of the war, and the gamekeepers laid off, taking a salmon from the river was still technically a crime, but this would only have added a taste of adventure for the seventeen year old fisherman. On any other balmy Sunday evening in May he would have enjoyed the view across the river and the lush meadows to the Gap of Dunloe, and the rugged McGillycuddy's Reeks mountain range beyond. On this pleasant Sunday evening however, while he went competently about landing the fish, there were other things on William Quinlan's mind.

During a short lull in his fight with the salmon he turned around and looked up the hill to where the roof and chimney pots of the house were visible above the trees. Soon after the outbreak of war in 1914 the aristocratic owner of the house had been called out of retirement to take up a senior post in the newly formed Ministry of Munitions in London. Soon afterwards, when it became obvious that the war would drag on, his family had left to join him leaving the house empty for the duration. And it was not only the gamekeepers who had been laid off as a result. William's father, Michael, who had been employed as the coachman at Beaufort had suffered

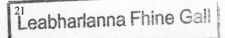

a similar fate. So Michael and another of his sons, James, had, along with thousands of other Irish 'navvies', gone to seek work on building a gigantic new munitions factory at Gretna in Scotland. This journey to Scotland had, however, ended in tragedy.

It was over a month now since Michael Quinlan had died, officially as the result of a heart attack, while working at the great munitions factory 'across the water'.

Because 'The Easter Rising' – the armed rebellion against British rule – had been raging in Ireland at the time of Michael's death the tragic news had not reached home for several days. 'The Rising' had disrupted communications and caused the British Government to declare martial law in Ireland. So Michael's body could not be returned to Beaufort for burial, and he had been buried in a pauper's grave in Carlisle before his family had even learned of his death. The Rising had also prevented James, who had been obliged to deal with all of the arrangements at Gretna including the inquest and burial, from immediately returning home.

But the fact that James had not returned for some weeks after The Rising had been suppressed and normal travel arrangements restored, alerted William to the possibility of there being more to his father's death than appeared at first sight. In a way he was glad that his mother was so overcome with grief at the loss of her husband, a grief compounded by the fact that she had been prevented from attending his funeral, she was unable to think too deeply about the circumstances of his death.

But today James had finally, and unexpectedly, returned home. When the Quinlan family came home from Mass that Sunday morning they found him waiting for them in the kitchen in the kitchen of the cottage by the river close to Beaufort Bridge. William hardly recognised his brother. In the five short months since he had left home James had not only developed physically, he had also lost much of the youthful impetuousness which had been so much a part of his make-up. Even their mother had remarked that James had gone away a boy and come home a man.

As he continued to play the salmon, it occurred to William that it was not only James who seemed to have been transformed by recent events. The early months of 1916 had brought about momentous changes in Ireland, changes which had a profound effect on the lives and the attitudes of the Irish people. The Easter Rising, and in particular the reprisals exacted by the British authorities following the suppression of the rebellion, had served to unify Irish opinion. Summary arrests and executions had aroused anti-British feeling and reinforced the desire for a truly independent Irish Republic. Before the events of Easter Week talk of armed insurrection against British rule had received only limited support. The majority of Irish people had been of the opinion that Irishmen should be joining Britain in the war against Germany. In the first two years of the war thousands of Irishmen had volunteered to fight in Britain's armed forces, but now, within a few short weeks, all that had changed. Previously armed rebellion had been spoken of only behind closed doors by a few committed adherents to 'The Cause'. Now it was preached openly to large and receptive gatherings.

That very evening a man had come from Dublin to speak at Devlin's public house in Beaufort village on the subject of further armed resistance to British Rule. Six months previously that same Man from Dublin had spoken to a mere handful of committed supporters in the back kitchen of the public house which doubled as a farmhouse, but tonight he would find the yard behind the pub crowded with eager listeners.

Had it not been for James, William would have been there himself.

The salmon rose again and the sound of the splash brought him back to the business at hand. At this point on its journey to the sea the Laune was deep and slow running, and the banks were clear of bushes. He was able to play the fish in this deep water for a further fifteen minutes before finally landing his prize. It proved to be a fine spring salmon that he estimated would weigh at least fifteen pounds. He gutted the fish then wrapped it carefully in reeds to keep it as fresh as possible until he could take it to the Great Southern Hotel in Killarney, where the chef was usually prepared to buy a fish on the cheap, even though he knew it had been poached. Over the months that his father and brother had been working in Scotland they had regularly sent money home. While they were away whenever he had sold a fish or a snared rabbit, he had been able to pocket the money for himself. But with his father dead, and with James back home, and for the moment at least seemingly unemployed, money would be tight again. His mother would have to support herself and the three younger children on William's earnings from his job on a local farm, so he could in conscience no longer keep the proceeds of his hunting and fishing activities for himself.

With the death of her husband Annie Quinlan seemed to have aged and lost much of her zest for life, but now that James was home William fervently hoped she would to return to something approaching her former confident self.

But as he dismantled his rod and packed away his fishing tackle William was still at a loss to understand his brother's change of attitude towards the Irish nationalist cause. When The Man from Dublin had last visited Beaufort, James had been one of the most enthusiastic of those who attended the covert meeting in the pub kitchen. William was certain that had James not been forced to accompany his father to Scotland he would have joined in The Rising. But earlier today when he had suggested that they go to tonight's meeting together, James had demurred and made excuses. William could accept his brother saying that as he had only just returned home he should spend the evening with his mother, but when she had suggested that her sons go to Devlin's together, James' excuses ceased to ring true. Later when William was preparing to set off for the pub by himself James had quite forcibly asked him not to go.

This worried William and he failed to understand James' attitude. But his brother continued to be evasive and seemed determined to dissuade him from going to the Nationalist meeting.

"But sure weren't you always a great one for fighting for The Republic, Jim," he said. "The last time The Man from Dublin was here in Beaufort you were all set to join the rebels. If it hadn't been for Da taking you off over the water you would have been in The Rising itself. Something must have happened over there at the munitions factory to change your mind about fighting for Irish freedom."

"Oh I still believe in the right for Ireland to be free of British rule," said James. "So did Da, God rest his soul, but he was dead against blood being spilled to get it. And I tell you Bill, having seen some of the wounded soldiers coming back from France I can see his point. But it's not the idea of fighting for freedom that I am against: it's some of these people doing all the talking and persuading other men to do the fighting and dying that I don't like."

Both brothers could see that their mother was getting upset by the argument and so William did not press James further for a more plausible explanation. Rather than go to the meeting he decided to spend a few hours on the riverbank to gather his thoughts.

The light was fading as he picked up his tackle and started for home. He had not gone far before he saw the unmistakable figure of James coming to meet him. They stood for a while without saying anything. James lit a cigarette, something that William had not seen him do before.

James broke the silence. "That's a grand looking salmon you have there, Bill."

"It is so, a good fifteen pounds," said William. He could see that James had something he needed to get off his chest. "What's up Jim? Why were you dead set against going to the meeting at Devlin's?"

"It's a long story Bill. I'll tell you the gist of it but for God's sake don't say a word to Ma, she's still crying over Da and it would only make things harder on her if she knew the whole story."

William was surprised to see the previously carefree James expressing such deep concern and having difficulty in speaking his mind. "Is it about that fella down from Dublin, Jim?" he asked.

"It is so Bill," replied James. "I went to Mass at the Cathedral in Killarney on my way home this morning and he was talking to the people outside after. Bad luck to him. Sure I don't trust him one bit, and I have to stay well out of his way."

William thought for a minute before replying. Then he voiced the thought that had been worrying him: "Something happened over there in Scotland, didn't it? Was it something that was to do with Da dying of a heart attack? Ma knew that something was wrong when you didn't come straight home after the funeral. She was even thinking that you had taken up with that girl you met over there. Da wrote to her about that."

He let that sink in then continued: "Let me in on the truth Jim or I won't know what to say to her if she asks me about it again."

James laughed, "ah sure that thing with the girl never came to anything."

He was silent for several minutes. Finally he said: "do you remember Liam Daly?"

"Sure of course I do." William remembered Daly as a local jarvey, a jaunting car driver, who was also a committed nationalist rebel. When their father had been coachman at Beaufort House he had suspected Daly of stealing a harness from the stables and reported him, making a dangerous enemy of the man.

"He always had it in for Da, but what about him?"

"Well," said James. "He was over at the factory in Scotland, and him and your man from Dublin tried to start some kind of trouble there at the time of The Rising. I never heard the full story, but it all fell to bits when Daly lost his head and killed an old Scotsman. He shot him dead, and in the church of all places. Me and Da were there at the time and we saw it all, so Daly took us as hostages. He was out of his head and he was all set to do for us too, until a security man shot him. But that fella from Dublin got away. Honest to God Bill you never saw anything like it."

James solemnly crossed himself, and William was amazed to see a tear in his brother's eye. "An old fella called Alistair McGregor it was. And him and Da were grand friends too; I never saw Da hit it off so well with anyone. Daly killed him without blinking an eye. The worst of it was that Daly was aiming the gun at me at the time and Alistair got in the way. That's two people that saved my life over there Bill."

"Christ Almighty!" It was not like William to take The Lord's name in vain, but he was profoundly shocked by what he heard. "Is that what killed Da, was he shot too?"

"No, Da died of a heart attack all right, but it was what Daly and that bastard from Dublin did that brought it on for sure."

It was William's turn to cross himself. "So that's why you didn't come home as soon as The Rising was over, did you have to stay over there while the cops looked into it?"

"No," said James. "Sure there was no investigation at all by the cops. It all happened at an important munitions factory and so the British security people kept it quiet. No, the reason I didn't come home was because that fella from Dublin got away and he knows I saw everything that happened. The security people were sure that he made it home to Ireland and they told me to wait for a while over there until things were settled here. And they were right too, he did come back. So it's not safe for me here yet with him still around. I'm hoping he thinks that Daly killed me, but if he finds out that I'm still alive he'll have every rebel in the country after me to stop me telling what I know about him. And there won't be anybody around to save me the next time. But I'll tell you this Bill, if I ever get him on his own he'll pay for what he did to Da."

William had never in his life seen James taking anything so seriously. A thirst for vengeance had never been part of his nature. It took a few minutes for the reality of the situation to sink in. "Christ Jim, you'll have to lie low until he goes back to Dublin. And you're right. It'll be better all round if Ma never finds out about it."

"That's right Bill. But that's not the worst of it, there's a good chance that he'll tell Pat Devlin and the rest of them what happened, so I can't stop around here any longer or they'll be sure to find me. Ma won't like it but I'll have to leave first thing in the morning. I told her that I have to go straight back over the water or I'll lose my job. But I wish to God that I could tell her the truth about why I'm going so soon."

"What will you do Jim?"

"Well I don't want to go back to Gretna that's for sure. I've had enough of that place. When the war is over I might go to America, I have a friend there who'll help me to get fixed up. But I'll have to put some cash together first and I want to keep sending money home to Ma. So it'll have to wait until after the war and Jack comes home."

James was referring to their elder brother who had volunteered and was now fighting against the Turks in Mesopotamia.

He showed William a small silver badge bearing crossed cannons and a crown with the words 'War Munitions Volunteer'. "They gave us these to stop the girls over there handing us white feathers for not being in uniform. It'll get me a job in another munitions factory. I'll let you know which one as soon as I'm fixed up. But for Christ's sake don't let on to anybody where I am. If people like Pat Devlin find out I'll have to go on the run."

"What'll we tell Ma?" asked William.

"I'll tell her that there's a danger I might be moved to another factory and not to worry if she doesn't hear from me for a while."

"Ma's no fool, Jim," said William. "I might have to tell her some of the story. Anyway you'll come home again before you go to America."

"Sure of course I will," said James. "I'll have to see Ma." His voice hardened: "and I still want to settle up with that bastard who was responsible for what happened to Da."

A full Irish moon was rising as they made their way home.

# Chapter 2

"Things went well tonight Pat." The Man from Dublin and Pat Devlin were sitting in the kitchen of Devin's pub in Beaufort with a bottle of Irish whisky on the table between them.

"You're right there," said Devlin. "A lot more turned up than the last time you were in Beaufort."

From their point of view the meeting, some might have termed it 'the lecture', had certainly been a great success. The pub bar had been too small to accommodate the numbers present and so they had gathered in the large open yard at the back where The Man stood on an upturned beer crate to address them. Most of the gathering were men but, unusually for a time and place where 'politics' were largely a male preserve, a number of women were also present. Adopting a schoolmasterly pose with his thumbs hooked in the armholes of his waistcoat The Man from Dublin had little difficulty in fuelling resentment against the British authorities in Ireland. On his last visit to Beaufort some months before The Rising he had found little support for armed rebellion, but now the mood of the Irish people had changed. British reprisals, in which at least one totally innocent local man had been arrested and interned, had achieved everything the leaders of the insurrection had hoped it would.

The Man and his host sat and smoked and drank their whisky. "If it hadn't been for Casement being taken, and the guns lost, the 'boys' would have won," said Devlin. "And Pearse and Connolly would be sitting up there in Dublin Castle as the first leaders of the Irish Republic."

He was referring to the capture of the former British diplomat, Sir Roger Casement, who had brokered a deal with the German military to supply arms to the Irish rebels. Casement had been captured soon after landing from a German submarine in Tralee Bay, and the ship carrying the consignment of German rifles had been scuttled by her German crew following discovery by the Royal Navy.

"No Pat," said The Man, "that's not the truth of it at all. Pearse and Connolly knew very well that when it came to a fight they would be no match for the British Empire, German guns or no German guns. Now for Christ's sake keep this under your hat, but the real purpose behind The Rising was to create a new crop of Irish martyrs to arouse the anger of the Irish people and the sympathy of the rest of the world. You saw for yourself here tonight how people feel about the Brits now, and I can tell you that over there across the Atlantic the Yanks are having second thoughts about joining the war. Tell me this Pat: how is it I am here with you tonight instead of being dead or in gaol waiting execution?"

"I thought about that," said Devlin.

"Before The Rising, while I was setting up a bit of business at a munitions factory over in Scotland, Pearse and Connolly told me all about their plans to become martyrs. They ordered me to lie low while the fighting was going on and when it was all over to start stoking up feeling against the Brits. The reprisals have made that job easy."

The Man was right in that after The Rising the rebel leaders including Padraig Pearse and James Connolly had been tried and convicted of treason rather than being treated as prisoners of war. Their executions soon followed, and in death they achieved more than they could have hoped for at the beginning of The Rising.

Devlin sat quietly while he reflected on what he had just heard. Eventually he changed the subject and brought up another matter that had been occupying his mind. "Tell me now, have you seen Liam Daly at all since the pair of you were over there at that munitions place. Is he still there or was he by any chance one of them killed in The Rising?"

"Sure wasn't it his fault that the plan to sabotage the factory over there was buggered," said The Man with uncharacteristic passion. "The stupid bastard went wild with a gun and shot an old Scotsman, in a catholic church of all places. The last I saw of him he was trying to escape with a couple of hostages. That old coachman from around here, Quinlan, and his son it was. Daly had it in for the old fella so I suppose he shot the pair of them. But I don't know whether he got away or not, and to tell you the truth Pat, I couldn't care less."

"That's queer," said Galvin. "I heard that Michael Quinlan died of a heart attack over there and they couldn't bring his body home because of The Rising and martial law being declared. I know for a fact that the news came from his son James. Mrs. Quinlan told Mrs. Connor, the postmaster's wife, after Mass about a month ago. At first the Connor woman thought the telegram was to say that the other Quinlan lad, Jack, was killed in the war."

The Man from Dublin sat up in alarm. "Are you dead sure about this Pat? Are you telling me young Quinlan is still alive? If he's alive and the old man really died of a bad heart it must mean that Daly is dead. Jesus Christ Pat, that young fella saw and heard a lot more than was good for him over there. Has he been home, have you seen him by any chance?"

He did not elaborate on exactly what James Quinlan had witnessed and he thought that Devlin, with a lifetime of involvement in the nationalist cause, would not expect a full explanation. The Beaufort publican would certainly understand if one was not forthcoming. But in this instance The Man had reasons of his own for keeping the full story from Devlin.

"No," said Devlin. "If he came home I'd know about it, this is a small place and sure you couldn't keep anything like Jim Quinlan coming home a secret for long."

"Well if he does come back here let me know the minute you hear about it Pat. There might not be anything in it but we can't afford to take chances, and the sooner we put him out of the picture the better I'll feel about things. In the meantime I'll send one of the lads over to Gretna to find out if Quinlan is still working there."

Devlin sat in silent thought and it was some minutes before he spoke again. "It would suit us a lot better if Jim Quinlan met his end over there in Scotland," he said. "The Quinlans are well known and well liked around here and there is a lot of sympathy for Annie over Michael's death. We could have trouble getting people to believe that one of them was an informer or something, and if it came out that we had a hand in killing young Jim it might turn a few people against us."

The Man considered this. He was less concerned about the actual damage young Quinlan could do to the rebel cause than he was about the effect it would have on his own reputation, should the full story of the events at the munitions factory ever come out. The failure of his mission to disrupt the working of such an important war factory, and turn the thousands of Irish navvies working there against the British, was ultimately his responsibility. But he was not about to tell Pat Devlin that. He knew that the British security service would have covered the incident up, so the only possible danger to his reputation and standing in the nationalist movement came from James Quinlan. He was not certain how much Quinlan actually knew, but he certainly knew enough to complicate matters, and at the very least arouse suspicion should he ever be allowed to speak out. The Man from Dublin could not afford to take the risk. That young man would have to be silenced. But The Man also realised that he would have to tread carefully.

"You could be right Pat," he said, "you know how the land lies around here. I'll try to get the job done over the water and that way we might even find a way to blame it on the Brits."

Devlin seemed satisfied and changed the subject: "I take it you'll be staying the night."

The Man from Dublin had originally intended to remain in Kerry for a few days and the quiet village of Beaufort was an ideal centre from which to visit the larger towns of Killorglin, Killarney and even Tralee. But hearing that James Quinlan was still alive had caused him to alter his plans.

"No Pat," he said. "Sure I haven't been home since before The Rising, I've been lying low up in the North. The sooner I find out what the situation is in Dublin the better I'll feel about things. So if you can get someone to run me into Killarney I'll catch the late night train."

The lie was obvious. From what he had said to the men at the meeting it was clear that The Man was well informed about what was happening in Ireland's capital, and of course he would have passed through Dublin on his way down from the north. But Devlin let it go.

"If I hear anything will you be wanting me send a telegram to 'Mr. Smith' as usual?" asked Devlin.

The question started The Man thinking. He felt that it would be wise to adopt a new name for the purposes of this particular exercise, and looked around for inspiration. His eyes rested on the whiskey bottle.

"No Pat," he said, "to be on the safe side I'll be using a different name from now on. Send the wire to 'John Jameson'." He gave an address in the Dublin suburb of Rathmines.

He decided to change the subject. "Talking about how things are around here, have you heard anything about the owner of Beaufort House? Does he ever come back to see how things are down here?"

"No," said Devlin, "His Lordship has an agent up in Dublin to look after things for him. I hear that he's a big wig in the British Government these days."

"He is so Pat," said The Man. "He's a big man in the Ministry of Munitions. Keep your ears open about him too and if you hear anything let me know. We're keeping tabs on people like him for future reference." He did not elaborate but Devlin caught the implication: 'His Lordship' was being singled out as a possible future kidnap, or perhaps even murder target.

After he had arranged transport to take The Man to the railway station in Killarney, the publican sat and considered the implications of what he had learned regarding James Quinlan. He knew nothing about a rebel plan to disrupt the British munitions factory except that it seemed to have failed, and that The Man was blaming Liam Daly. He knew Daly of old and it came as no surprise to learn that the former local jarvey had threatened to shoot Michael Quinlan. When Quinlan had been coachman at Beaufort House he had reported Daly for stealing from the stables and had made an enemy of the hot headed rebel. Like The Man from Dublin he would not shed a tear if it turned out that Daly was indeed dead, and he knew that if it emerged that the jarvey had been in some way connected with the death of the former coachman then local sympathy would lie firmly with the Quinlan family. Devlin realised that if that happened, he personally could then be placed in an awkward position.

While they had not been particularly friendly, it was well known locally that he and Daly were closely connected with the republican cause, and if Daly was held responsible for the death of Michael Quinlan, then in the minds of local people The Cause, and by association, Devlin himself, could well be implicated. It was not, however, just the effect on the struggle for an Irish republic that caused Devlin to be concerned. He was also a businessman. Attached to his public house was a grocer's shop, and both pub and shop relied on local support. And Beaufort House itself had been, and he hoped would be again, a most valued customer.

***

Ireland was fast becoming a land of divided loyalties. Only those who were totally committed to The Cause were able to set aside family, religious, or other responsibilities. William Quinlan felt the effect as he readied the pony and trap to drive his brother to Killarney railway station before the sun had fully risen the next morning. As he worked, his brother said an emotional farewell to their mother. William had been seriously thinking about joining one of the new Republican organisations being formed from the remnants of those defeated in The Easter Rising. Although a supporter of Home Rule for Ireland his father had always been against a complete separation from Britain, and especially by way of a full scale armed rebellion. Unlike James, William had accepted his father's argument that as a coachman he relied on wealthy British families with large estates in Ireland for his livelihood. But it was obvious to him that this situation was due to change. The World War which still raged and seemed set to last for some time yet would alter everything.

He dropped James off at the station to catch the Dublin train, unaware that The Man from Dublin, who now called himself 'Mr Jameson' had, a mere couple of hours before, caught an even earlier Dublin train. After the train left he went straight home, unharnessed and stabled the pony, and looked in on his mother for a minute to let her know that James was safely on his way. He then got his bicycle and left for work. Apart from the little money sent home by Jack from his meagre army pay, William now thought of himself as the sole breadwinner and could not afford to lose his job. On his way through the village he met Pat Devlin.

"Fine day Bill," said the publican.

"It is so Pat," replied William.

"How is your mother bearing up after hearing about your father, Lord have mercy on him." Devlin crossed himself as he spoke.

"Ah sure she's not too good Pat. It'll take a bit of time yet for her to get over it."

Devlin nodded sympathetically and said: "I'm sorry to hear it Bill. Tell me has she heard from your brother Jim at all?"

William had been expecting this. It was the kind of question any concerned neighbour would have asked. In view of what James had told him, however, and knowing that The Man from Dublin used Devlin's public house as his base in Beaufort, he was tempted to lie. But he knew that the lie would soon be found out. His mother or the younger children were sure to tell their friends of James' brief visit, and being caught out in the lie could easily point to him knowing about his brother's involvement in the affair at Gretna. This would then almost certainly lead to nationalist fingers being pointed at both himself and his brother. Besides, in spite of James' recent experience, he still believed in the Irish nationalist cause and still harboured thoughts of supporting it. So he decided to give Devlin a vague account of James' visit home while at the same time protecting his brother.

"Sure didn't he come home for the day yesterday. We came home from Mass and there he was in the kitchen there waiting for us. Ma was delighted to see him, but she was mad at him for not telling us he was coming."

"Ah sure that's grand Bill," said Devlin. "Tell him to look in at the pub and there will be a pint waiting for him."

"But sure isn't that the sad part of it Pat," said William. "He only stayed for the one night before he had to go back over to Scotland. They're working day and night at that munitions place. I'm only back this minute from taking him to the station in Killarney."

"Jesus, but that sounds like hard work over there all right," said Devlin.

"It is so Pat," said William, "but the pay is good. I'd go myself but I have to stay here and look after Ma and the young ones. And it's time I was thinking about going to work here in Beaufort or the boss will kick my arse if I don't turn up in time for the milking."

He was conscious of the fact that he had only managed to get a job as a farm labourer because one of the farmer's sons had joined up to fight in the war.

"You're right there Bill," said Devlin. "I have a bit to do myself this morning."

The parted and William pedalled off to work. Devlin went to fetch his own bicycle. He knew that if he sent his telegram from the post office in Beaufort the contents would soon be known all over the village. So he cycled to Killarney to wire the news to 'Mr Jameson'.

# Chapter 3

"Did you hear the news from home Jack?" The speaker was Private Patrick Coughlin of the 1st Battalion the Connaught Rangers.

"I did Pat," said his companion. Bombardier Jack Quinlan of the Royal Field Artillery knew that his friend was referring to the events of Easter Week in Ireland, but he was more concerned about the tragic news that he had recently received in his last letter from home. In the last batch of mail to reach his unit he was surprised to find a letter from his brother William, rather than from his mother. On opening it he immediately found out why: William had written because his mother was too distraught to tell him that his father had died. The news of his father's death would have been difficult for his mother to bear, but the fact that the body could not be taken back to Beaufort for burial must have distressed her beyond belief.

They were sitting on ammunition boxes among all the other paraphernalia of war in the heat of the arid desert surrounding the ancient city of Basra in Mesopotamia.

Mesopotamia formed part of the Turkish Ottoman Empire. At the outbreak of the war in September 1914 Britain sent units of the Indian Army with some Western troops to the area to secure the oil installations on which the Royal Navy depended. They were initially successful and captured Basra and its oilfields without encountering any sustained resistance from the Turks. This gave them impetus to move further up the Shatt-al-Arab and the town of Qurna fell to British forces in December 1914. Then in April 1915 a Turkish attack on Basra was repulsed and, as the enemy retreated British troops followed up and captured Amara in May. More troops were sent to Mesopotamia and it was decided that an attempt should be made to capture Baghdad, the city which marked the end of the line for the Constantinople-Baghdad railway. Built by the Germans the railway formed the principal Turkish supply line and her main link with Germany. British forces reached Kut-al-Amara in September, but at this point the advance faltered due to lack of supplies. Turkish reinforcements had also arrived, the British force was defeated and Kut was besieged by the Turks. Following several bloody battles in which British attempts to relieve the siege of Kut were repulsed with heavy losses, both the British and the Turks were re-grouping and reinforcing. So while the slaughter known as The Battle of the Somme raged on the Western Front the war in

Mesopotamia had reached a stalemate.

Jack Quinlan had joined up soon after the outbreak of war. When Kitchener launched his famous 'Your Country Needs You' recruiting campaign its impact was felt even in Ireland. Thousands of Irishmen answered the call to arms. Some volunteered because they genuinely felt they should support Great Britain in the fight against Germany; some joined through youthful enthusiasm and the promise of adventure; but many were simply seeking a way out of poverty and the endless grind of trying to scrape a living from tiny plots of poor land rented from absentee British landlords. A few, like Jack Quinlan, had volunteered out of a sense of duty - a sense which had not been so much Jack's own but that of his father. Michael Quinlan had been a senior member of the staff at Beaufort House and so it was expected that at least one of his sons would enlist. As the eldest, this responsibility had fallen to Jack. He did not complain; it was simply the way things were done. His one departure from convention was that rather than enlist in one of the numerous Irish infantry regiments he had opted to join the Royal Field Artillery.

Recent experiences were however, causing Jack to question the social order he had been brought up to observe.

He had arrived in Mesopotamia soon after the retreat from Kut-al-Amara and his battery was immediately attached to the Tigris Corps. This hastily assembled force, named after one of the two great rivers of biblical significance in the region, was assigned the task of relieving the Indian Army troops trapped by the Turks in Kut. But it soon became evident that nothing had been learned from the recent failures and that the Tigris Corps was ill-prepared for the task. Over the next several months Bombardier Jack Quinlan experienced the full horror of war.

There were shortages of everything. Men, food, and medical supplies, transport and high-explosive ammunition for the 18 pounder guns of the field artillery, were all in short supply. The weather conditions for the troops were atrocious: humid heat by day and freezing cold at night. Arid desert became mosquito ridden swampland when it rained and the rivers flooded. Heat, flies and mosquitoes caused as many casualties as did Turkish guns and bayonets. Just as importantly there was the unwillingness, or the inability, of the senior commanders to recognise the conditions and adapt their tactics accordingly. The infantry were sent in on totally uncoordinated frontal assaults against well defended Turkish positions. Jack and the other artillerymen watched in horror as the attackers were cut down in droves, and were driven to tears of frustration that the lack of appropriate ammunition prevented them from bombarding the enemy to any real effect. The idea of shelling enemy trenches using shrapnel instead of high explosive shells would have been laughed at on the Western Front. The gunners knew that had different tactics been adopted many lives could have been spared. What caused Jack even more distress was the plight of the wounded. Hundreds of badly injured men lay out in the open, sometimes for days, waiting for help from a medical service that would have been hard pressed to cope with half their number. He watched helpless as they were sometimes set upon, killed, and robbed by marauding Marsh Arabs while Turkish officers did little or nothing to prevent it.

Inevitably the attempt to relieve Kut failed, and the garrison was forced to surrender. The Tigris Corps retreated to lick its wounds, and as soon as they got back to Basra Jack received the news of the death of his father. In spite of all the death he had recently witnessed this news from home hit him hardest of all.

"From what I hear the boys at home made a good fist of it, but sure they never stood a chance," said Coughlin, resuming their conversation. "Haven't I been in the British Army long enough to know that small rebel forces will never beat them in a straight fight, it takes the likes of the Turks and the Germans to do that."

"I'd say that the leaders at home knew that when they started," said Jack.

"You could be right there Jack. But in the end it was all for nothing. Them brave fellas shooting down our countrymen at home would have been better employed out here giving us a hand against the Turks." As a regular British soldier serving in an Irish regiment, Coughlin failed to see the contradictions in his remark.

There was a pause before Coughlin spoke again. "In a way I think it would be a good thing if the boys had won, it's about time that Ireland was free."

Jack thought about home and his father's life as a coachman. "Oh Ireland will be free of British rule soon enough Pat," he said. "But it will be a long time before we are free of British money, a lot of us will still have to rely on them to earn a crust."

With his father's death he knew that he would have to work on the Beaufort estate in order to retain his family's home. He knew that 'His Lordship' was not a bad master; there were many other British landowners in Ireland who were far less caring of their native employees. But since he had left the confines of Beaufort, and seen some of the rest of the world, he had begun to question the accepted principle.

"Anyway there's nothing we can do about it," said his friend. "God knows we have troubles enough of our own and we're too far away from home for it to bother us."

"I wouldn't say that Pat," said Jack. He told his friend about his father's death and how the body couldn't be taken home for burial because of the Easter Rising.

"Jesus, I'm sorry to hear that Jack," Coughlin crossed himself. "I'll tell Father O'Connell when I see him, and he'll pray for your father's soul at Mass."

Unlike Jack who had joined up for the duration of the war, Patrick Coughlin was a regular soldier. Like tens of thousands of his countrymen over centuries of British rule he had enlisted in the British Army. Signing up to fight for 'The King's Shilling' was one of the very few (legal) ways of escaping from a life of poverty. Patrick, from a small village in Co. Galway, had joined the regiment long associated with Ireland's western province, The Connaught Rangers. On enlistment at the age of seventeen in 1910 his mind had been full of thoughts of travel, three square meals a day every day and a few shillings in his pocket. He had given little or no thought to having to earn his pay on the battlefield. Patrick's desire for travel had soon been satisfied. His first posting was to the 1st battalion serving in Ferozpore in India where he was stationed until the outbreak of war in 1914. The battalion then sailed from Karachi as part of the Indian Corps and landed at Marseilles in the south of France. They then served on the Western Front until December 1915 when they were sent to Mesopotamia.

This movement across the globe was nothing new to the men of the Connaught Rangers. Raised in the early eighteenth century, the regiment had served Britain with distinction for two hundred years. Their first battle honour was gained in the Egyptian Campaign, and more followed in The Peninsular War. Throughout the nineteenth century the regiment served in the Mediterranean, The West Indies and North America (Canada), they saw active service in The Crimean War, The Indian Mutiny and the Zulu Wars in South Africa. In its long history the regiment had spent very little time in Britain and virtually none in Ireland. The 'old sweat' regulars of the 1st Battalion, and at the age of twenty-three Pat Coughlin considered himself to be one of these, were immensely proud of their regiment and its traditions. But even so they never forgot the fact that they were Irishmen born and bred.

Being exclusively Irish, the regiment included a Roman Catholic chaplain among its staff while other units such as the field artillery did not. So, while encamped at Basra, at Church Parade on Sundays the 'RCs' including Jack Quinlan went to Mass with the 'Rangers'. This was where Jack first met Pat Coughlin and the two immediately hit it off. Since their first meeting, the artilleryman spent much of his free time at the Rangers lines. He found it pleasant to be with fellow Irishmen and it came as a refreshing change to be referred to by his proper Christian name rather than 'Paddy' as all Irishmen were invariably called in his own unit.

"Will you look at this, a good honest Connaught Ranger associating with a lowly artilleryman, and an NCO at that. What in God's name got into you Pat Coughlin to lead you to this?"

The tone was entirely good-natured and both Jack and Pat looked up from their ammunition box seats to find another 'Ranger' standing there.

The newcomer was introduced by Coughlin with some aplomb as 'Private James Joseph Daly himself, pride of the Connaught Rangers'.

Daly, in spite of his remarks, smiled and offered a firm handshake. "Put it there Jack, sure if you're a Kerryman you can't be all that bad in spite of the company you keep."

Then he lowered his voice "But listen Jack," he said. "Be careful not to flash that gunner's badge too boldly around here. Some of the lads were saying that it was the field artillery that did for the boys in The Rising at home."

"I heard that too," said Jack. "And by all accounts they had plenty of the right sort of ammunition to do the job. If we only had a few of them HE shells here a lot of good men would have been spared."

The infantrymen nodded in agreement.

"Please God they'll send you the right stuff the next time Jack," said Daly, "and between us we'll finish this war. I'm getting tired of fighting for King and Country, when all the time it's someone else's king and someone else's country."

"The sooner the pair of you do that the better I'll like it," said Coughlin. "Sure I might even give you a hand myself. I'll be glad when things go back to normal."

"I hope to God that nothing goes back to normal after this war, there's too many things that need changing in this world," said Daly.

"You're right there," said Jack. He was referring to the social order that had obliged him to volunteer for service. But he suspected that Daly meant an end to British rule in Ireland.

# Chapter 4

The summer of 1916 was a busy one for William Quinlan. As well as working long hours on the farm where he was employed, he helped his mother look after the cottage garden. At the rear of the cottage there was a potato patch and vegetable garden but Annie Quinlan was particularly anxious that the flower garden at the front should be kept as neat and colourful as possible.

The cottage on the banks of the Laune just by Beaufort Bridge was in fact the gatehouse to Beaufort House. It provided comfortable accommodation for the coachman, a senior member of the household staff, and his family. When the house had been closed and the coachman laid off the Quinlan family had been allowed to continue living there in anticipation of the world someday returning to normal. Occupation of the gatehouse, situated just inside the main gates guarding the long driveway up to the house, was conditional on the cottage and garden being kept neat and tidy in a manner befitting the gatehouse of a gentleman's country seat. Although the house was now empty and her husband dead, the coachman's widow was determined that standards must be kept up. To her mind it served as a memorial to the husband she mourned. So William helped her as much as he could, which left little time for his beloved fishing. He still managed to catch some fine brown trout of an evening from a pool just below the bridge within a few hundred yards of the cottage but, after the fish he landed on the Sunday of James' visit, the salmon would have to wait until the autumn. And there was another pressing matter to be attended to: peat for the fire had to be cut and stored for the coming winter.

Although there was firewood aplenty available in the woodland on the estate, the slow and even burning sods of turf provided a far superior fuel. Like all the other local people the Quinlan family cut their turf from an ancient Irish peat bog in the shadow of Carrantuohill, Ireland's highest mountain. A country road led up from the village towards Dunloe and past a group of ancient standing Ogham stones to where a narrow *boreen* branched off to the bog. Around the village the land was lush and green but as the road drew closer to the mountains the fields became smaller and the land poorer. Thick hedges gave way to dry stone walls. The peat bog itself was a vast expanse of heather-clad moorland potted with bog holes left behind by centuries of turf cutting and filled with dark peaty water. All but the newest of these holes were hidden under a thick blanket of soggy marsh plants and mosses which would bear little weight and so made the bog a treacherous place for the unwary.

In previous years, with all the men of the family there to help, turf cutting had been a carefree festive occasion carried out during school holidays; holidays timed in Ireland for just this purpose. There had been picnics in the heather with homemade bread, cakes and buttermilk. The men of the family cut the turf while Annie prepared the food and the smaller children played. This year, however, all that would have to change and, had he thought about it, William would have recognised this as yet another consequence of the war.

Michael Quinlan had been an acknowledged expert with the *slean*, the angled spade used for slicing and lifting the sods of turf from the bog, and before his death his sons been acquiring the skill. But this year that responsibility would be William's alone and he would have to complete his training on the job. There would be plenty of advice available as well as many genuine offers of help but William, although still only seventeen, was already developing his father's stocky build and powerful body and was determined that he could manage by himself. His mother noticed that he had also inherited much of Michael's independent nature. So he soon mastered the art and the family helped as best they could. William cut the turf, Annie and the children laid out the sods to dry in the summer sunshine. Once they had been turned and dried on both sides they were piled on end in little stooks, and later into larger clamps ready to be transported home. In the weeks between haymaking and harvest, when there was less work on the farm, the task was completed and an adequate supply of fuel built up outside the cottage for the coming year. William gave a sigh of relief, while his mother, although she kept it to herself, was immensely proud of him.

But there was little opportunity to relax. Harvest time brought the prospect of yet more back-breaking toil. Although some of the larger farms in the less mountainous counties of Ireland boasted modern reaper-and–binder machines, the corn in the small fields of Co. Kerry was still cut in the age-old way using the scythe. Men worked in twos and threes one behind the other their arms rising and falling in unison as they swung their scythes. Other men, helped by the women and children, gathered up the cut corn and tied it in bundles with ropes of twisted straw to form sheaves. The sheaves were stood on end in rows of stooks to await transport to the farmyard in overflowing carts drawn by sweating horses. Threshing was a communal event. The panting steam traction engine pulled the threshing machine from farm to farm followed by the men and hordes of children. When the machine was set up in a farmyard all the farmers, farmers sons, and farm workers in the parish lent a hand until the hot dusty work was done. Then the entire company moved on to the next farm. Farmers wives and daughters competed with each other to see who could provide the finest food and drink. The harvest was vitally important and in unfavourable weather the Catholic Church would sometimes even grant a dispensation for the men to work on Sundays.

***

At harvest time in France that year the Battle of the Somme had reached a stalemate on the Western Front. It had cost hundreds of thousands of lives and resolved nothing.

***

After the hustle and bustle of the harvest, a fine Sunday in September found William back at a favourite spot on the riverbank. It would be his first full day's fishing for some time, and he left the cottage immediately after bringing the family home from an early Mass, putting away the trap, and caring for the pony. To maximise his time with the rod, he got his mother to prepare some sandwiches with a bottle of buttermilk to wash them down for his midday meal. He fished without success until hunger overcame him and he sat down to eat his lunch.

From where he sat he had a view across the river and over the meadows to the main Killarney to Killorglin road. As he watched a lorry passed, travelling from west to east towards Killarney, and carrying a detachment of soldiers. Since the beginning of the war soldiers had become a familiar sight in the area. Several local lads had joined up and came home on leave in their uniforms. But this was different; these men were on active duty. Before The Rising law-enforcement had been solely the responsibility of The Royal Irish Constabulary, the civilian police. But now, although it meant little outside the cities and larger towns, martial law was still in force and the British army had become much more conspicuous, even in rural areas. The sight of the soldiers turned his mind to thoughts of the rise of nationalist feeling throughout the country. Although his father would not have approved, and his brother had fallen foul of the rebels, he still had a good deal of sympathy with those calling for an Irish Republic. Like most of his contemporaries he had to some extent been carried along on the tide of anti-British feeling that began with the reprisals following The Rising. But William was no hothead, he took after his mother in that respect, and unlike his brother James, he would stop to consider things. He was not old enough to vote, but had he been, he thought that he would have opted for Sinn Fein. The party, although not directly involved in The Rising, advocated the establishment of an independent republic. It was rapidly growing in popularity and was expected to sweep the board in the next election at the expense of the incumbent Home Rule Party.

But he realised that there was little he could do about it at present, he had his mother and the younger children to support, and that had to be his main objective at least until one or both of his brothers came home. And the prospects of that happening soon were not at all certain, Jack was in the thick of the fighting in Mesopotamia, and James was God knew where? Keeping out of the way of The Man from Dublin. His mother was becoming increasingly worried about James. She had heard nothing from him since his flying visit in June, and although William did his best to reassure her that James was fine, he was beginning to get a little anxious himself. With a sigh he went back to his search for a salmon.

\*\*\*

Annie Quinlan was indeed worried about her second son. She knew that he was not very proficient at letter writing but she thought that she would have heard something from him by now. When they were together at Gretna it was Michael who had done all of the writing and she had received weekly letters, all of them containing some money. News from Jack in Mesopotamia was also slow in arriving and the safety of her sons was the focus of her prayers.

With William fishing, the two little girls playing and their brother, 'young' Michael, doing his school homework, Annie went out into the front garden. There was little that required urgent attention, but she needed something to occupy her mind. The therapy failed to work however, and she could not shake off the worry about her two eldest sons. She almost missed the sound of footsteps on the gravel drive and the female voice addressing her:

"Excuse me mam, but would you by any chance be Mrs Quinlan?"

Annie looked up in surprise. She stood up and studied the speaker, an extremely pretty dark haired girl of medium height in her late teens or early twenties. The girl wore a well cut green dress and carried a light summer coat over her arm. She appeared hot and dusty and looked as if she had walked some way in the warm sun.

"Yes," said Annie. "I'm Mrs Quinlan."

The girl smiled and extended her hand. "That's grand," she said, "I walked out from Killarney and I was afraid I wouldn't be able to find you.

I'm over for a holiday from a munitions factory in Scotland and I'm staying with my uncle in town."

Annie's face lit up. "Oh you must know my son James." She thought for a moment. "Sure you must be Kate, the girl he's courting over there, his father wrote and told me all about you."

"Oh no mam," said the girl hurriedly. "I'm sorry I should have told you at first. My name is Maureen Ryan. But I know Kate and I met James a few times. When she heard that I would be in Killarney Kate asked me to look him up. Is he around by any chance?"

Annie's smile disappeared and her face clouded over. "God in Heaven, are you saying that he's not over there in Scotland either."

The girl looked mystified: "No", she said, "we haven't seen him around the factory since he left after what happened to his father, Lord have mercy on him." She hurriedly crossed herself.

There was silence while Annie collected her thoughts. Her mind raced but she was determined to stay calm and look at things rationally.

But the girl seemed flustered, and she spoke hesitantly: "God knows I'm sorry to have troubled you like this mam. If I had known it would cause you to worry I wouldn't have come at all." She turned to go. "I'll be on my way and leave you in peace."

But Annie had recovered, and her inbred sense of traditional Irish hospitality came to the fore. "You'll do no such thing Miss Ryan. You walked all the way out from Killarney to ask after James and the least I can do is make you a cup of tea. Come on in now and we'll have a chat about that son of mine, and when William comes home from fishing sure he'll run you back into town in the trap."

"Thank you mam," said the girl. "A cup of tea would be grand, so I won't say no."

They went into the large cottage kitchen and Annie sat the girl down in one of the 'best' chairs. 'Young' Michael looked up from the table and was about to get up but Annie told him to get on with his schoolwork. He was now the only one of her four sons that could fulfil her dream by becoming a priest, and she was determined that he should have the requisite schooling. She got out the best china and made some tea. The two little girls, Elizabeth and Mary, came in to gawp at the stranger, but their mother gave them thick slices of soda bread liberally spread with homemade jam and shooed them back outside.

When they were settled with their tea and homemade fruit cake, they chatted and Annie told the girl what James had said to her about munitions workers being moved to other factories at short notice.

"Ah sure that will be it," said her visitor. "The men do get moved

43

around a lot, so he's sure to be at one of the other factories."

"Well the young blackguard should let his mother know where he is," said Annie with feeling.

"Ah sure you'll be hearing from him any day now." said the girl.

Annie then asked another question that had been on her mind since finding out that the girl worked at Gretna. But before she did she told 'young' Michael to go and finish his homework in his room.

"Tell me Miss Ryan did you meet my husband at all over there in Scotland?"

"No mam," said the girl. "Sure I only saw Mr Quinlan a few times at Mass. But we were all sorry about what happened to him. There were prayers said for him at the church."

They sat in silence until they heard the sound of someone approaching the cottage and a small voice asking: "How many fishes have you catched William?"

"Ah sure there were no fish at all in the river, they were all at school to-day," came the reply.

"There's a lady in the kitchen with Ma," said another voice, "I think she came looking for James."

A mystified William entered by the back door and stepped back in surprise at the sight of the pretty stranger drinking tea with his mother.

"Come in here now William," said Annie. "This is Miss Ryan, sure isn't she a friend of James' over on a holiday from the factory in Scotland."

"Oh I'm afraid that I'm only a friend of a friend of your brother's," said the girl.

A suddenly bashful William took the offered hand and muttered a traditional greeting: "Welcome here miss."

Annie smiled inwardly at William's embarrassment in the presence of a beautiful girl. "She walked all the way out from Killarney to look for him," she said. "The young rogue never went back to the factory when he left here in so much of a hurry, and no one at all knows where he is."

"I told your mother that he must have been moved to another factory," said the girl. "Sure isn't it happening all the time?"

"That's right Ma," said William, "he said the very same thing himself before he left home."

Annie was not convinced but let it pass. "I told Miss Ryan that you would run her back to her uncle's in town. We can't let the poor girl walk all the way to Killarney again. So hurry up now and harness the pony or you won't get her there before dark."

William had eaten nothing since he had his sandwiches on the river bank. He had planned on having some supper and then rescuing something from his day's fishing by taking a few trout from the pool below the bridge. But he did as his mother told him.

Although still feeling awkward and uncomfortable in her presence, he found it a pleasant experience sitting with the girl in the trap in the warm Autumnal evening. He half hoped that some of his friends would see him, and half hoped that they wouldn't because he'd never hear the end of it if they did. After a couple of miles of silence Maureen Ryan spoke:

"I'm afraid that I troubled your mother coming on her like that without any warning, and asking after James," she said. "If you could drop me at the Cathedral I'll shoot in and say a quick one for her and one for your father too. And sure it's only a short step from there to my uncle Pat's."

William could not very well argue with that, and all he could say was: "Ma will be very glad about that Miss."

They reached Killarney, and he halted the pony at the Cathedral gates. She stepped down lightly from the trap.

"Thanks for the lift William," she said. "And when you hear from James would you tell him that Kate over in Gretna would like to know how he is. I didn't like to say any more about that in front of your mother." With that she disappeared into the Cathedral.

William turned the trap round and headed for home. As soon as he was out of sight Maureen Ryan came back out of the Cathedral and, instead of going to her 'uncle's', she hurried to the station and caught a late train for Dublin.

# Chapter 5

Maureen Ryan was a member of *Cumann na mBan*, the Irish Republican Women's organisation, and she had taken part in the actual fighting during The Rising in Dublin. She had carried dispatches from the Nationalist Head Quarters in the General Post Office to the other rebel strongholds across the city. Prior to surrendering on Friday April 28th the rebel leader, Padraig Pearse, had ordered all the women volunteers to leave, and so Maureen had managed to slip away and avoid capture and subsequent internment. She came from a staunchly republican family. Her father had been badly injured in a police baton charge during the infamous Dublin lock-out of 1913, and one of her brothers had been killed in The Rising. Another brother was now interned by the British in North Wales. These facts alone were enough to convince her of the righteousness of the Republican cause and, in spite of her tender years and delicate beauty, she was considered to be a seasoned campaigner.

She was perfectly suited for the task The Man from Dublin, now calling himself 'Mr Jameson' had set her.

"Did you believe the mother when she said that she had no word at all from him?" They were sitting in the parlour of 'Mr Jameson's' house in Rathmines, a quiet middle-class Dublin suburb, which had escaped the battering other parts of the city had suffered from the British artillery.

"I'm sure she was telling the truth," said Maureen. It was a mere two hours since she had arrived back in Dublin from Killarney, and although she had only slept intermittently on the train, she looked fresh and alert. "Sure the poor woman nearly burst into tears when she heard that he wasn't at the munitions place across the water."

'Mr Jameson' noticed a note of sympathy in Maureen's voice but made no comment. He put it down to no more than empathy between two women who were at that moment mourning the loss of family members.

"What about the brother, William you said his name was, does he know anything?"

"I think he might," she answered, "he's a quiet one and hasn't much to say for himself." She laughed, "I think that being around a strange girl brought out the shyness in him, and I think I might be able to get something out of him. I started the ball rolling by telling him that the girl in Gretna wants to know if they get word from his brother, but I think I could get him to tell me first."

"All right," said 'Mr Jameson'. "But I don't want you to go back to Beaufort again for a while or they'll get the notion that this is more than someone asking casual questions. Anyway I have someone else keeping an eye on things down there."

Maureen waited to be told who the 'someone else' was, but the information was not forthcoming.

"Ok," he said, "for the present we'll assume that they've had no word from him at home, and you're telling me that there's no sign of him over in Gretna either. They think at home that he might be working at one of the other munitions factories, but they don't know which one. Tell me again about your trip over to Scotland."

She went over the details of her visit to the munitions factory once again. She had arrived in Gretna and found the place teeming with humanity. To her it seemed as densely overpopulated as the worst areas of her native Dublin, a city which boasted some of the poorest and most overcrowded slums in Europe. The thousands of Irish navvies who had built the sprawling munitions factory, which stretched for nine miles over the English border, were now employed in building an infrastructure and amenities for the thousands of factory workers drawn from all over the British Empire. A complete new town was under construction at Eastriggs with houses, shops, a cinema and other leisure facilities for the workers. 'Mr. Jameson' had already given her some idea of what it would be like, and had assured her that she would find it easy to mingle with the factory workers without arousing the least suspicion.

"Just pretend to be one of the women munitions workers, 'The Gretna Girls' they call themselves," he had told her. "God knows you'll never be able to pass yourself off as a navvy," he had added with a rare touch of humour.

By a stroke of luck she had managed to find temporary lodging in Carlisle. It could only be on a temporary basis because the girl who occupied the bed was currently working on the nightshift, and when she resumed daytime working Maureen would have to find other accommodation. Having been brought up with a sister and two brothers in a very small house in Dublin she was not at all fazed by the arrangement. She spent her first few days travelling to and from Gretna on the crowded workers' trains and strolling around the town to get her bearings. Her *Cumann na mBan* training had taught her to familiarise herself with her surroundings whenever she found herself in a potentially hostile area. But it had soon become evident that searching for one individual among so many was effectively looking for the proverbial needle in a haystack.

She thought that she might enjoy some success by going to the Catholic Church and talking to the local priest, as she was sure that Michael Quinlan would have gone to Mass while he was there. And, assuming that he was still there, his son would be doing so now. Her story that she was looking for her brother who had not been home for some time was plausible enough, but the priest was new to Gretna and hadn't yet become familiar with all his parishioners. He told her that he was a replacement for the previous priest who had been hurt in some kind of trouble involving factory workers. However, he had heard the name 'Quinlan' mentioned and thought it might be in connection with the same incident, but this had all happened 'before his time'.

"Your best chance of finding your brother young lady," he had advised her, "is to go to the local police. I'm sure they will be able to offer you a lot more help than I can."

Maureen Ryan had been brought up to be suspicious of the police. At home in Dublin, the Royal Irish Constabulary represented British authority and as such were regarded as 'the enemy'. To her mind the police in Scotland would be no different, and anyway the man she was now working for had warned her against enlisting the help of the authorities. He knew that his failed attempt to sabotage the factory would have been covered up, but anyone making enquiries about Michael Quinlan at the local police station would immediately arouse suspicion. Maureen knew nothing of this, but she followed orders and did not take up the priest's suggestion. She went back to striking up casual conversations with people and asking if they had heard of her 'brother'.

After a fruitless week she began to lose heart, and she would soon have to look for other accommodation. She was about ready to give up her seemingly impossible search and return to Dublin when she had a stroke of good fortune.

The Institute in Gretna was a popular meeting place for the factory workers, and particularly for the Gretna Girls who went there to relax, read, drink tea, write letters and catch up on the latest gossip. Maureen, at a loss to know what to do next and worrying about having to go home and report her failure, was sitting idly drinking a cup of tea. She was half listening to the chatter of a group of young women, obviously factory workers, at a nearby table

A chance remark grabbed her immediate attention: "Whatever happened to that young man you were walking out with Kate, James I think he was called, is that great romance over?"

"Oh I haven't seen him since he went home to Ireland after his father died," replied the girl called Kate. "He said he was coming back to Gretna,

48

but I never thought that he would."

Maureen was by now fully alert. She took a deep breath and approached the group.

"Would you be talking about James Quinlan, by any chance?" she asked.

The girls looked up and carefully inspected the stranger. Eventually, seeming having satisfied herself that she was addressing a fellow factory worker, Kate spoke:

"Why, do you know him?" she said.

"Well if he's James Quinlan from Beaufort sure of course I know him, didn't we go to school together. I'd like to tell him how sorry I was to hear about his father, do you know where I can find him?"

The girls looked at each other and shrugged their shoulders. It was obvious that none of them knew where he was.

"It was tragic about James' father," said Maureen. "Do you know exactly how it happened?"

By now she had their confidence.

"Oh poor Mr. Quinlan died of a heart attack. On a train it was," said Kate. "They couldn't take his body back to Ireland because of the trouble over there and so he's buried in Carlisle." Following some thought she added: "The best person to ask about all that is Sarah Birks."

"Where can I find her?" said Maureen, "I'm new here and I might look her up when I have time."

"Oh everyone knows Sarah," said Kate. "Just go to the main office and they'll tell you where to find her."

Maureen would have liked to question the girls further but was wary of arousing suspicion. So she looked up at the clock, thanked them and hurried off as if she was late for work. The Gretna Girls went back to their gossip.

She was relieved that she had at least one positive piece of information to take back to Dublin: she had established that Michael Quinlan had in fact died from a heart attack. She had no idea of why this particular piece of information was of any importance, but she had been directed to find out and she had managed to do so. With any luck she might now accomplish the main part of her mission by discovering the whereabouts of James Quinlan. On leaving the Institute she headed straight for the main factory office building. She was full of confidence, but was due for a disturbing shock.

Had she known that Sarah Birks was an inspector in the Ministry of Munitions Women's Police, Maureen Ryan would not have gone anywhere near the factory. But by the time she realised her mistake it was too late and she was being ushered in to see the policewoman. She was greeted with a friendly smile, invited to sit and asked how the factory police could be of assistance. Maureen, now woefully out of her depth, could only manage to stumble through her story that she was a friend of the Quinlan family and was looking for James whom she hadn't seen since his father died. She said that she was anxious to pass on her condolences. There was a small but perceptible change in the policewoman's attitude and Maureen found herself having to answer some searching questions. How long had she known James? How well did she know his family? And, more pointedly, did she work at HM Factory Gretna or had she come here especially to find James.

In spite of being flustered Maureen was aware that if she lied she could be in trouble. She admitted that she did not work at the factory, and she concocted a story that she was on her way home to Ireland and had decided to look James up at Gretna on the way.

Eventually Inspector Birks had told Maureen that as far as she knew Mr. Quinlan no longer worked at the factory, but if Miss Ryan would like to wait she would double check. Maureen rapidly made her excuses and left. She mumbled that she did not want to put them to any further trouble and that she had to be on her way or she would miss her train. She hurried to the station, caught a train to Carlisle, picked up her bag and set off back to Ireland.

As she hadn't found James Quinlan in Gretna she had gone directly to Killarney as directed, to check if his family knew where he was.

"So you think the policewoman was suspicious and knew more than she was letting on," said 'Mr. Jameson'.

"I don't think Quinlan is there now or those girls would know it," said Maureen. "But from the way that copper quizzed me, and from what the priest said, I'd say that something happened over there and that he was part of it. If we could find out what it was, we'd be well on our way to finding out where he is. And sure there are loads of people around who can help us to do that."

"No!" said 'Mr. Jameson' emphatically. What she said confirmed his first impression that this girl had more brains than most, and so it had been wise not to tell her more than he needed her to know.

"I don't want anyone else involved in this yet. So remember now, not a word to a single soul about what you're doing for me, it's too important to The Cause. Do you hear me now Maureen?"

"Yes," she said, and under the circumstances felt it appropriate to add, "sir."

***

Maureen left and made her way home feeling more than a little puzzled by 'Mr. Jameson's' attitude. She was experienced enough to know that with the authorities fully alert following The Rising the need for secrecy was paramount, but the demand that positively no one else should be told what she was doing seemed extreme even by Irish Republican standards. If this man Quinlan had done something serious against The Cause why weren't several of 'the boys' trying to hunt him down? She would have liked to talk to her father and ask his opinion, but she worried that if there was a simple explanation he might be angry with her for breaking the golden rule of silence.

But when she got home she put her concerns aside as she heard the news her father had for her: The death sentence given to the leader of *Cumin an man*, Countess Constance Markievicz, for her part in The Rising, had been commuted to penal servitude for life.

"The Brits got cold feet about executing a woman," said Maureen's father from his chair by the fire.

He was talking about Constance Gore-Booth, the daughter of the wealthy land owner Sir Henry Gore-Booth. Constance had married the Polish nobleman, Count Markievicz, and in spite of her position and background she was a confirmed Irish Nationalist. Maureen had met the Countess, and when the *Cumann na mBan* leader was sentenced to death for treason after The Rising, she had prayed for her. Now it seemed that her prayers had been answered.

'Mr. Jameson' was also cheered by the news of another death sentence being rescinded: that of Eamonn de Valera. 'Dev', as he was known, was by now one of the most senior nationalist leaders still alive. As a relatively junior rebel commander during The Rising, he had been the last to surrender. He had been sentenced to death with the other leaders but, because he had been born in America, his sentence too was commuted to life imprisonment. For reasons of his own, 'Mr. Jameson' was heartened by the fact that the original sentence had not been carried out.

The Easter Rising was over, and although the military action had failed, the main objective had been achieved in that the seeds of Republicanism had been firmly sown. He was convinced that the British government would soon have to consider some degree of freedom for the Irish, and it did not really matter to him whether this came in the form of Home Rule or a fully independent Republic. With all of the senior nationalist leaders either dead or serving long prison sentences, there would be a political vacuum. He was sure that in their present mood the electorate would no longer support the incumbent Irish Parliamentary Party because they represented the old order, and he saw an opportunity to gain a position of real power for himself as part of an alternative political force.

Most of his life and work for The Cause had been spent in the shadowy world behind the scenes. So he was not known to many outside of the inner circles of the movement, and no one, except Pat Devlin, would as yet have heard of 'Mr. John Jameson'. But now, as he began the mission entrusted to him by the executed leaders of The Rising, that of rousing public resentment against British rule, he was hopeful that this name would become widely recognised. He knew, however, that Eamonn de Valera also had political ambitions and, had he been free, 'Dev' would have been a popular choice to lead the country. Now, however, with de Valera alive, but safely behind bars, 'Mr Jameson' was confident that he could use the situation to work his way into a position of power by acting as the public face of the man serving life imprisonment. And, given the chance, he might eventually replace him.

But in order to achieve his goal it became even more important that the one blot on his record, the failure of his attempt to sabotage the Gretna factory, be removed. To achieve that, James Quinlan would have to be found and silenced.

# Chapter 6

In Gretna, Inspector Sarah Birks knew a lot more about the whereabouts of James Quinlan than she had told Maureen Ryan. Immediately the Irish girl left her office she contacted her superior, Commander Wilson, the head of security at the factory.

Sarah knew James quite well and, more to the point, she was one of the very few people who knew where to find him. She had been working undercover with a good friend of James', Pete Casey, during the Irish nationalist attempt to sabotage the factory, and when James and his father, Michael, had become unwittingly involved in the plot Sarah had helped Pete to rescue them when they were taken hostage. After his father's death she had been one of those who persuaded James not to go home immediately in case the rebels found out that he had survived and blamed him for the failure of the plot. When James had eventually gone home Sarah had been convinced that he would never return to Gretna, but a mere four days later, while she was working late he turned up at her office totally unannounced.

"Good God! Jim," she had greeted him. "I never expected to see you again so soon, something must be very wrong."

James told her about arriving at Killarney and finding the rebel they still referred to as 'The Man from Dublin' not only there but due to speak in Beaufort that very evening.

"I didn't want to hang around with him there," he said, "I'd put Ma and Bill and the young ones in danger. So the only thing I could think of was to come back here. If that fella man knows that Daly didn't kill me, he'll be looking for me. He's sure to look for me here as well, but I was hoping that you could help me to get a job in one of the other factories until the war is over. After that I might go to America like Pete."

"Of course we'll help Jim, it's the least we can do," she told him. "Come on we'll go and see Commander Wilson, I know he's still on site and I'm sure he'll know what to do."

Commander Wilson, head of factory security, had only met James briefly but the lad's father had been a member of the commander's staff. He was also acutely aware that James' father had worked at the Irish country house belonging to his superior at the Ministry in London. And in spite of his current wartime duty as head of security at a munitions factory, Wilson was still officially a serving officer in the Royal Navy and as such he considered that Michael Quinlan had died under his command. He was, therefore, anxious to help.

They had looked up the locations and products of all the current munitions factories and picked out the one they thought best suited their purpose. Wilson had provided James with a reference and, they had sent him on his way.

Now, just a few weeks later, the problem again reared its head. The visit of Maureen Ryan clearly indicated that the matter of James Quinlan's safety was far from being resolved.

When Sarah told him about the visit of Maureen Ryan, Wilson at first feared that another attempt by Irish nationalists to disrupt the factory was being planned, but on reflection this seemed unlikely so soon after the rebel defeat in the Easter Rising. But neither he nor Sarah Birks were prepared to risk accepting the Irish girl's story that she was a concerned friend trying to find James Quinlan. They were agreed that the rebel leader who had escaped, and whom James could identify, was trying to ensure that his secret remained safe.

"Very well Inspector, you had better warn young Quinlan about this," said the Commander.

Sarah sat down to write to James but changed her mind and decided to go and see him instead. Because he still felt some measure of responsibility for the death of James' father, Commander Wilson agreed, but cautioned her to be careful. They could not be certain that there were no other rebel agents in the area and so she would have to make sure she was not followed. Wilson, who had learned from his previous brush with Irish nationalists, and unaware that James Quinlan was being sought by only one man, feared that if James were discovered by the rebels they would use it as a propaganda ploy. And he still feared that given the current mood in Ireland they would use any and every opportunity to cause trouble among the Irish workers here at his factory. In the interests of factory security he made some arrangements to try and eliminate any possibility of Sarah being watched and followed on her way to warn James.

So, early next morning, dressed in civilian clothes, she was driven out of the factory in Wilson's private car. At Carlisle she caught a train to Newcastle-upon-Time where she went directly to the police station. She changed into her uniform and was driven in a police vehicle to the village of Birtley near Gateshead. On arrival at Birtley she entered one of the munitions factories located there.

There were two British First World War munitions factories in Birtley, one producing artillery shells and the other making cartridge cases. What made them unique was that they were managed and staffed entirely by

54

Belgians. In 1915, to help redress the shortage of munitions reaching the soldiers in the field, the British Government had commissioned Armstrong-Whitworth to build the factories. But with nearly all able-bodied men either in uniform or engaged in other essential war-work, labour presented a problem. It was the Belgian government-in-exile who provided the answer: The Belgians agreed to manage and staff the factories while the British provided money and materials. By late 1916 the factories were almost exclusively manned by Belgian refugees and soldiers too badly wounded to return to the front.

James Quinlan was one of the very few non-Belgian munitions workers at Birtley, and he was the only Irishman. It seemed to be the ideal hiding place, which was why Wilson and Sarah had recommended it to him. Like all the Belgians workers, James lived in Elisabethville.

In keeping with the policy adopted for wartime munitions factories, accommodation had to be provided for the workers. This necessitated the construction of a complete self-contained new town like the one being built at Gretna. Named after the Queen of the Belgians, Elisabethville was designed to house some 3,000 men, many of them with their families. The new town boasted cottages complete with small gardens for the families, hostels for the single men, a school, a church and a cemetery

They were seated with cups of tea in the works canteen when Sarah told James about Maureen Ryan's visit and expressed her fear that the man they knew only as 'The Man from Dublin' was searching for him. She warned him to be ultra careful, and his previous experiences had left him in no doubt that she was right, but he had one concern:

"I'll have to write home soon," he said, "Ma will be worried and wanting to know whether I'm all right. But I can't tell her that without telling her where I am, and she'll want to write back. And the minute she does that the news will be all over Beaufort. If they are looking for me in Gretna they're sure to be looking there too. I don't want to put Ma and the rest in any danger."

"Yes I see your problem Jim," said Sarah. She thought for a while then came up with a solution: "We'll set up a relay system."

He looked puzzled, but she went on. "It's simple really. You give me a letter and I'll post it on from Gretna. Then your mother can post her reply back to me and I'll send it on to you here. I'll act as a go-between and you'll be able to keep in touch with your family without anybody knowing where you are."

They discussed it and agreed on a plan of action. "And Jim," she added with a laugh, "you won't have any excuse now for not writing home."

Before she left, James asked if she had heard from Peter Casey. Pete

in 1909 he joined the Irish Republican Brotherhood. On his return to Ireland in 1916 he took part in The Rising and served as an officer in the defence of the General Post Office where he fought alongside Padraig Pearse. He was arrested after the rebel surrender but was not considered senior enough to be tried for treason. While interned at Fron-goch he demonstrated exceptional organisational skills and was largely responsible for the large numbers recruited to the republican cause at the camp. On his release in December 1916 he went back to Ireland and turned his organisational skills to promoting The Cause. Collins' release was in effect the beginning of the next phase of armed resistance to British rule.

William Quinlan, although still only seventeen had, as a result of his efforts to support his mother, younger brother and sisters, come to be regarded in the Beaufort area as a grown man. It caused little comment therefore when he attended the homecoming 'hooley' held at Devlin's pub for the returning internees. Even his mother had raised no objections. With her husband dead and her two eldest sons having been away from home for over a year, save for James' all too brief visit home, she had come to accept William as the man of the family.

On arrival at the pub he was greeted with a glass of stout 'on the house' and joined a small group of local men standing together in a corner of the large lamp-lit and smoke filled room. The rest of the bar was packed with men, and the crowd overflowed into the grocery shop at the front of the premises. The few women present congregated in the kitchen. Before long his group, as William had expected it would be, was approached by Pat Devlin.

"'Evening men," said their host. He looked at William. "And how is your mother these days Bill? Is the poor woman showing any sign of getting over the loss of your father, God rest his soul?"

There was a shuffling of feet and some sympathetic murmurings among the group.

"Ah sure she's a whole lot better now Pat since she heard from Jim."

William knew that he wasn't telling Devlin anything that wasn't already common knowledge in the area. Mrs Connor, the postmaster's wife, carefully monitored all incoming mail and anything of the least interest was relayed to her friends in her weekly report to the ladies of the village every Sunday morning after Mass. So by now it was widely known that a letter had arrived for Annie Quinlan, which did not bear an official stamp as it would have done had it come from her son Jack. Mrs Connor had therefore deduced that it could only have been sent by James.

"And how is the bold Jim Quinlan getting on these days Bill?" Michael Flynn had joined the group. He was older than both William and James and had gone to school with Jack, but James had worked for the Flynn's on their farm and so Michael knew him well. "Is he still working at that munitions place over the water?"

"Ay he's still at it Mick," said William, "and the last we heard he's grand, thanks be to God. He even sent a bit of cash home to Ma."

"Is he still at the same place as he was when your father died?" said Devlin.

"No," said William, "sure isn't he gallivanting around all over the place over there, I don't think he knows where he will be from one day to the next."

"Jim was always a great one for gallivanting," said a member of the group, and they laughed.

William did not want to venture any further information but he realised that Devlin might well know that his mother had recently posted a letter addressed to 'Inspector Birks' at HM Factory Gretna in Scotland.

"The thing of it is it's hard to keep in touch with him," he said. "Ma sent a letter to someone Da and Jim knew at the first place they were at in the hope that they would pass it on to him. It eased her mind to write it, but I'd say that the chances of Jim getting it are small." He made a mental note to try and ensure that his mother's next letter to 'Inspector Birks' was posted from Killarney.

There was silence while this piece of information was digested.

Michael Flynn, as if suddenly remembering something, turned to William. "Jesus Bill," he said, "I was sorry to hear about your father. I never knew a thing about it until I came home yesterday. It must have been hard on your mother when she couldn't bring him home to be buried. Will you tell her that I'm sorry for her trouble?"

William could see that the concern was genuine, and was touched that Michael should have been thoughtful enough to mention it even though he had troubles aplenty of his own.

"Sure of course I will Mick," he said.

"Come on now lads drink up," said Devlin. "There's a barrel of good porter on the counter over there to be drunk before anyone thinks of buying a pint."

When they had replenished their glasses most of the group gathered around one of the other returned internees who began regaling them with tales of his exploits during The Rising and his consequent internment. With the aid of the strong porter he went on to denounce the British and call on everyone present to support 'The Cause'. It seemed to William, standing at the back of the group with Michael Flynn, that the words and phrases used sounded far more eloquent than anything he would have expected from the

Sean Murphy he had known for years.

"Sean must have gone back to school to learn all them big words while he was over there in Wales," he said.

"Ah sure he learned all that off by heart from your man, Michael Collins, in the camp," Michael replied.

"Jesus it must have been hell for you to be picked up and carted off like that Mick. What was it like to be in the prison camp?" said William. "Were you put on at all by the Brits, what was life like there?"

Michael Flynn was conscious of the fact that William Quinlan was the only person, outside of his family, who had shown the slightest interest in the actual conditions at Fron-goch internment camp. Most were more concerned with the circumstances that had landed him there. They were intent on building him up into a nationalist hero, irrespective of the fact that he had not played even the smallest part in The Rising.

"Ah sure it wasn't too bad at all," he said. "We had enough to eat and the huts were dry. The country over there is a lot like here, and you could see the mountains. There were a few of the soldiers you had to steer clear of, but most of them were decent enough fellas. They knew they were a lot better off guarding us than they would be on the Western Front."

He went on to explain that the camp was split into two parts: one section was an old abandoned distillery where most of those who had been tried and sentenced to long terms of imprisonment were housed. The other part of the camp was made up of rough wooden huts to accommodate the other internees. Fron-goch had originally been used to house German prisoners of war but, after The Rising, the Germans were moved elsewhere to make room for the Irish. William listened intently as Flynn told him about Michael Collins and his recruitment campaign.

"Did you join yourself Mick?" said William.

"I did so Bill," Michael replied. "But it wasn't what Collins said that made me do it. It was the way I was picked up and carted off over to Wales by the British Army, without ever having lifted a finger against them. We'll have to put a stop to that kind of thing happening in Ireland once and for all."

William noted the bitterness in Michael's tone, a bitterness that was unusual for the normally easy-going farmer's son. "Do you think that this fella Collins is the man to do it?" he said.

"He might be," said Michael. "I'd say that he'll lead the next rebellion, and if Collins has any say in it, there's sure to be one. But when it comes down to it I'd rather see Eamonn de Valera in charge. I saw him on the ship when we were being transported over the water. He tried to talk to us before the soldiers dragged him off. But I'll tell you this Bill: there is a man who could really lead Ireland to freedom. It's a terrible pity that he's serving life in Lewes Gaol. God knows we need him here."

They sipped some porter. "And what about yourself Bill where do you stand?"

William had been expecting the question. For some time now he had been mulling things over in his mind and trying to reconcile his various responsibilities. He was certain that he wanted to see Ireland free of British rule and he sincerely believed that he should play a part. But there was his mother and the young ones to think of. And there was James' problem with 'The Man from Dublin' and he had to tread carefully in order protect his brother. He was also conscious of how Jack would feel if he came home from the war and found William armed and ready to kill British soldiers. Jack had gone off to war to fulfil what amounted to a feudal duty. When the war was over, and Beaufort House reopened, at least one member of the Quinlan family would have to go to work there in order to justify their occupation of the cottage. In all probability that responsibility would fall to Jack, and it might not be well received if William was found to be an active member of an armed republican faction.

"I'm all for an independent Ireland Mick. I hope to God that we can get it by peaceful means, but if the worst comes to the worst I'll be ready."

"Good man yourself I'm with you there," said Michael.

The porter flowed, the speeches were soon over and the party had moved on to lustily sung rebel songs. In the early hours William and Michael, both of whom were careful about how much they drank, made their separate ways home in the moonlight. A bond of sorts had been formed between them.

\*\*\*

In Dublin, Christmas 1916 for Maureen Ryan was, in spite of being in mourning for one brother, a joyous time. Her other brother had been released from the internment camp. After lunch on Christmas Day she sat by the kitchen fire with her father and her brother, Kevin, while her mother and sister cleared up. Kevin related to them his experience of life as an internee.

"I suppose that all the lads that were taken over to Wales were the ones that held up the great British Army for a whole week here in Dublin." said John Ryan.

"Not at all Da," said Kevin. "Sure some of them never took part at all in The Rising, but the Brits lifted them all the same. There was one fella in the same hut as me from a place called Beaufort down in County Kerry who had nothing at all to do with the ructions. But I'll tell you this, after what the Brits did to him he'll be with us the next time."

At the mention of Beaufort Maureen sat up in her chair and before she could stop herself she said: "Oh sure I know Beaufort, I was down there myself a couple of months ago."

"And what would you be doing down in the County Kerry?" said her father in surprise. "Was it part of what you were doing for the fella over in Rathmines? And while we're on the subject, I could see that you weren't altogether happy with what you were doing for him."

"You're right there Da, sure I couldn't make head nor tail of what any of it was about." She took a deep breath. "Look Da, I know I'm not supposed to say anything to anybody, but I'm sure that I can trust yourself and Kevin."

She told them about her travels to look for someone called James Quinlan, and concluded by saying: "The queer thing is Da, if that fella did something terrible against The Cause, why aren't all the lads after him, and not just that man and me?"

Her father thought about for a while. Eventually he looked at her with concern in his eyes:

"Be very careful Maureen darlin'," he said. "I know about your man over in Rathmines, and he's one to be watched. Oh he works hard for Ireland all right, there's no doubt about that, but I'd say this thing he has you doing is nothing at all to do with The Cause. He's after this fella Quinlan for personal reasons. Quinlan did something, or saw something, or knows something that your man wants kept quiet. So you watch yourself because if he ever got the notion that you know what that secret is, he'd do for you just as quick as he would our friend Quinlan."

***

In Beaufort it was the first Christmas since Michael had died. Annie hoped that James would come home for the festival yet she knew in her heart that this was not to be. But just in time Christmas a letter arrived which served to bring her at least some seasonal cheer.

Jack's letter from Mesopotamia included a photograph of himself together with two other soldiers in tropical dress. It was given pride of place on the mantelpiece. Jack's two companions were identified as Patrick Coughlin and James Daly of the Connaught Rangers.

# Chapter 8

Bombardier Jack Quinlan ducked involuntarily as the shell whistled over his head. It plunged down and exploded with a 'crump' just short of the Turkish position and well to the left of its designated target.

"Add 50, go right 100," said the OP officer, a young lieutenant who exhibited a calmness beyond his years and experience.

"Add 50, go right 100." Jack relayed the fire order to the guns over the field telephone.

The order was repeated back by the gunner manning the telephone at the battery gun site. In his mind's eye Jack could picture the actions the order would have instigated around number one gun. During the time it took to reload, the necessary traverse and elevation alterations would be calculated by the man on the Artillery Board and the settings on the gun adjusted accordingly. An officer would give the order to fire. The 18 pounder would buck and recoil and send the next round on its murderous way.

Fifteen seconds later Jack ducked again as the shell went over and this time landed on the exact spot, right on top of the enemy trench.

"On target," said the OP officer.

"On target," repeated Jack into the telephone.

Up and down the line the same exercise was being carried out, and soon all the guns, the 18 pounder field pieces and the heavy 5 inch guns behind them, were registered on target. Jack and the lieutenant crouched down among the rocks where their observation post was sited, and the British artillery opened up all along the front.

The Tigris Corps had a new commander in Major General Stanley Maud, and the Corps had been refitted and reinforced. Lessons had been learned from the previous year's failure to relieve the siege of Kut-al-Amara. The Corps had been resupplied with more men, more and better equipment, improved medical facilities and transport. So that now, for the first time in the campaign, British forces outnumbered and outgunned the Turks. One reason for the efforts being made to build up the army in Mesopotamia was that Britain badly needed a victory to bolster moral at home where the stalemate and horrific casualties on the Western Front was sapping the resolve of the people. Under Maud, who had the reputation for being a cautious commander, there would be no more hastily planned and ill-coordinated mass infantry attacks made on heavily defended enemy positions. Time would now be taken for proper planning, and this time around the planners would take into account the atrocious local conditions. Winter and spring in Mesopotamia meant rain, and when it stopped raining the ground was a quagmire until the sun and the wind dried it brick hard. The drying process produced a clinging mist which obscured everything. In the hot humid air when the troops were not soaked by the rain they were drenched with their own sweat. At night it was freezing cold. The only things that thrived in Mesopotamia were the mosquitoes and the flies. No military planners, however skilled, could possibly devise a method of overcoming these conditions but at least they were now taken into account rather than being ignored as had happened in the past.

In December 1916 Kut was retaken and by January the following year the march on Baghdad was under way

Jack and the OP officer, Lieutenant Elliott, crouched in their cramped little rocky fortress and did their best to ignore the noise. Every so often, by the light of the fires and the sound of the explosions, the lieutenant checked on the accuracy of the shelling and passed adjustments via Jack back to the guns. Occasionally a shell dropped short and the ground trembled. A detachment of infantry were in position to protect the OP and there were skirmishes with Turkish patrols as they attempted to put the British observation post out of action. When the Turkish artillery tried to come into action some of the British guns were redeployed to silence them. There was little time to worry about the wet and the cold.

In the reorganisation of the Tigris Corps Jack had been retrained as a signaller and had 'drawn the short straw' in being assigned to serve at the observation post. He had been in action before, and undergone some extensive training, but no amount of practise could fully prepare him for the horrors of battle. There was no hiding place in the OP, you were a target for both enemy artillery and infantry, and in the forward positions snipers posed a particular danger. Jack and the young lieutenant bolstered each other's confidence by speculating on how much worse things were for the Turks who were to be on the receiving end of an unrelenting rain of high explosives. Although there could never be a significant friendship between the commissioned and non-commissioned officers they had developed an understanding, and worked well together.

At dawn the barrage was lifted and the rain came down. There was a deafening silence for a few moments. Then a series of shrill whistles signalled the beginning of the infantry attack. The noise of the artillery was replaced by the rattle of machine guns, the crack of rifles and the shouts of men as the first wave made a frontal assault across the muddy ground. Soon the shouts were joined by screams. From Jack's position it was difficult to see what was happening in the Turkish trenches through the rain and the smoke, where he knew that men would be locked in desperate hand-to-hand fighting. But the British second wave went in on schedule, and by noon the Turks were in full retreat.

Getting used to the thunder of the bombardment was one thing, but getting used to what followed the infantry attack was something else entirely. The actual assault was shrouded by the rain and smoke, but once the Turkish trenches had been taken and the smoke cleared, the sight of the battleground littered with dead and wounded was something that would live with Jack Quinlan for the rest of his life. He knew that Lieutenant Elliott was similarly affected, and that he too had difficulty in dragging his gaze away in order to concentrate on his principal duties as OP officer. The still bodies of the obviously dead were easy to discern as they lay limp and still, but it was the plight of the wounded writhing in the mud or wandering about helplessly that was so pitiful. Even with the improved medical services there was clearly still a severe lack of experienced orderlies, stretcher bearers and field ambulances. What frustrated Jack and the lieutenant most was that they could do absolutely nothing to help. Although the retreating Turks were now out of sight, and other field artillery units equipped with the light 13 pounders had moved forward in support of the advancing infantry, they had to remain at their posts and be ready to direct fire in the event of an enemy counter-attack. So they waited and watched and drank some of the stale lukewarm water from their canteens. Neither man had the stomach to eat their field rations.

"What's the chance of a counter-attack sir," asked Jack.

"Pretty slim I should think," said the officer. "Hopefully we might be relieved in an hour or two. If anyone remembers that we are still out here that is," he added with a grin.

The lieutenant went back to looking through his binoculars at something in the far distance while Jack gazed morosely over the scene in front and said some silent prayers for the dead and wounded.

Some way off an infantryman was trying to help an obviously seriously wounded comrade and calling for stretcher bearers. There was something vaguely familiar about them.

"Can I have a loan of the binoculars sir?" he said.

The lieutenant handed the glasses over and Jack focused them on the two infantrymen.

"Oh Jesus no," he exclaimed. Pat Coughlin was lying on the ground clearly badly hurt and James Daly, who also seemed to be covered in blood, was trying to help him.

"What's the matter Quinlan?" said the officer.

"I know the two wounded infantrymen over there sir," said Jack. "They're good friends of mine, is there any chance at all that I can go and help them sir?" he pleaded.

Lieutenant Elliott thought hard. He knew that he should follow orders and deny the request. But, although he did not know these men, by sending Jack to help them he might at least relieve some of his own frustration at not being able to do anything for the wounded. He took the binoculars from Jack and looked for himself.

"It looks as if the man on the ground is quite badly hit," he said.

He made up his mind: "All right Quinlan, see if you and the other chap can manage to get him back here. But be quick about it. I'll get the medical kit ready."

"Yes sir, thank you sir," said Jack. And with that he was gone.

"Jesus Jack, where did you come from," said James Daly as Jack came running up to him.

"I was in the OP over there," said Jack. He looked down and almost recoiled in shock as he saw that Coughlin's leg was a mass of blood, raw flesh and bone. The wounded man was breathing but had passed out.

"What happened to him Jim?" he asked Daly.

"A bloody heathen Turk threw a bomb at us, and Pat got the worst of it," said Daly.

"Can we move him," said Jack. "If we can move him over our OP, Lieutenant Elliott has a medical kit there."

"Well we can't leave him here in the bloody mud getting soaked with the rain," said Daly. "If we wait for stretcher bearers we'll be here till Saint Patrick's Day. Come on give us a hand. We'll make a seat for him with our arms under his arse and carry him sitting up. But you'll have to take that side Jack, the bastard with the bomb got me in this arm and broke it."

Jack noticed that Daly's left arm was dangling uselessly at his side.

They managed to get the groaning Coughlin up and made their way to the OP. "I hope to God that the poor bugger doesn't wake up. He's better off not knowing a thing about this," said Daly.

After a struggle they reached the OP. The lieutenant gave Coughlin an injection from the medical kit to relieve the pain and held a canteen to his lips.

"That's all we can do for him here I'm afraid," he said. "I'd be very reluctant to touch that leg without the proper equipment, even if I was sure of what I was doing."

He turned to Daly: "Now what about that arm Private, it's obviously broken but you appear to be able to walk pretty well. You should make your way to a dressing station before you become infected."

"Ah sure don't I know already that its broken sir, but it'll have do till we get poor old Pat there fixed up. Until then I'd rather stop here with him if it's all right with you sir." Daly was obviously reluctant to leave his friend.

"No, private," said the lieutenant. "The best way to help your friend is to find the nearest dressing station and tell them to send someone back here to attend to him. Tell them that Lieutenant Elliott said to come to the artillery OP. Quinlan and I can't leave here, so it is all up to you."

"He's right Jim," said Jack. "You can't do Pat any good with a broken arm. Sure we'll look after him until you send us back some help."

As Daly was leaving he saluted with his good arm and said: "God bless you for your help sir, sure don't I know well that you've done more than you should have." He looked at Jack: "We'll have a drink together the three of us when this is over Jack."

"We will too Jim," said Jack.

Coughlin stirred and groaned. Lieutenant Elliott looked on in sympathy as Jack unashamedly crossed himself and said a prayer for his friend.

Eventually two stretcher bearers came up. They gently loaded Coughlin onto the stretcher and carried him back to a regimental aid post. If they thought anything about finding a badly wounded Connaught Ranger at an artillery observation post they said nothing about it. There was little that could be done at the aid post except give him another injection and send him back to an advanced dressing station. From there he was taken by field ambulance to a casualty clearing station and eventually back to the base hospital at Basra.

Some weeks later when Jack's battery had been relieved, and he was sent back to the base at Basra, he made his way the Connaught Rangers' lines. He found James Daly with his arm in a sling doing light duties. Daly was delighted to see him:

"Good man yourself Jack. I knew you'd make it."

"How is Pat? Did they manage to save him?" said Jack.

"Sure isn't he living the life of luxury in the hospital being looked after by all those lovely nurses? They saved his leg and they're going to send the blackguard home. He's going to the hospital in Blighty, and then to the barracks in Tipperary of all places."

"Ah sure that's grand," said a very relieved Jack.

Daly grew serious: "I'll say this Jack, if it wasn't for you, and that young officer of yours, Pat wouldn't be alive today. Sure I'd never have got him out of it on my own."

They went to the hospital together and found Coughlin being prepared for movement with other soldiers who had received a 'Blighty one'. They would soon be taken down the Tigris by boat to a hospital ship bound for Britain.

Before he left for home Coughlin promised to visit both of his friends' families when he was up and about and on sick leave in Ireland. He also promised Daly that he would find out what he could about the situation in Ireland regarding independence. Something which Jack noted seemed to be of growing importance to his friend.

"And for Christ's sake don't tell anyone that a Connaught Ranger had to have his arse saved by two bloody gunners, or we'll never live it down," was Daly's parting shot.

# Chapter 9

Things were not working out as 'Mr Jameson' had been hoping they would. A year had passed since his failure to sabotage the Gretna factory and the only witness to his part in the fiasco, at least the only living witness who was not bound to secrecy by British security, was not to be found. James Quinlan could ruin his political ambitions if he were allowed to tell what he knew, and recent developments meant that silencing Quinlan was becoming more important than ever.

Soon after the release of the republican internees he had been contacted by Michael Collins who was in the process of setting up a republican spy network and needed 'Mr Jameson's' years of experience in undercover operations. This was not the future he had mapped out for himself. His ambition was to become involved in Irish frontline politics, and to this end he was beginning to make a name for himself speaking to groups all over the country. He was also coming to the attention of the authorities, which to him was no bad thing as it would serve to add to his credibility as an ardent republican. It did not, however, suit Michael Collins' purpose. Collins needed him to help set up covert operations, which meant that he would have to go back into the shadows. He dare not refuse because Collins was fast building a reputation for ruthlessness and would not hesitate to eliminate anyone he even considered to be standing in his way. So 'Mr Jameson' agreed to work with Collins, conscious that if it came to light that he had failed The Cause once he would never again be trusted. And it was not only his political ambitions that would be at an end – he might well forfeit his life into the bargain. He had to find James Quinlan.

Maureen Ryan had by now visited several of the dozens of wartime munitions factories on the British mainland, but without success. 'Mr. Jameson' had heard of the existence of the factory at Birtley but had dismissed the possibility of his quarry being there because, according to his information, all the employees were Belgians. Not only had Maureen's quest been fruitless, it had also proved to be expensive. Although he had access to the Irish nationalist movement's funds, most of which were coming from America, he would not have been able to draw on them without providing a valid reason and this he would find very difficult to do. So he was obliged to pay for Maureen's trips 'across the water' out of his own pocket, although he left her under the impression that The Cause was footing the bill. Finally he reached the conclusion that the only way he could trap young Quinlan was to lie in wait for him in Beaufort and deal with him there when he eventually returned home; irrespective of what Pat Devlin might have to say.

But how best to achieve this? He reasoned that there was every possibility of James Quinlan returning home in the near future. It would be Easter in a few weeks, the anniversary of his father's death, and Quinlan might feel a need to come and comfort his mother. But it was obvious from the way he had gone to ground that he was aware of the fact that he was being hunted. 'Mr Jameson' suspected that he had been spotted by Quinlan when they were both in Beaufort and that this was the reason for the lad's sudden departure. It seemed that he was also being helped by the policewoman at Gretna, otherwise why would his mother have written to 'Inspector Birks' as had been reported by Pat Devlin. Another disturbing aspect of Devlin's last report was that the Beaufort publican thought Quinlan's younger brother also knew much more than he was letting on.

"He's a smart one young Bill Quinlan. I'd say that even if he doesn't know where his brother is, he knows how to get in touch with him," said Devlin as they were seated over a pint of porter in a pub in Killarney. 'Mr. Jameson' did not want to be seen too frequently in Beaufort.

"Do you suppose that his brother told him what happened over in Gretna?" he asked Devlin.

"I wouldn't put it past him," said Devlin. He was keenly aware that he himself did not know what had 'happened over in Gretna', but the way things were shaping up he had decided that he definitely did not want to know. The more he saw of this man's extraordinary efforts to find James Quinlan the more he was convinced that anyone else who was even suspected of knowing about the happenings at Gretna was in mortal danger. And, as a result of what he had just told 'Mr Jameson', that now included James' brother, William.

'Mr Jameson' sensed Devlin's unease. When he returned to Dublin he worried that should Quinlan come home at some point he could easily be there and gone before Devlin knew about it, as had happened on the previous occasion. Reluctantly he decided that he would have to enlist further help. But who could he trust?

It was Maureen Ryan who provided the answer: He was in the process of telling her that he had decided to abandon the search for Quinlan on the British mainland, and concentrate on laying in wait for him when he returned home to Beaufort, when she made a chance remark:

"My brother, Kevin, was in the internment camp in Wales with a fella from Beaufort," she said.

'Mr Jameson' immediately took notice. "Was this one of the boys who fought in The Rising and was captured?" he said.

"No," said Maureen, "according to my brother he was one of the people picked up off the street for no reason at all and sent to the camp with the rest."

The Man was disappointed. "Ah sure it's a pity he's not one of us."

"He might be now," she said, "Kevin says he's mad at the Brits for the way he was treated, and Michael Collins recruited him into The Volunteers while he was in the camp. I don't know his name but I could ask Kevin if you want me to."

The Man's obsession with secrecy surfaced: "Don't do that, didn't I tell you not to say anything to anybody," he said sharply.

He regained his composure: "All right Maureen, leave it to me for a while. I'll call you when I need you again."

After she left he contacted Pat Devlin and learned that Michael Flynn had gone to school with one of James Quinlan's brothers and was friendly with another. And it could be significant that Quinlan had worked for the Flynn family on their farm. It sounded as if he had found his man, but how best to use him? That was the question.

*&ast;*

To the south of the village of Beaufort the Gap of Dunloe cut through the MacGillycuddy's Reeks mountain range to the area known as The Black Valley. It was a wild sparsely populated place. In winter it was bleak and almost completely deserted, but in summer it was renowned for its spectacular beauty. Before the war, tourists would be driven out from Killarney in jaunting cars to Kate Kearney's Cottage where they would hire ponies for the ride through 'The Gap' to view the scenery. But through the whole of 1917 this trade had virtually dried up. Most people in Britain were too preoccupied with the war to worry about visiting the Lakes of Killarney and, since the sinking of the *SS Lusitania*, few Americans would brave the German u-boats and cross the Atlantic purely for pleasure. This made 'the Gap' the perfect location for training a secret army.

Here in 'The Gap' the survivors of The Rising, freed from internment and with new recruits to The Irish Republican Brotherhood and The Volunteers, met to regroup and plan the next phase in the fight for Irish freedom. Few weapons and no uniforms had been salvaged from the failure of Easter 1916, but even before the release of the internees men met here to march and train by moonlight; talk about The Cause, and make plans for the next armed rebellion.

Although not officially a member of any of the republican organisations William Quinlan was aware of their clandestine activities. He knew the area well. In summer he spent what little spare time he had on the riverbank, but in winter he would wander around the Gap looking for deer and visiting the mountain tributaries of the Laune to watch the salmon spawn.

Since the night of the party to welcome home the internees he had become friendly with Michael Flynn. They shared many of the same interests, particularly fishing. William knew that Michael was involved with the rebels and he was gradually drawn in to their activities. Michael's mother was worried about his association with the 'the boys' as they became known, she had already endured his internment and feared that next time she would lose him for good. So William would call for Michael on the pretext that they were going fishing or hunting for rabbits, but instead they would go 'up the Gap' where Michael would join in the training exercises, and William would follow his own pursuits. By the spring of 1917, however, he had begun to accompany Michael and was a rebel in all but name.

# Chapter 10

It was the second Sunday in March, the one immediately preceding St. Patrick's Day, and on that great Irish Saint's day the salmon fishing season was deemed to open. There was an official opening date a few weeks earlier, but for as long as anyone could remember March 17th, a public holiday, had been considered a more convenient time to begin. The spawning season was over, the spring floods were receding and the days were getting longer. Even the salmon seemed to be happy with the arrangement and one or two were invariably caught on 'Patrick's Day'. On this particular Sunday there was a definite hint of spring in the air, and the afternoon had been set aside by William Quinlan and Michael Flynn for checking their fishing tackle in preparation for the opening day. It had been decided that they would meet at William's home by the river.

Maureen Ryan waited until she was certain they were both inside the Quinlan cottage before crossing the bridge.

It was Annie who answered the door. She started in surprise to find Maureen standing there, but soon recovered and greeted her unexpected visitor with a smile.

"Sure if it isn't yourself Miss Ryan, James' friend from the munitions place," she said. "But if you're looking for him I'm afraid that you're having no more luck than the last time you came. I'm sorry to say he's not here."

They stood for a moment until Annie was struck by an awful thought and quickly crossed herself: "Oh Holy Mother of God," she cried, "don't tell me that something else terrible has happened over there at that factory. I always knew no good would come out of that place."

"Oh no, no Mrs Quinlan," said Maureen quickly. "It's nothing at all like that. Sure I haven't been in Gretna myself for ages now, I left there months ago and I'm working in Killarney now. I just called in on the chance that James might be here. I thought he could tell me how things are over there and how some of the people I knew there are getting on."

Annie breathed a sigh of relief: "Thanks be to God," she said. "I'm afraid that since Michael died and Jack and James went away, I'm forever expecting bad news."

"I'm sorry to have worried you again Mrs. Quinlan," said Maureen. "I seem to be doing it every time I come here. I'm sure that James is all right though. Have you heard from him at all?"

Annie had regained her composure: "Ah sure I'm getting letters from him all the time. But will you look at the pair of us standing here at the door, come on in now and I'll make a cup of tea."

Maureen was surprised to find the kitchen deserted.

"The young ones are out playing with their friends and 'young' Michael is up at the church with Father O'Brien getting ready for the big Mass on St. Patrick's Day. But William is around somewhere with a friend of his sorting out their fishing tackle."

Annie went to the back door and called out: "Come in here this minute William, look who's come back to see us."

"It's Miss Ryan again, looking for James," she said as William entered, closely followed by Michael.

Before William could say anything Maureen rose and held out her hand. "Hello William, it's grand to see you again," she said, and looked expectantly at Michael Flynn.

"This handsome fella is Michael Flynn," said Annie. "He's a friend of William's.

Michael blushed but found pleasure in briefly holding Maureen's hand in his.

"Michael is a friend of James too," said Annie, "and he went to school with Jack. That's Jack there in the picture," she added proudly, pointing to the photograph on the mantelpiece. She failed to notice the look of distaste that passed over Maureen's face as she looked at the picture of the three soldiers, but it was picked up by William.

"Have you seen James at all over there in Gretna, Miss Ryan?" said William. "We hear from him sometimes but we don't know where he is. Sure he's travelling around the whole country over there and is never in the same place for any time at all. His letters are sent on to us by someone at Gretna. Did you ever come across an Inspector Birks at the factory miss?"

William was intent on telling her the same story he told everybody else before his mother could give her embellished version. He noticed that Maureen Ryan showed a brief moment of alarm at the mention of the factory policewoman's name.

Annie saved her from having to answer William's question: "Oh sure Miss Ryan doesn't work over there anymore. She left that terrible place long ago. She's working in Killarney now," she said.

"Well I'm not exactly working there yet," said Maureen, "but I start at the Great Southern Hotel tomorrow morning. They're only taking me on until after Easter, but if the tourist trade picks up I have the promise of a job there for the summer."

For reasons he couldn't quite understand this news pleased Michael. He was dying to join in the conversation but, "ah sure that's grand Miss Ryan," was all he could think to say.

"Tell me, why did you decide to leave the factory?" said William. Something about Miss Ryan had begun to bother him but he couldn't put his finger on what.

Maureen was silent for a few moments. Then as if having made her mind up about something she said. "Well it was like this. My brother was arrested after The Rising last year and taken to one of those horrible internment camps. My mother took it very hard, and Da is a cripple, so I came home to be with them."

"But he's out now thank God," she added brightly, "so I had to find another job. There's nothing at all going in Dublin these days, so here I am in Killarney."

Annie looked up from making the tea. "Sure wasn't Michael there arrested, and put in one of them camps himself," she said.

Maureen feigned surprise. "Is that right Michael?" she said. "Where did they have you locked up?"

"Over in Wales," he said. "A place called Fron-goch."

She continued to play her part well. Her surprise seemed authentic: "But sure that's the same place as my brother was. Maybe you knew him. Now that I think about it, he said there were some lads from around here in the camp with him. His name is Kevin, Kevin Ryan."

Michael was stunned. He felt an attraction to this girl and the thought that he knew her brother was more than he could have hoped for. "Kevin Ryan from Dublin," he exclaimed. "Sure of course I know him! Weren't we in the same hut together? He was telling me all about his family up in Dublin."

A look of concern crossed his face. "But he told me he had brother who was killed in The Rising."

"Yes," she said. "Sean was killed in the troubles. Murdered by the British," she added bitterly.

Annie crossed herself. "Mother of God pray for us," she said, "is there to be no end to it at all. We have Irishmen like Jack fighting for the British against the Turks and the Germans, and other Irishmen all set to fight to the British. And all the rest of us can do is say our Rosary and pray that God spares us."

They drank their tea in silence.

When they had finished Maureen stood up and said: "Well I'll have to be on my way, I have to get ready to go to work in the morning. Thanks for the tea Mrs Quinlan."

She looked at Michael and held out her hand: "It was nice to meet you Michael. Maybe we'll get the chance sometime to have a chat about yourself and Kevin and the internment camp."

Before Michael could answer she turned to William and said: "I don't like to ask, but if it's no bother could you give me a lift into Killarney again William?"

William nodded but then had a thought. He looked over to where Michael was standing trying not to stare too hard at Maureen. "Sure why don't you run her into Killarney yourself Mick. You can have a loan of the pony and trap, can't he Ma?"

"William is right Michael," said Annie. "You could have that chat about your brother on the way there Miss Ryan."

"That would be grand," said Maureen. "Are you sure you don't mind Michael."

Michael didn't mind in the least. "Sure it's no trouble at all, I'd be glad to take you to into Killarney Miss Ryan," he said.

"Thank you Michael, and please call me Maureen," she said.

When they left Annie looked at William: "I think you did Michael a favour by letting him drive her into Killarney," she said. "He could hardly take his eyes off of her. But I can't say that I blame him sure she's a lovely looking girl."

"That might be so Ma," William answered. "But don't forget she was here twice now looking for Jim. But when you wrote to him about it he sent back to say that he'd never heard of her. Did you see the face she pulled when she saw Jack's picture, and when I asked her about Jim's friend Inspector Birks she had a worried look about her."

\*\*\*

In the trap on the Killarney road, Michael was at first a little tongue-tied but she soon put him at ease. They talked about her brother and the internment camp for a while before she brought up the subject that had really brought her to Beaufort.

"Mrs Quinlan said that you went to school with her son James," she said.

"No, that was Jack," said Michael, "but I know Jim too, he used to work for my father."

"Would you let me know when he comes home to visit?" said Maureen.

"Sure of course I will," he said. He opened his mouth to speak again, but he paused and a look of disappointment gradually replaced his smile. "Ah sure I see it now, you're sweet on Jim Quinlan. Were you going with him over the water?"

Much to her own surprise, Maureen sought to quickly deny that suggestion. She reached over and touched his arm: "Oh no Michael, that's not it at all, sure I hardly knew him at all. I only met him a couple of times. He was walking out with a friend of mine and she hasn't heard from him since he left after his father died. When she heard I was coming to Killarney she asked me to look him up."

Michael was so relieved that he failed to see any of the flaws in her story: "Sure I'll let you know the minute I set eyes on him Maureen."

"Thanks Michael," she said. "And promise me that if you do see James you won't say a word to him about me. It might embarrass him if too many people know he was courting a girl over there and that she's still keen on him. It'll be better that we keep this between the two of us until we see how things work out."

Having something to keep 'between the two of them' and sharing a secret with Maureen Ryan was something that suited Michael very well. "Sure you can rely on me all the way Maureen," he said. "But how will I let you know if he turns up?"

"Give me a few days to settle in and find out what hours I'm on, and I'll leave a note for you at the reception in The Great Southern," she said.

After he dropped her off in Killarney Maureen watched him out of sight. There was something about him that she had not expected, and it bothered her when she could not but her finger on what it was.

That night she penned a short note to 'Mr. Jameson' in Dublin to let him know that she had made contact with the person she assumed to be 'his' man in Beaufort. But she did not tell him that the meeting had not gone as she had imagined it would. As she thought things over, she realised that she had expected to meet a fully committed republican rebel ready to die for The Cause like her father and brother, and indeed, most of the men she knew in Dublin. Michael Flynn had, however, turned out to be a pleasant easy-going country man, and although she had detected the note of bitterness when he spoke of his internment, he was not at all the kind of person she would have expected to be working for 'Mr Jameson'. Furthermore it was evident that Flynn was a close friend of the Quinlan family. These thoughts disturbed her. She failed to see how this fitted in with 'Mr Jameson's' plan, whatever that was.

She also found herself being drawn into thinking of Michael Flynn in a far more personal context; something she knew was against all the principles of undercover work for The Cause.

# Chapter 11

After Maureen had stepped lightly down from the trap outside the Great Southern Hotel on Sunday evening Michael Flynn knew that he simply had to see her again. She had said that she would leave a note for him at the hotel reception 'in a few days' and those few days seemed to take forever to pass. St Patrick's Day arrived, and after Mass he went fishing with William, but it was clear that his mind was not on the fish. Had they not agreed to share the catch, he would have gone home with nothing.

Back at the Quinlan cottage he could not avoid Annie's knowing looks and smiles. William could see that his friend was besotted. He would have liked to warn Michael about his suspicions regarding Maureen Ryan, but could not find a way of doing so without revealing the whole story of James and 'The Man from Dublin'. Although he trusted Michael to keep it to himself, he felt that the fewer people who got involved in James' predicament the better.

By Wednesday Michael could wait no longer. After milking and completing his morning chores on the farm he excused himself and muttered something about having to go into Killarney. Although the thousands of small Irish farmers who rented poor land from rich landowners still struggled to make a living, people like the Flynn's who owned their own land, were doing well out of the war. There was a now a ready market for their produce 'across the water' in war-torn Britain. As Michael was their only son, the Flynn's had been forced to hire a farmhand to cope with the extra work. In the first instance that man had been James Quinlan. But James had gone to work at the munitions factory in Scotland, and soon after that Michael had been interred. So two hired men had been required to work on the Flynn farm, and even after Michael's return home these had been kept on. So he could easily be spared for a few hours from work on the farm

When he first told his mother that he was going to Killarney she hoped that the trip had nothing to do with 'the boys' as the rebels were known. But as he cycled off, she was gratified to see that he was wearing his best suit, something he would not have done to go 'up The Gap'. So she thought nothing further about it.

For her part, Maureen Ryan soon settled into working in a hotel. The Great Southern was the largest and best appointed hotel in Killarney. It stood opposite the station and was owned and operated by the railway company of the same name. Even though the tourist trade had been badly hit by the war, The Great Southern still enjoyed a good trade from rail passengers. When 'Mr. Jameson' had used his Nationalist contacts to secure a job for her there Maureen had asked if she was meant to watch the comings and goings at the station, but he had said no. She was not to do anything to attract attention to her. Her job, he said, was to get Michael Flynn to tell her when James Quinlan came home to Beaufort, and when she heard this news, to contact him immediately. In truth, he would have liked her to watch the station, but he had not of course told his contacts what Maureen's real purpose was in Killarney. She had simply been described as a 'niece' who needed a job. So she was expected to earn her wages, and he could not afford for her to be dismissed for paying more attention to the station than to her work.

But as the days went by she found herself thinking more and more about Michael Flynn, and she began to hope that she might somehow spot James Quinlan herself if he arrived in Killarney. Having met William, and now that she had seen a photograph of Jack, she was certain that she would recognise their brother. She began to think that if could she spot him when he arrived in Killarney she could report his presence to 'her uncle' without ever involving Michael Flynn. To her surprise, she did not relish the thought of Michael knowing that she was merely using him to find James Quinlan. If the fugitive came home and was killed, and there was no longer any doubt in her mind about what 'Mr Jameson' intended to do when he eventually caught up with James Quinlan, she would prefer it if Michael did not know that she was involved. She had only known Michael for a very short time but she felt that something had happened between them. Something she did not want to end. So she worried about how he would react to her being implicated in the murder of someone he knew well. And she was rapidly coming to the conclusion that this would be a cold-blooded murder rather than a republican 'execution'.

As she penned a note to Michael she was disturbed to realise that these thoughts bothered her. Ever since she was a little girl her life had been dominated by the nationalist cause. Her father had been crippled for it, her brother had died for it, and she had seen death at first hand during The Rising. This situation, however, seemed somehow different. But did she dare ignore the explicit orders of 'her uncle'?

Maureen had Wednesday afternoon off and decided to have a look around the town she had previously only passed through. She left her note for Michael at the desk, but as she came out of the hotel she was pleasantly surprised to see him coming up the street towards her on his bicycle. Rather than wait and have the hotel doorman ask who he was, she walked down the street to meet him.

"Hello Michael," she said, "I didn't think I'd see you again so soon."

Although he had fervently hoped to see her today the sudden meeting took him by surprise. He dismounted rather clumsily and made to shake her hand. "Sure wasn't I coming into town today anyway and I was going to The Great Southern to see if you had left me a message."

"Oh", she said, "and there was I thinking that you came here especially to see me." It surprised her to find that she actually meant it. "But anyway you'll find a note waiting for you at the desk."

His disappointment showed and he started to get back on his bicycle. "Ah sure the truth of it is Maureen I was hoping I'd see you."

She smiled: "Ah sure I was only codding," she said. "Come on, leave that bike here and show me around Killarney."

Michael parked his bicycle against a wall and they set off to explore the small town of Killarney. They walked down Fair Hill past the Friary to Emmett's Road then turned left into St. Anne's Road and came into High Street. He pointed out some of the shops and businesses he had known since he was a child and found to his relief that, although a virtual stranger, she was easy to talk to and he felt at ease with her. He thought about taking her along High Street where most of the larger shops were located but, wishing to prolong the pleasure of walking with her, he headed down New Road to St. Mary's Cathedral instead. They went in, dipped their fingers in the holy water font inside the door, genuflected, and sat in a pew at the back. Michael was too absorbed in his companion to notice anything else, but Maureen said a silent prayer for her brother. On emerging they walked around Cathedral Place and along New Street which brought them back into High Street. The walk had taken less than an hour and Michael wondered what to do next.

Where the road curved back around towards the station Maureen spotted the horse-drawn jaunting cars parked and waiting for custom. At the moment there were only three of the traditional Irish vehicles standing in the rank, but Michael explained that when the tourist season proper began in a few weeks time there would be a long line of them touting for custom. In the years before the war, he told her, there were queues of tourists waiting to be taken to the world renowned beauty spots in the area. But this year, he said, business was expected to be bad. The Irish jaunting car had a seat at the front for the driver, known as a 'jarvey', which also accommodated one passenger. There were double seats facing outwards over the wheels on each side, and a further double seat facing backwards. Steps were fixed to the car to allow the passengers to reach the seats.

"Are there no jaunting cars at all up there in Dublin?" asked Michael.

"No," she said, "not now anyway. We have omnibuses and trams. A lot of the rich people have motor cars or take the taxi cabs, but the poor have to walk."

She turned to Michael: "Will you take me for a ride on one Michael", she said. "But only if it's not too dear," she added quickly.

"Sure of course I will," said Michael.

Michael approached a jarvey leaning lazily against the wall and the man looked up in surprise. "Sure is it yourself Michael Flynn," he said. "Don't tell me you were thinking of taking this poor girl for a ride on one of Killarney's famous jaunting cars. Does your mother know what you're at when you're out of her sight?"

"I am too," said Michael with a laugh, "what are you charging to-day Pat?"

Michael didn't care what the jarvey was charging just as long as he could take Maureen for a ride on the car. He was confident that he wouldn't be charged the 'tourist' rate, but he thought that she would expect him to ask.

"Wait now while I think," said Pat. "There's the hay and oats for the horse, and fags and porter for me to be paid for, and it all costs a fortune these days. But as it's yourself Michael and there's nothing else going around here sure I'll take the two of you to Ross Castle and back for a tanner."

Michael helped Maureen up onto one of the side seats and then clambered up on the opposite side. He would have liked to sit beside her but did not want to appear too forward. It gave him immense pleasure however, to see how much she enjoyed the short ride down to where the ruins of Ross Castle stood by Lough Leanne, one of the famous 'Lakes of Killarney'. In the bright early spring afternoon, before the trees were fully in leaf, the high seat of the jaunting car provided spectacular views of the countryside with the lakes and mountains behind. Maureen chatted and joked with the jarvey, and old hand who knew exactly how to treat his customers. She greeted everyone they met with a smile and waved to people in the distance.

When they returned to town and Michael helped her down from the car she was still laughing. "Thank you Michael," she said, "that was grand, and thank you too Pat," she added shaking the jarvey's hand.

"Did you know miss," said Pat as he accepted the sixpenny fare from Michael, "that when a fella takes his girl for a drive on a jaunting car it means he's engaged and he has to marry her. So you make sure that this blackguard Flynn does his duty."

Maureen laughed and Michael blushed. She looked at the clock on the Town Hall: "Will you look at the time Michael," she said. "I'll have to go back to the hotel; they'll soon be getting ready to serve dinner. But sure I had a grand time."

As they walked back to where he had left his bicycle she linked her arm in his. "I'll leave you here Michael," she said. "I don't want anyone at the hotel to see me walking out with a man and me only being there for less than a week."

Michael took a deep breath: "Is there any chance of doing this again Maureen?" he said.

She laughed: "Would you be asking me for a date Mister Flynn?"

"I would so Miss Ryan," he said firmly.

"I'm off again next Wednesday if you are free yourself," she said. "I'll meet you down by the jaunting cars at about two, and you can take me for another drive."

Michael would make very sure that he was free. "I'll be there," he said.

As he turned to get his bicycle she suddenly grabbed his arm: "Watch out Michael," she said urgently. "There's a copper coming across the road and he's heading straight for us."

Michael looked round and saw a member of the Royal Irish Constabulary coming across the street. He turned to tell Maureen that it was just an old friend coming to say 'hello' but she had already turned on her heel and was hurrying away. As she neared the hotel she looked back and her heart sank to see Michael chatting amicably with the R.I.C man.

Later that night when she lay in bed she tried to think logically about the events of the afternoon. She had to admit to herself that she had enjoyed Michael's company, and the jaunting car ride had been an unexpected and pleasant experience. But the incident involving the policeman had rather spoiled it for her. For as long as she could remember she had been taught to regard the R.I.C as agents of the hated British authorities, and as such not to be trusted. She failed to understand how Michael, who had been interned for no reason by those same authorities, could possibly do anything other than despise them, let alone be friendly with one of them.

Each of them spent the following week in worried thought. Maureen knew that her duty demanded that she put her relationship with Michael Flynn back on a more business-like footing. If necessary she was to flirt and lead him on, but that was as far as it was supposed to go. As the days went by, however, she realised that she was really looking forward to being with him again, and it never occurred to her not to keep their date. Although she had been courted by young men in the past, all of them from strictly nationalist backgrounds, she was perplexed to find that Michael Flynn attracted her quite differently.

For his part Michael was deeply concerned about the manner of their parting. He tried to convince himself that she had been forced to hurry in order to get back to work at the hotel on time, but the next seven days proved to be an anxious wait for him.

When the following Wednesday afternoon finally came around she was still curious, and asked him how he could justify being friendly with 'a copper'. He in turn, was surprised that she should take the incident so seriously, and could not understand why being interned by the army should make him shun someone he had known all his life.

"Sure he's an old friend, and he only came to ask after my mother," he told her.

"Well don't let him think that he could ever be a friend of mine," she said tartly, "him or any other copper. You say that you are ready to fight for Irish freedom, but what will you do if you have to fight against the likes of him? "

"I'm ready to fight for freedom all right Maureen," he said. "But sure when the fighting is over won't we all have to live together in the same country again."

Maureen was taken aback. For her entire life all she had heard about was fighting for Ireland as if it were an end in itself. She realised that she had never heard anyone talk about what would happen when Ireland was eventually free, and it caused her to see yet another side to Michael Flynn.

The tension between them eased. In his presence her mood soon mellowed and the incident was forgotten.

# Chapter 12

James Quinlan did not go home for Easter as 'Mr Jameson' hoped he would. Neither had he appeared in Beaufort during the following months. As a result 'Mr. Jameson' was by now well beyond feeling edgy. He was getting quite desperate. Following the release of internees the previous December, the London Government had gradually allowed several more of those prisoners who had not been put on trial to return home. Finally a general amnesty was declared and the remaining prisoners, including those sentenced to life imprisonment, were released. Among them was Eamonn de Valera.

'Mr Jameson's' political ambitions had already been shelved as a result of his having been forced into helping Michael Collins set up his spy network. Working for the 'Big Fella', as Collins had come to be known, meant that he could not put his name forward as a Sinn Fein candidate in the by-elections scheduled for later in the year. At first he thought that the release of de Valera would put an end to his political career before it began, because the well known and widely respected 'Dev' was an obvious choice to lead the political arm of the Nationalist movement. This, however, turned out not to be the case. 'Mr. Jameson's' gift for oratory was well known, and so his role was changed once again to promoting the Sinn Fein candidates. As a result he became a political insider, and his aspirations were back on track. He felt that with careful planning he would eventually be in a position to forge a political career for himself. But there still remained the same dark cloud on his horizon: James Quinlan.

He had not been able find his nemesis on the British mainland, although from the fact that his family were in contact with him, it was plain that Quinlan was over there somewhere. It was also obvious by now that the fugitive knew that he was being hunted, and had no intention of returning to Ireland anytime soon. So a different approach was required. He could of course go to Collins and ask for help from the covert organisation he had helped to build but, if the real purpose behind his search for Quinlan came to light, he could find himself in deep trouble.

After some consideration he opted for a different strategy: he would find a way of luring his quarry out of hiding and set a trap for him.

He considered bringing Maureen Ryan back from Killarney but decided against it. She was still working at The Great Southern Hotel and would be there for the entire summer season. And as she was paying her own way he did not have to support her financially. But, more importantly, he reasoned, as she was in what she would consider 'enemy territory' she would be more careful about what she said. She was less likely to disclose her connection with him there than she would in the familiar surrounds of Dublin.

Had he known the real situation in Killarney 'Mr Jameson' would not have been quite so complacent.

***

Maureen Ryan was now 'walking out' with Michael Flynn. They were meeting almost every time she was off duty at the hotel. He had kept his promise and taken her for another jaunting car ride to Ross Castle. Then the next time they met she had borrowed a bicycle from one of the other girls at the hotel, and they had cycled out to see some of the other local beauty spots. They enjoyed their first kiss in the moonlight beside Torc Waterfall.

She was pleased that he continued meeting and training with the rebel factions at The Gap of Dunloe, and was satisfied that he was not doing it just to please her. It provided a common interest and their discussions about the nationalist cause helped to strengthen the bond between them.

Gradually she came to realise how totally different life was here in Killarney from that she had known in Dublin, and she began to make comparisons. The obvious difference between the small town and the capital city was one of size, but there was more to it than that. Killarney had nothing to compare with the wide main streets of Dublin with their large stores and elegant Georgian buildings; but neither did it have anything approaching the overcrowded and disease ridden Dublin slums. Most of the people here were poor, especially in the mountainous areas to the south of the town, but there was none of the hunger and deprivation that was so rife in Ireland's capital. This was particularly noticeable in the children. Many of them might be poorly dressed, but they appeared to be well fed and exhibited a healthy glow. They did not have the sickly pallor of the children in the city with the highest infant mortality rate in Europe.

When Michael told her about life in the internment camp and how he had met her brother, Kevin, he also mentioned how he had met Michael Collins there. He mentioned how he had briefly seen Eamonn de Valera on the voyage to Wales, and now much he had been impressed by 'Dev'.

She told him of her own part in The Rising as a member of *Cumman na mBann*, and of her high regard for their leader, Countess Markievicz. "And I met 'the Big Fella' at the GPO," she said. "De Valera was in command at Boland's Bakery, but he was one of the commanders who wouldn't let women fight in the front line."

When 'Dev' and the Countess were both released from prison they celebrated by having a rare drink together.

But when Michael asked her about working at the munitions factory she tended to change the subject. She was finding it increasingly difficult to lie to him.

The spring and early summer of 1917 were proving to be the most pleasant time of her life. She still felt moments of disquiet whenever they met Michael's policeman friend, or came across other R.I.C men. But again she could see that, while Irish nationalism was alive and well in County Kerry, it too, was different from what she had known in Dublin. There, The Cause always seemed to be presented in terms of black and white, Irish or British, republican or loyalist, with nothing in between. Here, in an area where most people knew each other, as evinced by Michael knowing both the policeman and the local republican leaders, she realised that the lines were somewhat blurred.

Under the leadership of Michael Collins, the Republicans were beginning to flex their muscles again following the military defeat of 1916. Across the country R.I.C. barracks had been attacked and arms had been stolen. One such raid had taken place in nearby Tralee, and although Michael had not actually taken part, Maureen was proud of the fact that he was a member of one of the republican bands that had carried out the raid. Yet she still had difficulty accepting that he could continue to have a friendly word with a policeman. Nothing in her own background had prepared her for a situation like this, but she began to wonder if this was not the way many people throughout most of the country regarded the nationalist cause. And perhaps even in parts of Dublin.

But when they encountered British soldiers, Maureen would pull Michael across the street, her hatred of them being clearly evident: "They killed my brother and a lot of other good people in The Rising," she would say.

They rarely mentioned James Quinlan, and Maureen began to dread the thought of him eventually arriving home in Beaufort. She wondered if she would have the courage not to report it to 'her uncle' up in Dublin. She actually prayed that it would not become necessary for her to do so, because she feared that she might easily lose the man she was rapidly falling in love with.

For his part, between his work on the farm, seeing Maureen and training with the rebels, Michael still found time to go fishing with William Quinlan. To begin with Michael was too embarrassed to talk about Maureen, but when the conversation turned to the nationalist cause, he told his friend proudly about her part in The Rising. For a time William thought that this was what attracted Michael to the girl from Dublin, but he soon had to admit that this was not the case. There was obviously something deeper than that. William had never been 'one for the girls' but anybody could see that Michael had fallen hook, line, and sinker for Maureen Ryan. He again felt that he should warn Michael about his suspicions regarding the girl's real purpose in Killarney, but decided that it would have to wait until James came home. At that point he would have no choice but to tell Michael the whole story. He was confident that, in spite of his rebel activities and his love for Maureen, once he knew the truth Michael would do nothing to harm James.

# Chapter 13

The town of Tipperary had a special connection with that 'most Irish of Irish regiments' the Connaught Rangers. The second battalion had been stationed at the Tipperary Town Barracks from 1908 to 1910, but their most enduring link with the town came about through their favourite marching song, "It's a long way to Tipperary". In August 1914 they sang it as they marched in parade order through the French port of Boulogne on their way to the front. The scene was witnessed by the London Daily Mail war correspondent, George Curnock, and his account was printed in the paper a few days later. From that day on the catchy music hall song, originally written by Jack Judge, became popular with both the British forces and the civilian population.

Private Patrick Coughlin arrived at the Town Barracks, now a Command Depot, in the summer of 1917. After being shipped back to Britain, he had spent several weeks in a military hospital where his leg responded well to treatment. From there he was sent to Holywell Convalescent Hospital in Belfast, where he was eventually passed fit for duty and sent to Tipperary to await posting back to his unit.

What really struck Patrick on his return to 'Blighty' were the differing attitudes exhibited by the civilian populations of the various countries of the United Kingdom towards wounded soldiers. On the British mainland the homecoming wounded from Mesopotamia were treated as heroes. Baghdad had recently been taken from the Turks, a rare decisive victory which gripped the popular imagination and raised the moral of the war-weary people. In Belfast, and throughout the largely Unionist north of Ireland, they were treated with respect. Troops from the area had suffered particularly high casualty rates, and the 36th division, largely made up of Ulstermen had been decimated at the Battle of the Somme. In the almost exclusively Nationalist south of Ireland things were very different.

Patrick had not been home for over two years, when he had enjoyed a short leave before the 'Rangers' were posted to Mesopotamia. Then there had been general support for the war. Recruitment was good and large numbers of Irishmen were volunteering. British soldiers were generally welcomed. But the reprisals following The Rising had changed all that. Irishmen serving in the British armed forces wounded or not, were either ignored, treated with suspicion, or even faced outright hostility depending on the strength of nationalist feeling of the observer. Even at home Pat felt that he was something of an embarrassment to certain members of his family.

All of which made his welcome by Jack Quinlan's family, particularly by Jack's mother, all the more pleasant.

Since Jack's letter had arrived to tell her that his friend Patrick Coughlin had been wounded and was being shipped home, Annie had waited with bated breath for him to visit her, as Jack had promised that he would. At first she thought that her expected visitor would still be suffering the effects of his wounds, and she began to worry about how best to accommodate an invalid. She took it for granted that her guest would stay overnight. Eventually William managed to re-assure her that Patrick Coughlin would have to be fully recovered before the army would allow him to travel unattended. Nevertheless, everything that could be done was done to ensure that Jack's friend was welcomed in the proper manner. The photograph of Jack, Patrick and James Daly was moved to a more prominent position. William explained that Patrick would not be wearing shorts and a pith helmet like he was in the picture, tropical dress, he said, was the last thing that a soldier needed in Ireland. Eventually a letter came from Patrick to say he was coming to visit and would indeed stay for a night. Annie decided that he would use one of the beds she kept made up in anticipation of the day Jack and James came home.

It was a Sunday in late July and the family went to the early Mass. Immediately after they came home from the church William left to pick their visitor up from Killarney station. Patrick was wearing his Connaught Rangers uniform and they were aware of the puzzled looks William got from people who knew him, both in town and on the road home to Beaufort. One or two friends thought that it was Jack in the trap with him, and were surprised to find that it was not. William had to explain that the soldier was in fact his brother's friend.

"I'm afraid that there will be a lot of talk around here when news gets out that you had a British soldier in the pony and trap with you Bill," said Pat. "Will it cause any trouble for you?"

"Ah sure there will be a few that might have something to say, but most of them will be curious and let it go at that," said William.

"I'll tell you this Bill," said Patrick. "It's a different Ireland now to what it was the last time I was home."

"It is so," said William. "But listen Pat, my mother is dying to meet you and find out all about Jack and Mesopotamia. You're in for more questions than you've had in your whole life, because she'll want to know everything. But go easy when it comes to talking to her about the war."

Patrick laughed. "Sure haven't I been grilled by two experts already, once at home and once by Jim Daly's mother, and I'll tell your Ma the same pack of lies that I told them. By the time I'm done she'll think that Jack Quinlan is winning the war on his own, and he'll be a general in no time at all. God knows it'll keep me out of heaven but it'll stop her from worrying about him."

"That's grand Pat," said William. He was beginning to see how Jack would have made a friend of this amiable 'Ranger'.

Once they arrived in Beaufort, Annie plied Patrick with tea and homemade scones. She had prepared a special Sunday meal served on the 'best' crockery. After lunch the inquisition began in earnest. He did his best to reassure her that Jack was well away from the fighting, and in no immediate danger. In fact the war in Mesopotamia was portrayed as being a bed of roses compared to the Western Front. But Annie Quinlan was no fool. She waited until the girls went out to play, and 'young' Michael started doing his school homework, before bringing up the subject of his wound. If things were as easy out there as he made out, why had he been hurt badly enough to be sent home. Even in the southwest of Ireland they had heard of 'Blighty ones'. But he wouldn't tell her anything about the actual fighting and concentrated on Jack's part in his rescue.

"I'll say this Mrs Quinlan," he said. "If it wasn't for Jack I wouldn't be here today, and Jim Daly would be a goner too. Jack got the pair of us out of a deep hole. Anyway, now that we have taken Baghdad from the Turks, I'd say that things will be as quiet as a church over there."

During a lull in the conversation, while Annie made yet more tea, Patrick went to the 'outhouse'. When he returned he said to William: "I saw the rods outside Bill, is it yourself who is the fisherman?"

"It is so Pat," said William.

"Ah sure it must be five years now since I drowned a worm or hooked a trout myself. What's the fishing like around here?"

"Ah well," said William, "there's not much chance of a salmon at this time of year, the weather is too hot and the water's too low. But there's plenty of trout waiting to be caught."

"Sure I can't remember the last time I tasted a good Irish trout," said Pat. "The army doesn't serve them to the other ranks. I don't know what kind of fish it is they give us on a Friday, but to be sure it's not Irish trout."

Annie came with cups of tea. "Well," she said, "I never knew that they observed the Friday fast in the British Army." It pleased her to think that Jack was still able to keep up his catholic duty of Friday abstinence.

"They do for the Irish regiments when we're in barracks because nearly all of us are good catholic lads," said Patrick. "I don't know if it's the same for the British regiments, but it might be, because there are a lot of Irishmen like Jack in all the mobs these days. But in the field it's the same for all of us, we eat what we get handed. I don't know what they put into them field rations, but sure I think I'm better off not knowing."

He was about to make further disparaging comments about army field rations but checked himself. "But it must be something good." He pointed at the photograph: "Look at Jack and your man Daly there, sure aren't they thriving on it?"

Annie gave him an old-fashioned look, but had to admit that the trio in the picture did not look underfed. She turned to William:

"Why don't you take Patrick fishing for a few hours if he'd like to go," she said. "And maybe Michael Flynn might like to go too, if he's not out courting the Ryan girl."

"That would be grand," said Patrick. He hesitated for a minute. "But would you do me a small favour William (he thought it prudent not to use 'Bill' in front of Annie). Have you any old civvy clothes I could have a loan of? I don't want to go back to Tipp with my lovely new uniform smelling like the Dublin fish market."

William guessed the real reason behind the request: Patrick did not want him to suffer any embarrassment by being seen with a British soldier. But all he said was: "sure that's no trouble at all Pat."

William sent his young brother off on his bicycle to see if Michael Flynn was home and ask him if he wanted to go fishing. While they waited Annie found Patrick some of Jack's old clothes, she thought would fit better than anything belonging to the stockier William. It also seemed more appropriate to her that Patrick should wear Jack's things. Patrick changed and they went outside to sort out the fishing tackle.

"This fella Flynn," said Patrick, "is he likely to take exception to fishing with a British soldier, uniform or no uniform?"

"Not at all Pat," said William. "Sure doesn't he know Jack well and it never bothers him for people to know it, and the last thing he'd do is cause trouble for anybody staying in Ma's house. But he's a good Irish Republican all the same, and he has good reason to hate the British."

He told Patrick about Michael's unwarranted arrest and internment after The Rising.

"God save us!" said Patrick, "what's coming over Ireland these days."

Michael was at first a little uncertain when he received the invitation to go fishing with William and 'the fella in the picture with Jack'. He knew that Maureen would not approve, but he was curious to meet and talk to a British soldier, especially one from an Irish regiment. And this man was a close friend of Jack Quinlan, his old schoolmate. He decided that he would go, and if Maureen was upset he would explain that he thought it would be useful to The Cause for him find out how an Irishman serving in the war felt about the situation at home.

Patrick was still apprehensive but when Michael arrived he was soon put at ease: "Put it there Pat," Michael said, "sure I'd know you anywhere from the picture of yourself and Jack on the mantelpiece there. Hasn't Mrs Quinlan been telling me all about you for weeks now?"

They made the short walk to one of William's favourite spots on the riverbank. Although he tried his best to hide it, Patrick's limp was still noticeable. They fished for a while without success. The conversation mostly involved William and Michael giving the obviously out-of-practice Patrick some hints and tips. The Connaught Ranger was plainly enjoying himself but after about half an hour with nothing to show for their efforts William called a halt.

"It's too early yet lads," he said, "we'll have to wait until the cool of the evening. Then you'll see the trout rising all around here Pat, and we'll have a few with the flies."

The others took his word for it. So they put the rods down and stretched out on the grassy bank in the warm early evening sunshine.

"Tell me now Pat," said Michael, "how is the bold Jack Quinlan these days?"

"Ah sure he's fine Mick," said Patrick. "He asked to be remembered to everyone I met around here. I was telling Bill and his mother that if it wasn't for Jack I wouldn't be here today. And neither would Jim Daly, because that eejit would have stayed there with me even though he could have walked out of it. He had a broken arm but his legs were fine. It was teeming with rain and the bearers were nowhere to be seen. There was no moon that night and if we were still there after dark the bloody Marsh Arabs would have had us for sure. "

He told them the whole story of the rescue by Jack and the artillery OP officer.

"That's Jack Quinlan all right," said Michael. "You're a lucky man he was there Pat."

"I am so," said Patrick. "But here's the queer thing. Here I am living the life of Reilly stretched out in God's green Irish grass with a fishing rod by the side of me, but half of me wants to be back out there with the lads, in the sand and the heat and the camel shit and the bloody mosquitoes."

There was silence for a few minutes while they digested this.

"So, Mick," said Patrick after a while. "Bill here was telling me about you being interned with the boys who took part in the troubles last year."

"I was that," said Michael warily.

"Jesus Mick," said Patrick, "I was sorry to hear that. I knew there was trouble here, they can't keep it all from us, even over in Mesopotamia. But we didn't know how bad things are. Sure the only news we get is from old British newspapers and they only tell one side of the story."

"But what about letters from home?" said William, "I was telling Jack a bit about how things are the last time I wrote to him."

"That's where most of the real news comes from all right," said Patrick. "But you have to remember that when the people here at home write to us they have more important things on their minds than politics, so all we hear is a bit about it. And anyway, if there's too much information in the letters the bloody censors blot it out. Sure don't they keep an eye on all news from Ireland and especially letters to Irish regiments like the Connaught Rangers?"

"So," said Michael, "you're finding things different here now Pat."

"You're right there Mick," said Patrick. "It's easy to see that a British uniform is not welcome in Ireland anymore, and from what happened to fellas like yourself I can't say that I blame the people here. Sure I wouldn't blame you if you tried to drown me in the river there."

William and Michael exchanged glances of surprise, and William thought it was time to change the subject. "What will you do when the war is over Pat?" he said.

"Maybe he'll come back here to help us in fight for Irish freedom Bill," said Michael. "A few fellas with Pat's sort of experience would come in handy."

The response again surprised Michael. "Some of the lads like Jack, who are only in for the duration might do that Mick," said Patrick. "But men like myself and Jim Daly are regular soldiers, we joined up for the King's Shilling and we're stuck with it. If we left the army and came home before our enlistment is up we'd be posted as deserters and either shot or locked up for a long time." He thought for a moment then continued. "Mind you, there are a few who might take the chance, and I wouldn't put it past your man Private James Joseph Daly to be one of them. And if that was to happen sure I'd have to come too to watch out for the eejit."

"Will they by any chance send you back here to fight against us," said Michael.

"No chance at all Mick," said Patrick with some conviction. "They won't let the Connaught Rangers anywhere near Ireland, and they won't leave us in England for very long either. No, you can bet that as soon as the war is over, it'll be overseas again for us. Back to the bloody Grim, or some other God forsaken shithole."

"The Grim, where's that? I never heard of it," said William.

"The Northwest bloody Frontier of bloody India," said Patrick. "British soldiers call it 'The Grim' for good reason, nothing but rocks and sand and bloody flies, and fellas who could shoot your eye out from half a mile away.."

"What will you be doing out there?" said Michael.

"Defending the great British Empire from people who want nothing more than their independence," said Patrick.

"Apart from the rocks and the sand and the flies sure it sounds just like Ireland," said Michael.

"You might have a point there Mick," said Patrick. "But if them Pathan tribesmen weren't fighting us sure they'd be cutting each other's throats."

"It sounds a bit like Ireland all right," said William, and to his relief the others laughed. "Come on lads," he added, "there's trout jumping all around us. We'll see how good a fisherman you are now Pat."

Later that evening as they ate a supper of fresh brown trout expertly cooked by Annie, Patrick said: "Wait till I tell the lads about this, sure they won't believe a word of it. Thanks for a grand night lads, and thank you for putting me up Mrs Quinlan."

"Ah sure we're glad to have you here Patrick," said Annie. "Please God yourself and Jack and your friend James Daly will all be here together before long."

"What time do you have to go to-morrow Pat," said William. "I'll give you a lift back to the station."

"I have to be in barracks by midnight," said Patrick. "There's a train from Killarney about five."

"I'm going to town myself to-morrow evening," said Michael. "I'll take you in myself Pat, if I can have a loan of the trap from Bill. I have a date with Maureen Ryan and I might take her for a drive, it'll be cheaper than a jaunting car."

As he cycled home Michael thought about the things Patrick Coughlin had said. He realised that when dealing with the British Army things were not as black and white as Maureen seemed to think. There seemed to be Irishmen serving in the army who were still Irish through and through, in spite of the uniform they wore. But he wondered if she would ever be prepared to even discuss it with him.

# Chapter 14

The plan devised by 'Mr. Jameson' to entice James Quinlan out of hiding was in essence quite simple. Putting it into operation, however, would carry an element of risk.

Phase one of the scheme was the easy part. It involved placing Quinlan in a position where he would either have to come back to Ireland, or face putting other members of his family in mortal danger. What he had gleaned from his conversations with Pat Devlin convinced 'Mr Jameson' that Quinlan's brother William knew what had happened at the Gretna munitions factory, and that he also knew how to contact the fugitive. All 'Mr. Jameson' had to do was make it clear to William that unless James came out of hiding and returned to Beaufort, their family would be made to suffer. It was well known that republican militants often resorted to this kind of coercion, and so he was in no doubt that William and his brother would take his threats seriously. And he considered it to be a pretty safe bet that the brothers would not hesitate to put their own lives in jeopardy in order to save their family.

To ensure that there was a definite end to the whole affair he had decided that both Quinlan brothers would have to die. This meant that the killing would have to take place in Beaufort or, if at all possible, somewhere in the bogs or foothills of the nearby mountains; and in any case it would suit him better if the event took place well away from Dublin. Pat Devlin might not be happy about this, but 'Mr Jameson' knew that the Beaufort publican would have no choice but to accept it.

Although he considered his plan to be workable, he would require help to carry it out. It would be relatively easy for him to travel to Beaufort by himself and issue his ultimatum to William, but if two rebels were seen to be involved it would add credence to the threat. He could not wait around in Beaufort until Quinlan came home, as this would arouse suspicion down there and, more seriously, he would be missed from Dublin – the last thing he wanted was to have Michael Collins questioning his absence. And, while he would certainly have no qualms about killing Quinlan himself, wherever possible he had always considered it better to get someone else to actually pull the trigger. He would be able to use Pat Devlin to let him know when James Quinlan came home, and he could make it part of his threat to William that he inform Devlin as soon as his brother finally arrived. But he knew that the Beaufort publican would be reluctant to go further than that; Devlin would not want to become involved in the murder of two local men. So he needed to find someone more fully committed. And it had to be someone he could trust, which in his world meant someone he had some kind of hold over.

He had Maureen Ryan in position in Killarney but he was beginning to question her commitment. Her reports were becoming fewer and less detailed, and he wondered if she had things other than his interests at heart. A few simple enquiries about how his 'niece' was getting on revealed that she appeared to be fine, but much to his annoyance, it was said that she was courting a young local man. From there it was easy to determine that the man in question was Michael Flynn, the former internee that Devlin had mentioned, and the man he had instructed Maureen to inveigle into helping her. It seemed that she had followed that part of his instructions rather too closely. Things were obviously getting out of hand down there and Maureen would have to be brought home. The fact that she was romantically involved with a man, even a former internee and confirmed nationalist, meant that she could no longer be trusted not to do or say something inappropriate. He was well aware that she had fought bravely in The Rising, but he certainly would never trust her to commit murder for him. It was time, therefore, to bring her back to Dublin where he could keep a closer eye on her, and if necessary remove her from the scene entirely. That particular job he would have to do by himself but, although it went against his usual practice, he was prepared to accept the fact.

After some thought he decided that Maureen's brother, Kevin Ryan, was the man he needed for the job in Beaufort. Ryan was a member of Michael Collin's secret organisation; he had fought in the front line in The Rising and would not hesitate to kill for The Cause. It would be risky, but if Ryan needed any further incentive to do as he was told, and keep his mouth shut afterwards, he could be told that the orders had come directly from Collins himself. He could tell Ryan that they were in Beaufort to investigate the possibility of either kidnapping or eliminating the owner of Beaufort House, a high ranking member of the British government. He could even make a show of nosing around the grounds, and looking over the house itself from a safe distance, to cover his back in the unlikely event of his being questioned at a later date. 'Mr. Jameson' was confident that Ryan knew the ropes well enough not to question Collins' orders, and would certainly not discuss the operation with his colleagues if ordered not to. There was an added bonus in having both Ryan's involved: he could bring them into line by playing one against the other.

What he did not know was that Kevin had been present when Maureen had told their father of her concerns about working for 'Mr. Jameson'. Kevin knew about the hunt for James Quinlan, and was aware of his father's opinion that this was a personal affair and nothing whatsoever to do with The Cause.

Maureen was serving breakfast at the Great Southern hotel when the porter found her and handed her the telegram from her 'uncle'. She asked to be excused, went to her room and stared at the envelope, her thoughts racing. Without opening it she knew what the wire would say. It would be an order from Dublin to return home immediately. When she eventually opened it, the telegram simply said that there had been a 'family bereavement', but she knew that this was just a ruse to provide her with an excuse for leaving her job at short notice.

It was the message she had come to dread receiving. The last few months with Michael Flynn had been the happiest of her life. She had convinced herself that she could have a life outside of The Cause, and she had begun to hope that such a life would be possible with Michael Flynn. But in her heart she had always feared that the day would come when she would have to face the reality of her situation, and that her idyllic time in Killarney would be brought to an abrupt end. She had fervently prayed that when that day came she would be able to find a way of keeping on the right side of 'her uncle' while at the same time continuing to be with Michael.

Now, out of the blue, the fateful day had actually arrived. And she was not prepared for it.

She sat on her bed and tried to collect her thoughts. Her first inclination was to disobey, to ignore the telegram and stay in Killarney. She would talk things over with Michael, tell him the truth and hope that their love for each other would see them through. But it was an impossible dream. Maureen knew very well that she was trapped, and that there was no way out. She had to face the reality of her situation. She was too deeply involved in 'Mr Jameson's' affairs, and she knew too much to be allowed to simply walk away. At the first hint of anything less than wholehearted commitment on her part he would have her eliminated. In 'Mr. Jameson's' world once in, you were never allowed to get out alive. If she did not do precisely as she was told her life would be forfeit, and worse, probably Michael's as well.

She lay on her bed and agonised over what to do. She could simply leave without a word, but she knew that Michael would come to Dublin to find her, and in doing so put them both in danger. For everyone's sake she knew that she should make a clean break from him, but could not bring herself to do so. Eventually she managed to reach a form of compromise. Although she knew that she would hate herself afterwards, she would tell

Michael yet more lies. She would not go directly to Dublin on the first available train as ordered; she would risk delaying her return home until she had seen Michael, shown him the telegram, and promised to come back to Killarney as quickly as she could. It was the only way she could see of ensuring that both of them survived. But the thought of never seeing Michael again brought tears, and she lay on her bed and cried.

When she had pulled herself together she went to the hotel manager, showed him the telegram and told him she had to leave to-day. It was plain to see that she had been crying so the manager assumed that the wire was meant to tell her of the death of someone close, and was kind. He expressed his condolences. He paid her up to date, and told her that he would miss her. If things worked out favourably for her, he said, he would be pleased to employ her again. In a daze she packed her things and left the hotel. It would be several hours yet before she was due to meet Michael so she had time on her hands. She wandered around Killarney, but no matter where she went around the town she found that it was somewhere she had been with him, and she had to move on. It seemed to be more difficult to escape from Michael Flynn than it was to break free from 'her uncle'.

Eventually she went into the cathedral and sat there in quiet solitude to wait.

# Chapter 15

In Beaufort, Patrick Coughlin rose early on the Monday morning and had breakfast with the Quinlan family before William left for work. Soon afterwards, the children, who were on school holidays, went off to play. Following William's suggestion, he took one of the rods and went off to 'drown a few worms' while Annie did her weeks washing. From his childhood days Patrick remembered that this Monday ritual would be unalterable, and he felt a moment of nostalgia for days gone by. On the river bank he thoroughly enjoyed himself for an hour or two and managed to catch a few trout, but eventually his mind began to wander and he sat to reflect.

What Michael Flynn had told him about being interned for six long months for no reason other than being in the wrong place at the wrong time, had left a disturbing impression on his mind. He decided to question Michael further about it on the journey into Killarney later in the day. And when he finally caught up with the Connaught Rangers it was something he would talk over with James Daly. Patrick had the uncomfortable feeling that if he was right about his regiment being sent to India after the war, they too might well be involved in interning people without trial, just like the troops in Ireland. To make this more likely there were rumours of unrest among the tribesmen of the Northwest Frontier Province. This was nothing new for that turbulent corner of the British Empire, and Patrick knew that Britain would react in the usual way by reinforcing the troops who policed that vast, barren, mountainous area. In his view it was ten to one that the Connaught Rangers would be involved.

Back at the cottage he was putting the fishing gear away when he noticed the turf-cutting *slean* leaning against the wall obviously being prepared for use, and picked it up. William came home for 'the dinner' that day rather than eating at the farm, and they chatted for a while about cutting the winter supply of turf. For a regular British soldier Patrick exhibited a surprising knowledge of the subject, and spoke nostalgically about his experiences as a boy cutting turf at home. From William he learned that the peat in the Beaufort area was close to the surface. All that was required was to remove the top layer of heather from the bog to reach it. They could then cut down to six or eight feet before hitting the bottom, at which point the resulting bog hole would soon fill up with brown peaty water. Patrick said that it was about the same at home in County Galway, but he knew of parts of Ireland where cuttable turf went down to three times that depth.

Annie came to call them for dinner and heard what they were saying. "William cut every single sod of turf all on his own last year," she said proudly. "But this year, thanks be to God, he'll have Michael Flynn to help him."

It was the first William had heard of this arrangement. He glanced at his mother and received a look in return that left him in no doubt that the deal had been struck and could not be altered. So he let it go without argument.

After dinner Annie wanted to talk some more about Jack. It was clear that she was worried, and Patrick did his best to put her mind at rest. She found him easy to talk to and began to tell him about her husband. He listened to the story of how the coachman had been laid off and gone 'over the water' with James to work at the munitions factory. It was eighteen months now since Michael's death and she still found it difficult to talk about it, but she managed to tell Patrick the story as she knew it, and she felt better for having done so.

"Jack told us about it, and sorry we were to hear the news Mrs Quinlan," said Patrick. "We had prayers said for his father at Mass."

The thought of soldiers in the middle of a war thousands of miles away saying prayers for her dead husband brought a tear to her eye. They were on their third pot of tea when Michael Flynn came to take Patrick to the station.

On the way to Killarney, Michael, in answer to his questions, explained to Patrick a bit more about his internment and about what had happened in Ireland since The Rising the previous year. Although it was soon obvious that he was reluctant to say very much about his personal involvement with 'the boys', he did mention meeting Michael Collins in the camp at Frongoch.

"If it comes to a fight," he said, "I'd say that Collins is the man to lead it."

"What about after the fighting is over, what will happen then?" said Coughlin.

"Eamonn de Valera is the man to lead an independent Ireland." Michael answered, and with that he lapsed into silence.

Eventually Patrick said: "Ah sure I can see that you're not too keen to say a lot about them things to a fella in a British uniform Mick. And I'm ashamed to say I can't blame you."

"I have nothing against yourself Pat, and I can see how you'd hit it off with Jack Quinlan," said Michael, "but the way things are in this country now it's a lot better for a fella to keep some things to himself. And it's very easy to get someone else into trouble as well as yourself."

"Jesus, sure Ireland is going to the dogs altogether," said Patrick. He had a sudden thought: "If Ireland is Independent some day, what will happen to British regiments like The Connaught Rangers? I suppose that we'll be disbanded and myself and Jim Daly will be kicked out without any chance of a pension."

It was his turn to sit in silence. Eventually he brightened up: "Why don't we talk about something a bit easier to handle. Tell me about this girl you're so keen to see."

This was a subject Michael was more than ready to discuss, but in the event it was Patrick who monopolised the conversation by telling Michael about the girls he had known in various places around the world. So the remainder of the journey passed off pleasantly enough. Eventually they reached the station where Patrick would catch the train back to Tipperary.

***

In the cathedral Maureen suddenly realised that she would have to hurry to meet Michael. As she came out she noticed a familiar pony and trap disappearing around Cathedral Close. She hurried after it and saw that it was indeed William Quinlan's trap, but it was being driven by Michael Flynn. In shocked surprise she saw that the passenger Michael was chatting with in such a friendly fashion was a British soldier. She followed them to the station. On the platform Michael was shaking hands with the soldier and seeing him on to the train.

Something inside Maureen snapped. All the emotions, all the pent up tension of the day, suddenly boiled over. Love inexplicably turned to hate. As Michael turned and began walking back down the platform she dashed up and slapped his face.

"You bastard!" she yelled at him. "After all I said to you about my poor dead brother and my crippled father and Kevin, what do I find you at? Talking to a Brit soldier and even shaking hands with him. Well that's the last I ever want to see of you Michael Flynn!"

With that she turned on her heel and stormed off.

# Chapter 16

The car was a 1912 Morris Oxford and Kevin Ryan was at the wheel, driving was one of the skills he had been taught as a member of Michael Collins' underground movement. They had picked the car up outside the station in Killarney, where it had been left ready for them by Pat Devlin. As they drove out of town they caused little comment, it was just another rich tourist being driven out to see the sights. To avoid being recognised 'Mr Jameson' wore a large trilby hat with colourful coat and trousers, which he hoped would mark him as an American. Although the weather was fine, the hood of the vehicle was raised. He had opted to drive out to Beaufort so that he could get there, complete his business, and get back with the least possible delay. The sooner he got back to Dublin the less likelihood there was of his being missed.

Beside him in the driver's seat, Kevin tried to shake off the feeling of unease he felt about the mission he had been handed. He had been told that all he had to do was drive, look out for any unwelcome interference, and be ready to react immediately and without question. The orders, he was given to understand, came directly from Michael Collins. Their mission was described as 'top secret' and was not to be discussed with anyone, even other members of the movement. This kind of arrangement was by now familiar operating procedure to Kevin; he had taken part in several republican operations which had involved raids on police stations, and even one in which a suspected informer had been 'executed'. He had fought bravely in The Rising and was ready to die for The Cause, but this was different. He believed the story about the owner of Beaufort House being targeted by Collins - that was the way 'the war' was currently being fought - but he suspected that there was more to it than that. And he was worried that his sister Maureen might well be involved. She was in Killarney working for the man sitting in the passenger seat, and it was too much of a coincidence to suppose that he had two operations running in the area at the same time.

So, like Maureen, he had broken the rules and consulted his father.

"I still think that your man is up to some personal devilment," said Sean Ryan from his seat by the fire, "so mind out for yourself Kevin. And for Christ's sake look out for Maureen. She's in this too and I'd say she knows more about it than is good for her. From her letters home it looks to me like she's getting fed up with the whole thing and would like a way out. She talks a lot about that fella Michael Flynn you met in the camp in Wales, and I think she's sweet on him."

"Would you say that I'd be better off not going down there at all Da?" said Kevin.

"Jesus no Kevin," said his father. "If there is any chance at all that Collins is in this you'll have to go. You can't go against the 'Big Fella' and don't forget that someone has to look out for your sister."

It was late afternoon when they arrived in Beaufort and went first to Devlin's public house. 'Mr Jameson' left Kevin in the car and went in. He only stayed long enough to find out where he might find William Quinlan at this time of day, tell Devlin that James Quinlan would soon be coming home, and to send a telegram immediately Quinlan arrived in Beaufort. He also collected two Webley service revolvers, recently stolen from the RIC barracks in Tralee.

When he came out he directed Kevin to drive up towards the Gap of Dunloe. Ryan noted that they had passed Beaufort House on their way to Devlin's and were now heading in the opposite direction, but he said nothing.

# Chapter 17

Michael had not considered the possibility of Maureen actually seeing him with Patrick Coughlin. When she slapped his face he had been left standing in shocked silence, completely stunned by her sudden and totally unexpected outburst, it took him several seconds to collect his thoughts. All he could think of doing was to set off after her, and as he came out of the station he saw her disappearing into the Great Southern Hotel. He started to follow her in but was stopped in his tracks by the burly doorman. The doorman knew that this young countryman was not a hotel employee, and he was certainly not a guest, so he was not about to allow him into 'his' hotel. A scuffle broke out as Michael tried to push his way past and the duty manager came out to see what was disturbing the jealously guarded peace and serenity of The Great Southern. When Michael explained that all he wanted to do was speak to Maureen Ryan he was told that Miss Ryan had received bad news from home and had given up her job to go back to Dublin. The manager added firmly that if Michael didn't leave immediately the police would be called. The doorman was about to say that he had just seen Maureen run past him into the foyer, but the manager had left and he was not about to impart any information to this 'country mug'.

Michael waited around the station for well over an hour watching the hotel in case she came out, but she failed to appear. He walked around the town in the vain hope that he might find her, but eventually had to give up; collect the pony and trap, and make his lonely way back to Beaufort.

He put up the pony and trap at Quinlan's and, unusually for him, failed to go for a quick word before cycling home. He knew that he would not be able to hide his distress and couldn't bear the thought of having to answer their concerned questions.

He went home in a daze and spent a sleepless night wrestling with emotions that varied between deep despair and bitter anger. What hurt him most was that he did not understand; he simply could not think of a rational explanation for Maureen's angry outburst and sudden departure from the station. He knew of her loathing for British soldiers, and he could have accepted her being angry with him. Had she waited and questioned him about being with Patrick Coughlin he would have at least have had the opportunity to offer an explanation; and even if she was not prepared to accept it they could at least have talked it over. But the violence of her reaction was totally unexpected. He looked for solutions and thought of writing to her, but he realised that he did not have a home address. He had borne the trials of internment in Wales without complaint, but this was practically unbearable, and eventually he gave up in helpless frustration.

Next morning he said nothing to his family. He ate little for breakfast and went about his farm chores with little obvious thought for what he was doing. His worried mother watched as he stood and stared blankly into space for several minutes, and then went feverishly to work like a man possessed. She pleaded with him to tell her what was wrong, and although she got little response, she guessed that it must have something to do with 'the Ryan one'. Like all Irish mothers she was very protective of her son where girls were concerned.

After dinner he had all the questioning he could stand and went in search of William Quinlan.

William was chatting to his employer in the farmyard when Michael cycled up. The trio exchanged greetings and made small talk for a few minutes before Michael mentioned the purpose of his visit:

"Your mother was asking me to give you a hand with the turf this year Bill," he said. "There's not much doing at home for a while and I was thinking maybe we could start on it tomorrow."

William glanced at his boss, who nodded. "Ah sure that'll be grand Bill, we'll be all right here for the rest of the week." It would have been unheard of for a farmer not to grant time off to his men for turf cutting.

Next morning Michael arrived at the Quinlan cottage before they had finished breakfast and he wore every sign of having spent a sleepless night. As they made their way to the bog William broached the subject he and his mother had discussed two nights before:

"So Mick," he said, "why was it you didn't come in for a chat with Ma when you brought the trap back on Monday night?"

"It's a long story Bill, and I'm not all that sure myself how it all happened, but I'll tell about it while we're at the turf." Michael was obviously working up to tell him something and William realised that he would have to be patient.

They began cutting turf and took turns at using the *slean*. When it was his turn to cut, Michael set about the work as if his life depended on it and it was all William could do to keep up. By the time Annie and the children arrived in the pony and trap with the midday meal, they had worked down several levels, and there were sods of turf lying all around the bog hole drying in the sun.

They worked on into the afternoon and by then water was beginning to seep into the hole from the surrounding bog. Soon Michael was working almost up to his knees in brown peaty water and William called a halt, he knew that the water would rise further and that they had extracted all the turf they could from that particular bog hole.

The tolling of the evening Angelus bell could just be heard as it drifted across the bog on the evening breeze. The other turf cutters were packing up and leaving. Annie and the children left to prepare an evening meal. They drove down the *boreen* and turned onto the road. As they did so a car came up and to Annie's surprise it turned and drove up the *boreen* towards the bog.

"Some more tourists taking the wrong road," she said to the children, and they laughed.

As they tidied up ready to go home Michael told William about the incident with Maureen Ryan, and his difficulty in understanding 'what came over her'. By the time he had finished dusk was falling and they were alone on the bog. William was torn between sympathising with his friend and telling him of his original suspicions regarding Maureen. But before he could say anything he noticed the car speeding up the *boreen* throwing up a cloud of dust.

At the end of the *boreen* were the roofless ruins of an old stone cottage standing in the middle of a small paddock, and surrounded by a dilapidated stone wall. It was all that remained of a smallholding probably abandoned some seventy-odd years before during the great famine, when the Irish potato crop failed.

The car came to a halt by the ruins and two men got out. William immediately recognised one of them.

"Christ Almighty!" he exclaimed. "It's that fella from Dublin who's after Jim. Come on Mick we'll have to run before they spot us."

He turned to run but Michael grabbed his arm. "No it's all right Bill," he said. "Sure it's only Maureen's brother Kevin, wait till I ask him where she is."

"I tell you they're after us Mick," William shouted at his friend. "Come on, they know nothing about bogs, if we run like hares they'll never catch us."

William tried to pull Michael away but it was too late. When he looked round he found himself staring into the barrel of a revolver.

# Chapter 18

When Maureen ran out of the station and dashed into the hotel she knew that Michael would have difficulty in following her. She rushed through towards the staff toilets and on the way bumped into one of the waitresses.

"Sure I thought you went back home to Dublin Maureen," said the girl in some surprise.

"I'm going tonight Mary," said the breathless Maureen, "but can I have a loan of your room for a bit while I wait for the train. But please don't let on to anyone that you saw me."

"All right," said the mystified waitress.

Maureen went up to her friend's room and lay down on the bed to think. Gradually it dawned on her what had just happened and slowly she came to bitterly regret her actions. As she came to terms with what she had done she began to realise that she had made a terrible mistake. She really did love Michael Flynn, and the thought that she had almost certainly have driven him away forever dismayed and frightened her. She resolved to find him and make things right between them.

She left the hotel by a back way and walked around town looking for him. After a fruitless search it dawned on her that in her haste she had forgotten that he had left Quinlan's pony and trap outside the station. But by the time she got there it had gone. She had lost him. She got on the Dublin train, sat in the corner of an empty compartment and cried.

It was a slow overnight train that seemed to stop at every station on the way, so it was morning before she arrived in Dublin. She knew that the first thing she ought to go was report to 'her uncle', and she boarded a tram for Rathmines. But halfway there, in a moment of defiance, she changed her mind and went home instead. She badly wanted to talk to someone, and the only person she could face at the moment, and who she knew would give her a sympathetic ear, was her father. Everything else would have to wait until later, and never mind the consequences.

When she arrived home she found her father drinking his after breakfast cup of tea by the fire. He almost choked when he saw her.

"Ah Maureen darling," he said as he tried, and as usual failed, to rise. "Sure you're a sight for sore eyes. Thank God they had the good sense to send you home before the ructions started. Sit down here now, have a cup of tea and tell me the score."

Maureen was mystified: "What ructions Da? What's happening?"

"You mean you don't know?" her father said. "Ah sure that's your man over in Rathmines all right, not letting anybody know the score if he doesn't have to."

Even though still feeling the effects of the last twenty-four hours Maureen sat up in alarm. Something was not right and she was worried: "What's happening Da? Tell me please."

"Sure hasn't himself gone running off down to Killarney, and taken Kevin along with him. They're supposed to be checking out someplace called Beaufort House for Michael Collins. But I think that maybe that fella he had you looking for has come home. I still say this is something personal, but he told Kevin that Collins is behind it all, so he had to go with him. Kevin wasn't too keen on going down to Kerry, but I told him to go so that he could watch out for you."

Maureen's thoughts raced. If James Quinlan had finally surfaced and 'her uncle' and Kevin had gone down to Beaufort to kill him, William Quinlan would surely try to intervene. And she knew what that would lead to. Michael Flynn would go to his friend's aid.

"Holy Mother of God," she cried, "they'll kill Michael too." She was out of the house before her father could say another word. She had to do something to prevent anything happening to Michael.

She waited impatiently for a train back to Killarney. The by now familiar journey to the southwest seemed to take an age but eventually she arrived. As she left the station she spotted her waitress friend, Mary, cycling up the street towards the hotel.

Maureen stepped out into the road and stopped her: "I need a loan of your bike Mary," she said. Before the astonished girl could react Maureen had grabbed the bicycle and was peddling furiously through the town.

As she reached Beaufort she met Annie and the children coming back from the turf cutting. "Do you know where I can find Michael Flynn, Mrs Quinlan?" she said breathlessly.

"Michael Flynn? Sure he's up at the bog cutting turf with William," said Annie.

"Which way is that?"

Annie gave her directions and she set off again, leaving Annie wondering what could have caused her to be in such a flustered hurry.

\*\*\*

The light was beginning to fade out on the bog. Michael, still holding the heavy *slean,* stared in surprise at Kevin Ryan.

"Jesus Christ Kevin, what are you doing here?" said Michael.

"I know well what they're doing Mick." William made a threatening move towards the man he still knew only as 'The Man from Dublin', but was stopped by a menacing movement of the revolver.

He felt his anger towards 'The Man' rising and, undeterred, he went on: "They're looking for Jim. This bastard here was responsible for what happened to Da. He was one of a gang that killed an old fella in a church over in Scotland, and Jim and Da saw them do it. They took them hostage and Da died of a heart attack because of it."

'Mr. Jameson' thought rapidly. His suspicion that Quinlan's brother knew the whole story had been confirmed. Now it looked as if this man Flynn also knew about it, and his first priority was to prevent anything more being said in front of Kevin Ryan. He made a quick modification to his plans. It was possible to get rid of William Quinlan and Michael Flynn immediately without it interfering too much with his final objective.

"I came down here to make you bring your brother out of hiding," he said. "But sure he'll come home for your funeral just as quick. We'll have to get shot of the two of them Kevin. You watch Flynn while I finish this one off first."

He had gone past worrying about who did the actual shooting, and in any case he wanted to make absolutely sure that he left both of them dead.

"No Kevin!" None of them had noticed Maureen cycling up the *boreen* and dropping the bicycle by the stone wall. She was running as hard as she could across the bog to where they stood. The heather grabbed at her skirt as if to prevent her reaching them in time.

"Maureen!" Michael and Kevin spoke simultaneously.

Kevin recovered first. "Christ Almighty, where did you come from Maureen? But whatever it is you're after you can't stop here. This is Michael Collins' business and you have to stay out of it, so get away from here as quick as you can."

"Listen to me Kevin," said Maureen urgently. She pointed at 'her uncle'. "Didn't Da say that this business was something personal to this lying shite, and that the 'Big Fella' has nothing at all to do with it? Sure don't you know very well that Collins was still in the British internment camp along with yourself and Michael when I was sent to look for William's brother?"

'The Man from Dublin' immediately turned on Maureen his face livid with rage. Obviously beyond control he raised the revolver. His finger tightened on the trigger: "I'll shut your mouth for good you bitch; now you'll be the first one to go."

They were the last words he ever uttered.

Seeing Maureen threatened by the pistol, and hearing the arrogant tone of the gunman's voice when he shouted at her, caused something to snap in Michael Flynn's mind. He didn't hesitate. He swung the heavy *slean* round in a vicious circle. It caught the 'Mr Jameson' behind the ear just underneath his hat brim. There was a crunch of metal on bone. The revolver fell to the heather. He remained standing for several seconds, then toppled slowly over and fell with a splash into the dark peaty water of the bog hole.

Kevin Ryan instinctively wheeled around and brought his gun to bear on Michael, but Maureen jumped in front of him and grabbed his arm.

"For Gods' sake don't do it Kevin. Can't you see that Michael just saved my life? If it wasn't for him I'd be stone dead. I won't let you shoot him, or William either for that matter."

She moved across and stood defiantly by the shaking Michael, who instinctively placed a protective arm around her.

Her brother stared at her for several minutes then slowly lowered the gun.

For all of two minutes none of them moved, they just stood and stared at the spot where the gunman had been standing as if he were still there. No one uttered a word. Even Maureen seemed dumbstruck and clung to Michael.

Slowly realisation dawned on William. He shook off the feeling of horror at what he had just witnessed. "Quick lads, give us a hand," he said urgently. "We'll have to pull him out of the water before he drowns."

He and Kevin Ryan jumped down into the still rising murky water and struggled to pull 'Mr Jameson' out of the hole. When they eventually managed to get him out and onto the dry heather they could see that it was no use. He had been dead even before he went into the water. One side of his face was a horrible mess of blood and peat. His head hung at an unnatural angle and it was obvious that his neck was broken.

Michael was beginning come to his senses. "God help me," he said "sure I never meant to kill him. I don't know what came over me." He crossed himself and the others, as if at Mass, automatically did the same.

Kevin Ryan looked at the body and his face went white. "Jesus Christ!" he said. "What are we going to do now? There'll be ructions when Michael Collins finds out about this. We'll all be found dead in a ditch."

Maureen had regained some of her capacity to think clearly and her voice remained steady. "Listen Kevin, didn't I tell you that Collins knows nothing at all about it," she said. "And the only thing we can do now is to make sure he never finds out."

She pointed briefly at the body without actually looking at it. "What were you supposed to do here before I came, and does anyone else know

110

what's going on."

Kevin told her that all he knew about it was that they had picked up the car in Killarney, and that he was to drive 'Mr. Jameson' out to Beaufort to investigate the possibility of 'targeting' the owner of Beaufort House. After that they were to drive back to town and leave the car where they found it, with the two revolvers hidden under a seat. Nothing had been said about killing anybody. But it suddenly came to him that he should have known that he would not have been given a gun unless there was a distinct possibility of him having to use to use it.

"There you have it" said Maureen. "Sure hasn't Beaufort House been closed up with nobody at all there for years, and it will stay that way until the war is over. So that was all a pack of lies. Are you sure that's all you had to do?"

"Only that we stopped at a pub on the way here. He went in and picked up the guns, but I stayed in the car. I don't think that the fella in the pub saw me at all," said Kevin, catching on.

She took her brother's arm and began firmly leading him back towards the ruined cottage and the car. "So all you have to do is to leave the car and the guns at the station and go back to Dublin," she said. "Go home Kevin, talk to Da and let him know that I'm grand. As long as you don't say a word to another soul sure you'll be all right. The rest of us will think about what to do here."

Kevin could see the logic of what his sister was saying, and he felt that the sooner he was away from here the better. He nodded, picked up the second revolver, went back in the car and was soon on his way back to Killarney.

# Chapter 19

"We'll have to call out the cops," said Michael, still recovering from the shock. "I'll go to the barracks in Killarney and tell them what happened."

"No Michael," said Maureen, "if we get the authorities involved there will be all kinds of questions, and the 'Big Fella' will find out for sure. If we're not very careful we'll have the cops and 'the boys' all after us at the same time. And the way things are none of them will be bothering about looking for the truth."

"We could take him over behind the wall there and just say that we found him," said William. "Sure nobody will know that it was you that did it Mick. And anyway they wouldn't blame you if they did find out. You saved all our lives when you hit him and you had every right to do it."

"That's no good," said Maureen. "There were lots of people around here all day. The cops will want to know why no one else found him."

William forced himself to look at the body: "I know that he was the blackguard who was responsible for my father's death, and for Jim being on the run," he said. "I'm not a bit sorry that he's dead. But even so he should have a Christian burial."

"You're right there Bill," said Michael. "Look, there's no need for yourself or Maureen to have anything more to do with this, so go home the pair of you. I'll go and see Father O'Brien. Sure he'll know how to handle this."

"That won't work either Michael," said Maureen. "If you tell the priest he'll say that you should go to the cops and it will all come out anyway. You could tell him in confession if you like, and then he wouldn't say a word, but that would be of no help to us now. And anyway sure you have nothing to confess to, killing him was no sin, you did the only thing you could."

Not one of the three wanted to voice what they were all thinking. It was Michael who eventually broke the silence: "She's right Bill," he said. "God forgive me but all we can do is leave him here for somebody to find him. You take Maureen home with you and I'll move him somewhere else so that nobody will connect him with your bit of the bog."

By now night had fallen. A full moon had risen over Macgillycuddy's Reeks and bathed the bog in a silvery light. The other turf cutters had long gone home and there was not another soul around. They were alone on the bog. The hole continued to fill up as the surrounding bog drained into it, and it was by now half full.

Maureen was still thinking clearly. She had seen enough violent death during The Rising not to be put off by one more dead body.

"It would be a lot safer if we put him somewhere where he could never be found. We could put him back in that hole," she said. "Or better still another hole somewhere away from here. There seems to be plenty of them around. And I'm not leaving you here to do it alone Michael, I'm staying with you."

"I'm stopping here too," said William. "Sure wasn't it me he was after when he came here. You saved me from him, so I can't leave it all up to you Mick."

All three were reluctant to face doing what it seemed had to be done. For both Michael and William it went against every aspect of their strict Catholic upbringing. Maureen too had been brought up to honour the Church's teaching, and even after what she had witnessed during The Rising, she baulked at the thought of burying a body in a lonely bog. She well knew that in Ireland's troubled land it was not uncommon for dead bodies to be discovered in fields and ditches, but when found, these were always given a decent funeral.

Eventually they made up their minds. They searched around until they found an old bog hole, one that was well covered with green soggy moss and almost completely hidden in the heather.

In the soft Irish moonlight they weighed the body down with stones from the nearby ruins, and slipped it into the hole. They stood quietly by the watery makeshift grave, and said a silent prayer.

# Part Two

## The Call

*That every year I have cried, 'At length My Darling understands it all,*
*Because I have come into my strength, And words obey my call'.*
**(W.B.Yeats – from 'Words')**

# Chapter 20

After they had prayed for the soul of the man they had consigned to the bog, they made their way back to the cottage in silence. Each had their own private thoughts and none were prepared to voice them.

By now it was getting quite late and Annie was becoming increasingly worried. The sight of William and Michael wet through with filthy water from the bog did nothing to ease her mind, and she was anxious to know what had happened. William lied and told her that the *slean* had fallen into the bog-hole and it had taken them a long time to recover it. The others nodded their agreement. From their general demeanor and facial expressions, however, she could tell that this was not the whole truth. It certainly did not explain why Maureen had been so anxious to find Michael Flynn, and what she was doing cycling off to the bog as if her life depended on it? But Annie held her peace and resolved to question William about it later. She made them sit and eat, although none of them had much appetite. She fussed over Maureen and would not hear of her going back to Killarney, or anywhere else that night. Room would be made for her to stay at the cottage and that was that.

When Michael left to go home, Maureen went out with him as far as the gate. For the moment they were too overjoyed at being together again to waste time in complicated explanations; but she promised to tell him the whole story of how she came to be at the bog when they met again the next day. She resolved that she would also tell him the whole truth about her involvement with the 'The Man from Dublin' and her search for James Quinlan.

They embraced in the moonlight. Minutes passed. When eventually Maureen looked up at him she noticed a cloud pass over Michael's face. The relief of being with her again could not entirely erase the thought of what he had done earlier that evening.

"I killed a man Maureen," he said quietly. "I could never have let him harm you, but all the same I wish to God that I never had to kill him like that."

This, added to the emotions brought on by the last two days, proved to be too much for him. As she held him tight she could feel his body racked with sobs. Tears fell from his eyes. "A grand soldier for Ireland I'll make," he said. "Will you look at me now, crying like a baby after killing a man.

God knows what you will be thinking of me."

By now she was crying too. She sensed that it was not just the killing at the bog that had brought the tears. "Hush love," she said tenderly, "sure wouldn't I rather have you than any other man in the whole wide world. And as for being a soldier, well you acted on the spot when you had to. Most men would have hesitated until it was too late, and we would all have been killed for sure. Oh Michael, I love you and I'm so proud of you."

"And Michael," she added with some feeling, "it's true that I want you to help The Cause, but God knows I don't want you to die for it."

They would have liked to spend the night together, but in rural Ireland that would not have been possible, and certainly not under Annie Quinlan's roof. And wagging tongues would have raised more questions requiring more untruthful answers.

While the three of them had been together, they had benefitted from mutual support and had managed to deal with the events of the evening. But now that they were alone, each had to cope with their individual thoughts by themselves.

Despite not having slept properly for two nights, Maureen could not manage to drop off. She was too relieved and excited by the thought of finding Michael again when all had seemed lost. But her happiness was tinged with apprehension, and to her surprise, she suffered pangs of guilt for the way in which they had disposed of the body. Although it had been the only solution they could think of to the problem they had been faced with, she felt a need to say a private Act of Contrition and pray for forgiveness. But the guilt she felt over what had happened at the bog failed to reach the depths of the guilt she felt for having deceived Michael. As the night wore on she prayed harder than she had ever done that, when he heard the whole story, he would be able to forgive her.

She thought about what she had said to him about dying for the cause, and it brought back memories of her brother. When he had been killed during The Rising her overriding feeling had been one of anger. But if Michael were to be killed she suspected that it would generate much different emotions, she did not know quite what they would be, but she prayed to God that she would never be obliged to experience them.

William too lay awake, his mind churning over the events of the evening. The sudden appearance of 'The Man from Dublin' had served to remind him of the troubles that his family had been obliged to live through over the past year. Had it not been for that man his father might still be alive, and his brother would not be in hiding and in fear for his life. He was satisfied that Michael's swift action had saved their lives and, thinking about it now, he asked himself that if he had been the one holding that *slean,* would he have reacted as decisively. But like his companions, he found that the manner in which they had disposed of the body preyed on his conscience. Even though he told himself that it had been the only thing to do, consigning someone's body to a hole in the bog was to his mind a mortal sin. He knew that one day he would have to confess it, although he realised that he could never make reparation. The thought occurred to him that, as a result of 'The Man's' actions, his own father had been laid to rest in an unmarked pauper's grave a long way from home. He tried telling himself that being dumped in a bog was no more than the villain deserved. But he found little consolation in that.

There was, however, at least one saving grace to come out of the whole affair: he could now write to his brother and assure him that it was safe for him to come home. It gave him some comfort to think of how pleased his mother would be to see James again. She would probably never know the debt they owed to Michael Flynn for that, but he promised himself that somehow the debt would be repaid.

Holding Maureen in his arms, and hearing her say that she loved him, had meant the world to Michael. When he got home he found his mother waiting up for him. He told her the same story they had told Annie Quinlan, but unlike Annie, Mrs Flynn was happy to believe her son. For the last few days he had seemed so sad and distant, and it had worried her. Tonight that sorrow seemed to have been lifted from him, and in her relief she did not question him further.

Although Michael's thoughts that night were almost entirely on Maureen, one niggling worry invaded the recesses at the back of his mind. He would have to question his commitment to fighting for Irish freedom. He had killed one man, and he was not at all sure that he was ready to repeat the experience.

At the Quinlan cottage, Annie knew that William was keeping something from her, especially when he was adamant that there was no need for her and the children to help with drying the turf and bringing it home.

"Sure you have enough to do here Ma with Michael and the girls going back to school," he said. "Myself and Mick Flynn can manage it easy, Mick is going to use his horse and cart, so we won't even need the pony."

He was not looking forward to going back to the bog so soon. Neither was Michael, but it had to be done. To her credit, and to William's surprise, Maureen insisted on accompanying them. At first he thought that she might have some ghoulish notion about returning to the scene of the crime. It soon became clear, however, that her only motive was to support Michael. They went quietly about the work but, no matter how hard they tried, they could not resist an occasional glance across the bog. It was as if they expected a ghostly apparition to rise from it at any moment.

Maureen was totally inexperienced in this kind of manual labour. She found it hard going but stuck to her task well. She had returned to Killarney where the manager of the Great Southern hotel had been as good as his word and re-employed her. He even allowed her to delay starting work for a few days 'to clear up a few things'. The traumas of her recent experiences had brought home to her how much she needed to be with Michael Flynn, and how, by her own confused actions, she had come so close to losing him. She was determined not to let it happen again, and she began to wonder if a city girl born and bred, especially one brought up to dedicate her life to the nationalist cause, could possibly find happiness as a farmer's wife. To her delight Michael had completely forgiven her when she told him the story of her hunt for James Quinlan, and the way in which she had set out to involve him in the scheme.

"The best thing to do is to forget all about that love, sure it's all in the past now," he told her.

So she tried her best at helping with the turf and was soon pulling her weight.

Eventually the turf was in and built into a weatherproof clamp behind the cottage. Annie was ready to approach William and demand some straight answers when a letter arrived from James promising to come home for Christmas this year. All thoughts of chastising William were immediately put aside.

# Chapter 21

In Dublin Michael Collins was becoming concerned about what had happened to one of his senior planners. 'John Jameson' had not surfaced for several weeks and no one had seen or heard from him. In Rathmines, his housekeeper was complaining that she had not been paid for some time. It was at first feared that he had been secretly picked up by the authorities and was undergoing interrogation at Dublin Castle, but Collins was soon satisfied that this was not the case. Much of his effort since his release from internment had been directed at establishing an efficient nationalist spy network, and he even had agents inside 'The Castle' itself. He was satisfied that if his man had been arrested he would have known about it. After several more weeks had passed with no definite news, Collins formed the opinion that 'John Jameson's' disappearance had been caused by the settlement of some long standing personal dispute. His investigations pointed to the fact that his planner had not been involved in any 'official business' that could have possibly resulted in his going missing for so long. But anyone with such a long history of undercover work for The Cause was, he reasoned, sure to have made enemies along the way. 'John Jameson' would not have been the first, and as things stood in Ireland at present, he would certainly not be the last, to mysteriously disappear as a result of an old score being settled. It was a hazard they all lived with, including himself, and he doubted if he would ever learn the truth. So while he issued instructions for everyone to keep their eyes and ears open he had more pressing matters to attend to.

In October 1917 Sinn Fein had been re-formed and Eamonn de Valera had been elected president of the party. He had also taken over leadership of the Irish Volunteers. The party was now committed to working for the establishment of an Irish Republic, and their policies proved to be successful in that three Sinn Fein candidates, including De Valera himself, won parliamentary by-elections. But the party had adopted an abstentionist policy which meant that all three of those elected refused to take their seats in the House of Commons.

Throughout the rest of the country the preparations for armed resistance were gaining momentum, and nowhere more than in the southwest. But there would be no repeat of Easter 1916. The leaders of that ill-fated rebellion had known that they stood no chance in a pitched battle against the

British army; their main objective of that 'blood sacrifice' had been to awaken the Irish people. That was now no longer necessary, anti-British feeling was rife. There was no longer a need for a pitched battle and the next war would be fought using guerrilla tactics, and all preparations were being geared to this end. Training was becoming better organised, and appropriate programmes, procedures and practices were being put in place.

In training with the rebels William, was merely going through the motions but Michael had begun to take it very seriously indeed. At first William thought that he was merely trying to impress Maureen, and while there was an element of truth in this, it did not tell the whole story. On top of his experiences in the internment camp, Michael's thinking was deeply affected by what had happened at the bog. He thought it over carefully and came to the conclusion that similar tragedies would continue to occur as long as Ireland remained part of the United Kingdom. While that situation persisted there would always be conflict; there would always be Irishmen prepared to resist British rule, and as a consequence men like the one they had buried in the bog would continue to command an important place in Irish affairs. And people like himself, William, and Maureen, would continue to be caught up in situations totally out of their control. To himself, Michael reiterated what he had said to William, he was determined to do what he could to help make Ireland free. But as he threw himself wholeheartedly into the training, he was still uncertain about whether he was really cut out to be a front line soldier. It was not long, however, before he was given an opportunity to find out.

There were people still alive in Ireland who remembered the Great Famine. As a result, the memory of the famine, in which an estimated million people had starved to death, remained fresh in the Irish consciousness. The fact that death on such a scale could have been easily avoided still rankled. In the mid-nineteenth century for the poor farmers of the south and west potatoes formed the staple diet. All other crops went to pay the rent and people were faced with a terrible choice: they either lost their homes and livelihoods or they starved. Thousands died of one of the many and various diseases caused by malnutrition. The real tragedy was that the worst effects of the famine could easily have been avoided: there was food aplenty available in the country but no attempt whatsoever was made by the government in London to see that it was fairly distributed.

Many Irishmen, therefore, were deeply concerned about the amount of food being sent 'over the water' to bolster the British war effort. The Nationalists, and particularly Sinn Fein, recognised an opportunity to embarrass the authorities while at the same time building support for the party. As well as raiding R.I.C. barracks for arms, they began stealing cattle destined for export and passing them on to local butchers for slaughter and distribution to the people. Michael Flynn took part in one of these raids in County Cork.

The raid was carried out on a quiet back road as the cattle were being driven along it to the port of Queenstown. It was mounted after the farmers had received payment but before the cattle reached the docks, where armed police could be expected to intervene. To begin with things went according to plan, the rebel cattle thieves lay in wait, and when they sprang their trap the drovers offered no resistance. But as the cattle were being driven off, a man, obviously an agent for the buyers coming to supervise the rest of the drive, caught up with the raiders. He began to protest loudly and was shot out of hand by one of the rebels.

Michael was shocked. When the raid was being planned nothing had been said about killing anyone, in fact it had been stressed on the men carrying out the plan that the drovers were not to be harmed; killing Irish farmhands would prove to be counterproductive for The Cause. But even though one man had clearly overstepped the mark, Michael noted that nobody in the rebel band questioned the action or made any protest. Killing, he thought, was becoming all too acceptable in Ireland; and both sides were equally guilty.

"At least when I killed a man I was forced into doing it," he told Maureen. "I still want to do my bit for Irish freedom because until we are free of British rule the killing will only get worse. But even so, sure I could never shoot someone for no reason at all."

\*\*\*

Although he agreed with Michael as far as Irish freedom was concerned, for William things were not quite so clear cut. For one thing he had seen a man killed. And, although he was not entirely comfortable with the thought, he was satisfied that if it ever came to the point where it was completely unavoidable, if it came to outright war, he felt that he would be prepared to fight for The Cause. But he also had his family to consider. James was sending money home on a regular basis, but William still saw himself as the main breadwinner, as well as being responsible for all the manual tasks connected with family life. There was the cottage to think about too. He knew that when he came home, Jack would see it as his place to go to work at Beaufort House. That would ensure that his mother and the children would continue to have a roof over their heads. But what if, God forbid, Jack was killed, or too badly wounded to work? He doubted if, having lived abroad for over a year now, James would agree to work at

Beaufort. He was certain that after the war James would go to America as he had said he would do, and that would leave William as the only one left to take on the responsibility.

And, the way things were shaping up in Ireland, working at Beaufort House might well not prove to be as straightforward as it seemed. William had been thinking about the remarks made at the bog by Kevin Ryan about the rebels 'targeting' Beaufort's British owner. According to Maureen that had been 'a pack of lies', but it could have contained an element of truth. In view of 'His Lordship's' position there was a distinct possibility that it could become fact. If that were to happen, then anyone directly connected with Beaufort House, and especially the Quinlan family, could be caught in the middle of the conflict between the Irish nationalists and the British authorities.

And yet another matter continued to bother William, the debt he still felt he owed Michael Flynn. The strain was beginning to tell. He did not feel trapped exactly, but he began to think about his future and question what life in Beaufort had to offer him. Letters from James and Jack served to fuel the feeling that he was being left behind. The world seemed to be calling him; he was beginning to feel that it was time to spread his wings.

\*\*\*

In November, Patrick Coughlin paid another short visit to Beaufort before embarking on a troopship back to Mesopotamia where the fighting still went on in spite of the fall of Baghdad. The fishing season was over, but he and Michael sat by the fire with William late into the night when the others were in bed, and chatted about the political situation. Patrick was anxious to gain as much information as he could to take back to James Daly.

In the hope of avoiding the problem that had arisen on Patrick's previous visit Michael had decided to take a chance and tell Maureen that he would again be meeting the Connaught Ranger. He finally managed to explain to her how he had been surprised by the British soldier's attitude towards Ireland's troubles and how, in his opinion, there were many more Irishmen serving in the war who saw themselves as fighting against Germany rather than for Britain. When it came to a fight with British troops, he told her, they could prove to be valuable allies. Although she remained sceptical, and declined the invitation to meet Patrick in person, she was determined not to do anything that might cause friction between herself and the man she loved. So she accepted the fact that Michael liked the Connaught Ranger, and that he was anxious to talk with him again.

When he left to return to the war, Patrick carried with him three small medals bearing images of The Blessed Virgin. They had been given to him by Annie with a sincere show of faith, and so he had accepted them graciously. He knew that he would be able to hand James Daly his in person, but he was not at all certain about seeing Jack. The artilleryman might be in a totally different part of Mesopotamia when he got there, but he said nothing of this to Annie and promised her that he would deliver the gift.

\*\*\*

James came home the day before Christmas and his mother cried with joy. As well as the tears, however, William could not help but notice that several years seemed to have suddenly fallen from her. James brought presents for everybody: a purse for his mother, a cap for William, a coat for 'young' Michael, and rag dolls for the girls. All of which, he told them, had been hand made by the Belgians he was working with at Birtley. This was the first that his mother had heard of the Belgian munitions factory, and he had to quickly explain to her that he was no longer travelling between factories but had been sent to work there permanently. William said nothing to contradict his brother. They all listened with rapt attention as James explained that he was the only Irishman there and described what life was like working with the Belgians. He told them all he could without letting slip that he had actually been in hiding, and he and William exchanged knowing glances. To keep the conversation light he taught the girls a few words from the smattering of French he had picked up, and they could not wait to go and say *bonjour* to their friends.

After Mass on Christmas morning he was greeted by many old friends and acquaintances. Several mentioned that they remembered his father and expressed sorrow about what had happened, but the atmosphere was generally jovial. 'Happy Christmas' was the order of the day. Annie too was a centre of attention and she revelled in showing off her handsome son. People remarked upon how much James had changed, how 'grown up' he had become.

The changes in James had not of course escaped either Annie's or William's notice. Gone was the reckless youth who not long before had been trying to decide whether to join the British army like his older brother, or the Irish rebels like some of his friends. In his place was a much more mature and thoughtful person who had endured some hard times and had become a better man because of them. Although Annie missed her husband and Jack, Christmas 1917 in the Quinlan home was a joyous time.

But in much of the world at large 'peace on earth' still remained an unknown concept, and the mass killing went on.

# Chapter 22

The day after Christmas, St. Stephen's Day in Ireland, dawned bright and frosty. William and James managed to get out for a morning walk, which provided them with the opportunity to discuss recent events out of their mother's hearing.

When William had finished telling his brother the whole story about the death of 'The Man from Dublin', James said: "You're lucky to be alive, Bill. If Mick Flynn hadn't given that fella a belt with the *slean* he would have shot you for sure. And Mick and that girl as well, even with her brother there."

"It's not Mick killing him that bothers me Jim," said William, "but weighing him down with stones and putting him into the bog wasn't right."

"He had it coming to him Bill," said James with conviction. "Sure he would have left Da and me at the bottom of the Solway Firth and thought nothing of it. I tell you now that I'll shed no tears for him. And don't forget that because of him Da never had a wake, or the decent funeral he was entitled to."

William digested this. "I suppose you're right Jim," he said. "But, God knows, it still bothers me a bit. In any case we all owe Mick Flynn a lot. I only hope I get the chance to make it up to him."

"The way things are here in Ireland you might get the chance any day," said James.

He changed the subject: "So" he said, "what about Mick and this girl? If he's well in with 'the boys' these days, and she was working for your man in the bog, is there any chance they'll tell someone about it. I don't want to have them after me again. And I suppose seeing as your man always went to Devlin's when he was in Beaufort, Pat must have been in on it with him."

"No chance at all of that Jim. Mick Flynn will say nothing to anyone about it, and Maureen Ryan was glad as any of us to see that fella killed. And sure Pat Devlin knows nothing. Your man made sure that no one except Maureen knew that he was looking for you, and she knows now that if he found you he would have killed her as well as you because of what she knew about him."

"Jesus" said James, "it's a different Ireland altogether now. Over the water there they think that The Rising put an end of all the troubles, but sure it was only the start of a whole lot more."

"You're right there Jim. And there's bound to be more trouble before long. Most of the lads around here are getting ready for it."

"Are you going to be in it with them Bill? Sure wasn't I all set to join them myself the last time, only Da took me off to Scotland with him."

"I don't know Jim. But I can't do anything until either yourself or Jack comes home for good. After that I'll think about it. What about yourself, what are you going to do now?"

"I'm not going to join the rebels if that's what you're asking," said James. "After what happened to Da I'll have nothing to do with them. But I won't hold it against you or anybody else if you want to join the fight for Ireland. I definitely can't blame people like Mick Flynn after the way they were treated. But it's not for me anymore."

"So, what will you do?"

"I'll see the war out with the Belgians so that I can send a bit more money home for Ma, and then it's America for me. The fella I told you about from Gretna, Pete Casey, is over in the States and he says he'll help me get fixed up."

It was what William expected, but not exactly what wanted to hear. "You won't go before Jack comes home will you Jim?" he said. "The truth of it is I was thinking that I might try my hand at a bit of travelling myself after the war."

"All right Bill, I don't blame you, sure there's nothing here in Beaufort for you. But we can't leave Ma, and the young ones here on their own, so I'll wait until after Jack comes home."

The thought that Jack might not live to come home occurred to both of them but was left unsaid.

That evening James wanted to renew acquaintance with some old friends, so they went to Devlin's pub where William had arranged to meet Michael Flynn. In the pub James was greeted in friendly fashion by the majority of the drinkers in the bar, and by Pat Devlin himself, but there were also a few suspicious glances. There was nothing like the euphoria that had marked the arrival home of the internees the year before. James' homecoming had already been noted by the pub owner and he was planning to report the fact to 'Mr. Jameson' by telegram from Killarney the following day; and he hoped to pick up a bit more useful information to-night. He was talking to one of the more diehard republicans at the bar when Michael came up to order drinks.

"Jesus Christ Mick," said the rebel drinker, "what's a fella like you doing drinking porter with Jim Quinlan. Sure isn't he working for the bloody Brits."

"Ah sure Jim's not working for the Brits at all," said Michael. "He's working for the Belgians."

"The Belgians?" said Devlin. "But I thought that they were occupied by the Germans, how in the name of God can he be working for them?"

"Ah well," said Michael, "according to Jim they weren't all captured by the Germans. A lot of them escaped to England and set up their own munitions factory there."

"Ah well I suppose there's all kinds of queer things going on in this war." Devlin's interest was aroused and he decided it would be useful to learn more by striking up a conversation with James himself. The other drinker had moved away and Devlin made a start to this process by waving Michael's money away:

"These are on the house Mick, to welcome Jim home."

The three friends stood and chatted in a corner. Periodically men came over to greet James and several offered to buy them drinks. None of the three were heavy drinkers, so the offers were politely turned down by James. William brought up the subject of Patrick Coughlin's visit and their fishing trip. Annie had already told James about Patrick's visit, and what he had told her about Jack and Mesopotamia, but Michael only wanted to talk about the soldier's views on the Irish political situation. When they had exhausted that subject James wanted to ask Michael about Maureen Ryan – his mother was still under the impression that he had been friends with her at Gretna – but before he could do so they were approached by Devlin bearing drinks which could not very well be refused.

"So Jim," said the publican. "Your mother was looking happy to have you at Mass yesterday morning. Are you home for good now?"

"No Pat," said James, "I'm only here for a few days. I have to be back over the water before the week is out."

"Mick here tells me that you're working for the Belgians now."

"I am so Pat."

"Jesus I never heard about them having a factory over there," said Devlin. "How did you get in with them? Bill there was telling me that you were running around all over the country working for the Brit munitions people."

"Ah sure I got fed up with that," said James, "I never knew where I was half the time. But being in the trade as they say, I got a job with the Belgians. And between you and me Pat, while I was working at the British factory, I was always in danger of being conscripted into the army."

This was not true, but James felt it added authenticity to his story, and gave him an opportunity of changing the subject.

"And I wouldn't put it past them to bring in conscription here in Ireland as well," he said.

"If they do Eamonn de Valera will have a bit to say about it," said Michael.

This started a heated discussion with several others joining in. Devlin thought that he had gleaned enough information, certainly as much as could be included in a telegram, so he left them to it.

When they left the pub and were out of earshot of the other drinkers Michael turned to James. "Would you be fit to go into Killarney with me in the morning Jim?" he said. "Maureen Ryan would like a word with you."

***

Maureen now had a permanent job at The Great Southern. The hotel remained open over Christmas but did little business. What work there was to do was carried out by those staff who lived locally, so she was able to go home for a few days over the holiday.

At home she learned from Kevin that the disappearance of 'the fella from Rathmines' had been put down to the settlement of an old score, which in a way was not far from the truth. As far as her father and Kevin were concerned that was the end of the matter, but Maureen still had something to do before she could put it behind her: She had to meet and talk to James Quinlan. If she was to have any hope of enjoying a happy future with Michael Flynn down in Beaufort she would have to make her peace with James.

It was not something she was looking forward to. Thinking about it reminded her of how she felt when she went to talk to the priest in confession, a practice she still kept up. Like the majority of Irish people involved in the nationalist struggle she did not suffer from a conflict of conscience between her duty to The Cause and her duty to The Church; to her mind they were one and the same. But, unlike the requirements of the confessional, she did not feel that her involvement in the search for James Quinlan demanded that she make an act of contrition. She had been carrying out her duty as she saw it at the time, and the fact that she had been duped into doing it was immaterial. And she was determined not to make that mistake again.

What she would apologise to James for, however, was deceiving his mother. She also felt that she had to make some form of reparation, and that James was entitled to hear the full story behind what had happened, and her role in it. Michael and William had already been given a full account of her part in the search for James, and had offered to tell him themselves, but she was determined that it was something she had to do by herself. She was

129

beginning a new life and there must be no bitterness or recriminations hanging over from the past. That did not mean that she was any less committed to the struggle for Irish freedom, she would never abandon that; it simply meant that her role in it would change. From now on her all efforts would be in support of Michael.

In spite of being reassured by Michael, she spent many anxious hours before finally meeting the man she had expended so much effort in attempting to lead to his death.

She need not have worried. When they met in a cafe in Killarney on the morning following St. Stephen's Day, James Quinlan was surprisingly sympathetic. He was taller than William but was quite evidently a Quinlan. Had events taken a different course she knew that she would have recognised him. Even though James told her that it was not necessary, she was determined to tell him the whole story.

When she had finished he said: "There's no call to blame yourself Maureen, you weren't the first person to be taken in by that fella. And I'll tell you this; I'm glad you'll be the last."

"What about your mother," she said, "will she hold it against me for telling her a pack of lies?"

It was the one point that James seemed to take seriously. "It'll be better for Ma if she never finds out anything at all about it," he said. "She's only just getting over what happened to Da, and it won't do any good at all to tell her anything about what happened over there in Gretna. We all think that the best thing is to keep it from her."

She looked at Michael who nodded in assent. "All right James," she said, "I won't say anything to her about it."

They chatted for a while longer but Maureen wanted to give Michael the latest news from Dublin, so James left them alone and went to have his first real look around Killarney for two years. He noticed Pat Devlin going into the Post Office. The Beaufort publican was going to send a telegram to 'Mr Jameson'; one that that would never be delivered.

After James left to go back to Birtley, William spent many hours thinking about how his brother had described working with the Belgians, and of the things he had seen and learned. He thought of Jack and Patrick Coughlin in Mesopotamia, and in spite of the danger he knew they were in, he was a little envious. What stories Jack would have to tell when he came home.

He looked forward to the coming New Year. Maybe 1918 would be the year the war would eventually come to end, Jack would come home, and he would have the opportunity do make a mark on the world for himself. And hopefully that would help to put all thought the body lying in the bog behind him.

# Chapter 23

"Will you listen to him now, Jack?" said Private James Daly, "to hear him talk sure you'd think he was the finest fisherman since Saint Peter himself."

Patrick Coughlin had arrived back in Mesopotamia and rejoined his colleagues in the Connaught Rangers. Daly had also fully recovered from his wounds and both were ready to return to the front line. Christmas 1917 had passed off quietly in Baghdad, and at New Year 1918 they were delighted to receive a visit from Jack Quinlan.

Coughlin had already told James about his visit to the Daly family and was now enthusiastically recounting the story of his visit to Beaufort. "Sure it's the truth I'm telling you, we didn't leave a single trout in the whole of the river Laune," he said.

They laughed, and he continued in a more serious tone: "I'll say this Jack, the Laune is a grand water for the fishing, and that brother of yours knows how to handle a rod. What about yourself, do you like to drown a few worms?"

"No," said Jack, "Bill is the fisherman in the family. I don't know where he gets it from because none of the rest of us ever took to it."

Daly had things other than fishing on his mind. "Pat was saying that his fella Flynn who was locked up with the rest of the lads after The Rising was a friend of yours Jack," he said.

"That he was," said Jack, "sure didn't we go to school together."

"Even if he wasn't in The Rising itself he must have been well in with 'the boys' to get picked up and interred like that," said Daly.

"From what he was telling me he never once gave a thought to joining in The Rising," said Coughlin. "The truth of it is that one minute he was minding his own business in Killarney and the next thing he knew he was behind barbed wire in Wales".

"Jesus, but that was hard lines for him," said Daly.

"I'd say Pat is right about him not being in on The Rising," said Jack. "I never once heard Mick Flynn say a word about Home Rule, or anything else to do with politics. Sure he's the last man in the world you'd expect to see with a gun in his hand."

"That'll all change now, I can tell you," said Coughlin. "Since he was locked up for doing nothing he's all for setting Ireland free. He was telling me that he would rather it happened by peaceful means, but if it comes to a fight he'll be there."

"What about the rest of the country Pat?" said Daly. "From what you saw at home would you say that there's much support for another rising. Is there any chance that it will come to that again?"

"Ah sure the country is changed altogether since the last time we were home, Jim," came the reply. "After what happened as soon as The Rising was over, with the executions and martial law and people like Mick Flynn being interred, I'd say the whole country would be behind them if the lads tried again."

"That all sounds grand," said Jack. "But sure they won't have any more chance of winning than they had the last time."

"I wouldn't bet on that Jack," said Coughlin. "They learned their lesson in 1916. They know very well that they can't beat the British Army in a pitched battle and they won't try that again. From what I heard they'll be using guerrilla tactics. They'll hit and run, and Jim here can tell you how hard it is for a regular army to catch people who fight like that."

"He's right there Jack," said Daly. "Sure didn't we spend enough years fighting the Pathans and the rest of them tribesmen out there in The Grim with no chance at all of catching the canny buggers. If the lads in Ireland do the same thing it'll be just as hard for the British army to beat them. There's places galore to hide a guerrilla force in the South and the West. But I suppose they won't try to do anything until after the war now. "

"I don't know about that Jim," said Coughlin, "from what I saw it's already started. Sure wasn't there a raid on a police barracks near Tipperary itself while I was there. No one was killed, but there were a few sore heads when it was over and the lads got away with some hand guns."

Daly nodded his head, seemingly in satisfaction. Coughlin went on: "And here's another thing. The fact is that the army is running short of men, and conscription is being stepped up. I wouldn't put it past the government to try and introduce conscription in Ireland, and if they start calling up Irishmen there'll be ructions."

"Did anyone tell you who might be leading the country if we do win independence?" said Daly.

"According to Mick Flynn this fella de Valera is the man for the job, with Michael Collins to help him," said Coughlin.

Coughlin and Daly continued to discuss the tactics involved in guerrilla warfare, but Jack was barely listening. His mind turned to something closer to home, and he eventually asked the question that had been bothering him:

"Did you get any notion that my brother Bill might join the fight for Irish independence, Pat?" he asked.

"Oh Bill is all for Irish freedom all right Jack," said Coughlin. "I'd say that he'd be ready to fight for it. But he says that he has to stay at home to look out for your mother and the children. And from what I saw he's making a grand job of it too."

"Sure Bill was only a boy when I left home, and he was all set to join up with me, but Da wouldn't let him. It's hard to think that he must be a man now," said Jack.

"Well he's a man now sure enough," said Coughlin.

"I hope to God you're wrong about conscription Pat, I don't know what my mother would do if Bill was to be called up."

"Sure with the money that yourself and your brother are sending home your family are doing fine, and you have no worries there Jack," said Coughlin.

Jack thought about this for a while before commenting: "It's not only money that's keeping him there, it's the cottage as well. It was tied to Da's job, and with him gone, Lord have mercy on him, at least one of the rest of us will have to work up at Beaufort House to keep a roof over our heads. I was hoping that the war might change all that, but I'm afraid we'll be stuck with it for a few years yet."

"We have to rent the farm from a fella we never even saw," said Daly vehemently. "There were too many of us for the land to feed and that's why I 'took the shilling'. The only thing that will change things in Ireland will be freedom from British rule."

"It was the same here," said Coughlin. "But the way I see it is I joined up, and now I'll have to see it out. I was telling Mick Flynn and Bill in Beaufort that if there is any sign of trouble at home after the war they won't let regiments like the 'Rangers' anywhere near Ireland. It'll be The Grim or somewhere else far away for us."

"You're right there Pat," said Daly. "And then we'll be the one's rounding up some poor buggers for internment without trial, just like that fella Flynn at home."

There was silence while they digested that sobering thought. Then Coughlin said. "What about yourself Jack? Please God this war will end sometime soon and you'll be going home, what will you do then? Will you join in the fight for Ireland?"

Jack thought long and hard before answering. "I don't know about that," he said. "To be sure I think that the only thing that will cure Ireland's trouble is independence. On the other hand I suppose I'll be the one that'll have to go and work up at Beaufort House. If nothing else, I owe it to Bill to take that load off him. And the truth of it is I've had my fill of fighting, for a while anyway."

"Don't count your chickens yet Jack," said Daly. "You might see a lot more of it before this war is over. Sure I know that things are quiet here for the time being, but the Turks are still a long way from being beaten. And I'd say that we'll have a few more dances with them yet."

"There were great celebrations at home over the capture of Jerusalem a few days before I left Tipp," said Coughlin. "And aren't they telling us that the Russians are coming down from the north to put pressure on the Turks, and anyway these fellas in the armoured cars have them running like rabbits all over the place. Maybe they'll send us a few of them new tanks as well, and that will be the finish of the Turks."

"I wouldn't put have any faith at all in these new machines myself," said Daly. "Fair play to the boys in the armoured cars, they're doing a good job, but sure them bloody big tanks would sink in the sand or run out of petrol in this bloody desert before they got anywhere near the Turks. And God knows at the end of the day it'll still be down to us poor bastards with the bayonets."

"But don't forget about your man, what's his name? Lawrence?" said Jack, "I hear that he has them on the run too. If he has them beat sure we can all go home."

"I wouldn't bet a penny on that Jack," said Daly. "Even if the war here is over soon, it'll take a long time yet before we beat the Germans. And as long as the war against them lasts there'll be no going home for any of us. From what you were saying about conscription and the shortage of manpower Pat, we'll be back on the bloody Western Front again before we have time to scratch our arses."

They lapsed into silence, each one with his own private thoughts.

"Ah well, Happy New Year Lads," said Jack Quinlan.

# Chapter 24

If, during the first months of 1918, things were relatively quiet in Mesopotamia, the war of attrition showed no signs of reaching a conclusion on the Western Front, and the killing went on without a pause.

As a result both James Quinlan and Patrick Coughlin were proved to be correct in their predictions: Conscription was stepped up on the British mainland and the London Government attempted to introduce a similar system in Ireland. Eamonn De Valera, as a Member of Parliament, albeit one who refused to sit in the House of Commons, vehemently spoke out against it and rallied support throughout the country. He composed a declaration opposing conscription which was posted on every church door inviting signatures. Thousands signed it. Even the bishops opposed the move to conscript Irishmen. The level of opposition was such that the London Government, while not abandoning the idea, did little to enforce it. But one outcome was that several republican leaders were arrested. De Valera himself was imprisoned in Lincoln Jail.

***

Some months later, Maureen Ryan was serving dinner at The Great Southern hotel in Killarney when to her amazement she saw a face she instantly recognised. The last time she had seen Countess Markievicz was during The Rising. Then they had both worn the uniform of *Cumman na mBann* and the Countess had carried a revolver. Now, seated in the hotel dining room, she looked every inch the aristocratic lady she in fact was. She seemed equally surprised to see Maureen and waved her over to where she sat alone at a corner table. It was with a feeling of trepidation that Maureen approached the lone diner. But The Countess greeted her in friendly fashion.

"Why hello Maureen," she said, "what a pleasant surprise. Fancy my seeing you here of all places. Are you well?"

Although Maureen had served with the leader of *Cumann na mBann* during The Rising and had shared the dangers with her, on this occasion she thought it better to keep their relationship on a more formal footing. She curtseyed as would be expected of a waitress approaching a diner of high rank.

"Yes thank you Madam," she said, "I'm grand."

The head waiter had seen The Countess call Maureen over, and in case the diner was about to make a complaint, he came to the table himself.

"Is everything all right Madam?"

"Oh yes everything is quite satisfactory thank you," said The Countess. "I've known Miss Ryan here for some time and was just enquiring after her health, but if she is busy then I'll have a word with her later."

Maureen felt that this was her signal to leave, and she went back to her work. The head waiter also turned to go but as he left the Countess called him back.

"My girl has been taken ill," she said, "and as the Ryan girl used to work for me and knows my requirements, I was wondering if I might borrow her for the rest of my stay here."

The head waiter knew very well who the diner was, and was aware of her reputation, so he was not about to say or do anything without recourse to a higher authority.

"I'm sure that could be arranged Madam," he said. "But it will be up to the hotel manager. Would you like me to have a word with him?"

"Yes please, do that," said the Countess.

The hotel manager also knew who Countess Markievicz was and what she represented. It was of course common knowledge that she had been found guilty of treason and sentenced to death for her part in The Rising. The fact that the death sentence had been commuted to life imprisonment, and that she had subsequently been released during the general amnesty, had if anything, only served to increase her notoriety. This presented the hotel manager with something of a dilemma: The vast majority of his guests were rich tourists, well-to-do land owners or industrialists. A great many of them were English and very few would have any sympathy with the Countess's well publicised republican views. So whatever the manager's personal leanings, it would not help his career to exhibit nationalist tendencies himself. On the other hand the Countess was the wife of a well known and highly respected foreign nobleman, and as such she was accepted by the hotel clientele. But the manager was aware of the underlying tensions, which the lady herself was known to enjoy fuelling, and so whatever he did would require him to tread carefully.

Eventually he decided that he must accede to the Countess's wishes. But he warned the head waiter to be careful, and inform the Countess quietly that she could 'borrow' Miss Ryan for the rest of her stay at the hotel.

"And tell the Ryan girl that she is not to say anything to anybody about this," were his last words to the head waiter. Both men were aware that the length of the Countess's stay had not been specified, but neither mentioned this inconvenient anomaly.

The Countess smiled quietly to herself when the head waiter told her that Miss Ryan's services were at her disposal for the remainder of her stay at the hotel. She had known before she arrived in Killarney that she would meet Maureen, that was the purpose of her visit, and that the hotel management would allow her to commandeer the girl's services.

"Thank you," she said, "please ask Miss Ryan to come to my suite when she has finished serving dinner."

Maureen's mind raced as she somehow got through serving dinner. What did Constance Markievicz want with her? She knew the Countess well enough to suspect that meeting her here could not be put down to pure coincidence. What if, she thought, the *Cumann na mBan* leader's visit to Killarney was somehow connected with the disappearance of 'Mr Jameson'? Would she be able to convince the Countess that she knew nothing about it? One thing she was determined to avoid, however, was any suggestion that Michael Flynn had been involved in the disappearance of the rebel conspirator.

Although no formal announcement had been made, by now it was accepted that she and Michael would eventually marry. Maureen had even been accepted by Michael's mother, the woman who had previously refused to concede that a waitress from Dublin was a fitting match for her only son. Mrs Flynn's conversion had been brought about by a chance remark made by William Quinlan to his own mother. Annie was telling him about Mrs Flynn's opposition to any suggestion that Michael might marry 'the Ryan one' and his comment was. "Ah sure if he gets married to Maureen he won't have time to go marching with the Volunteers up at The Gap."

When this opinion was relayed to Mrs Flynn via the Sunday after-Mass grapevine, it caused her to have an immediate change of heart.

So Maureen had now completely regained the happiness she once feared she had lost, and she was looking forward to a blissful future with Michael. She had come to terms with what would be expected of her as a farmer's wife, and was confident that she could be content in the role. By the time she knocked on The Countess's door she was resolved that whatever happened she would do or say nothing that might put that future at risk.

The Countess greeted her with a kiss and invited her to sit. "I can't tell you how pleased I am that you managed to avoid arrest during the unpleasantness in Dublin after The Rising, Maureen. But how did you come to end up here in Killarney?"

"I have a friend down here Madam," Maureen decided that it would be wise to continue to address The Countess as 'Madam' rather than call her by her first name of 'Constance' as she had done during The Rising. "The truth is we're thinking of getting married."

To Maureen's relief The Countess didn't seem to be the least put out by this. "I'm delighted to hear that Maureen and I certainly wish you all the best. Tell me how exactly did you meet your intended?"

"Sure he's a friend of my brother Kevin, Madam. They were in the internment camp together."

The Countess nodded in satisfaction. Maureen's answers confirmed what she had already learned. She had been making enquiries about several missing members of *Cumman Na mBann,* who were now scattered far and wide, when the need for someone to carry out a special mission for The Cause had arisen. Maureen Ryan had been high on her list. She had spoken to Kevin Ryan, and it was what she gleaned from him that prompted her to make the trip to Killarney.

"Ah yes, internment," she said and paused. "Still I'm relieved to hear that the man you intend to marry must be a staunch Irish Nationalist. What's his name by the way?"

"Michael Flynn, Madam and he's one of the lads all right," said Maureen with some pride. She was beginning to relax. "He was one of those interned even though he had nothing at all to do with The Rising, but sure since then he's all for doing his best for The Cause." And she thought it safe to tell the Countess about Michael having taken part in a cattle raid.

"Well now Maureen," said the Countess. "To tell you the truth, Michael Collins and I are looking for someone to do a little job for us, and this young man of yours might just fit the part." She noticed the look of alarm that crossed Maureen's face and quickly went on: "Oh it's nothing dangerous. This task does not involve guns. In fact any sort of violence would ruin the whole scheme. I take it that you and Michael have heard about what has happened to Eamonn de Valera."

"Oh yes Madam," said Maureen, her confidence growing as she realised that whatever The Countess wanted did not involve the disappearance of 'her uncle', Michael Collins' late associate. And she believed her former commander when she said that Michael's life would not be endangered.

"We were sorry to hear that 'Dev' was put in jail again," she said. "Michael met him on the boat going over to Wales and was very taken with him."

"That's excellent," said the Countess. "If Michael knows and would recognise Mr de Valera that would be a great help. Now I'm sure you understand Maureen, that what I'm about to tell you is in strict confidence."

"Sure I know the way of it well enough Madam," answered Maureen.

"Good girl," said the Countess. "Very soon now we will need to send a top secret message to Mr de Valera over there in Lincoln Jail, and we will require a reliable messenger."

At first Maureen thought that she had misheard The Countess earlier, and that it was she herself who had been selected for the operation. But the Countess went on: "Do you think your young man would be willing to do this for us?"

This was something Maureen had to think seriously about. Since the cattle raid she and Michael had often discussed how they would help 'The Cause'. They had agreed that they would do whatever was required of them as long as it did not involve coldblooded murder, which they both knew Michael could not, and would not, commit; and neither would they would do anything which might pose a threat to their future life together. Nevertheless, now that the call had actually come, and prospect of being actively involved had arrived, her first thought was to protect Michael. "Ah sure I could do that for you myself Madam."

"Oh I know you could Maureen," said the Countess. "But both Michael Collins and I are agreed that this is a job for a man. The prison authorities will certainly expect us to try and contact such an important prisoner as Eamonn de Valera, and a pretty girl turning up to visit him would immediately arouse their suspicions. It's the oldest trick in the book, and they would watch you like hawks. No, what we need is someone who can legitimately meet with a prisoner in relative privacy. And of course it has to be someone who would not be recognised. The fact that Michael was one of thousands of unfortunate internees does not mean that he is actually known to the authorities."

Maureen began to worry about what was coming next and her heart sank as the Countess dropped the final bombshell: "How do you think Michael would react if we asked him to visit the prison posing as a priest?"

# Chapter 25

A small group within the British Government realised that the proposal to introduce conscription in Ireland had always been doomed to failure. They reasoned that, in the prevailing political climate, with the rise in popularity of Sinn Fein and increasing numbers joining the various rebel militant factions, a great many potential conscripts would simply refuse to be drafted. Most would probably opt to join the Volunteers or the Brotherhood instead, which they were bound to feel would offer them the best form of protection. But these Members of Parliament were in the minority. Attempts were made by the government to enforce the Defence of the Realm Act by banning not only military parades, but also Irish lessons, Gaelic football matches and even Irish dancing competitions. These efforts only added fuel to the fire and one result was a marked increase in Volunteer raids on police barracks. The objections to conscription put forward in Ireland were also being voiced in America, and Anglo-American relations began to suffer at a time when Britain had a particular need of her powerful transatlantic ally.

So what had, for the first two years of the war, been a fruitful recruiting ground was now a barren desert. In the mainly Nationalist south the mere mention of conscription caused recruitment to virtually dry up completely, but in the largely Unionist north a good number still answered Kitchener's call to arms.

But for William Quinlan the failure to introduce conscription was a mixed blessing. He was becoming increasingly dissatisfied with life in Beaufort and had even considered the possibility joining up. For centuries Irishmen had taken the 'King's Shilling' as a way of escaping poverty, but William considered it as a way of escaping from what was for him a seemingly dead end existence. Conscription would have offered a valid excuse to make an immediate break; but he knew in his heart that he could not leave before Jack came home, and he felt ashamed for having entertained the thought of doing otherwise. While joining the British Army did hold a certain appeal, the idea of being conscripted was not, however, something that sat easily on his mind. For one thing as a lowly farm worker he would in all likelihood have been drafted into one of the many Irish infantry regiments, and William felt that he should set his sights a little higher. He had seen the flickering silent images of modern war machines on the cinema screen in Killarney and had been fascinated by them. It seemed obvious to him that the use of motor transport would increase rapidly after the war and he wanted to be part of the revolution. It struck him that even Maureen's brother, Kevin, was already able to drive, having been taught as part of his training for service with Michael Collins' rebel organisation. He wondered if he too could learn by becoming fully committed to the rebel cause, but soon realised that it would be a long time before a country boy from the far southwest could rise to a position where it would become necessary for him to be able to drive a car.

His desire to get away from Beaufort was further fuelled by constant reminders of the events of a few months before. The memory of the body still lying in the bog would not go away. He was very conscious of the fact that, barring the extremely unlikely event of the war ending soon, turf cutting would once again be his sole responsibility this year. And he was not looking forward to returning to the bog. He had spoken of this to Michael Flynn, and although Michael's time was now almost fully occupied with courting Maureen and training with the Volunteers, William had obtained a promise of his friend's help again. In a way William envied Michael and Maureen, not just for their obvious happiness, but also because they had something positive to look forward to, while he seemed to be stuck in a rut. And there was still the added complication of the debt he felt he owed Michael for solving the problem of 'The Man from Dublin'.

He worried that the circumstances surrounding 'The Man's' disappearance might somehow come to light. Pat Devlin had been asking about James, and when William answered that his brother was doing well he noticed a brief look of puzzlement pass over the publican's face. He wondered how much Devlin knew of the actual events, and William was determined not to add to his knowledge, however much the pub owner already knew or suspected.

For his part, Devlin was well aware that 'Mr Jameson' planned to kill James and had come to Beaufort to threaten William in an attempt to force his brother into the open. The fact that James had indeed come home and that the car and guns had been returned as planned seemed to indicate that the scheme had worked. But nothing had happened to James when he had come home Beaufort for Christmas. Letters were still arriving from him at regular intervals and Devlin knew that they contained money for Mrs Quinlan. So it was obvious that James Quinlan was still alive but, unless he was contacted by 'Mr Jameson', Devlin had no way of knowing how or why. He dared not ask William what had happened when 'Jameson' had last come to Beaufort because this would mean that his own involvement in the affair could be made public. Devlin's reputation locally was too important to him to risk people knowing that he had helped in a plot in which a member of the Quinlan family was to be killed. So all he could do was wait and see what developed.

# Chapter 26

Michael Flynn listened attentively as Countess Markievicz outlined what she and Michael Collins wanted him to do for The Cause. She was careful to tell him only enough to enable him to decide whether he was prepared to accept the assignment, the details would come later. She could of course have dispensed with these formalities and simply told him that if he did not do as she wished it would go hard with Maureen, but while she had learned enough of their relationship to know that this would have been enough to bring Michael into line, it was not her favoured way of getting things done. Underhandedness was not part of her make-up and she had enough experience to know that the loyalty of pressed men was always in question. So she told him what she wanted and suggested that he talk it over with Maureen before making up his mind – knowing that he would do so, whether she sanctioned it or not. In essence Michael was simply required to visit Eamonn de Valera in Lincoln Prison and let him know that efforts would be made to facilitate his escape. He would then bring back bring back the prisoner's reply. The Countess was at pains to point out that this was not intended to be a one-off visit 'across the water'. Depending on how plans for the escape attempt developed, Michael would be asked to make further visits to update the Sinn Fein leader. To ensure that they could meet in relative privacy Michael was to be dressed as a priest and to pose as the prisoner's personal confessor.

This was the aspect of the plan that the Countess feared Michael might object to. The thought of impersonating a priest would, she reasoned, be abhorrent his to Catholic beliefs; as would be the case with the vast majority of Irishmen of the time. And for Michael also, this was true, but in spite of his experiences at the bog and on the cattle raid, he was as keen as ever to become more deeply involved in The Cause. For one thing there was the thought that Maureen had already placed her life on the line for Irish freedom and at the back of his mind he felt that he still had prove himself worthy of her. And even though it didn't show, the memory of his internment still rankled. What he had experienced so far had made him question his suitability for service as a front line soldier in a guerrilla army with a duty to kill without compunction, but the task proposed by the Countess presented him with an opportunity of playing an important role without the necessity of causing bloodshed.

Had the prisoner in Lincoln Prison been anyone other than Eamonn de Valera he might have thought further, but under the circumstances he felt prepared, albeit reluctantly, to set his religious scruples aside and accept the Countess' mission.

These, however, were not the only aspects of the assignment he had to consider, and it was Maureen who pointed out some of the more practical consequences of his becoming involved in the plan.

"I'd trust Constance Markievicz with my life, and I know that she would look out for you if anything went wrong, Michael," she told him. "But some of the others, and that includes the 'Big Fella' himself, wouldn't think twice about leaving you over there on your own, high and dry with nobody at all to turn to for help."

Before Michael could think of a reply Maureen went on: "The other thing you have to think about my love is that once you do something like this for The Cause, you're in it for good. You can never back out. This isn't like going on cattle raid with a few of the local boys, or even being interned with a lot of other men. You will become known to some of the most important people in the movement, and if this scheme works out you can bet your life that it won't be the last time they will be calling on you."

"And don't forget that you won't be able to breathe a word to anyone about this, and no one will ever know what you did for Ireland," she added.

Michael thought for a moment: "Sure I wouldn't want anyone to know about me pretending to be a priest, most of all, my mother," he said. "And didn't Jim Quinlan tell us that the fella in the bog did the same thing once. I wouldn't want Bill or anyone else to think that I was as bad as him."

"Ah sure no one would ever think that of you Michael," said Maureen gently.

"And aren't you in it for life yourself, Maureen," said Michael, "and as long as you are I want to be in it with you."

She held his arm and looked him directly in the eye. "Oh Michael," she said, "you don't have to do anything like this just to impress me. Sure I wouldn't think any less of you if you refused to do what they're asking."

But Michael's mind was made up. He put his arms around her. "Well I'm going to take no chances at all of that ever happening," he said.

For the first time in months he brought up the question of his part in the killing of the man at the bog. What if someone, by whatever means, discovered something? What if the finger was pointed at him? But Maureen had spoken to her brother, Kevin, and was confident that, bearing in mind the length of time that elapsed, there was no chance of that ever happening.

So Michael answered his country's call and was instructed to stand by until he was needed.

As Michael waited for the Countess to summon him to action, life went on around him. He would have liked to tell William what he had been selected to do for The Cause. This desire was not motivated by any feeling of pride; Michael genuinely felt that he owed it to his friend to warn him of the possibility of not being able to join him on fishing trips next spring and summer.

Not that William himself would have much time to follow his favourite pastime that year. He was by now an extremely competent farmhand and as such was entrusted with many of the more important tasks on the farm. At spring ploughing he no longer just did odd jobs, but carried out that strenuous activity himself. After a long day of walking up and down with one foot on the unploughed ground and one in the furrow, steadying the plough to keep a straight furrow while at the same time holding the reins and guiding the horses, he was too tired to even think of fishing. When a field was ploughed it was harrowed to prepare it for planting with wheat, oats, barley or potatoes. Like threshing the corn in the autumn, potato planting was something of a local ritual in spring. Everybody lent a hand. The seed potatoes were sliced into halves, and sometimes thirds or even quarters, depending upon how many 'eyes' the original seed possessed. Shallow trenches were opened up using a specially adapted plough with double mould boards, and well rotted farm manure was spread in the bottom of these 'drills'. The seed potato segments were then laid individually by hand on top of the manure. Women and children helped with this back-breaking task, and great pride was taken in planting the segments at regularly spaced intervals. Once a row had been planted the 'drill' was closed using the plough. Corn was still sown by hand. Women and children walked over the finely harrowed earth scattering the seed from special sacks hanging from their shoulders. The scattered seed was then harrowed in.

It was hard, relentless work, but William realised that for people on these larger farms, where horses provided the power for farm implements, life was relatively easy. Closer to the mountains around 'The Gap' there were many hill farms and smallholdings with tiny stone strewn fields, where tilling was still carried out by hand using spades and shovels.

It was easy to imagine the resentment fuelled when much of the result of this backbreaking toil went to pay rent to absent landlords.

***

It was in fact some months before Michael actually received his summons from the Countess. He had begun to think that there might have been a change of plan, or that a more suitable candidate had been found to play his role. Then at last he received the call. The message was sent to Maureen at The Great Southern and it was she who gave Michael his initial instructions. He was directed to report immediately to an address in the city of Dublin. Here he would be thoroughly briefed on his part in the plan to free de Valera. But first he would have undergo a crash training course.

The time spent in waiting for the Countess to make contact had not been wasted. It afforded Michael and Maureen an opportunity to prepare the ground. The main problem they faced was concocting a plausible explanation for Michael's absence from Beaufort. They were particularly anxious about how his mother would react when he told her that he might have to leave home for a while. Michael was content to simply make up a reasonably believable story and leave it at that. He knew that she would question whatever excuse he made, but this was a price he was prepared to pay to carry out the task he had been assigned for The Cause. Hundreds of others were, he said, paying a much higher price. And many Irish mothers were being obliged to stand by while husbands and sons left to join the fight. He cited the case of Annie Quinlan who had lost her husband and currently had two sons far away from home, and was left with no certain knowledge of when, or indeed if, they would return.

Maureen, however, was not at all happy with this arrangement. Mrs Flynn had by now come to accept the city girl who, on her frequent visits had shown a willingness to learn and to become involved in the various jobs around the farm which were traditionally carried out by the women of the family. She was always prepared to fetch and carry, help with housework and prepare meals, churn butter, feed chickens, and she even tried her hand at milking. After the initial period of caution the farmer's wife warmed to her son's 'intended', and she began to look forward to having another woman around to talk to. But Maureen knew that if she and Michael were to suddenly go away without a thoroughly plausible explanation all that would change. Michael's mother would immediately jump to the conclusion that they had either run off to get married behind her back, or were 'up to some devilment' with the rebels. In either case she would suffer as she had done when Michael was interned, and in spite of her current high opinion of the girl, she would blame Maureen. And forgiveness would be a long time coming.

"I'd hate to fall out with your mother, Michael," she said. "We've been through so much together, and one day soon I want to marry you. Sure it'll be a lot easier for us to do that with your mother on our side. Some day you'll have to take over the farm from your father, and we'll have to live there. Please God your mother will still be alive, and it would be hard for all of us if she wanted to have nothing to do with me."

Two years previously, had anyone told Maureen that she would think and talk like she this she would have laughed at them. She had never been required to even think about how her own mother would react to her involvement with The Cause. On the contrary, working for Irish freedom was something that was expected of her. But now she had come to realise that not all Irish families were like that, life for the majority of people could not be viewed in such simple terms. She had learned that, in any kind of war, while some did the fighting, others were left behind to cope with everyday life as best they could. Not everyone could, or would, devote their entire lives to the fight for freedom.

Even in the midst of Ireland's troubles the land still had to be tilled and crops grown, turf still had to be cut, and in her case, hotel tables still had to be laid and meals served. And lives would have to be picked up again once the war was over.

She was anxious that whatever happened, they should avoid causing a rift in Michael's family.

Ironically it was the determination of the authorities to enforce the Defence of the Realm Act that provided them with a workable solution.

News was reaching Beaufort that arrests were being stepped up, and that many of those arrested were former internees. Although men were not being forcibly conscripted, the clampdown was designed to remind the Irish that, in spite of all opposition, conscription could still be introduced. It seemed obvious that what was happening across the rest of the country would soon spread to Beaufort.

Although Michael's parents rarely spoke of the political situation, they were not ignorant of the fact that the 'troubles' touched everyone, and Mr Flynn in particular had thought about what the immediate future held for them. He could not by any means be considered a nationalist sympathiser, and he had determined not to take sides. But Michael's arrest and internment had affected him and caused him to question this position. He felt that he should warn his wife, and expressed a concern that in the current climate Michael might be in danger of being picked on again. When Michael was approached by his worried mother, he suggested that it would be better if he were to go away for a while so that in the event of the authorities coming to look for him he would not be home. He said that he could stay with Maureen's family in Dublin for a few weeks, and his mother seemed relieved to accept what he said. As Maureen would remain in Killarney, and would visit her as usual, Mrs Flynn could be certain that her son would not stay away for a minute longer than was necessary.

# Chapter 27

At the eleventh hour on the eleventh day of the eleventh month 1918 the armistice came into force and the guns fell silent on the Western Front. Soon afterwards the Turks surrendered and the Great War was over. On the British mainland there was a moment of almost stunned disbelief as the news sank in. Then there came a feeling of profound relief, closely followed by a spontaneous explosion of unbridled joy.

In Ireland, the celebrations were much more low key but none the less heartfelt. In spite of what had happened in the aftermath of The Rising there were still tens of thousands of Irishmen, including many from the southern counties, in uniform and serving in every one of the various theatres of war. There were also thousands who lay buried in makeshift graves all over the world who would never return home. In all 206,000 Irishmen had volunteered and 30,000 of them had died. Those survivors who would soon be coming home could not expect the rapturous welcome veterans from other parts of the British Empire would receive, but in family homes all over Ireland there were private celebrations and no less a sense of profound relief. This however had to be balanced against those families where the sense of loss seemed all the more difficult to bear because of it. Prayers and Masses of Thanksgiving were interspersed with Requiems. In the Roman Catholic Church, November is traditionally observed as the month of the dead.

In Beaufort the Quinlan family planned a private celebration and, in spite of the nationalistic mood of the country, many friends and neighbours came to share Annie's joy at her son Jack's deliverance from danger. Although now fully committed to working undercover for Michael Collins in the scheme to free Eamonn de Valera from prison, Michael Flynn was genuinely pleased that Jack would be coming home and expressed as much to Annie and William. Maureen Ryan was, somewhat surprisingly for a born Nationalist, also pleased about Jack's pending return: As well as being pleased for Michael, she found that through everything that had happened since she first met them, she felt an affinity with the Quinlan family. William had double cause for celebration: A letter arrived from Jack in time for Christmas confirming that he would be coming home. Added to the pleasure of his brother's pending safe return was the news from the agent in Dublin that Beaufort House was to be reopened. The owners would be coming back, and in recognition of his war service, Jack was to be offered the senior position of 'steward' – in effect estate manager. If all of this came about William would be free to leave his job on the farm and plough a different furrow of his own.

Following close on the heels of the private celebrations marking the end of the war, there was reason for a much more public demonstration in Ireland which threatened to rival the victory celebrations elsewhere in the world. In December 1918 Sinn Fein won a landslide victory in the General Election and became the major force in Irish politics. The party won an incredible 73 seats having previously held only 6, while the Irish Parliamentary Party was virtually wiped out when their number of successful candidates tumbled from 68 to 7. It was a clear indication that the Irish electorate were in favour of a much greater degree of independence than the limited Home Rule proposal supported by the IPP. Even the predominately Unionist north seemed to have turned against Home Rule, which proved to be a rather embarrassing blow to the government in London.

Immediately following the election, Sinn Fein set about attempting to fulfil its election promises to the Irish people. In January 1919 the successful candidates were summoned to a meeting at the Mansion House in Dublin. This was the first meeting of *Dail Eireann,* the government of the new and independent Irish Republic promised by Sinn Fein. The members present approved a provisional Irish Constitution and ratified three historic statements: The first proclaimed the foundation of an Irish Republic; the second was an appeal to the 'free nations of the world' for recognition of the *Dail* as the legitimate government of Ireland; and the third stated that Ireland was to be governed by principles of 'Liberty, Equality and Justice'. There was an immediate reaction throughout the country and particularly from the militant factions. The Volunteers had by now developed into a well prepared guerrilla army armed with weapons mostly stolen from the Royal Irish Constabulary. They had been formed into independent groups adopting a cell system whereby only the leaders of one cell were aware of the members and activities of another. The basic military formation was the 'Flying Column' – a group of well equipped and uniformed, mostly unemployed, men who were sustained and supported by the local population. For them the meeting of the *Dail* represented a call to arms.

One major difficulty, however, confronted the first meeting of the *Dail:* only twenty-seven of its members were able to attend. The remainder were in prison either in Ireland or on the British mainland. In spite of his still being held in Lincoln Jail, Eamonn de Valera, was elected *Priomh Aire* – First Minister. Other members of his cabinet were: Arthur Griffiths – Vice

President and Home Affairs. Michael Collins (Finance and, unofficially, Intelligence) Cathal Brugha (Defence) W.T. Cosgrave (Local Government) and Countess Markievicz (Labour)

The Countess became the first woman in Europe to be appointed to an, albeit unrecognised, cabinet post.

Many of the earliest military actions in what was to become known as 'The Irish War of Independence' or 'The Anglo-Irish War', depending on individual affiliations, were instigated by Michael Collins. 'The Big Fella' was now faced with the problem of freeing not only de Valera, but also several other prominent Sinn Fein members held in various prisons. It was particularly important that as many as possible of the imprisoned members of the *Dail* be set free.

Given that the authorities were by now fully alerted, and had stepped up security across the country, Collins was surprisingly successful: Twenty prisoners broke out of Mountjoy Jail in Dublin using a rope ladder; five more simply walked out by pretending to be armed with revolvers which later turned out to be spoons; six men escaped over the wall at Strangeways Prison on the mainland while Volunteers held up the traffic and helped them get away. There was a riot at Crumlin Road Jail in Belfast when Republican prisoners took over one wing, having laid in provisions beforehand. Orange mobs threatened violence in protest, which only added to the authorities' problems. The dispute was solved when one prisoner, John Doran, was granted political status and separated from the criminal inmates. Doran may have been only one man but it handed Sinn Fein a major propaganda victory.

Collins was careful to keep Michael Flynn well away from these events. Michael's sole concern was to act as liaison with de Valera in Lincoln jail, a task he was carrying out competently and with increasing confidence. It would not do to have him arrested while taking part in some other illegal activity. For his part Michael, while glad to be playing an important role in the struggle for Irish freedom, was anxious for the matter to be settled. Just as soon as he completed his assignment and, 'Dev' had been successfully freed, he intended ask Maureen to marry him. He still harboured hopes of Irish Independence being achieved without the need for bloodshed, and Maureen, in what for her represented a change of heart, now agreed with him. These hopes were soon to be shattered.

The Irish Volunteers now became officially known as The Irish Republican Army. At the village of Soloheadbeg in County Tipperary an IRA flying column held up a party of RIC men escorting a consignment of gelignite and two policemen were deliberately killed. The Anglo-Irish War had now begun in earnest.

For an already war-weary Britain this was a conflict they could well have done without. In the immediate post world war era her army was all but exhausted and in need of rest and recuperation. British forces were scattered all over the world and the logistic nightmare of bringing some home, while still maintaining a presence in the former battlefields, had begun. At home the hospitals were crowded with thousands of wounded, many of whom would never fully recover. There were some troops stationed in Ireland but these were not front line units. So there was little option but to wait and hope that things calmed down, and in the meantime the responsibility for containing the republican actions fell on the RIC.

And to exacerbate the situation, a further complication was about to arise half-way around the world in one of the remotest outposts of the British Empire.

# Chapter 28

Shortly before the armistice, Michael Flynn had, as directed, presented himself at a certain house in Dublin. His first lesson had been, as Maureen had said it would be, a severe warning that the mere acceptance of the mission meant that he was now inextricably tied to the Irish Nationalist Cause for life; a life that would be forfeit if he were to show the slightest sign of disloyalty.

An elderly man and a woman of indeterminate age, neither of whom offered him with a name, told him that they had been instructed to 'train him for the priesthood'. He was fitted out with a dark suit and overcoat, and shown how to wear a clerical collar. Some preliminary work had obviously been done and the well-tailored suit fitted perfectly. It was not however, brand new, that might have invited comment, and Michael wondered if the previous wearer had been a real priest. The only problem was finding shoes to fit and several pairs had to be tried before a satisfactory pair was found. As someone whose usual daily dress did not call for a collar-and-tie, he found the stiff Roman collar uncomfortable, but was told he would have to get used to it. Priests were a common sight in Ireland so he was given nothing more than a few brief instructions on how to conduct himself.

Then, and long before he considered himself to be anything approaching ready, he was sent out to rehearse his role by walking around the streets of Dublin, in costume and carrying a thick leather-bound prayer book in his hand; and under the impression that he had been left entirely on his own.

Feeling decidedly uncomfortable and self-conscious at first, he chose to walk some of the quieter, well-to-do residential streets. Gradually his confidence grew and he stepped out more boldly onto some of the city's busier thoroughfares. Soon he got used to being greeted as a priest: 'Good morning Father' and 'Fine day Father' or 'Excuse me Father' when almost colliding with someone, even though the fault was usually his. He began to answer with a smile and even on occasion plucked up the courage to say "God bless you'. He had been told that many of Dublin's priests came from remote country areas and that he should not worry about his Kerry accent or farmer's gait. All the while he maintained a careful look-out for genuine priests to avoid being drawn into conversation with them as he had been instructed. He wondered what would happen if he were to somehow slip up and be challenged by someone who saw through his disguise and it struck him that if he was questioned by the police he would not be able to give any more that vague descriptions of his mentors.

He had been assigned reasonable lodgings, and had been warned that neither his landlady nor the other lodgers knew his real identity. It was important, he was told, that he learned to play the part of a priest twenty-four hours a day. A request to pay a brief visit to Maureen's family was immediately and forcibly turned down.

While he remained in the city centre he felt secure in his role and even began to enjoy the sights and sounds of Ireland's capital. But when he inadvertently wandered into one of Dublin's poorer areas things took a decidedly different turn.

Maureen had warned him about the Dublin slums, but nothing could have prepared him for his first experience of the real thing. The squalor and disease, the nauseating smells, and especially the air of hopelessness would remain with him for the rest of his life. He wished he had more to give to the dozens of obviously hungry, pale and ragged children that stood with outstretched hands and pleading eyes waiting for alms from a priest.

Then he was approached by a 'shawlie' – a young woman carrying a baby wrapped in her shawl.

"Would you bless the child for me Father?" she said, "the poor thing is ailing and if he doesn't see out the night sure your blessing will ease his way into Heaven."

Michael almost turned and bolted. But somehow, he wasn't sure how, he brought himself to raise his hand, make a Sign of the Cross, and mutter a few words of prayer.

The act of deceiving the woman weighed on his conscience. But the sight of people, supposedly at liberty, forced to live in conditions far worse than anything he had experienced in the internment camp, gave him an added sense of purpose and stiffened his resolve. This was the kind of injustice, he thought, that only a fully independent Ireland could right.

Michael did not know it but throughout this phase of his training he was constantly watched. After several days he was deemed to be sufficiently competent to carry out his mission and sent to yet another address where he met Michael Collins.

'The Big Fella' was friendly and told Michael that he remembered him from the internment camp. He thanked him for undertaking this important mission, the only person Michael had met so far that had thought to do so. There then followed a detailed explanation of how vital it was to Ireland's political future that Eamonn de Valera was free and able to play his part in the process. The Sinn Fein leader, said Collins, would obviously not be able to remain in Ireland, but would travel abroad as an ambassador to promote The Cause, especially in America. Following the lecture, Collins handed Michael a prayer book identical to the one he already carried and gave him detailed instructions on how it was to be used. To back up his story of being de Valera's personal confessor he was given a letter from 'Dev' to 'Father Flaherty' asking the priest if he would visit him in prison. This, he was told, was in case he was required to produce some proof of identity. A reply had been sent and permission for the visit granted by the prison authorities. He was then handed some money to cover his travel expenses and sent on his way to Lincoln Jail.

Armistice celebrations were still in progress when Michael got off the boat at Holyhead. The Irish Sea had, as usual, behaved badly and the ferry had been buffeted by high winds and squalls of rain as it ploughed through rough seas. On board the steamer he had suffered from seasickness brought on by the both the weather conditions and the anxiety he felt about his mission which caused him to have butterflies in his stomach. But on the train journey to Crewe he recovered, and he began to reflect on how different this trip was from the last one he had taken through North Wales. Then he had been a prisoner on his way to internment, now he was free and on his way to visit a far more important prisoner. But he fervently prayed that both journeys would not end in similar circumstances, and see him again behind bars.

The trains were, as he expected, crowded with soldiers. Although they did not treat him with the same degree of reverence that he had experienced in Ireland, they were polite and seemed friendly enough. Like the rest of the country, they were still gripped by the feeling of euphoria brought about by the ending of the war. On that November morning, the towns, villages, railway stations, and even individual houses that the train passed were still decked with flags and bunting. Newspaper headlines still proclaimed 'Victory'. Even Michael could not avoid being affected by the general mood of excitement. He changed trains at Crewe and again at Ely. The train now crossed the flat fenland and headed north. Soon he could make out the imposing bulk of Lincoln cathedral lording it over the city from the crest of its hill. It brought him abruptly back to the task in hand.

Full of apprehension, he found his way to the prison, a forbidding stone fortress surrounded by a high wall. Security was not as tight as he had been told to expect and he was allowed through a small door in the massive gates without the intense questioning he had feared. At the reception area inside the walls he gave his name, stated his business and was, somewhat carelessly he thought, searched. There did not seem to be the strict demonstration of efficiency and attention to detail that he had been given to expect. Soon, to his relief, he discovered the reason for such laxity: the air of euphoria that followed the armistice had found its way into Lincoln Jail. Even the usually alert prison warders had been affected by it.

Michael was ushered into a large room divided in two by a metal grill that stretched to the high ceiling. Chairs were placed at intervals on either side of several evenly spaced small square openings in the grill. A few of the chairs were occupied by visitors speaking to prisoners through the openings.

He recognised de Valera the instant the Sinn Fein leader was led through a door at the back of the room on the other side of the grill. 'Dev' was as Michael remembered him from the brief sighting on the internment boat to Wales. There were the same bushy black hair and eyebrows. A heavy black moustache sat underneath a large sharp nose which supported round thick glasses. His tall loose frame had earned him the nickname of 'The Long Fella' when he had lectured in mathematics at Maynooth College.

As the prisoner was ushered across the room he said something to the prison guard out of Michael's hearing. The guard shook his head, but de Valera seemed to speak sharply to him and the guard, with a shrug of the shoulders, unlocked and removed the handcuffs. 'Dev' then walked purposefully across to where Michael waited, reached through the grill, and warmly shook his visitor's hand.

"Good of you to come, Father Flaherty," he said, "I trust you had a pleasant journey. How have you been since I last saw you?"

In spite of being told what to expect and how to conduct himself, Michael was momentarily thrown off balance and de Valera had to increase the grip on his hand to prompt a reply.

"I'm grand thanks, Eamonn," he finally managed to reply. He made a show of looking around the room. "But God knows I'm sorry to see you like this."

'Dev' said nothing but the intelligent eyes behind the spectacles examined Michael closely. He had of course been expecting a visit from his friend 'Father Flaherty' and was making sure that Michael looked the part. The would-be priest's outward appearance seemed authentic enough but 'Dev' sensed Michael's nervousness and hoped that the guards would put it down to the anxiety usually exhibited by all prison visitors.

He opened his mouth to speak but stopped himself. He turned and stared hard at the guard who hovered nearby. "I thought that you were told that this was to be a private visit," he said.

The guard, somewhat reluctantly, moved away. He had, along with his colleagues, been briefed on the background and importance of this particular prisoner, and told that the tall Irishman was to be kept under strict supervision at all times. But the request for a visit from the prisoner's personal confessor had presented the authorities with a problem. They were under strict instructions not to hand de Valera and his Sinn Fein colleagues the least opportunity for propaganda, and to deny the prisoner the right to a private confession could well be used for just such a purpose. If the news was circulated that the privacy of the confessional had been compromised, public opinion in Catholic Ireland, and perhaps among Catholics across the world, would have been inflamed and an already volatile situation made worse.

So de Valera and 'Father Flaherty' were left alone. The whispered 'confession' consisted of Michael passing on the message he had been given by Collins. This took less than a minute, so in order to stretch the time to what a real confession would take, 'Dev' questioned Michael about his background and asked how he came to be involved in the scheme to free him. He nodded knowingly when told that Michael had been one of the internees at Fron-goch. He echoed Michael's own sentiments:

"This must never again be allowed to happen in Ireland."

Finally de Valera rose to his feet. "You have something for me Father Flaherty?" he said loudly enough for the prison guard to hear.

Michael passed the prayer book through the grill opening, de Valera accepted it and turned to the guard. "Father Flaherty has kindly brought this for me," he said, "I suppose you will want to inspect it to ensure that it is not a bomb."

The guard checked the book and handed it back, he thought that it would be more than his job was worth to confiscate it. Michael raised his hand and gave de Valera a priestly blessing, the guard replaced the handcuffs on the prisoner and took him away.

Michael managed to hold his composure until after he had passed through the gates. Once outside, it took a supreme effort of willpower not to run as fast as he could away from the prison. At the railway station he went to the toilet and was sick. He found a deserted bench where he sat and almost fainted with relief that he had got away with it. A woman asked if he felt unwell and it was all he could do to assure her that he was not. He was on the train back to Ely before his stomach began to settle down and he could believe that everything had gone to plan. But the train was pulling into Crewe before he felt completely relaxed and was able to think of anything else. The nearer he got to Ireland the more confident he became that he would be able to return to Lincoln.

Michael Flynn had successfully answered the call and completed his first assignment for The Cause.

# Chapter 29

"Boys oh boys," said Patrick Coughlin, "there'll be ructions out there now."

"And we'll be the ones who'll be sent to defend the grand British Raj and make sure the sun never sets on the glorious bloody Empire," said James Daly.

"The Raj, would that be some place in India?" asked Jack Quinlan.

"That's right Jack," said Daly. "And if what they say is true, me and Pat here will be coming back this way before long to defend it."

He flicked the stub of his cigarette over the rail of the troopship into the water of the Suez Canal.

"It's true all right," said Jack, "I asked Lieutenant Elliott and he said that the Afghans have invaded India. Why would they be doing that?"

"For nothing but pure devilment Jack," said Daly. "And I'll bet you any money you like that the first regiment sent out there will be the Connaught Rangers."

Daly's 'pure devilment' was in fact not far from the truth. According to the terms of a treaty signed after the Second Afghan War in the late nineteenth century, Great Britain was granted sole responsibility for Afghanistan's foreign affairs. But these waters had become extremely muddied during the Great War. The Amir of Afghanistan had accepted a Turkish military mission together with a supply of arms and ammunition, and soon the Germans too were playing their part in Afghan affairs. After the armistice, the Afghans considered that they were now an independent nation and demanded participation in the Versailles peace talks. Great Britain refused, and to complicate matters the Amir was killed in somewhat suspicious circumstances, leaving his sons to squabble over the throne. Amanullah Khan, the third son, proclaimed himself Amir, but the army suspected his complicity in his father's death. In order to give the army something else to think about, and to generate support at home, the new Amir decided to create a diversion abroad and launched an invasion of India through the Khyber Pass. The result was to be the Third Afghan War.

Great Britain had been at peace for a mere few months when, on top of the Anglo-Irish war, she found herself embroiled in yet another armed conflict. Although these outbreaks of violence could be considered as mere skirmishes when compared with the Great War, they were wars nonetheless, and as such required resources of fresh well supplied and equipped troops, all of which were in short supply in post war Britain. Her army was exhausted. Many of the British troops in India were due to return home, and most of the Indian native troops were also worn out from having served in theatres of war all over the world. Indeed a great many were still waiting to return to India. But something had to be done to preserve this important part of The Empire.

As a prelude to the invasion the Amir enlisted the aid of dissident Indian revolutionaries, and inflammatory leaflets were distributed throughout the Northwest Frontier Province, and in the Punjab, urging the people to 'use every possible means to kill the British'. Rioting and looting became widespread. The actual invasion force, however, proved to be not much more than a large group of belligerent but undisciplined tribesmen, which was held up by native troops at Landi Kotal near the Afghan entrance to the Khyber Pass. Men of the Somerset Light Infantry sent to reinforce the native troops were smuggled in covered lorries past the hostile tribesmen in The Pass, and the invasion stalled. But it sparked off a series of raids by Afghan and local tribesmen which was to last for years, leaving The Northwest Frontier – 'The Grim' to British soldiers – more lawless than ever.

"You're right about the 'Rangers going back to India, Jim," said Coughlin. "But sure it'll be like going home for us."

"Jesus, and here was I thinking that the war was over," said Jack.

The troopship home from Mesopotamia exited the canal and entered the Mediterranean Sea. Daly was silent while he considered what Coughlin had said about going back to India being like going home. It was obvious to his two companions that the remark had struck a chord.

"You could say that I suppose Pat," he said. "Sure haven't we spent enough time there to think of it as home all right, but the truth of it is that it's not home at all. Ireland is still my home and it always will be. And God knows there's the same kind of trouble there as there is in 'The Grim'."

"From what I hear things are starting to boil up in Ireland all right," said Jack.

"Things were bad enough when I was there after being wounded," said Coughlin, "and I'd say that they'll be worse now with your man, de Valera, still in jail; there'll be no peace until he gets out."

"After the last four years you'd think that people would have had their fill of war." Deep down, Jack knew that he for one had seen enough of the futility of war, and wanted no more to do with it, however valid the cause or plausible the excuse.

"There will always be people ready to go to war, Jack," said Daly. "That's why there will always be work for the likes of myself and Pat here.

God help us, but sure soldiering is the only thing we know anything at all about."

His wistful mood changed and in a rare moment of frustration he kicked the ship's rail. "Jesus Christ Almighty! I think I've spent my whole life fighting for the British Bloody Empire, and I can't get it out of my head that all the time I should have been at home fighting for Ireland."

They let the outburst pass. Then Coughlin spoke in a calmer tone: "I know what you mean Jim, but we 'took the shilling' and swore an oath, and since then sure 'The Rangers' is the only home we have."

Daly remained unconvinced, but he did not want to argue with his friends. He forced himself to laugh: "Well the next time I'm drinking a pint with your man, George V, sure won't I tell him to stick his shilling up his arse."

They laughed and paused to light fresh cigarettes. Jack was thinking of home. "Maybe it won't be as bad as we think at home," he said hopefully.

"However bad it gets, you stop out of it Jack," said Coughlin. "You have a grand family to think about, so just look out for them and forget about war and politics."

"Watch out for yourself too," said Daly. "From what Pat was telling me British soldiers weren't welcome in Ireland last year, and they'll be even less welcome now, no matter how many will be coming home from the war. Don't expect to be greeted as a hero outside of your own house."

"And for Christ's sake don't let on that you were in the artillery," said Coughlin. "After what happened in Dublin in The Rising, there are people over there ready and waiting to do for any British gunner they come across."

"You stood by us in Mesopotamia Jack," said Daly, "but we might not be around to return the compliment, if you get my drift."

When the troopship docked at Southampton, military discipline was resumed. Jack stood with several other 'odd bods' due for demobilisation, and watched as his friends fell in with the rest of the Connaught Rangers on the quayside. Dolan and Coughlin looked back at him with blank faces as they slung their rifles and shouldered their kit bags and marched off to board a train for the Army Depot at Dover. They had parted with handshakes and promises to keep in touch. Daly in particular was anxious that Jack keep him informed of events in Ireland, so they would certainly write occasionally. But Jack, with sadness, felt it was unlikely that he would ever see either of the two 'Rangers' again.

With several hundred others he was processed through a demobilisation centre, provided with a suit of civilian clothes, some money and a travel warrant, and sent on his way. Mindful of Coughlin's warning, he did not join in the high spirited drinking of the other ex-servicemen on the boat home but kept very much to himself. At Kingstown there was a general stampede to get off the boat. A few of the returning former soldiers were joyously met by family members, but for the rest there were only silent stares and even a few derisory remarks from the dock workers and casual bystanders. In their 'demob' suits they might as well have still been in uniform, so they remained grouped together as they boarded a train into Dublin city.

Jack hung back and waited until the rush was over. He left the port area and adjacent railway station and wandered into the town. Having just returned from the Middle East his body was not ready for the damp chill of the Irish early spring. As he walked past a pawnshop he noticed an overcoat hanging in the window and he went in and bought it for a mere few shillings. As well as keeping him warm it covered his tell-tale suit. But it could not disguise his weather-beaten features deeply tanned by the desert sun. On the tram into the city a man remarked on it, and Jack told him that he was returning home on holiday from South Africa. The man seemed satisfied and they reached Sackville Street before he had a chance to ask further questions. Jack went into the battle-scarred General Post Office, now fully functioning but still bearing clear signs of the bombardment it had endured during The Rising. He sent a telegram home to Beaufort and went to catch a train south for Killarney. On the way to the station he could not help but notice the other ruined buildings, gaunt legacies of the British artillery employed to quell the rebellion, and he was reminded of Pat Coughlin's warning about not letting on that he was a former gunner.

As the train steamed southwards, however, his mood changed and he began to look forward to going home and being with the family he had not seen for well over three years. What until now had seemed to be a far-off dream gradually developed into a reality, and he wondered if his telegram had reached his mother, and if William would be there with the pony and trap to meet him at Killarney.

In the event both his brother and his mother were there, Annie had decided that she would not be denied the pleasure of being the first to welcome her son home. She laughed and cried in turn as she hugged him, while William stood by trying to make his mind up whether he too should hug his brother, which might be viewed as unmanly, or formally shake his hand. It was Jack who resolved the dilemma by slapping William on the back and wrestling him playfully to the ground.

Outside the station, Jack stood and took his first look at Killarney for over three years. He was intrigued to find that a mood of celebration seemed to prevail, and people were standing around laughing and chatting excitedly.

He smiled to himself, but he knew that whatever the good news being circulated might be, it had nothing to do with his return. William and his mother were equally mystified and shrugged their shoulders.

Maureen Ryan came out of The Great Southern Hotel and walked across to say 'hello'. William, who knew of her aversion to British soldiers, wondered what her reaction would be to meeting Jack, but she too seemed to have been caught up in the joyous atmosphere, and she greeted him with a friendly smile. William asked her if she knew the reason for all the 'great gas' everybody seemed to be enjoying.

"Oh," she said, "you haven't heard the news. Eamonn de Valera is out. He escaped from the jail over in England this morning."

She looked at Annie and laughed. "And Michael is home as well, isn't it grand."

# Chapter 30

As William and Annie took Jack home to Beaufort, Eamonn de Valera was sitting in a safe house in Manchester. News of his escape had spread rapidly and celebrations were spontaneously arranged all over Ireland. Rumours abounded regarding the manner in which his freedom had been accomplished; wild stories about how his escape had been accomplished circulated; opinions on how it was done ranged from his having bribed the prison guards to a full scale raid being mounted by Michael Collins. Everyone had 'inside information and everybody had something to say. What all were agreed on, however, was that the British authorities would never publish an accurate account of what had actually happened, and that the Irish republicans would make the most of the propaganda opportunity. In doing so they would concoct the most sensational story possible. It could be years before the truth came out and so the rumour-mongers were set to have a field day.

One of the very few people to know the absolute truth was Michael Flynn.

He had not seen Maureen since Christmas when they had met briefly at Maureen's home in Dublin. In recognition of the successful completion of his first visit to Lincoln it was thought that he could now be fully trusted, and he was allowed a greater degree of freedom by his 'handlers'. While he was in Dublin he was no longer required to masquerade as a priest; his lodgings were changed and, through republican channels, he was given casual work at Dublin's North Wall docks. Going home to Beaufort before his job was finished could not, however, be countenanced, but he was allowed to write home and put his Mother's mind at ease. It was known that he had been interned with Kevin Ryan and so he was permitted to visit the Ryan family and have a chat with Maureen's brother. The usual warnings about keeping his mouth shut were issued, but Kevin knew enough not to ask what Michael was doing in Dublin. And in any case they had other things to discuss.

Kevin assured Michael that the subject of the disappearance of 'Mr Jameson' had not come up for some time. Collins seemed convinced that the rebel had fallen victim to someone settling an old score, and while he still instructed his people to keep their eyes and ears open, he seemed satisfied.

"The only danger to us that I can see, Mick," said Kevin, "is your man Quinlan opening his gob."

"Ah sure there's no chance at all of that, Kevin," said Michael, "I'd put my life on Bill Quinlan. Anyway if he did say anything about it sure wouldn't he have to tell people the real reason behind why it all happened? And he wouldn't do that because it would go hard on his mother if she ever heard the truth."

They agreed that their secret was safe and they went back to reminiscing about their time in the internment camp.

Maureen came to visit her parents at Christmas. Like Kevin, she was experienced enough not to question Michael about his work for The Cause in front of others, even her own family. So she was forced to contain her curiosity until they were able to get away and spend a few hours alone.

Michael told her about his visit to Lincoln and about meeting Eamonn de Valera. He was confident that Countess Markievicz would not object to him sharing his story with Maureen, who already knew some of the details. So he held nothing back. She heard about his meeting with the young mother with the sick baby, and how it had stiffened his resolve. When he tried to explain his feelings before and after the prison visit she held him close and felt a deep concern for his safety, deeper even than the fear she had felt for her brothers and her friends during The Rising itself.

"Oh Michael," she said, "I wish to God that you didn't have to go back there again."

"Ah sure it'll be alright now love," he said. "They told me that the first time would be the worst, and as I wasn't found out that time I'd have every chance of getting away with it again. And I'll tell you this Maureen, that fella de Valera is a real gentleman and I'll do my very best for him."

"I know you will Michael," she said. "But you can't believe everything they tell you, so please be careful my love."

Some six weeks later he was finally on his way back to Beaufort. On the train to Killarney from Dublin, he felt a mixture of satisfaction and relief that the job was successfully completed, and was excited by the prospect of seeing her again. As he relaxed on the journey he began to compare the empty Irish countryside and small towns, with the more heavily populated areas and large cities he had passed through in England, and it felt good to be going home.

His second visit to Lincoln Jail had taken place over the New Year holiday 1919. It was obviously timed to coincide with the celebrations to mark the beginning of the first year of peace. He donned his priest's clothing once more, and moved back to his first lodgings where he was known only as 'Father Flaherty'. The weather was clear and frosty with good visibility and he was able to see more of the English landscape. As anticipated, security at the prison was not as stringent as it might have been and he was allowed through the door in the prison gates without question. He was processed through the visiting procedure with a minimum of fuss and led into the large room with the metal grill. Being a public holiday, the room was more crowded than on his first visit but there were some free seats at the far end away from the door. De Valera was brought in as on the previous occasion, and the handcuffs were removed. The prison guards were convinced that, as nothing untoward had come of 'Father Flaherty's' first visit, there was nothing to fear from him now, so Michael was left alone with 'Dev'.

Michael heard de Valera's 'confession' and they held a whispered conversation. The Sinn Fein leader plied his visitor with questions about the situation in Ireland. He was clearly becoming tired of life in prison and he confided in Michael that he wanted to be out and doing something useful for The Cause. Nobody, especially not the guards, noticed that before Michael left he and de Valera had swapped prayer books.

There was an anxious wait at the prison entrance where a more conscientious guard seemed to be carrying out closer inspections of the departing visitors, who were waiting in line to be allowed out through the door in the gates. As Michael neared the end of the queue a group of laughing women visitors came out of the prison building and joined the line. The guard seemed to take exception to their apparently carefree attitude to prison visiting. He turned to them and waved a much relieved 'Father Flaherty' through.

In an otherwise deserted compartment of the train back from Lincoln, Michael's heartbeat slowed sufficiently for him to check the prayer book. The wax impressions of two keys nestled safely in the hollowed out centre of the book.

Back in Dublin he followed instructions and handed the book to Michael Collins in person.

He spent the remainder of the month of January working on the Dublin docks. It was cold hard labour but Michael welcomed the diversion and it helped to keep his mind occupied. He went to visit the Ryan family again to have a chat with Kevin. But he found that the word had gone out to the effect that Michael Flynn was not to be seen associating with known republican sympathisers, so he could not stay. Maureen's crippled father had quickly put two and two together and realised that Michael Flynn must be 'one of Collins' special boys'.

As Michael was leaving he held out his hand and said: "Put it there Michael, sure I always knew that Maureen would fall for a decent republican some day."

At the beginning of February he went back to Lincoln for the third, and last, time. As the situation in Ireland deteriorated with more and bolder rebel raids on RIC establishments, and even some of the smaller army posts, security arrangements for nationalist prisoners on the mainland were tightened. De Valera's cell was searched but nothing remotely suspicious was found. It was reasoned that if 'Father Flaherty' was not all that he was supposed to be, he was not bringing anything into the prisoner, and therefore he must be taking something out. So orders were issued to search the priest thoroughly before he left; and any consequences arising from harassing a genuine priest would have to be accepted.

When this was communicated to the guards they took it to mean that there was no need search Michael on his way into the prison, and he was allowed to go directly to the visitor's area. He was subjected to a comprehensive search as he left. Nothing was found and he accepted the prison authorities' apology. The exchange of prayer books between visitor and prisoner had again gone unnoticed.

In the early hours of the following morning the prisoner used the keys Michael had delivered hidden in the prayer book. He slipped quietly out of his cell and made his way across the deserted yard to the main gate. A noisy drunken demonstration in the road outside diverted the guard's attention and Eamonn de Valera stepped to freedom through the door in the gates. He was met outside, and immediately spirited away to a safe house in Manchester.

***

They were sitting in the parlour of Flynn's farmhouse. Much to the relief of his parents Michael had returned home safe and sound. His mother was thankful to learn that the danger of his being interred again had passed, and that he was home for good. After an emotional welcome he and Maureen were left alone in the parlour. He finished telling her the rest of the story of his part in de Valera's escape from Lincoln Gaol.

"There's a do on over at Devlin's pub tonight to celebrate him getting out," she said. "I won't mind a bit if you want to go, Michael."

Michael was well aware that it would not have been considered seemly in rural Ireland for her to accompany him to such a gathering. But he also had personal reasons for not attending.

"No love," he answered. "Sure I'd find it hard to stop laughing at what some of those eejits will be saying about it, half of them will be swearing blind that they were in on it. I might even get cross if any of them has a wrong word to say about 'Dev'. And sure aren't you a lot better looking than anyone I'm likely to meet in a pub. So I think I'll stop here and ask you to marry me."

Maureen marveled at how he had grown in confidence. She put it down to his experiences of the last few months. "Well it took you long enough," she said. "But weren't you supposed to do that after the first time you took me for jaunting car ride?"

At the pub, Pat Devlin was following his usual practice of circulating and keeping his ears open for any snippets of information that might prove to be useful to The Cause. He had recently picked up several items, but was becoming concerned that he had not heard from his usual contact in the movement for some time. 'John Jameson', seemed to have disappeared off the face of the earth. It was nothing unusual for the nationalist agitator to lie low for a spell, but this was different. In view of the fact that he had sent a second telegram to 'Mr Jameson' to inform him that James Quinlan had been home and was, contrary to what Devlin had expected, still alive and well, he felt that he would have received some word from Dublin. The thought that 'Mr Jameson' might be dead did not enter his head. He was confident that his rebel contact would surface again. But in the meantime he had the feeling that something was going on that he was not a part of. While he had no intention of ever playing a front line role in nationalist affairs, he had too many other irons in the fire for that, he did not like being left out of things entirely. Being friendly with 'Mr Jameson' had allowed him to play what could have been a dangerous game in relative safety.

Tonight one of the local Volunteer commanders, who had taken a few too many, had let slip that an order had come down from Michael Collins himself to the effect that Michael Flynn was working exclusively for him and was not to be included in arms raids or any other operations. This was supposed to be a well kept secret, but according to the inebriated local commander 'sure doesn't Pat Devlin know very well how to keep things to himself'. Devlin had wondered at Flynn's absence from Beaufort, and he had not quite accepted the story that Michael was trying to avoid being re-arrested and interned. Now that he had found out that Flynn was working for Michael Collins he knew that he should report the lapse in security by the local man. But how, and who should he report it to? It was too important to entrust to a telegram and he had no other way of contacting 'Mr Jameson'.

The only solution he could think of was to talk directly to Michael Flynn. The former internee was obviously 'well in' with Collins and would know what to do. It surprised him that Flynn was not at the 'hooley' to mark 'Dev's' escape, but he decided that at the first opportunity, he would tell Michael what he had heard about him and Collins. He also intended to ask him if he knew the whereabouts of 'Mr Jameson'; and what was happening between 'Jameson' and James Quinlan.

***

As the celebrations were at their height in Beaufort, in Dublin and at the safe house in Manchester an argument was brewing.

De Valera did not want to risk going back to Ireland. He wanted to go directly to America as Ireland's *Priomh Aire* and begin the work of generating political support for the newly declared Irish Republic by mobilising the considerable Irish-American lobby. Collins, however, considered that he could minimise the risk of de Valera being arrested again if he returned to Dublin for a brief visit before crossing the Atlantic. The propaganda value, he argued, to be gained from 'Dev' appearing openly at a well orchestrated rally would be immense. It would be helpful when he landed in America to be able to demonstrate the depth of feeling in 'the old country'.

It was not the first time that Collins and de Valera had disagreed: 'Dev' was becoming increasingly concerned by Collins' seemingly total reliance on armed struggle as being the only road to Irish independence. While he was not averse to a fight, as he had proved during The Rising, he saw a political solution as being the best way forward in the long run. The political climate in a war-weary world in the immediate post-war period would, he thought, provide an excellent opportunity to achieve independence without the need for bloodshed. One of his objectives in America was to argue the Irish case for a seat at the Peace Conference. And he secretly suspected that Collins might use his visit to Dublin to provoke a strong reaction from the authorities, which as things stood could easily lead to people being killed.

Eventually, however, he was persuaded to travel secretly to Dublin where he was given a rapturous welcome. Much to his relief the event passed off peacefully. He was smuggled back to Liverpool and then aboard the liner *Celtic* for the voyage to America.

# Chapter 31

In Beaufort, Jack Quinlan was not caught up in the euphoria surrounding de Valera's escape. For the first few days since his return home from Mesopotamia he had not strayed far from the cottage by the river. Part of the reason for this was that he was unsure of the reception he would receive locally. He was not unduly worried for himself, and he knew that he would have to venture out at some stage, but there had been many incidents where returning soldier's families had suffered harassment.

His principle reason, however, for remaining close to home was that, before he did anything else, he felt that he should spend time with his family and particularly with his mother. He soon realised that it would take time for them to get used to having him home, and he needed to come to terms with how the three younger children had grown since he last saw them, and to accept that his brother, William, was now a full grown man. So many things had changed, not least of which was the fact that his father was no longer with them. For the first time since he had received the news in Mesopotamia, the reality of the family's loss made itself felt. It soon became obvious that his return had served to rekindle his mother's pain, but it was only when they were alone together that she felt able to talk to him about his father's death. She did not want the children to see her in tears again after so long.

When Jack had first received the news of his father's death he had sensed that there was something not quite straightforward about how it had happened. There were some subtle differences between the account he had got from his mother, and the story contained in William's letter; a letter which had been written after James' brief visit home. Jack suspected that William had not told him the whole truth, and he urgently wanted to talk things over with his brother.

William too, was aware that he would soon have to talk to Jack about their father, and he realised that he would have to tell his brother the whole truth. It would be no use trying to hold anything back because James would soon be coming home, and he was sure to tell Jack everything. But he could not see a way of telling Jack the whole story without including the parts played by Michael Flynn and Maureen Ryan. Like Pat Devlin, he was not convinced by the story that Michael had been forced to leave Beaufort because he feared being interned again. He thought it was very unlikely that

Michael would go away like that without a word, and even more unlikely that he would leave Maureen behind when he left. He didn't know the details of the cattle raid, but he knew that Michael had been involved in something and was not talking about it. William thought that this might be the reason for his friend's sudden departure, but he had said nothing to anyone about it in case it got back to Michael's mother. He had not seen Michael since his return home, but put this down to the fact that his friend was catching up for lost time with Maureen. It would be Sunday tomorrow, and he would make it his business to have a word with Michael after Mass.

As they came out of the church the following morning several people came across to talk to Jack. For the most part the ex-soldier was warmly welcomed home. But, while there was no outright animosity, several former friends pointedly ignored him. William managed to slip away to look for Michael, but was troubled to find him in close conversation with Pat Devlin. What disturbed William was not the fact that Michael was talking to Devlin, there was nothing strange about that as they obviously knew each other; it was the worried look on Michael's face that bothered him.

The Quinlan family was just leaving for home when Michael ran after them to say hello to Jack. The two old school friends greeted each other with obvious pleasure.

After much back slapping Michael said. "Christ, Jack, it's grand to see that you're back safe and sound."

"From what I hear you were in the wars a bit yourself Mick," Jack replied. "I heard all about it from Pat Coughlin."

"Listen Jack," said Michael, "we'll have to have a real chat. Is it all right if I call in after dinner today Mrs Quinlan?"

"Of course it is Michael," said Annie, "sure you know very well that you're welcome anytime."

Michael caught William's eye. "And maybe we could go and have a look at the river, Bill. Sure I'm dying to see how the fish are doing."

"That's grand Mick," William answered. It struck him that these were the first words they had spoken for several months.

That afternoon Michael, Jack and William sat in the cottage kitchen and talked over old times. William noted that Michael seemed agitated, as if he had other things on his mind. He too, was pre-occupied and anxious to talk to Michael about what to tell Jack about his father and 'The Man from Dublin'.

The conversation came around to Patrick Coughlin's visit, and Michael brought up what the Connaught Ranger had said regarding the political situation in Ireland. He was not at all certain what Jack's attitude to the nationalist cause would be, having spent nearly four years in the British army, and in all probability soon to be working for a former British Government Minister.

"I was surprised to hear a British soldier saying that he was all for the Irish Republic," said Michael.

"I'd say that a few of the Connaught Rangers would be for it, Mick," said Jack. "Did Pat tell you about Jim Daly?"

"He told us all about how you saved both their lives," said William.

"Ah sure I suppose Pat made more of thing of it than it was," said Jack. "He's a great one with for telling stories."

Michael wanted to come back to the subject of The Cause. "Pat told us that this fella Daly was keen to know all about what's happening here."

"He is too, Mick," William had told Jack that Michael had adopted nationalist leanings since his internment, but he was content to wait until he knew more before forming his own opinion. "He made me swear that I would write and give him all the news."

"What will you tell him?" asked Michael.

"To be honest with you I don't know yet Mick," Jack answered. "I'm only just home, and I haven't had a chance to catch up with things. But I do know this much: Pat was right when he told us that it's a different Ireland altogether now from what it was before the war. I was sorry to hear that you got arrested and put in jail,"

To William's surprise Michael seemed content to leave it at that. Annie made some tea and they drank in silence. When they finished Michael rose as if to leave, but instead looked at William.

"Maybe we could take a walk down to have a look at the river, Bill," he said. "The season will be on us soon and I'd like to see what our chance of a salmon might be."

By now he was halfway to the door so William had little choice but to follow him. They got their coats and went out, leaving Jack and his mother wondering what had got into them.

"Michael has been away since before Christmas, working at the docks up in Dublin," said Annie. "So I suppose they have a lot to talk about."

Jack could only shrug his shoulders. "Ah sure that'll be it, Ma," he said.

By now it was late afternoon and the light would soon be fading. They went down to the riverbank and William immediately brought up the subject that had been worrying him.

"Listen Mick," he said. "I'll have to let Jack know about how Da died, and what happened to that fella from Dublin. And I'll have to tell him everything about it, because if I don't sure Jim is bound to tell him the whole story when he comes home."

Michael looked worried. "Sure isn't that what I had on my mind too,

Bill," he said. "I see what you mean about Jack. But we always knew that this was bound to come up as soon as he came home. I'd say that the only thing we can do is to tell Jack the truth."

"You're saying to tell him the whole thing, Mick? Tell him about yourself and Maureen and the fella in the bog and all?"

"Ay Bill, Jack will have to have the whole story, he'd know if you left anything out and ask Jim about it." Michael thought for a moment. "Look Bill I'd say that we can trust Jack to keep it to himself when he knows how it could harm your mother and Jim if it came out. This is what we'll do. I'll have a word with Maureen first, I'm seeing her tonight, and then the two of us will tell Jack together."

"Ah sure there's no call for you to say anything, Mick, I can tell him myself."

"No, Bill." Michael was adamant. "I'm the one that killed that fella, and I'm the one that'll have to tell Jack about it."

He paused before continuing: "Anyway Bill, I'm thinking that we could soon be having a whole lot more to worry about than trusting Jack not to say anything. Did you see me talking to Pat Devlin after Mass?"

"I did," said William, "what did Pat want with you Mick?"

"Jesus Christ, Bill." It was unusual for Michael to talk like that. "Devlin asked me if I knew anything about what happened to the very same fella, your man in the bog. 'John Jameson' Pat called him. It hit me hard I can tell you, and for a minute there I didn't know what to say. "

William was stunned. "God Almighty, Mick. Does he know what happened?"

"No I don't think so, Bill," Michael replied, "but he has an idea that something is not right. You know how the fella always went to Devlin's when he was here in Beaufort, and they were as thick as thieves. Well I think that your man 'Jameson' told Pat something about what he was doing the last time he was here. I'm sure Devlin doesn't know the whole of it, but he knows enough, because he told me that he thought it had something to do with yourself and Jim."

"Oh God, Mick, is the whole game up? Will they be after Jim again? And sure they know where he is now."

"I don't think it's as bad as that yet Bill," said Michael. "All Pat is worried about is that he can't find 'Jameson' to tell him all the news from Beaufort, the way he's been doing for years. I told him that I knew nothing about it, but that I'll try to find out. That'll keep him quiet for a while."

William breathed a sigh of relief, but then a frown crossed his face and he again expressed concern. "But why would Pat be asking you about it Mick, if he didn't know that you had a hand it?"

Michael had expected the question and had his answer ready: "The eejit has a notion that I was doing something for The Cause while I was up in Dublin. And he thinks that I'm well in with the boys up there. God knows where he got that idea from, but as long as he keeps thinking it I'll be able to keep him quiet."

"Is that what you were doing in Dublin, Mick?" said William. "I didn't believe for a minute that you were frightened about getting arrested a second time, or that you had a job at the docks. Is it true that you're well in up there?"

"Oh I was working on the docks all right," answered Michael. "And sure the only one of the boys I know up there is Kevin Ryan. Kevin is the one who is well in, and he told me that nobody at all up there knows a thing about what happened here. And sure we know he won't say anything because of Maureen. But listen to me now Bill, we'll have to watch out, and if anything comes of this we'll all have to stick together and say nothing."

William knew Michael well enough to know that he was not being told everything, but he let it go without comment. However, he could see that Michael was worried, and that gave him real cause for concern.

\*\*\*

Pat Devlin was cycling home from Killarney. He stopped for a breather on Beaufort Bridge and leaned his bicycle against the parapet. As he looked over the wall he spotted two men in close conversation on the riverbank, and did not altogether like what he saw. It disturbed him to see Michael Flynn in close conversation with William Quinlan. He knew that when 'Mr Jameson' had last come to Beaufort he was looking for Quinlan, and that presumably this had something to do with Quinlan's brother James. He had asked Michael Flynn, who was now apparently 'one of the boys', about it and got nowhere. Now here were Flynn and Quinlan holding an animated and obviously secret conversation.

Something did not add up and Devlin was determined to get to the bottom of it.

# Chapter 32

"We should be hearing from Jack soon," said Private James Daly, "he said he'd write and tell us how things are at home,"

"Ah sure won't he be living the life of Reilly at home now, running after the girls and forgetting all about the likes of us," replied Private Patrick Coughlin.

They were sitting on a cliff top just outside the port of Dover and looking out over the English Channel. The distant coast of France was barely visible through a light haze. It was not a sight that many British soldiers took any delight in so soon after the war. Both regular battalions of the Connaught Rangers were being reorganised and brought up to strength at the nearby Army Depot. No official orders had so far been issued, but to old hands like Daly and Coughlin this could only mean one thing: the regiment was being readied for service overseas.

"No, Jack will write," said Daly. "He promised to let us know how things are at home, and Jack Quinlan is a man of his word."

Coughlin nodded in assent, then, after a pause he said: "Anyway, it won't be long now before we'll be going home for a while ourselves. Sure any eejit can see that we'll soon be off on the high seas again bound for God knows where, and before we go they'll have to let us have some home leave. We must be owed months of it by now."

"You're right there, Pat," Daly replied, "but it's not only God who knows where we'll be going. I can tell you now that it will be bloody India again for us. And sure doesn't everybody know that 'The Grim' can never be put right without the Rangers being there."

"But I thought the Afghans were beat Jim, I heard that we sent in aeroplanes to bomb Kabul and that was it,"

"Don't be an eejit Pat," said Dolan, "the war with Afghanistan is over but you know very well that doesn't mean anything at all to them bloodthirsty tribesmen on The Frontier. And from what I hear that Rowlett Act has them hopping mad."

The Rowlett Act was a law passed in India in March 1919. The Colonial government's intention was to extend indefinitely the 'emergency powers' brought in during the war to help control public unrest and root out conspiracy. This act gave the British Imperial Authorities the power to imprison without trial anyone suspected of causing unrest, and to use all necessary force to quell revolutionary activities. Introduction of The Act led to widespread indignation from both Indian political leaders and general public, which caused the government to implement even more repressive measures. Indian leaders, such as Mahatma Ghandi, were left powerless to oppose the Act by constitutional means. A 'hatal' was organised, and all Indian business was suspended, but tensions were running too high for peaceful means to have any effect, and rioting soon became widespread.

"I'd say you're right Jim," said Coughlin. "It's a bit like that 'Defence of the Realm Act in Ireland. And did you hear what happened at Amritsar?"

News of the Amritsar Massacre was rapidly becoming public knowledge in Britain: A British officer, General Dyer, discovered a large crowd gathered in a walled plaza in the city of Amritsar to protest against the enactment of the Rowlett Act. Under orders from Dyer, troops opened fire and reportedly killed over three hundred unarmed people who could not escape from the enclosed area. General Dyer was later removed from his post, but the damage had been done. The consequences of the massacre would cloud Anglo-Indian relations for decades.

"I heard about it all right Pat, and I'll tell you this," said Daly. "If I'm ever called on to do anything like that when we go back to India, the only one I'll shoot will be the bastard who gives me the order."

Coughlin could see that his friend was deadly serious. He sought to lighten the mood. "Anyway we'll be going home first and we'll find out for ourselves how things are in Ireland."

"Maybe so Pat," said Daly, "but aren't the two of us in the army long enough now to know that it always pays to make sure of your ground before making a move. And I'd like to hear from Jack first before I go back to Ireland so that I know what kind of a welcome I might get."

"It's an awful pity some of the brass in this army never learned that lesson," said Coughlin. "They could do a lot worse than to promote Private James Joseph Daly all the way up to General."

\*\*\*

At home in Beaufort, Jack had every intention of writing to the two 'Rangers' and had begun to get to grips with the current state of affairs regarding the fight for an Irish Republic; his main source of information being Michael Flynn. So much had changed since his last visit home. That visit had been for a short spell of leave prior to going to Mesopotamia. Then he had walked proudly around Beaufort in uniform, now he was loath to wear even his 'de-mob' suit. The changes that had occurred in his family he could attribute to time, everyone was now nearly four years older, and of course there was the loss of his father. But the changes in attitude of the Irish people generally were much more difficult to get to the bottom of. Michael Flynn told him that it was bound to be hard for anyone who not been in Ireland during The Rising to understand how that momentous event had altered perspectives.

One of the biggest changes that Jack noted, however, was the way in which Michael Flynn himself had grown in both stature and confidence. Gone was the easy-going carefree Flynn he had known at school and as a youth. In his place was a much more serious young man with a definite goal in life: that of seeing Ireland free of British rule. Jack put this transformation partly down to Michael's internment, but he also suspected that Maureen Ryan had somehow had a hand in it too. When he was introduced to Maureen at the Quinlan home she seemed friendly enough on the surface, but underneath he detected a trace of animosity. To Jack she seemed to be trying just that bit too hard to be nice, and was only doing so for Michael's sake. Which, Jack thought, spoke volumes for the way she felt about his old friend; the man she was going to marry. And he was pleased to note that she did seem to have a genuine affection for his own mother.

With raids and ambushes on RIC and army barracks by IRA flying columns, followed by arrests and reprisals by the British authorities, now almost a daily occurrence, Jack felt that he had stepped out of one war and straight into another. But what really brought home to him the seriousness of the current situation in Ireland was finding out about what had happened to his father. William and Michael told him the whole story about 'The Man from Dublin', the hunt for James and the final reckoning at the bog.

The only thing they decided not to disclose was the fact that Pat Devlin seemed to suspect something and had started to ask questions.

Before Jack had fully considered the implications of what had happened to his father and brothers, and its likely effects on him, a letter arrived from the Irish agent representing the owner of Beaufort House. His appointment as steward – effectively estate manager – was confirmed and the agent would shortly be visiting to discuss arrangements for preparing the house and grounds for the owner's return.

The house itself was showing every sign of having been left empty for the four long years of war. When Jack and the agent first entered they were met by the musty smell generated by all unlived in houses. But on opening the windows to the soft spring air, and removing the dust sheets from the furniture, they found little sign of any serious damage. The grounds, however, presented a much different aspect. The only part of the entire estate to have been properly maintained and kept up to its former well kept state was the area around the main gates. Annie Quinlan's insistence on keeping the cottage and garden as neat and tidy as it had always been was noted by the agent and he promised to mention the fact to 'His Lordship'. The rest of grounds, however, were in a sorry state and exhibited all the signs of neglect. The once carefully tended flower beds and lawns around the house were overgrown and the vegetable garden was a tangle of weeds. The home farm remained un-stocked and untilled and the farm buildings were in urgent need of repair.

Jack and the agent made a preliminary list of what needed to be done and attempted to identify the priorities. To begin with, the house would have to be made habitable and the gardens tidied up and put into some sort of order before the 'family' could even think of coming home. The farm would have to wait until later. Then there was the question of employing enough staff to complete these tasks.

When the house was closed the owners had taken the butler, the ladies' personal maids, and the children's governess to England with them. All of the other house staff, most of them local women and girls had been laid off. The agent suggested that as many of these as possible should be re-employed and suggested that they ask 'His Lordship' if the butler could be sent over to supervise putting the house back into order. Jack agreed to help by contacting as many of the former maids and others as possible before the butler, who would be responsible for actually employing them, arrived. It would be Jack's responsibility to hire farm and garden staff and this presented an immediate difficulty:

'His Lordship' had requested that as far as possible when employing 'outside' workers for the farm and gardens preference was to be given to men who had served in the war. Although falling into this category himself, Jack considered that, in the current political climate, adopting such a policy would be a mistake and could lead to trouble.

He outlined his reasons for 'His Lordship's' agent: With feelings in Ireland running ever higher against Britain and her Empire much of the animosity was currently being directed at ex-servicemen. Being seen to give them special treatment was, Jack reasoned, bound to fuel resentment locally, and many former soldiers might also be reluctant to risk themselves and their families being further ostracised. The owners of Beaufort House had previously enjoyed extremely good relations with the local population, and he felt that they would not wish to damage their standing when they returned to their Irish home. There were also practical reasons for not restricting employment at Beaufort House to ex-servicemen: Jack sensed a need for urgency and the agent agreed, so time was of the essence. In an almost exclusively agricultural area he could soon find experienced farm workers, but if the grounds were to be brought up to an acceptable standard quickly he would need men with some experience in gardening. He pressed the agent to allow him to hire men who had previously worked at Beaufort, and who knew what was required, irrespective of whether they had served in the war or not.

There was yet another aspect that Jack considered worth raising with the agent: Many of the men, some of them were mere boys, who had volunteered to fight came from the larger family farms in the lush lowland by the river. After the war the survivors had returned to the life they had left and would not be seeking other employment. Those who had joined up to escape poverty on the small rented hill farms, or simply in the search for adventure, had now seen some of the great wide world, and many of them would no longer be satisfied with life in and around a small Irish village. The great post war European exodus across the Atlantic was beginning to gain momentum and Jack had already heard of several local men with ambitions to seek a better life in the new promised land of America. His own brother James, he knew, planned to join them. And at least some of those who did not emigrate, Jack feared, might well join the rebels and fight against their former colleagues.

Jack considered telling the agent what William had told him about what had been said during the confrontation at the bog about Beaufort House being 'targeted' by the rebels, but decided against saying anything for the time being. This, he felt, he should keep to himself until he could speak privately to 'His Lordship'. His employer was a former government minister and would certainly know of the potential danger to himself and his family and he might not appreciate Jack discussing it with anyone else.

Eventually these arguments were enough to convince the agent, and he felt that 'His Lordship' would also accept his new steward's assessment of the situation. As a result Jack was given carte blanche to hire the most suitable men he could find. There was no shortage of applicants and he was able hire enough reliable men. The butler arrived from England to supervise putting the domestic arrangements in order and Beaufort House began to come to life again.

As the work proceeded, Annie Quinlan walked up from the cottage to see how they were progressing. She went around to the stables and the coach-house which had once been her husband's scrupulously guarded and maintained domain. Where the two carriages had once stood she found an empty space. Jack gently broke the news that a coach and horses would no longer have a place at Beaufort. When the owners came home it would be a horseless carriage that would provide transport. And the coachman would be replaced by a chauffeur.

# Chapter 33

Annie Quinlan gazed out of the back door of the cottage and down to the riverbank to where her three eldest sons sat and talked in the Sunday afternoon sunshine. The significance of the scene generated a mixture of emotions. James had now come home, and it gave her immense pleasure to see the three of them together again for the first time in four years. But she was well aware that she might never see them like this again, and the thought brought with it a tear. James would soon be leaving to start a new life in America, and she had a premonition that William would also be leaving her as well. They were out of earshot and she knew that she must not go closer to hear what was being said. They would tell her when the time was right.

"Sure you won't find a better offer around here Bill, or anywhere else in the whole of County Kerry. And sure there's no better man in all Ireland to do the job."

Jack had offered to take his brother on 'up at the house'. He guessed that William would be loath to accept, but he felt that the offer should be made. And besides, what he said was true, he was confident that he would not find a better candidate for the post he had in mind.

"Sure don't you know very well you can't take me on, Jack." William sounded adamant. "What will people say if you go around giving out jobs to your own brothers? It would look bad, and neither one of us would feel right about it. And what would 'His Lordship' have to say about it."

"Listen to me now Bill." Jack's tone reminded William of their father. "Nobody would say a word about you getting the job of water bailiff. Sure doesn't everybody around know that you are the best man for the job, and 'His Lordship' will want someone like you who knows the river like the back of his hand. You know where the banks have to be cleared and things like that. And the minute he has a fly into a salmon he'll forget all about you being my brother."

Before William could reply, James butted in: "And you know very well that you'd take to it like a duck to water Bill, I don't know why you're taking so long to make your mind up."

"I know what's keeping him from jumping at the chance, Jim," said Jack. "He's thinking the same thing that you and me were thinking a few years ago. He wants to leave Beaufort and see the world,"

He slapped William on the back and turned to James: "We owe it to him Jim," he said, "and we can't stop him. Sure didn't this fella here do a grand job of looking out for Ma and the young ones while you and me were away. Ma told me herself that she doesn't know what she would have done without him, and especially after Da died, Lord have mercy on him."

The sombre silence that followed allowed William time to consider his current position: He was out of a job. The farmer's son had returned from the war and so one of the farmhands had to be laid off. Had he chosen to argue the point, William would have been the one to be kept on as he had worked there longer, but in truth he was glad to be the one to go. He had nothing against his former employer who had always treated him fairly, or against farming in general; in rural Ireland farm work was a well regarded occupation followed by the majority of the male population. His excuse for quietly accepting the loss of his employment was that the other man had a family to support and needed the job more than he did. His real reason was that continuing to work for the farmer would have involved him making a long term commitment to his employer, and that he was not prepared to do. In reality he regarded leaving his job as his opportunity to break away and make his mark on the world – a world that seemed to be rapidly passing him by.

He had listened to Jack and James comparing their experiences, one in the war and the other in the munitions industry, and had felt totally left out of things. He could not even begin to match them. Even Michael Flynn seemed to be making his way up in the republican movement; his friend was certainly involved in something that William was not a part of. And Michael was soon to be married, which was bound to further limit their fishing activities. Not that there was any serious fishing to be had now that Beaufort House had re-opened and the 'water' jealously guarded.

For a time he had entertained the idea of accompanying James to America. He was confident that his brother would agree to take him, but James already had friends in 'The States', friends he had made away from Beaufort at the munitions factory, and might not fully appreciate having his brother tagging along. He was convinced that he could easily cope on his own in a foreign land, but even so he felt that he would always be regarded as the younger brother. And, much as he cared for James, he did not like the idea of somehow being in his debt. The same applied to Jack and his offer of a job up at 'the house'. Attractive as the prospect of having sole charge of everything to do with fishing at Beaufort House undoubtedly was, he would still be playing second fiddle to Jack.

He badly wanted to be his own man, and to do that he would have to leave Beaufort and build a new life by himself.

One thing, however, that might have persuaded him to stay would have been the possibility of being trained as a chauffeur at Beaufort House. But he knew that this was an impossible dream. First he would have to learn to drive a motor car. He did not foresee any particular difficulty in learning that particular skill; he had read about how it was done, and given the opportunity, he was confident that he could manage to teach himself. But he realised that being a gentleman's chauffeur required much more than just being able to drive, and there was no one around Beaufort with either the time, or indeed the inclination, to teach him the finer points.

The more he thought about it the more he was fascinated by the unstoppable advance of the motor car and he was determined that whatever the future held for him it would revolve around the internal combustion engine.

As if to add salt to that particular wound, the first private motor car had just arrived in the village of Beaufort. Although not as grand as the magnificent Rolls Royce at Beaufort House, Pat Devlin's new Model 'T' Ford was the talk of the parish. And following a few introductory lessons from the dealers in Cork, Pat seemed to be coping nicely.

He brought his mind back to the present: "You're right Jack," he said. "I have a mind to leave here."

Jack nodded his understanding.

"Where will you go?" Jim asked.

"I'm thinking of joining the army. A lot of people around here won't think much of me for it, but it's what I want to do. Sure isn't the army getting rid of horses and turning entirely to motor transport? They're on the lookout for fellas to train up as drivers, and I'm thinking that I could be one of them."

The half-expected arguments against his decision failed to materialise.

"When were you thinking of leaving for America, Jim?" Jack asked.

"Sure I'm ready to go anytime," James answered. "But I think I'll wait until after the wedding."

"So will I," said William, "sure it's the least we can do for Mick Flynn."

***

One Irishman already in America was Eamonn de Valera. 'Dev' was working with the considerable Irish-American lobby for recognition of *The Dail* as the legally elected Parliament and Government of the Irish Republic. He also wanted the new republic to have a seat at the peace talks in Paris. President Wilson was known to have sympathy for small nations, but was suspicious of the Irish-American leaders whom he considered to be pro-German. Wilson knew that a solution to the 'Irish problem' would have to be found, but much of his advice on the subject came from British sources. The Irish cause suffered a setback when a Sinn Fein delegation, which included Michael Collins, failed to get a meeting with the president when he passed through London on his way to Paris.

At home, in de Valera's absence, a decision made by *The Dail* was to lead to trouble: All members of the Royal Irish Constabulary were to be regarded as agents of the 'British Occupation Forces' and ostracised by the Irish people. Collins discovered that all intelligence collected by the police went to a special group of detectives at Dublin Castle known as 'G Division'. If this force could be eliminated, the British intelligence gathering system would be paralysed. These 'G men' were approached by members of the Volunteers and warned of the consequences of continuing to collate political information for the authorities. Some of them recognised the seriousness of their situation and complied, but others did not. These decisions were a recipe for trouble and would eventually lead to fatal results.

# Part Three

## That Old Perplexity

*The intellect of man is forced to choose Perfection of the life, or of the work,*
*And if it take the second must refuse*
*A heavenly mansion, raging in the dark. When all that story's finished,*
*what's the news?*
*In luck or out the toil has left its mark: That old perplexity an empty purse,*
*Or the day's vanity, the night's remorse.*
**(W.B.Yeats – 'The Choice')**

# Chapter 34

There was something vaguely familiar about the young man sitting opposite him but Pat Devlin could not quite put his finger on exactly what it was. They were sitting at window table in a bar in Tralee; the young man had suggested that they meet in Killarney but Devlin had insisted – as far as anyone could insist with someone claiming to be an emissary from Michael Collins - on Tralee. He did not know what the meeting was going to be about, but he didn't think that, with Collins involved, it could be about anything even remotely trivial. So just to be on the safe side he wanted to meet with the young rebel as far from Beaufort as was practicable. If things turned out badly as a result of what was said here he wanted to be as far removed from things as he possibly could; especially as his various businesses in Beaufort were picking up now that the war was over. He was slightly surprised, however, and not a little pleased with himself, when his suggestion of Tralee had been so readily accepted. Had he known what was to be discussed, however, he would not have so smug.

The journey to Tralee in his new car had afforded Devlin the opportunity to hone his newly acquired driving skills. He had parked it in full view outside the pub in an attempt to impress on this man from Dublin the fact that Pat Devlin was a man to be reckoned with. In an effort to further impress, he had even memorised some of the Ford's technical specifications - his actual understanding of these terms was nil, but he hoped that this would not be evident.

To break the ice Devlin bought the Dublin man a pint of porter and asked him if he had a pleasant journey down from the city. When the man sent by Collins assured him that he had, Pat pointed to the Model 'T', now annoyingly covered in dust from the dry unpaved roads, and said that he had driven all the way from Beaufort in his own motor car. He proceeded to inform his companion that the 'T' had a top speed of 40-45 miles an hour; it had an inline four-cylinder *en-bloc* engine; this particular model ran on gasoline and would do between 13 and 20 miles to the gallon.

The young man from Dublin was not, however, impressed. Devlin's attempts failed, and if anything, only served to place him at a disadvantage: Kevin Ryan knew more about motor cars than Pat Devlin would ever learn. He also knew a great deal more about Devlin than the Beaufort publican would have been comfortable with had he been aware of it.

Kevin had stopped off in Killarney before coming to Tralee, where he met with his sister, Maureen. So he already knew that Devlin had been asking questions about what had happened to 'Mr Jameson' and he suspected that he too would be questioned about the dead rebel when he met the Beaufort man later in the day. Before that happened he needed to know all that he could learn about Devlin, and who better to teach him than Maureen? On his way to Tralee, therefore, Kevin had sufficient information to enable him to think about how best to handle the situation, and he saw a possible way of preventing Devlin from pursuing his enquiries about the man who had been left dead in the Kerry bog.

That Kevin Ryan had been sent down to the southwest by Michael Collins was true. 'The Big Fella' was aware of the part the owner of Beaufort House had played in the Ministry of Munitions during the war, and as such 'His Lordship' had been immediately marked down as a possible target for kidnapping or murder. Someone of his importance could prove to be invaluable should the need for a high profile hostage arise; or if a murder victim was required to set an example to other British men of influence living in Ireland. Collins had no intention of making an immediate move against the British official whom he knew to be still actively involved in government business; he wanted him 'kept on ice' as he termed it, in anticipation of a more opportune moment. But in the meantime he needed to gather as much information as he could about the situation in Beaufort, and after that to be kept informed of 'His Lordship's movements.

Collins of course knew that Michael Flynn lived in Beaufort and could simply have employed him to keep an eye on Beaufort House but, although Michael did not know it, he too was being 'kept on ice'. The way Michael had carried out his role in de Valera's escape had impressed Collins, and he did not want his latest recruit involved in day-to-day operations where he would be in danger of coming to the attention of the authorities. He did not know Pat Devlin personally but had heard his name mentioned several times. A few enquiries confirmed that the publican was a good sound nationalist and, as a local businessman, he even had access to Beaufort House. Collins, ever the meticulous planner, needed someone to set up a properly functioning information system in Beaufort, and Devlin seemed to be a likely candidate. But it was not his way to place his faith in someone who had not been thoroughly vetted, as Michael Flynn had been by Countess Markevitz, so he was not prepared to leave everything to Devlin just yet. 'The Big Fella' concluded that as Kevin Ryan had sister in the area who was apparently about to marry Michael Flynn, he would be the ideal man to check Devlin's real credentials. Kevin would have a valid reason for visiting Beaufort occasionally and while he was there it would not look anything out of the ordinary for him to visit the local pub. After further thought Collins felt that he could also involve Michael Flynn without compromising Michael's position: He would have Devlin report to Michael, who could use his local knowledge to verify the information before passing it on to him. And, just as importantly, it would do no harm at all for Devlin to know that he was being watched even when Kevin Ryan was not around. Michael Collins liked to consider all possible eventualities.

In the Tralee bar, Kevin looked Devlin in the eye. "So Pat," he said, "you know that what I have to say comes straight from 'The Big Fella' himself. And you know that as soon as I tell you a single bit about it you'll be in, and there's only one way out. So if you don't want to hear it, tell me now and I'll be on my way with no hard feelings."

Having recognised his mistake in trying to impress Collins' man, Devlin was already beginning to have misgivings. Things had definitely been tightened up since the largely disorganised days before The Rising. This young man did not have the easy-going ways of 'Mr Jameson', and however ruthless that individual might have been, he was always ready to share a drink and a yarn. The man sitting opposite him now showed every sign of being one of Collins' reportedly elite group of killers. There was no doubt whatsoever in Devlin's mind that, no matter what had been said about there being 'no hard feelings', if he walked away now he would never be trusted by 'the boys' again. His days of working for The Cause would be over, and that did not fit in with Devlin's ambitions at all. Gone were the days when he had embraced the Nationalist cause purely for idealistic reasons, these days he took a much more pragmatic view. In the months since the armistice the shop attached to his pub had done exceptionally well and, with the reopening of Beaufort House, it was set to do even better. Devlin now had plans to expand his business interests. While much of his trade was coming from people known to be opposed to nationalism he was certain than the republicans would eventually win, and it would do him no harm at all to been seen as having supported them.

He took a deep breath before replying: "Sure won't anybody tell you that when it comes to working for The Cause, Pat Devlin is your man. I'm always ready to do anything 'The Big Fella' wants."

Kevin knew that Devlin was devious but he had his orders from Collins and so, without including the purpose, he outlined what was required regarding keeping an eye on the owner Beaufort House.

"And make sure that you handle all the deliveries to the house yourself," Kevin suspected that Devlin would already be doing that in his new car, "and keep your eyes and ears open."

To begin with Devlin was actually quite relieved. He was under no illusions about what Collins' had in mind, but what was being asked of him was in fact something he was already doing on behalf on 'Mr Jameson'. And this might give him the opportunity to find out what had happened to his old contact.

"How do I pass on anything I might find out to 'The Big Fella?" he asked. "In the past I always used to send telegrams to a fella in Dublin, but I haven't heard from him for a while. I don't suppose you know what happened to him?"

Kevin gave him a long look, as if not entirely happy to be questioned. "Did you now, what was his name and what do you know about him?"

Devlin's relief began to drain away, he realised that he had to tread carefully: "Lately he was calling himself 'John Jameson', he used to come to Beaufort to recruit lads for the fight. The only other thing I know about him is that he was doing something over the water while The Rising was on."

Instinct prevented him mentioning the search for James Quinlan to this particular man from Dublin. The way things were developing Collins' man might decide that it was something Devlin was not supposed to know anything about.

"I know nothing about that," Kevin lied, "maybe that's where he is now, over the water. Anyway," he added menacingly, "it won't do either of us any good to go around asking questions about it."

Devlin got the message. It was obvious that no information would be forthcoming and any attempt to labour the point would be fraught with danger. "So who do I send telegrams to now?" he asked. "By the way I always used to send them from Killarney. The postmaster's wife in Beaufort is a lot too nosy to trust."

"There'll be no more telegrams," said Kevin. "They're not safe anymore, there's too many spies around in Dublin these days. Do you know a fella called Michael Flynn?"

This took Devlin completely by surprise, and to Kevin's satisfaction, it showed. After taking a minute to collect himself the Beaufort man said: "Sure I know Mick Flynn well."

"So," said Kevin, "all you have to do is tell Mick what you find out and he'll make sure that it goes to the right people."

Devlin still didn't like the way things were developing. "Do you know Mick yourself?"

"Sure of course I do," said Kevin. "We were interred together over in Wales by the Brits, and sure any day now he's going to marry my sister."

Before Devlin could think of a reply Kevin stood up, downed the remains of his porter, and left.

As he drove back to Beaufort, Devlin was seething with anger. He was angry at the way he had been treated by that cocky young fella from Dublin; he was angry at the idea of his having to report to Michael Flynn. He did not particularly like what Collins was demanding from him; he did not like being in a position where he did not fully understand exactly what was going on; and he definitely did not like the fact that he could not see a way of turning the situation to his personal advantage.

He had always been aware that 'Mr Jameson' had only ever told him enough to enable him to do what was required, as had happened when he had arranged for the car and guns to be left outside the station in Killarney. But even so, he had always felt that he was central to the operation, and being able to report directly to Dublin meant that he was considered to be a man of some importance to 'the boys' in the Beaufort area. But now here was this upstart, Kevin Ryan, treating him as if he was not to be trusted and telling him to report to another Beaufort man, Michael Flynn. By naming Flynn as his contact, Ryan had confirmed what Devlin already suspected: Michael Flynn was better known to the senior members of the Republican movement than anyone around Beaufort was aware of. Was this simply because Flynn was Ryan's future brother-in-law, or was there more too it? And why hadn't Flynn himself been delegated to gather the required information? Devlin did not know and that rankled. It galled him to be relegated to what he considered to be a minor rule as a simple snooper. And having to report to someone in Beaufort meant that whatever he found out could, and would, be double checked, which stung Devlin's ego to the core.

Then there was the actual task itself: It was one thing to be sending snippets of information to 'Mr Jameson', but being under orders to spy for Michael Collins could prove to be a very dangerous game. It seemed obvious that Collins would be interested in the man at Beaufort House, but this was one area where Devlin would have preferred not to be involved. The owners had only recently returned and reopened the house so, as well as groceries, there were a number of household items required which Devlin had placed himself in a position to supply. If it ever became public knowledge that he was involved in a rebel operation against 'His Lordship' before Ireland was free of British rule, he stood to lose a lot of money. But he also knew that if he got on the wrong side of 'The Big Fella' he stood to lose a great deal more

He tried to put things into perspective and consider his options. He would have to tread carefully, but he was determined that he would somehow work his way back into a position where he was once again the master of his own destiny. He badly needed to find something he could use as a lever, and the only way to go about that was to find out more about what was actually going on.

***

They were sitting in an almost deserted bar in Killarney and Kevin told Michael what had transpired in Tralee.

"So 'The Big Fella' is dead serious about your man at Beaufort House," said Michael.

"He is so Mick," replied Kevin, "and sure after what he did in the war he's bound to be fair game."

But Michael was concerned. "There's a lot of innocent people working at the house now Kevin," he said. "I know most of them and I'd hate to see them get hurt."

"Ah sure there's no chance at all of that, Mick. The last thing Collins wants is for innocent Irishmen and women to get hurt, as long as they don't try anything stupid they'll be all right. But I can't say the same for anybody they brought over from England. Anyway, sure nothing at all might happen, 'The Big Fella' just wants to be ready in case your man at Beaufort ever comes in handy, if you get my drift."

Michael could do nothing other than accept that, but he was no happier about having to work with Devlin than the publican was about having to report to him. "I don't like the idea of getting too close to Pat Devlin; he'll only keep on at me about the fella I killed."

"I'd say that I gave him a fair warning about that," said Kevin. "But listen to me Mick, if he shows any sign at all of trying to find out any more about it, we'll have to fix him for good. There'll be nothing else for it because this could be the ruin of us all."

Michael knew that Kevin meant what he said and would be quite prepared to carry out his threat, but he still hoped it would not come to that.

Like Devlin, Michael was not happy about being drawn into whatever Collins had in mind regarding Beaufort House, but for very different reasons. Although Kevin had assured him that innocent people would not be in any danger, he had already witnessed on the cattle raid what could happen on the spur of the moment when guns were being used.

Later, when he was alone with Maureen he voiced these concerns to her, and added: "And I don't like the idea of being mixed up in something at Beaufort House behind Jack Quinlan's back. I know him well and I'll tell you this, if there's any danger of someone laying a hand on his boss, Jack will take a hand. I wish to God that I could warn him, but if I did that, sure I'd be no better than an informer."

"I know you'd never do that Michael," she said, "but sure it might not come to anything." In spite of her nationalist upbringing, she fervently hoped that she was right.

"Wasn't it yourself who told me that once I started I'd be stuck with it for the whole of my life love?" he said, "but I'm thinking that maybe I'd be better off fighting with a flying column. It's easy for fellas like Kevin, they chose their road years ago and they'll go where it leads."

Turning things over in his mind that night, Michael had a thought about how to resolve his problems involving Devlin and Beaufort House. And he did not altogether like himself for what he was thinking.

# Chapter 35

The actual wedding was held on a sunny Friday morning in a local parish church in Dublin. It was not one of the grandest in the city, but the Ryan family had worshipped there every Sunday for several generations. Flowers brought up from Kerry by Mr and Mrs Flynn brightened up the otherwise plain old building. Sunlight streamed through the high stained glass windows and shone on the couple making their vows before the altar. Most of the small congregation gathered for the Nuptial Mass and Marriage ceremony were members of the Ryan family or their friends, and many of them sported little harps or other emblems associated with the Irish Nationalist movement. Maureen's sister served her as her bridesmaid, her father sat uncomfortably to one side in a borrowed wheelchair; uncomfortable not because of the rudimentary nature of the chair, but rather because it was his first visit to the church for several years.

On the 'groom's side' were Michael's parents and a cousin who would act as best man.

Maureen, in a simple white dress and veil, carried a small bouquet of red roses and looked her loveliest. Michael, in his brand new wedding suit was immensely proud of her.

He would liked to have seen a few more people from Beaufort particularly some of the Quinlans, at his wedding, but for purely practical reasons, this was not possible. He was reluctant to put friends to the inconvenience, not to mention the expense, of travelling to Dublin on a working day at the height of the haymaking and turf-cutting seasons. Many of the local people that he knew had never travelled outside the confines of County Kerry and some of the older ones had never ventured further than Killarney. He had been surprised to learn that his own mother was one of these, the thought had never occurred to him, yet it helped to explain some of her fear of his being interned again. It took some persuasion to entice her onto a train, but eventually she had managed it and here she was crying at her son's wedding in a Dublin church. At the back of her mind, however, was a worry about how preparations for the party to be held on Sunday back at the farm were progressing without her being there to personally supervise. She had planned a grand affair to mark Michael's wedding and show off her beautiful new daughter-in-law, and the whole parish was expected to attend.

At the conclusion of the Mass the couple and principal guests left the church and went to a small local hotel for a formal wedding breakfast. In spite of the expense Mrs Ryan was determined that things would be seen to be done properly for her daughter's wedding. There was some hesitation over the unaccustomed food and the amount and variety of cutlery, but Maureen saved the day with whispered explanations based on the skills gleaned from her work at The Great Southern hotel. There were a few stumbled speeches and some genuinely heartfelt toasts after which the company retired to the Ryan house where a large crowd of friends and neighbours had gathered. In the time-honoured Dublin tradition the celebrations spilled out into the street.

Mrs Flynn was fascinated by the lack of space in the small terraced house. Although far from being the grandest and best appointed in the Beaufort area, the Flynn farmhouse was enormous by comparison. To her it felt almost claustrophobic and the close confines of the narrow street made her appreciate her own spacious farmyard. She had been in some of the town houses in Killarney and wondered how people could live in such close proximity to each other, but there was nothing there to prepare the countrywoman for the rabbit warren that was this area of Dublin. Maureen's mother could see Mrs Flynn comparing her home with what she imagined would be a grand mansion down in Beaufort. She was at a loss to know how to deal with the situation when a telegram addressed to Maureen was delivered by a boy on a bicycle.

The babble of conversation ceased and there was a moment of concern while Maureen opened the wire, telegrams being invariably associated with bad news. There was general relief, however, when a smile lit up her face.

She moved across to show it to her husband. "Look Michael," she said, "it's from Countess Markievicz, she sent it to congratulate us and wish us luck. Isn't that grand?"

"It is so darlin'," said Michael and put his arm around her shoulders.

The revelation about who had sent the telegram caused a stir, and glasses were raised to the Countess. Mrs Ryan felt vindicated that someone so famous had taken the trouble to send a telegram on her daughter's wedding day.

Michael noticed the mystified look on his own mother's face and whispered to Maureen: "I'll have to say something to Ma about who the Countess is, and how we come to know her."

"Let me do it Michael," she said, "I'll tell her that I used to work for the Countess."

Maureen was glad of the opportunity to talk to Mrs Flynn who she could see was feeling ill at ease, and she wanted to try and get her into conversation with her own mother. She was at a loss to find any common ground between them until she spotted Kevin talking to Michael. It gave her an idea. She got the two women together and casually remarked that they both had sons who had suffered internment. Although coming from totally different backgrounds, it was a topic on which the two mothers could easily empathise.

Over by the fire Michael's father was patiently listening to his opposite number, John Ryan, who by now had taken a few more drinks than were good for him. Mr Flynn listened politely but only managed to pick a little of what was being said. The general hubbub drowned out much of what the man was saying, and much of what Mr Flynn did pick up he failed to understand. When he had a drink in him John Ryan was apt to lapse into a confused mixture of English and Gaelic, all delivered in a strong Dublin accent. Michael's father did, however, get the gist of it and found what he heard disturbing. Maureen's father was obviously delighted with his new son-in-in law, but the reason for this seemed to stem from his idea that Michael was a well known and highly regarded member of the Irish Republican Brotherhood. He already suspected that Michael was 'running with the boys' and in view of his son's internment he did not entirely blame him. While personally he was prepared to allow Michael to go his own way, not that there would be much he could do to stop him, it was the effect this would have on his wife if she ever found out the whole truth that worried him. He could see her in conversation with Mrs Ryan and feared that she was being subjected to a similar diatribe.

The wedding party was by now developing into a full-blown nationalist rally, and there was a danger that the authorities might intervene. Both Michael and Maureen were becoming concerned about what his parents would make of it, but the time had almost arrived for them to leave for the station to catch the train back to Killarney. Kevin drove them in a car he had acquired from nobody knew who or where; and he was not prepared to talk about it.

On the train, Michael's father, who had been worried about how the Dublin wedding had affected his wife, was pleasantly surprised and relieved to hear her talking about how Maureen's mother had suffered the same agonies that she had over her son's internment. And, on top of that, Mrs Ryan had also been forced to bear the tragedy of having another son killed in The Rising. It was the first time that Mrs Flynn had talked at any length about how she felt about Michael's arrest, and it was obvious that the two mothers had found mutual support. Once that topic had been exhausted she turned to describing exactly what she had planned for the party to be held at the farm on Sunday. She was determined that it would be a fitting celebration for her son and beautiful new daughter-in-law. It was a pity that 'poor crippled Mr Ryan' wouldn't be able to come, but Maureen's brother and sister had managed to persuade their mother to travel to Beaufort with them.

When Kevin got back from the station, and had managed to elbow his way through the throng in the street, he found Michael looking thoughtfully at the telegram now proudly displayed on the mantelpiece.

"Tell me Kevin," he said. "How did she know that we were getting married today, and how did she know where to send it. I never said anything to her and neither did Maureen?"

"Neither did I Mick," Kevin answered. "I don't know what you did for herself and 'The Big Fella' but you made a name for yourself. But sure don't you know that they'll always be keeping their eyes on you now."

Maureen came across and stood close to Michael. She stood on tiptoe and whispered in his ear. Kevin took them back to the hotel where a room had been booked for their wedding night.

***

At Mass in Beaufort on the Sunday morning the priest blessed the happy and not a little embarrassed couple. Some of the congregation went home to carry out some essential chores before joining the others at Flynn's for the wedding celebrations. A picnic lunch had been prepared which would last well into the afternoon, and in the evening a local fiddler and accordionist had been engaged to provide music for dancing.

It was unheard of to send out formal invitations on such occasions, which were always open to all comers. Everyone in the area knew they were welcome, and everyone who possibly could, turned up. Inter-family feuds, and since the war and The Rising there had been a marked increase in these, were set aside for the day. Even a local Gaelic football match had been postponed.

The weather too had donned its Summer Sunday best and the sun shone. Tables of food were laid out in a cleared area of the large open barn and places had been laid in the parlour for the elderly and infirm. Several of them had struggled to get there but none, particularly the women, would have missed it for the world. The older men stood in groups and talked of the weather and the crops; some of the younger men found some suitably shaped sticks and held an improvised hurling match; when they tired of that they played pitch-and-toss for pennies; the children ran amok through the farmyard; the girls giggled, flirted with the young single men and cast envious glances at the bride.

The happy couple circulated. Michael had his back slapped and his leg pulled; Maureen smiled and occasionally blushed at the whispered advice, mostly old wives tales, handed out by the older women. Mrs Flynn, ably assisted by Mrs Ryan, plied the gathering with copious amounts of tea and Maureen was delighted to see that her mother was thoroughly enjoying herself.

Annie Quinlan grew tired of listening to the women in the parlour and moved outside. She found a quiet seat by the farmhouse door surveyed the happy scene. It reminded her of her own wedding and she brushed away a tear. She looked around for her sons. James and William were talking with a group of friends while Jack stood aside by himself. As she watched, the schoolmaster came across to talk to him. Annie noticed that he was not being spoken to with the same easy familiarity as his brothers and at first she thought that it was because he had served in the British army, but then she saw that there were other ex-servicemen there who were being treated in a perfectly friendly fashion. Then it dawned on her that it was because he now held the position of 'steward' at Beaufort House and as such was regarded as a man of some importance, on a par with the schoolmaster, the postmaster and the parish priest. She did not think that this would sit easily with Jack, but it was the way of things. Looking at her sons she wondered if she would ever see them married. She had no doubt that one day they would marry but she had a premonition that she would not see it happen. When James wed it would probably be in America, and William had broken the news that he too had chosen to leave home. Their leaving so soon after seeing all three reunited would hurt her to the core, yet she could understand their reasons for leaving. Unless they were content to spend their lives as farm labourers Beaufort had little to offer them. She drew some consolation from thinking that Michael, her late husband, would have approved of them trying to better themselves. But, had she known the full story behind their leaving, concern for their safety might have prompted her to urge them to leave.

Of her other children: 'young' Michael was now well on the road to becoming a Priest – Jack's position would help with that - and the girls were growing up rapidly. She envied them their carefree world.

A natural break in the festivities occurred in the late afternoon at milking time. Neither wars nor weddings would ever be permitted to interfere with this twice-daily ritual; the cows, like time and tide, waited for no man, and people left to attend to it on their own farms and smallholdings. After milking they reassembled at Flynn's for the dancing.

"Your man there thinks he's running the whole do, Mick. I wouldn't trust that blowhole one bit." The object of Kevin's derision was Pat Devlin who was dispensing glasses of stout from the barrel he had supplied and making a great show of it.

Michael was disturbed by the animosity clearly evident in Kevin's voice. "He's changed a lot lately, Kevin," he said. "Sure he's not the same Pat Devlin that we used to know. I'd say that all this new business he's doing has gone to his head. There was a time when you could trust him with your last penny, but I'm sorry to say, I don't think that's true anymore."

"Well the minute he takes a wrong turn I'll put him in the bog along with the other fella who was set to shoot yourself and Maureen."

"For God's sake watch yourself Kevin, the last thing we want is to get on the wrong side of 'The Big Fella', if we were to get rid of Devlin, and Michael Collins found out why we did it, we'd be in a lot worse trouble than we are now."

Michael was well aware that his real concern was not for Devlin, or indeed for Kevin, but for the effect any false move could have on Maureen.

"Anyway," he said, "sure nothing is going to happen here tonight."

"Something's going to happen somewhere," said Kevin. Like Michael he had noticed a few men slipping away. They were members of a local 'flying column' and were obviously setting off on some sort of 'operation'. When they returned they would say that they had been here all night, and no one would contradict them.

"Well I'm for a pint and a dance with a few of these lovely Kerry girls." Kevin wandered off and left Michael with his thoughts.

Although Michael was loath to think of such things at his wedding party, Kevin's attitude towards Devlin bothered him. He did not like the idea of Kevin killing the publican, something he knew his brother-in-law was quite capable of. If the whole truth were to emerge the repercussions could be disastrous. But what Devlin knew, or thought he knew, or might find out, was also a danger to them. And he had, at all costs, to protect his wife.

Then there was the question of what might happen at Beaufort House. He was not particularly concerned about the owners of the house, but he hated the thought of Jack Quinlan being caught up in a nationalist plot and the effect that could have on Jack's mother. It would prey on his conscience if they were to suffer when he might have been able to prevent it. He was torn between warning Jack, which would in effect make him an 'informer' despised by both sides, and letting events take their course.

Although he did not like the idea, Michael had thought of a way of dealing with both problems. And with Kevin primed for action and William Quinlan about to leave Beaufort he would have to move quickly.

# Chapter 36

Life at Beaufort House was settling down, and things were gradually getting back to some semblance of what they had been before the war. The interior had been brought up to a standard befitting an aristocratic family and, thanks to Jack Quinlan's hard work, the grounds were coming up to scratch. But everyone realised that, however hard they might wish for it, nothing would ever be exactly the same.

As far as the owner's family were concerned, one son had died in the war and a daughter had married and settled in London. 'His Lordship' still had duties to perform in the Ministry of Munitions, where he was now concerned with decommissioning munitions factories rather than building and administering them. Until this work was completed he could only spend weekends at Beaufort, arriving on Friday evenings and departing again on Monday mornings. 'Her Ladyship' meanwhile, still carried on as if nothing had changed. She was chauffeured to her many social engagements in Killarney, Cork city, and even Dublin. One of Jack's first tasks had been to prepare a garage for the 'Rolls' and repair the potholed drive. Had she cared to look, she would have noticed subtle changes in the attitudes of staff and tradesmen, and that not nearly as many caps were doffed as she drove by. One constant, however, was Annie Quinlan rushing to open the gates as 'Her Ladyship's' car approached.

The world at large too, had changed: people's attitudes to life and work had undergone a marked transformation. Expectations had been raised and millions of soldiers coming home to the promised 'land fit for heroes' were no longer satisfied with the social divisions and prejudices of the past. Even in southwest Ireland the effects of the social revolution brought about by the war were being felt. Jack had noticed the difference when recruiting staff for Beaufort. Once upon a time securing a job, however menial, at Beaufort House would have been a much sought after feather in the cap. Except for people like Pat Devlin and, Jack was honest enough to admit, himself, there had been little improvement in the material aspects of life, but working men were beginning to look at alternatives. Many were still tied to the land, but those who were not were looking further afield. Many were opting to emigrate to America, and Jack's brother James had already left. William proved to be the exception to the rule, he had chosen to go to England and join the British army.

Pat Devlin noted the happenings at Beaufort and reported either edited or enhanced versions to Michael Flynn. He need not have bothered, with local people working both inside and outside the house the whole area knew what was happening there. Devlin knew this and the thought made him angry. The notion that he was regarded as a minor player and being treated as an idiot gained strength. His anger found an outlet by blaming Michael Flynn, William Quinlan, and especially Kevin Ryan for his, largely imagined, troubles. His anger led him to do something he had always studiously avoided: he began to develop too much of a liking for the contents of the shelves behind the bar of his own public house.

He was drunk the night before William Quinlan left home. William and Michael met in the pub with a couple friends and Jack had promised to join them later. Although he had not been very clear on the subject, most people apart from his family and Michael assumed that William was bound for America like James. On a balmy August evening with the weather set fair there was haymaking and turf cutting to attend to, not to mention IRA training and raids, so the bar was sparsely populated. In any case departures for America were no longer rare events demanding elaborate send-offs. The group were seated around a table in the corner by the open fireplace when Devlin rolled unsteadily over to them.

"So you're running off to America after your brother, are you Quinlan?" The publican's words were slurred and his voice was louder than usual. "Well I have it all now. Your man from Dublin, John Jameson, had a word in your ears and hunted the two of you out of Ireland."

William, who had been avoiding Devlin since Michael had told him of the publican's questions about the events at the bog, bristled and stood up.

Devlin seemed not to notice: "I don't know yet why he had it in for you but I'll find out, and then we'll see who's the top dog around here."

William had heard enough. He charged at Devlin knocking a chair over as he did so, but was prevented by Michael from actually striking the publican. The other two at the table stood up in anticipation of fisticuffs.

"Shut up Pat!" Michael's voice was so uncharacteristically sharp that it stopped both combatants in their tracks.

In spite of the drink Devlin seemed to recover first. He turned his attention to Michael: "You stop out of it Flynn," he yelled. "You think you're the grand Irish rebel don't you, yourself and that bloody brother-in-law of yours. Making out you're well in with Michael Collins. Sure wasn't I fighting for Ireland before any of you young *spalpeens* were even born."

The bar had gone deathly quiet. Devlin suddenly seemed to realise that he had said too much, and began the process of sobering up. A voice from the doorway helped him complete the process.

"God bless all here." Jack Quinlan came into the bar offering the traditional greeting on entering a house.

With an effort Devlin forced himself to collect his wits. Events had suddenly taken an unexpected and entirely different turn, and it was one he had to deal with quickly. He wanted to increase his business with Beaufort House and the 'steward', therefore, was someone he felt he could not afford to get on the wrong side of. On the rare occasions that Jack visited the pub Devlin made a point of offering him a drink on the house. Although Jack had not yet been known to accept, it was important that the offer be made, and when the publican was not there in person, bar staff were under strict orders not to forget it.

"Ah sit down lads," he said, "sure wasn't I only codding, Bill." He turned to the newcomer: "Good man yourself Jack, come here and I'll stand all of you a pint."

William and Michael knew that he didn't mean a word of what he said, but now that the heat had gone out of the situation they were content to let things lie.

"I'll take you up on that some other time, Pat," Jack pretended not to have noticed anything amiss. "But tonight it's my shout," he said, inadvertently lapsing into using a term picked up in the army. "Bring us five pints for me and the lads here and don't forget one for yourself."

Devlin scurried off to get the drinks while Jack pulled a chair from an adjoining table and sat down. He didn't say anything about what he had seen on entering the bar; he knew that William and Michael would explain later.

They were chatting about William's departure when a girl brought the drinks.

"Where's himself?" said Jack as he paid her for the porter.

"Oh he forgot to pick up something from the station in Killarney and he ran out like a hare." The girl laughed and winked at William: "But I think it was yourself that put the thorn in his trousers, Bill."

Their laughter was interrupted by the sound of Devlin's car starting and speeding off down the road.

"Sure that eejit'll kill himself someday the way he drives around in that motor car he's so proud of," said one of the drinkers.

Later outside the pub Michael said good bye to William. As they parted he lowered his voice and said: "Don't forget to tell Jack what I told you, but for God's sake don't say where you got it from."

William was aware of the personal cost to Michael and the potential danger of what he was doing. He too had some misgivings, but he would do as he was asked. He saw it as a way of repaying some of the debt he still felt he owed.

***

As the brothers walked homeward Jack said: "What was all that carry on with Pat Devlin, Bill?"

"Sure that was only the drink talking. Pat has the look of a man that's hitting the gargle hard lately. But listen Jack, I have it from someone in the know that Devlin is nosing around the house and telling 'the boys' up in Dublin everything he finds out. That's God's truth Jack, and I'm telling you so that you can watch out for yourself and Ma."

Jack could easily see for himself the situation in Ireland generally, and he knew that there was a well supported active rebel group in the Beaufort area. He had already thought of the possible danger they posed to the occupants of Beaufort House, and he could not believe that 'His Lordship' too was not aware of it. But nothing had been said and on the surface no extra precautions seemed to have been put in place. He had assumed that his employer was trying to keep everything as normal as possible for 'Her Ladyship's' sake.

But he could see that his brother was being deadly serious, and hearing Michael Collins' name mentioned earlier tonight confirmed that the danger he already feared was very real. So he knew it was his duty to report what he heard.

"I'll have to pass that on Bill, but I know from my army days that they'll want to know where I got my information from. I suppose there's no chance at all of you telling me where you heard it."

"Sure all you can do is tell them the truth, Jack. Say that you got it from me. And sure I won't be around for anybody to ask me how I got a hold of it."

Jack realised what was happening and had to smile. "Well I have to hand it to Mick Flynn: he still remembers how to watch out for his friends, in spite of the company he's keeping these days."

# Chapter 37

To Maureen Flynn it all seemed to have happened long ago and far away. The heady days of The Rising with their elements of death and danger; her involvement in the hunt for James Quinlan including her trips 'over the water'; the unexpected meeting with the policewoman at Gretna; working at The Great Southern Hotel; and even her first meeting with Michael all seemed to have taken place in the distant past. Even the memory of the tragic events that night at the bog was beginning to fade. Only the thought of how she had, by her own confused actions nearly lost Michael remained fresh in her mind. But it had been rekindled recently by the news that William Quinlan had decided to join the British Army.

All the old prejudices resurfaced and it required some effort to dampen them down. The fact that she was able to do so was, she knew, a direct result of having married Michael.

Although she found that actually living at the farm was much different from merely visiting, the rebel girl from Dublin soon settled into life in the country and was perfectly content as a Kerry farmer's wife; albeit a farmer deeply involved in the nationalist struggle. To begin with there were some tensions, but gradually the Flynn household accepted their new family member, and she got to grips with the unaccustomed routine on the farm. Mrs Flynn in particular was happy to have her there, and even if she did not always understand the city girl's ways, she treated Maureen as the daughter she had always wished for. The couple had been given a specially prepared large room in a rarely used area at the back of the house, and the bride had insisted that they buy a few ornaments and small items of furniture so that they could turn it into a private world of their own.

She waited there for her husband to come home from having a last drink with William Quinlan - in Dublin it would have been acceptable for her to go into a bar with him but not in Beaufort. As she waited she examined herself in the mirror, and found that she had gained a little weight and her city pallor, not improved upon by working in the hotel, had been replaced by a healthy country glow. She smiled to herself as she thought that she was even beginning to look the part of a farmer's wife. It was certainly all a result of married life with Michael, which was proving to be even better than she had hoped.

That afternoon when she took buttermilk out to the men working in the field he had walked her back to the house, on the way they had slipped away and made love in the drying hay.

Life was good, but there could never be any complete escape from the underlying tensions and contradictions that were Ireland in 1919, and she wondered what the future held.

It was a rather relieved Michael who left the Quinlan brothers and cycled home. He still thought that the plan he had put into action was devious in the extreme and, not for the first time since his involvement in The Cause, his conscience bothered him. His scheme simply involved sending a warning to Jack Quinlan about the possibility of a rebel attack on his employer, and William, soon to be out of harm's way and impossible to be 'got at', was an ideal messenger. An equally unpalatable part of his plan was that, should any rebel move against the people at Beaufort House fail as a result of Jack being alerted, Michael would point the finger at Pat Devlin. He hoped that Devlin would merely lose all credibility with the republican movement, and any stories he told about the man Michael had killed would not be believed. Yet he had to face the undeniable truth that things were unlikely to end there and the publican would almost certainly lose his life. If, or more probably when, that happened at least it would be done on orders from Dublin, and Maureen's brother would not be tempted to put himself in the firing line by carrying out an impromptu execution of his own. Michael understood that, given the violent world Kevin inhabited, his brother-in-law would never feel safe as long as Devlin continued to question the disappearance of 'Mr. Jameson'. It was, however, some consolation to know that Devlin's drunken outburst meant that the publican might have in effect driven a nail into his own coffin. Although there had not been many men in the bar tonight he recognised a couple of 'the boys'. That Devlin could well have contributed to his own downfall provided Michael with some semblance of an excuse, but in reality he knew that it did not absolve him.

As they lay in bed in their private room at the farmhouse he told Maureen what had happened and how he felt about what he had done.

"Thank God Kevin wasn't there tonight," he said, "or he would have done for Pat there and then."

"You did what you could, the same as you did before, Michael, and you have nothing to blame yourself for."

"But I can't get away from the notion that I as good as killed him, Maureen," he said, "just as sure as if I hit him with a *slean*. And he's no stranger threatening you with a gun, but a man that I've known all my life."

Maureen was silent for a few minutes. She moved closer to him. "Is it because of me, Michael?" she said. "Is it meeting me that forced you into doing all these things?"

"Oh God no, Maureen," he said. "It's only the times that have to carry the blame. And it'll always be the same until Ireland is free."

***

Over the next several weeks some notable alterations were made to the arrangements and routines at Beaufort House. The staff were issued with a quiet but firm warning about carrying snippets of information about the lives and activities of the family and visitors. The effectiveness of this warning was always in question, but they were left in no doubt that anyone caught spreading tales would immediately lose their job. All sensitive and personal documents were placed under lock and key, and only the butler was allowed into 'His Lordship's' private study.

'His Lordship' no longer used the distinctive Rolls Royce or travelled by train. He was now driven directly to Dublin to catch the boat to England and brought back to Beaufort in an official car. The times and duration of his visits home were varied and his routes alternated. An extra passenger travelled in the car and stayed at Beaufort when 'His Lordship' was at home. Special quarters were prepared for him. He ate with the staff but did not mingle and avoided conversation with them, and he made no secret of the fact that he was armed. It was clear to all that he was a plain-clothed RIC officer.

But in spite of everything 'Her Ladyship' would not be moved: she could not be persuaded to change her routines and refused point blank to countenance any extra security precautions.

To rub salt into Pat Devlin's wounds, he was told that there was no longer any need for him to make deliveries to the house. In future the chauffeur would pick up anything needed from the shop.

Michael was sincere in his belief that while Ireland lived under British rule bitterness would continue to dominate life in the land once known as 'The Island of Saints and Scholars'. The evidence was all around him: increasingly murderous raids followed by increasingly harsh reprisals were the order of the day. His personal experiences: internment, the killing at the bog, the cattle raid, and especially the young Dublin woman with the dying baby, all served to strengthen his belief in the rightness of The Cause. Helping to free Eamonn de Valera from prison had given him hope that his dream could be achieved, and Maureen's love and support gave him the confidence to carry on. But the complications and contradictions persisted. He was tied to The Cause for reasons both practical: he would die if he ever tried to desert, and philosophical: he felt it his duty to do everything he could. He lived with the constant thought that he would certainly be called on again, and even without knowing where or when, he was prepared to answer that call. Yet he also knew that there were those who would consider him an informer, the most despicable term that could possibly be applied to an Irishman, if they knew that he had sent a warning to Jack Quinlan. He had been well aware of that when he made his decision to do so. It had been his choice and he would have to live with it. Now, however, the time had come for him deal with the consequences of his action.

He had reported to Michael Collins as accurately as he could the changes that had been put in place at Beaufort House, and had been forced to include the fact that Pat Devlin had in effect been banned from visiting there. He had not commented further on the publican, but he knew that Kevin Ryan would immediately blame Devlin for being careless and getting himself caught spying, or worse, even accuse him of putting his self-interest before his duty to The Cause and betraying them to the authorities. Rumours were rife about the fracas in Devlin's bar and Michael knew that these would get back to Kevin, and consequently, to Collins. He was perfectly happy to support Collins' plans regarding the British owner of Beaufort House, whatever that might involve, but in his heart he knew that he would have difficulty convincing himself that it was just an accident of war if innocent local people were harmed in the process.

The message to Collins was delivered to Kevin when he made his first visit to Beaufort since the wedding. It was Maureen, in the same firm tones that she had used at the bog, who persuaded her brother not to go anywhere near Devlin for the time being.

Soon afterwards, to Maureen's surprise she received a letter from Kevin inviting her and Michael up to Dublin for a few days. The letter said that an old friend would like to meet Michael for a chat. He knew that the 'old friend' could only be Michael Collins.

# Chapter 38

This time, unlike his previous visit to Dublin, there was no need for lies or cover stories. Now that he and Maureen were married it was perfectly normal for them to visit her parents. Apart from the brief visit for their wedding this was the first occasion they had been in Dublin together, and Maureen delighted in showing Michael parts of the city he had not seen or had barely glanced at when he had been preparing for his part in de Valera's escape.

She laughed when he worried about someone recognising him as the priest they had once spoken to, but she understood when he warned her against going anywhere the docks where he had once worked. There he would certainly be remembered. The city was at last showing signs of recovering from the ravages of The Rising. Buildings had been repaired and new ones were under construction; the piles of rubble left by the British artillery bombardment were being cleared away; and the trenches dug by the rebels in St Stephen's Green had been filled in. But the general atmosphere was still one of tension. The underlying sense of nervous apprehension was much more pronounced here in the city than it was in country areas. Maureen concentrated on showing him the places where the main actions had taken place, and where she herself had fought during that fateful Easter Week. She told him more than she had previously done about her own part in the fight. He began to grasp something of the significance of what had happened, but he knew that no one who had not been there in person could ever fully understand the feelings of those who had.

She grew quietly subdued and shed a tear as she remembered those who had died both during the fighting and in the reprisals that followed.

In an effort to lighten her mood Michael said. "Would there be any chance of taking you for a drive in a jaunting car Mrs Flynn?"

There were no jaunting cars but they found a carriage for hire and were driven in state around Phoenix Park.

Michael was in thoughtful mood when he returned from meeting with Collins. Alone with Maureen in an empty compartment on the train back to Killarney he explained why.

He admitted to being nervous at the thought of meeting the Irish Republican Brotherhood leader again, but was surprised by the easy familiarity with which Kevin approached Collins when his brother-in-law took him to meet the great man. The interview began with Michael being closely questioned about every possible aspect of what was happening in and around Beaufort. It soon became evident that the man from the British Ministry of Munitions was far higher on Collins' agenda than Michael had been led to believe. From time to time, when receiving an answer to a question, Collins glanced at Kevin as if seeking confirmation and it also became clear that Maureen's brother was far higher up the republican ladder than they had previously imagined. At the mention of Pat Devlin's name Collins scowled and Michael knew that Kevin had already made his feelings regarding the publican clear.

"It seems as if I might have been wrong about him," was, however, 'The Big Fella's' only comment.

With his questioning over, Collins outlined the current situation as he saw it: A growing number of Members of the British Parliament were anxious to move the Irish Home Rule Bill, first proposed in 1914, forward. There were signs that they were gaining ground over those members who were opposed to any break-up of the British Empire. The Home Rule Bill as it stood, Collins said, would not be acceptable to *The Dail* as it fell a long way short of recognising the Irish Republic, which was, for all intents and purposes, now a reality. But at least it was a significant step forward. Public opinion in Britain was also swinging in favour of a solution to 'the Irish question'.

As Michael listened he could not help but think that Collins was remarkably well informed.

The war, in this case the Anglo-Irish war, was, according to Collins, going well. The pressure against the British authorities was being kept up. Although the army still controlled the cities and larger towns, in country areas the RIC had sole responsibility for enforcing the law, and they were being constantly harassed to the point where they were on the brink of collapse. Michael knew that this was largely true, many smaller police stations and one-man outposts were being abandoned, and forces were being concentrated in the larger barracks.

"Now is the time," said Collins, "to increase the pressure. And 'your man' down there in Beaufort could provide us with an excellent opportunity of doing so. He is an important man and if we can prove that the RIC can't protect him it will really be a feather in our caps. At the very least it will force them to increase their security measures for such people and stretch their already thin resources even further."

Michael took all this in and said nothing, but felt some apprehension about what might be coming next.

"So," said Collins, "from what you have told us Michael, I gather that he changes his routes between Killarney and Dublin and sometimes travels to London via Cork. But there is only one road suitable for his large official car from Killarney to Beaufort. And anyway I don't think they would take the risk of driving on narrow country lanes, especially at night. So an attack would have to take place somewhere on the main Killarney road."

"What's wrong with hitting him at the house?" Kevin spoke for the first time since the meeting began. "With all them thick woods around we could steal up on him easy there. Or we could wait for him with a rifle when he goes fishing, and sure the whole RIC wouldn't be able to help him."

"No," said Collins, "It's good idea Kevin, but it's not as simple as that. We would have to have an expert marksman hanging around waiting for him in daylight. And you wouldn't be able to lie in wait in one place because he could decide to go fishing anywhere along the riverbank. You'd need someone inside the house to tip you off when he left to go fishing, and other people to watch for which way the target was heading. Don't forget that this is the countryside we're talking about, yes there are woods to hide in but it's not like being here in Dublin where you know the place like the back of your hand. You'd have trouble getting away, and we can't afford to have you getting caught, now can we Kevin? It would greatly reduce the propaganda value."

To Michael it was obvious that the plan was to kill rather than kidnap the Englishman, and the 'you' had not escaped his notice, it clearly pointed to Kevin being the nominated killer. He was, however, much relieved to find that Collins made no mention of security being stepped up around 'the target'.

"Besides," Collins continued, "for the present at least, we don't regard private houses like Beaufort as being legitimate military targets. As I said, there are signs that public opinion in Britain is beginning to swing our way, and there are British journalists beginning to ask why *The Dail* should not be recognised. We don't want to upset the applecart by attacking Ireland's British residents in their own homes just yet."

This obviously did not apply to RIC men who were always in danger of being attacked in their own homes.

"When will that happen?" asked Michael.

"If and when they are guarded by uniformed army or RIC men," replied Collins. "At that point they become military targets."

To Michael it all seemed to have been thought through with Collins' usual attention to detail. This being the case, he could not help but wonder where he personally fitted into the scheme of things. But he knew that it would be useless to ask, he would only be told when the time was right and until then he would have to be patient.

Kevin was not ready to be quite so patient. "That's all grand," he said, "but how are we going fix your man down in Beaufort?"

"As I said it should be done somewhere along the Killarney to Beaufort road," said Collins. "You will take charge of the operation Kevin, and I'm sure that Michael can help you find a suitable spot. I'll leave the details to you, but I suggest that you time your ambush for when the target is on his way back rather than leaving home. They will be relaxing as they near home and their guard will be down."

"Right," said Kevin. "I'll round up a few of the lads."

"No," Collins, "I don't want other members of The Squad involved in this. We don't want any friction between us and the organisation down there in Kerry, so it will be better if you use local men for the job. Michael will put you in touch with the local commander, and you'll have to work with him."

Before he left Michael asked Collins how Eamonn de Valera was getting on since his escape. 'The Big Fella's' face darkened and his only reply was a rather annoyed sounding "he's fine."

Michael asked Kevin about this afterwards:

"Dev doesn't altogether agree with our way of doing things," he said. "He thinks we're making it hard for him to persuade the Yanks to recognise the Republic and get us a place at the peace conference. But sure isn't it all right for him shaking hands with all the big men over there in the States, when he knows nothing at all about what's happening here at home."

On the train back to Killarney, as he gave Maureen a full account of what had happened, Michael wondered how many other members of the movement were lucky enough to have wives as understanding as his.

"What do you think, Michael?" she said.

"Oh I think it will work all right," he said, "and from what I saw up there in Dublin, I'd say that Kevin is the man for the job."

Maureen looked at him with some concern: "Sure you know very well that I didn't mean that at all. Tell me honestly now Michael, how do you feel about being part of an attack on someone in Beaufort?"

Michael was silent while he collected his thoughts. Eventually he was ready with an answer: "We're in a war and things like this have to be done or we'll never see Ireland free. And I can't have my cake and eat it Maureen. I made up my mind to join the fight and I can't run away from it now. The attack will be on the Killarney road so, thank God, Jack Quinlan and his mother and the youngsters won't get hurt. But there's sure to be reprisals and it's hard for me to think about that."

"What does 'The Big Fella' think about reprisals?" she said.

"I didn't ask him, but he knows there'll be reprisals all right, and I'd say that the harder they are the better he'll like it. He'll have a lot to say about it and he'll make sure that the British newspapers hear him."

Maureen digested that: "I think you're right Michael," she said. Then, after some thought she added: "You haven't said a word about whether you'll be in the fight itself."

No," he replied, "he only wants me to help Kevin out setting it up."

"Maybe 'The Big Fella' has something else in mind for you." Maureen sounded hopeful. "Something like you did to get de Valera out of jail."

"I don't know Maureen. I got the notion that Collins is only interested in the armed struggle these days. I'm afraid he doesn't think that Ireland can be set free any other way."

Maureen had been brought up to believe that 'the armed struggle' was the only way. But falling in love with Michael had made her stop and think. She was immensely proud of him for his part in de Valera's escape and she now believed that he could contribute a great deal to The Cause without ever carrying a rifle.

"Did 'The Big Fella' say that Kevin was one of 'the squad?" she asked. 'The Squad', as the group was called, was gaining notoriety as Collins' elite group of enforcers, kidnappers, and executioners. They were also becoming known as 'The Twelve Apostles'.

"I'm afraid he did Maureen," said Michael.

"He's my brother and I'm fond of him, but please Michael, I don't ever want you to become anything like him."

# Chapter 39

"Show a leg and show it lively." The bugle had already woken him and the orderly sergeant bursting through the doorway of the wooden hut prevented him from dropping off again. Not that rising at six o'clock in the morning was anything new to William Quinlan. At home when he worked on the farm he had been obliged to 'show a leg' just as early for morning milking, and on his rare days off he would get up early to go fishing or to check his snares.

Those days were over now. For the next seven years his mornings would be governed by a different, more stringent set of rules. He was in his third week of basic training at the Tank Corp Depot situated near Wareham in Dorset.

He got out of bed and made his way to 'the ablutions' where he visited the toilet, washed and shaved. The immediate availability of hot water at the turn of a tap was an unaccustomed luxury, at home he would have had to boil a kettle, and to his mild surprise he found that this applied to most of the new recruits. He had foolishly imagined that in England such conveniences were commonplace even among the working classes. It struck him that he had a lot to learn, not only about the army but also about the world in general. When he finished dressing, his blankets and bed boards had to be folded and stacked in the best military fashion, and after three weeks practice the clumsy country boy was becoming quite proficient at it. Breakfast was at seven. The food was good and plentiful. Many of the 'old sweats' among the recruits, some had been in the army for as long as six weeks, indulged in the private soldier's privilege of complaining about the food. But it was better than most of them had enjoyed at home during the war. Although it was different from the boiled eggs and homemade soda bread he was used to, William was satisfied.

After breakfast he went back to the wooden hut to help with cleaning and tidying up the barrack room. All the new recruits, the 'rookies', had to pitch in. It was William's first real experience of working as part of an organised team. It had only been at harvest time, turf cutting and a few other farm tasks, that he had been required to work in conjunction with others. He had spent a lot of time with friends and he had lived as part of a large family, but a great deal of his leisure time had been spent alone on the riverbank. He had never been one to take part in team sports. And after three weeks at the training depot he was coming to grips with the fact that part-time training with the Irish rebel irregulars did not compare with life in the British army. Training with the rebels was not a twenty-four hours a day job, they did not live, eat and sleep together like regular soldiers. Every aspect of army training, he was learning, was designed to instill the concept of teamwork, and that included cleaning the hut. By now the discipline and training was beginning to tell and the recruits were starting to think and act as a unit, irrespective of background, religion or social status. As the only Irishman, William had worried that he might face some form of prejudice because of what was currently happening at home, but this proved not to be the case.

He immediately became known as 'Paddy', a name he realised he would have to live with for the rest of his army service, but otherwise he was completely accepted; as were the 'Jocks', and the 'Taffs'.

The first parade of the day was at ten minutes past eight. The NCOs blew whistles, shouted "On parade, double up there', and the trainees lined up outside the hut. They were subjected to a close inspection by the squad sergeant and marched off to the parade ground for another inspection and 'square bashing'.

Boots had been energetically polished and buttons meticulously cleaned the previous night, but still the officer inspecting them managed to find fault, and couple of members of the squad were placed 'on orders'. Williams had so far avoided this form of punishment, which usually involved giving up free time for 'fatigues' in the cookhouse or tidying up around the camp. The inspection over, they began to learn the intricacies of rifle drill. This was the first time they had taken their rifles on parade and there was much excitement about this significant step forward in their training. It was hot sweaty work. The sergeant gave them a short breather to watch a more experienced squad at the other side of the square and they were moved to try and emulate them. At ten-forty there was a twenty minute break for a cup of tea and a smoke in the canteen. Then it was back to the rigours of rifle drill.

At midday they were released for a quick wash before dinner. The bugle sounded at twelve-thirty and the hungry squad headed for the cookhouse. Meat, greens and potatoes, followed by duff for pudding, were consumed with the appetites of healthy young men. Now at last they were allowed some time for themselves before going on parade again at two.

William opened his locker and took out the letter home that he had been working on for the last week. He had already written a short note to his mother to let her know that he had arrived safely and was well. Now, however, he was engaged in writing a longer account of life as a recruit, but every time he thought he had finished something new cropped up and had to be added. Today it was rifle drill.

In the afternoon there was PT. They were beginning to feel the beneficial effects of the exercise and the organised games. William had tried his hand at football and cricket without any great success, but one day in the gym he had been introduced to boxing and had been told by the PT instructor that, with the proper training, he might be able to 'do a bit'.

After the gym they were loaded onto a lorry and driven to the tank training camp at Bovington. Out on the heath they watched in fascinated excitement as a squadron of tanks were put through their noisy smoky paces. William watched and was more convinced than ever that this was the life for him.

***

In Beaufort, Jack grinned to himself as he read his brother's enthusiastic letter home. Jack was a little surprised, but greatly pleased, that William seemed to have taken so well to soldiering. He was pleased because his mother had worried when she heard that William intended to join up. Telling her that things were different now to when he had volunteered during the war, and that the peacetime army would give William the chance to realise his desire to learn to drive a motor car, had little effect. The war, and all the tragedy it had brought, was still fresh in her memory. But William's latest letter, without doubt the longest he had ever written, seemed to have settled her down.

A second letter had been delivered in the last few days, this one specifically addressed to Jack: The Connaught Rangers had been ordered to prepare for embarkation to India. But before they left, Privates Daly and Coughlin would be coming home on leave. And they would look up the former Bombardier Jack Quinlan when they arrived home in Ireland.

211

# Chapter 40

It was raining a soft but persistent west of Ireland rain, and the night was dark. Because of the weather the timing had gone badly awry and the car was late. They lay in wait, two concealed in the bushes, one on either side of the road about twenty yards before the crossroads. At the cross, a road branched off from on the main Killarney to Killorglin road which led over Beaufort Bridge to the village. A further two men were huddled up against the parapets of the bridge, and two others were positioned some seventy yards away at the other end of the bridge in case anything went wrong and the car and its occupants managed to survive the first attack. They were getting cramped and wet, and the waiting was beginning to play on their nerves.

The tension was even starting to get to Kevin Ryan. In spite of the cap and trench coat he wore he was getting wet through, and his city shoes were proving totally unsuitable for an operation in the country. His poor choice of footwear had attracted amused comments from the five local men, and he was beginning to lose his temper with both their attitude, and what he saw as their total incompetence.

For the fourth time in the last hour he checked the loads in his British army issue Webley revolver. His experience in the streets of Dublin had given him a preference for the more easily concealed hand gun over the .303 Lee-Enfield rifles the country men carried.

The ambush site had been carefully chosen. Although Michael was unhappy about the attack taking place so near to Beaufort, where the weight of the first reprisals would undoubtedly fall, he had to agree that Kevin had chosen his ground wisely. As the car came along the road from Killarney it would be forced to slow right down for the tight left-hander over the old stone bridge. The bridge itself had originally been built to accommodate only horse drawn vehicles and was barely wide enough to allow passage for the large official car. Immediately across the bridge was another left hand turn through the gates of Beaufort House. So there was a stretch of at least three hundred yards where the car would be obliged to travel at a snail's pace.

Kevin, who had stationed himself so that he would be the first man to spot the approaching car, stood up and shook off the rain which had collected in the folds of his coat. For the fourth or fifth time he crept round to check on his men. He found them even less enthusiastic than they had been before it started raining and one had left his post to shelter under the bridge not far from Annie Quinlan's cottage for a sinful smoke. Kevin cursed him roundly under his breath. He had become totally fed up with the attitude of the local flying column towards what they saw as his private operation. The area commander was supportive of an attack being made on such a high profile target in his territory, but he could not see why it required someone to come down from Dublin to carry it out. He felt that his authority was being undermined, and given Kevin Ryan's air of superiority, he probably had a point. The men of the column, unsurprisingly, agreed with their commander, and Kevin had to enlist Michael Flynn's help to convince them of the importance of the attack to The Cause, and that the orders had been issued by 'The Big Fella' himself. But it was only when Michael confided to them that Kevin was one of 'The Twelve Apostles' that they grudgingly accepted the authority of the Dublin man. But they still looked to their commander for confirmation whenever Kevin gave them an order. Things improved somewhat when it was revealed that the column commander would be the one to select the men to carry out the actual attack, and the prospect of action meant that there were sufficient volunteers. Eventually planning began to proceed more smoothly. The attack was rehearsed as thoroughly as was possible given that the men had to familiarise themselves with the chosen site individually; a group gathered around Beaufort Bridge would have looked far too suspicious. Finally, Kevin was satisfied that everything was ready and that the attack would succeed. The planning had been meticulous. Nothing could possibly go wrong.

The rain and the waiting had, however, dented even his confidence. He could see that the men were by now so fed up with waiting that they were dangerously close to mutiny and might soon pack up and go home. It never occurred to him that these men had been trained to use hit and run tactics. They were accustomed to attacking static positions such as RIC posts, and had no experience of sitting for hours in the rain waiting for a moving target to come to them.

He had just got back to his position when the headlights of an approaching car flashed across the sky as it came over the crest of a hill. The lights pierced the rain as it came around the bend. He blew his whistle to alert the men, but they had already seen the lights. The car sped towards him. He had a fleeting thought that it was going too fast to take the bend over the bridge, and he suddenly realised that something was wrong. As the car drew level he realised what it was. He shouted to the riflemen to hold their fire but it was too late. The shots rang out. The car swerved off the road, burst through the hedge and careered down the grassy slope towards the river.

The attackers ran towards the stricken vehicle. Kevin yelled at them to get back. But the plan called for them to surround the car and cover Kevin while he made sure there were no survivors, so they ignored him and did as they had been ordered. He scrambled down the slope to the car. The Model 'T' rested half in, half out, of the river. In the driver's seat Pat Devlin lay slumped over the steering wheel. There was a neat round hole in the side of his head where a .303 bullet had entered and a gaping, bloody wound on the other side where it had exited.

As he ran back up to the road Kevin shouted at them to get back into position, but the second car had rounded the bend before they had a chance to comply. Both the driver and the bodyguard reacted quickly as the headlights lit up the armed men in running around in the road. The guard drew his revolver, lowered the window and fired in their general direction to throw the rebels off guard. The driver accelerated and instead of turning left to cross the bridge the official car sped off down the Killorglin road. The stunned ambushers dived for cover. Only Kevin managed to fire a shot as he came running through the gap in the hedge, but without being able to steady himself, his revolver was totally ineffective.

\*\*\*

Annie Quinlan was sitting by the fire waiting for the sound of the approaching car. As soon as she heard it she would rush out and open the gate. Jack had told her to rest easy, he would see to the gate and there was no need for her to go out into the rain. But she would not hear of it, opening the gate was her job and she would do it.

When the sound of gunfire came from across the river she wondered what all the noise was. Jack immediately recognised the sharp crack of rifle fire, and trying not to alarm his mother, he told her to stay where she was while he went to see what eejit was out poaching rabbits in this weather. He went out the back door, down to the riverbank and stood concealed behind a willow. Through the foliage and the rain he saw the vague outline of the car tilting into the water on the opposite bank, and his heart sank. Michael Flynn's warning of an attack on 'His Lordship' had proved to be all too accurate. He was trying to decide what he should do when another car came along the road and suddenly increased its speed. There were some more shots which he knew came from a revolver, and the car disappeared at speed towards Killorglin. It came to him that it must be this second car that was his employer's official transport and that it had narrowly escaped the

214

ambush. And there was only one possible answer to the question of whose car was in the river: Pat Devlin owned the only other motor vehicle in the area.

After the pistol shots and the sound of the car accelerating there were a few minutes silence. Then the shouting started. With everyone yelling at once Jack couldn't quite make out what was being said, but from the tone of the voices there were curses and accusations. One voice eventually seemed to gain control; he called for the 'bloody useless bastards to calm down and follow the escape plan'.

There were the sounds of movements. Suddenly a different voice cried out in some alarm:

"Jesus Christ! Your man here is shot."

It was obvious that someone had been hurt, but whether it was an occupant of the car in the river or one of the ambushers Jack couldn't tell. His first instinct was to go and help but his army training took over and he waited. When he was reasonably sure that it was safe to move he left the riverbank and went around the cottage to the main gates. From the shelter of one of the massive pillars he could see across the bridge.

What he witnessed brought back memories of Mesopotamia: Through the rain he saw two men in trench coats and caps, wearing bandoliers across their chests, and with rifles slung on their shoulders. Between them they were supporting a clearly badly wounded colleague. Jack was well aware that in this situation, and given his position at Beaufort House, he would be foolish to become involved; yet he knew that he had to do something to help. During the war against the Turks, apart for the incident where he had helped his two 'Ranger friends, he had been under orders to hold his position and leave the wounded to their fate. Here, however, he was under no such constraints and he knew in his heart that he would have difficulty living with himself if he stood by and did nothing.

He took a deep breath, stepped out from behind the pillar and walked out onto the bridge with his hands held high above his head. As he walked towards the three rebels he silently prayed that whatever had happened across the bridge had not made them nervous and trigger-happy enough to shoot at anything and everything that moved. He had seen that happen even with experienced soldiers. As soon as they saw him one man let go of his wounded comrade, unslung his rifle and pointed it at Jack. A look of recognition crossed his face but the gun remained steadily trained.

"Stay back, Jack," he said, "this has nothing at all to do with you."

Jack pointed at the injured man who now lay groaning on the ground. "I only came to help him," he said. "I'm not going to stick my nose into anything else."

It suddenly occurred to him that he had placed himself in a potentially very dangerous position: These men would at some stage realise that he could identify them, and if he wasn't extremely careful he could become a marked man.

"Go home Jack," the rebel insisted, "sure aren't we well able to look out for him ourselves."

Jack decided that it would only make matters worse if he backed off. "And sure how many wounded men have you nursed before? I've seem more men shot than you will in your whole life. I can see from here that he's hit in the leg and he's losing blood like a stuck pig. If you drag him around anymore you'll kill him."

They kept looking back across the bridge and were obviously anxious to be away from there, but they didn't object to Jack laying their hurt colleague on the road to have a better look at his wound. Before he could begin, however, he had to remove the heavy revolver from the man's unsteady grasp and hand it to one of his companions. His knowledge of first aid was basic to say the least, mostly picked up from watching medical orderlies at work, but he had learned enough to know that the first requirement was to put the patient's mind at ease. He tried to look confident as he made a perfunctory inspection of the wound. He frowned as he spotted the man's sodden city shoes, but he removed them, took out the laces and used them as a rough tourniquet to stem the bleeding.

He stood up. "I was right," he said. "He was hit in the leg just above his knee, the bullet is still is there, but I've seen worse. If he has proper medical attention he'll be all right. And if you're any kind of an army at all you'll have some sort of an aid station or someone trained to treat the wounded."

"Sure of course we have," said the rebel with some pride, "but we can't stop here or the peelers will be on us any minute."

The second rebel, who had so far remained silent, spoke up, and in a less belligerent tone than that of his companion: "What can we do Jack?"

"Well," Jack replied, "if you keep dragging him around he'll bleed to death. We'll take him into the dry arch where we keep the turf. You'll have to carry him like this:" He showed them how he and James Daly had moved Patrick Coughlin on the battlefield in Mesopotamia.

Before they went through the gates, Jack went into the cottage where he knew his mother would be getting anxious.

"What's going on out there, Jack?" Annie asked as he went in.

"There was some sort of a motor car accident across the bridge, Ma," he said. "You keep the young ones inside while I find out a bit more about it."

Annie looked at him sceptically. She had heard the shots and knew that he wasn't telling her everything, but she realised that he was right about keeping the children indoors and didn't question him further.

When he got back to the dry arch under the bridge the rebels had laid the injured man on the floor and, with unexpected foresight, were building a wall of turf to hide him. The wounded man had passed out but was breathing steadily.

"What'll we do now, Jack?" They had clearly decided that they had to trust him.

Although Jack knew them, he had been careful not to mention their names. He also recognised the wounded man as Michael Flynn's brother-in-law.

"One of you take my bike and find Mick Flynn," he said. "He can bring the bike back here. The other fella can go back over the bridge and watch out for the RIC. While I'm waiting I'll harness the pony and when Mick comes he can take your man here to the dressing station in the trap."

They didn't argue. They were glad to have someone taking charge. But as they started to move Jack added sharply: "And get rid of them rifles and bandoliers, the only good they'll do now is get us all killed."

By now it was getting late and Michael's parents had gone to bed, but he and Maureen were still up. They were beginning to think that the ambush had succeeded and Kevin was on his way back to Dublin as he had planned to do before the authorities had the time to react. Then the breathless rebel arrived on Jack Quinlan's bicycle and began blurting out what had happened.

"For God's keep calm," said Michael, "and keep your voice down or you'll wake the whole house."

The messenger calmed down and told them what he knew: The whole thing had gone terribly wrong; Pat Devlin's motor car was in the river; 'your man down from Dublin' had been hit by a stray bullet from the target car and was lying wounded in Quinlan's turf house; Jack Quinlan had told him to come and find Michael Flynn.

When he finished his report, Michael and Maureen held a quick conference. Because she had some basic nursing experience from The Rising she wanted to come with him, but Michael persuaded her to stay. He said that if they failed to reach the rebel first aid post hidden up in the Black Valley he would have to bring Kevin here, and she should make some preparations. It was a lame excuse and she knew that he was merely trying to keep her out of danger. But, for a reason Michael could not quite fathom, she did as he wanted without argument.

Jack was becoming increasingly nervous. The RIC should have been here by now. He made the wounded man as comfortable as he could, and would have liked to be able to take him indoors but that was out of the

217

question. Whatever happened, his mother and the children had to be kept out of this. He had harnessed the pony and the trap stood ready outside the gate by the time Michael and the rebel arrived on bicycles. Mercifully the rain had stopped.

They got Kevin into the trap and made him as comfortable as they could with the blankets that were kept under the seat for use by the more usual passengers. The local flying column man cycled off on Michael's bicycle to alert the aid station.

Before he climbed into the trap Michael held out his hand: "I won't forget this, Jack," he said, "and neither will Maureen. You stuck your neck out for us farther than we have a right to expect."

Jack took the offered hand. "Forget it, Mick," he said, "sure don't we all owe you a lot more for what you did for Jim and Bill that night at the bog."

# Chapter 41

As soon as the escaping car reached Killorglin it was driven directly to the RIC barracks, where the inspector immediately contacted his colleagues in Killarney.

The reason for the Killarney RIC men being slow to arrive at the scene of the ambush was that they were waiting for an army unit to back them up and help to secure the area while they carried out a detailed inspection. The senior inspector in Killarney was aware of the importance of the man in the car that had just been ambushed. He knew the country around Beaufort and the Gap of Dunloe, and he was wary of deploying his men there at night; in the daytime his men could move around in relative safety but the nights belonged to the IRA flying columns. He also realised that he would need more men in order to mount any kind of effective search for those who had carried out the attack. And a thorough search would have to be carried out. His superiors in Dublin, and perhaps even in London, would demand it. It would do no good to tell them that the perpetrators would be long gone by now and that there was little chance of catching the right men. So he decided to share the responsibility and call in the army.

This allowed Michael enough time to get Kevin up to the Gap where members of the flying column took over. Following procedures copied from the British army, the patient was given some first aid treatment in a cottage in The Black Valley and then transferred to receive more comprehensive medical treatment by a sympathetic doctor in Muckross near Killarney. The transfer was carried out by boat across the famous Lakes of Killarney.

Michael took the Quinlan's pony and trap back to his own farm. The RIC would certainly by now be at Beaufort House and his arrival there at this time of night would certainly have invited some searching questions. He was sure that Jack Quinlan would corroborate any story he might invent, but it went against the grain to involve the Beaufort House steward any further. Jack would understand if he waited a day or two before returning the trap and pony. He put away the trap, stabled and fed the pony, and headed for the farmhouse. A thought struck him so he turned back and removed the blankets he had wrapped around Kevin and hid them under a pile of straw. They could well be covered in bloodstains, and he would get Maureen to wash them before taking them back. She had heard the pony and trap drive up, and having checked that it was her husband, she raked the

219

dying fire to life and put the kettle on.

"Thank God he's all right," she said when he had finished telling her what had happened. "And thank you too Michael," she added with feeling.

"We have Jack Quinlan to thank as well," he said. "He didn't have to lift a finger for Kevin, and it will be hard for him if his boss ever finds out what he did."

She was puzzled: "Why did he do it, Michael?" she asked.

"I don't know for sure Maureen," he replied. "He said it was because he owed me something for what happened at the bog, but I think there's more to it than that. This is the second time Jack put himself out to help wounded men."

Somewhat to Michael's surprise she seemed content to leave it at that.

At the crossroads by Beaufort Bridge, Jack, for the second time that night, was staring down the barrel of an Enfield rifle; this one in the hands of an obviously experienced British soldier. The army detachment had reached the ambush site and found him trying to pull a dead body out of a bullet-riddled car which had run into the river. The young lieutenant in charge was not prepared to take chances, and ordered him to be held at gunpoint until the police arrived. The RIC inspector in charge recognised 'His Lordship's' steward, but he too was not prepared to be seen taking the slightest risk and so Jack remained under arrest. It was not until the official car returned under escort from Killorglin that his identity was established. His employer immediately vouched for him and he was released.

Next morning the authorities began implementing their usual procedure following a raid. By this stage in the war it had become commonplace and everyone knew what to expect, but it was none the less intimidating for the local population. There were random searches which left homes, farms and businesses in disarray with furniture and equipment broken, but nothing was found; there were threats and people were warned of the consequences if the perpetrators were not apprehended, but no one offered the slightest piece of information; there were arrests without a shred of evidence; and life in general was made as difficult as possible in an effort to get someone to 'inform'. But all to no avail. Although the ambush itself had resulted in complete failure, the republican propaganda machine still went into action and concentrated on there being yet more British reprisals against innocent civilians following an attack on a 'legitimate military target'. The authorities countered by blaming the IRA for the death of an innocent civilian, in this case one Patrick Devlin, who was described as 'a well respected businessman'. In view of the importance of the man who had been attacked, however, and in answer to pressure from other possible targets, the senior officials at Dublin Castle felt that they had to do more.

Two detectives were drafted in from 'G Division' or Political Section of the RIC at Dublin Castle. These men were able detectives, but they belonged to the unit which had been singled out and threatened by Michael Collins. They were glad to have a break from Dublin, but they knew that Collins' influence reached across the entire country. In spite of this they had to be seen to have carried out a thorough investigation.

Jack Quinlan, as the only known witness was questioned at length. For the most part he told the truth, but maintained that he had not ventured over the bridge until he was absolutely certain that the coast was clear, and when he finally did so he had not seen anyone. He had suspected that the crashed car belonged to the local publican, Pat Devlin, and yes he knew a bullet wound when he saw it. He had seen enough of them in Mesopotamia. The detectives learned that he had been the one to warn his employer of the possibility of an attack and that the original information had come from his brother who had simply picked up vague references locally and brought them to him. Although what his brother told him was based only on local rumours he had felt it his duty to report it. His brother was now serving in the Tank Corps. Because much of their lives were spent dealing with vague hints and rumours Jack's story was a familiar one, and the detectives believed him.

Jack thanked his lucky stars that the rain had washed the blood from the bridge before it had a chance to dry and leave telltale stains. But he could not escape the fact that in Ireland these days, nobody, no matter who, could avoid becoming involved in this War of Independence.

Michael Flynn's father too, had similar thoughts when he wondered about the comings and goings in the night and the presence of Quinlan's pony and trap in his farmyard. He had of course heard of the events at Beaufort Bridge and the death of Pat Devlin; the whole parish knew about that almost as soon as it had happened. In his heart he knew that Michael was somehow involved, and Maureen too, and he could not hide from those facts for much longer.

The 'G men' turned their attention to interviewing and intimidating the men who had been arrested but, as usual, they got nowhere. They looked into Pat Devlin's past and learned that he had been a confirmed nationalist, that his wife had died several years ago and that his son would take over the shop, farm and pub. But they found nothing to provide them with a clue as to who had carried out the ambush. Eventually they came to the entirely reasonable conclusion that, bearing in mind the person involved, the raid had not been planned locally but at a much higher level in the Nationalist movement. Their reason for reaching this, not inaccurate, assessment was not based on detective work but on the mistake so often made by officers based at Dublin Castle: they badly underestimated the extent and thoroughness of the countrywide organisation set up and run by Michael Collins.

In the aftermath of the attack 'His Lordship' was approached by colleagues in London regarding the advisability of travelling backwards and forwards to Ireland. They expressed the strong opinion that he should move permanently back to London. His answer to that was that his wife would not hear of moving house again, and in any case he was not prepared to succumb to terrorist threats. He would resign before he would do that. The result was a directive to the RIC to increase security and alertness in the Killarney area. Reinforcements were sent, and a plain clothes unit established in the town.

Pat Devlin's funeral was attended almost as well as the Flynn wedding had been. The wake in the pub the night before was a riotous affair, one of which Devlin himself would undoubtedly have approved. The funeral service and Requiem Mass in the church were conducted solemnly and with dignity, but the actual internment in the churchyard took on a different aspect: In spite of the feelings he had expressed about the Beaufort publican, Collins ordered that the deceased should be buried with full military honours. The coffin was draped with the tricoloured flag of the Irish Republic, and men of the Irish Republican Army in full uniform fired a volley over it as it was lowered into the ground.

For different reasons neither Jack Quinlan nor Michael Flynn, who stood together at the graveside, were entirely happy with the show of force: Jack, because he had foolishly allowed himself to be lured into taking part in something he should have kept well clear of, and Michael because he still felt some responsibility for the publican's death.

At the doctor's house in Muckross the bullet was removed from Kevin Ryan's leg. Without recourse to a proper operating theatre the doctor did the best he could, and while Kevin was expected to make a full recovery, he could well be left with a pronounced limp. As soon as the patient was fit to be moved he would be taken to somewhere further away from Killarney and eventually back to Dublin. Michael and Maureen were kept in the picture regarding his progress but under no circumstances would they be allowed to visit. Kevin remembered being hit and the two flying column members helping him. There had been no reason why they should have done that: in the heat of the moment he had not realised how badly he had been wounded and had ordered his men to get away quickly, so they could quite easily have left him. He was grateful that they hadn't and was forced to rethink his opinion of the 'country culshies'. But he only had vague recollections of what had happened once they had half dragged half carried him across the bridge. It would be some time before he learned about the man who had saved his life by applying the tourniquet. From his point of view, however, the only good thing to come out of the whole affair had been the death of Pat Devlin.

He knew that he would have to provide Michael Collins with a full explanation when he got back to Dublin. But for the moment his main worry was that a limp might seriously limit his ability to continue functioning as one of 'The Twelve Apostles.

# Chapter 42

Tension was still running high among the RIC officers in Killarney, and keeping alert was the order of the day. The plain clothes officer on duty at the railway station noted the two men getting off the mid-afternoon train. They were each carrying light travelling bags and did not have the look of either farmers or businessmen, and such was their demeanour that for a moment he thought they might be fellow RIC officers. But had that been the case he would have been pre-warned, so he decided to keep an eye on them. He followed them into the buffet where they ordered cups of tea, and his suspicions were immediately aroused when he heard one of them asking the waitress for directions to Beaufort and where they could find some form of transport to get them there.

The RIC man sauntered out of the buffet then dashed into the station master's office and telephoned the barracks. When privates James Daly and Patrick Coughlin of the Connaught Rangers exited the station they found themselves surrounded by heavily armed policemen.

Private Daly protested loudly that they were British soldiers home on leave. As he reached inside his coat for his identification papers and leave pass a nervous young policeman knocked his arm aside with a rifle butt. At that, an already angry Daly became incensed. Completely oblivious of the threatening rifles he swung around, hit the policeman squarely in the mouth with his clenched fist and knocked him cold. Had it not been for the quick, and in the circumstances, courageous, action of the experienced RIC sergeant, Daly and Coughlin would have been shot down there and then. Taking his life in his hands the sergeant jumped in front of Daly and shouted "Hold your fire". Fortunately for both himself and the 'Rangers his men obeyed. After a scuffle Daly and Coughlin were handcuffed, marched off the RIC barracks, their bags were confiscated and they were thrown into a cell to cool off.

James Daly was furious about the way he had been treated, cursing the policemen and vowing vengeance on all concerned. He and Patrick Coughlin were nearing the end of their two week's embarkation leave and had simply been on their way to see Jack Quinlan when, for no reason they could think of, they had been surrounded by armed RIC officers. Since arriving in Ireland, Daly had carefully noted everything he saw and heard regarding the war being waged against the British authorities by the Irish

Nationalists in the form of the IRA. While waiting in the depot at Dover he had kept himself informed as best he could by reading the newspapers and letters from home, including those from Jack Quinlan. But his first real indication of what he could expect to find in his homeland came when the 'Rangers were given permission, and indeed advised, to wear civilian clothing when they went home. The more he observed what was happening in Ireland the more he became convinced of the justice of the Republican cause; and the more frustrated he became at not being able to do anything positive to help. As a professional soldier he knew that he had much to contribute, but as a British professional soldier he also knew that he had to obey orders, return to his unit, and embark for India. By the time they had reached Beaufort his frustration was fast approaching boiling point; and being arrested without any just cause had been the last straw.

The two prisoners were left to cool off in the cell off while the duty RIC inspector went through their identification papers and leave passes. Although not entirely familiar with army documents, he could find nothing amiss. And a search of their travelling bags seemed to support their claim to be army men. While he waited for Private Daly to calm down sufficiently to be interviewed the inspector considered his own position:

In spite of the situation in Killarney, arresting two British soldiers home on leave would not look good on his record. And to make matters worse, it would certainly provide the Nationalists with even more ammunition for the propaganda war. He was tempted to simply let the two 'Rangers go, but one of his own men had been injured in the fracas; and he would have to do something about that or the already fragile morale situation in the barracks would tumble to a new low.

In the cell, Patrick Coughlin watched as his friend's rage gradually abated and was replaced by a mood of cold, grim, determination.

"For Jesus' sake hold on to your temper now, Jim," he said quietly, "or we'll be spending the rest of our leave in this bloody cooler. And don't forget that if it wasn't for that sergeant, things might be a lot worse."

When they were eventually marched in handcuffs to the inspector's office to be interviewed they were surprised to find an army officer, a captain, waiting with the policeman. The inspector had resolved his dilemma: he had decided that as the prisoners were soldiers this was really an army matter.

Seeing the officer, the two privates immediately came to attention as smartly as the handcuffs would allow. The captain had been harbouring thoughts about stolen identification papers, it would not be the first time the rebels had done that, but he knew experienced soldiers when he saw them and ordered them to 'stand at ease'. He also suggested that the handcuffs be removed. The policeman reasserted his position by questioning them about what they were doing in Killarney, and why they had asked for directions to Beaufort. When he learned that the 'Rangers were simply on their way to visit an old friend they had served with in Mesopotamia, the soldier asked a few questions about the actions they had taken part in, and was satisfied that they were telling the truth about having served there. The inspector asked who the friend in Beaufort was, and he visibly started when he heard that it was Jack Quinlan. He suggested to the army man that they suspend the interview while the 'Rangers' statement was verified. The captain agreed, and to the surprise of the two privates, he asked the inspector if they could be taken to the canteen for a cup of tea rather than being returned to the cells. As it would be impossible for the prisoners to escape from the barracks, the inspector agreed, but he was also aware that in the event that the prisoners were proved to be friends of 'His Lordship's' steward it might be as well to treat them leniently. Before they were marched out by the RIC sergeant, the captain looked squarely at Daly and warned him that at the first sign of trouble he would be taken under close arrest to the army base.

In the canteen, Coughlin thanked the sergeant for his swift action outside the railway station and Daly, albeit grudgingly, concurred with a nod to the RIC man. In the office, the inspector explained to the army man who Jack Quinlan was, and that he had been the one to alert them to the possibility of the owner of Beaufort House being in danger of attack by the IRA. They discussed their options and agreed on a way forward.

Jack was supervising some of his men repairing the drive, while keeping one eye on the main gate in anticipation of the arrival of the two Connaught Rangers at Beaufort. One of the maids came from the house to tell him that there had been a telephone message asking him to go immediately to the police barracks in Killarney. Thinking that the summons had something to do with the ambush, he hurried to Killarney in the hope that he would be back by the time his friends arrived, and it came as a shock to find that they had been arrested. In the police barracks the two 'Rangers again stood rigidly to attention as Jack formally identified them. They were trying hard not to grin at the sight of their old friend who, from force of habit, was also standing to attention in the presence of the officer. The formalities over, they were ordered to stand at ease while the captain and inspector told them what had been decided:

Private Coughlin would not have to face any charges whatsoever and was free to go, but Private Daly had assaulted a policeman and would have to answer for that. Bearing in mind, however, that the Connaught Rangers were shortly due to embark for India, the case would have to be dealt with by his Battalion Commander. In the meantime he would forfeit what was left of his leave and immediately return to his unit. An old soldier like Private Coughlin was well aware that this did not strictly conform to King's Regulations, and he suspected that neither did it comply with civilian law, even the emergency powers in place in Ireland. But all in all he realised that they had got off relatively lightly.

The captain again looked pointedly at Daly: "Do you accept my findings private?" he asked. "If you don't you have a right to ask for a formal hearing which could well recommend that you face a court martial."

Daly came to attention. He definitely did not agree that he was guilty of anything, in fact he felt that it was he who had been assaulted, and that he had merely defended himself. He saw his arrest as the final proof of the wrongs being done by the British authorities in Ireland. But for now there was little he could do about it, and he had been up before his Battalion Commander enough times to know that this was an argument he couldn't possibly win.

"Yes sir," he said reluctantly.

"And you, Coughlin?" asked the captain.

Private Coughlin too came to attention: "Yes sir," he said. "But begging your pardon sir, I'd like to have a drink with Bombardier Quinlan here before I go back to Dover. He saved my life in the war, and it might be the last chance we'll have to meet for years. Private Daly was hurt out there too sir, so would it be all right if he comes with us? Sure won't the two of us go straight back to the regiment first thing in the morning." He briefly explained what had happened in Mesopotamia.

Neither the captain nor the inspector, were happy about Daly having a drink. They were convinced that it could only lead to trouble.

But the captain thought it over: "I'm prepared to allow you to spend a few hours with Mr Quinlan before returning to your unit, Daly," he said. "But there will be no drinking, and I'm certain that after what happened, the inspector's men will only be too happy to lock you up again if you even step inside a public house."

"Sure they'll be coming back to Beaufort with me sir," said Jack. "My mother has everything ready to put them up for the night. And anyway there's only one pub there, and British soldiers aren't welcome in it these days."

Since Pat Devlin's death this last wasn't strictly true, but it was enough to sway the captain. "All right, but I want you on your way back to your regiment in the morning, Private Daly."

"Sure won't I make sure of that sir," said Coughlin. With that their belongings were returned and they were dismissed.

Outside the barracks there was a proper reunion with handshakes and backslapping. Jack had his bicycle, but suggested that he could leave it in town and hire a jaunting car to take them to Beaufort. In spite of Daly being identified as a British soldier they knew that the police would be harbouring resentment over what had happened outside the station and Jack wanted to get him out of Killarney as soon as possible. It would only take a wrong word from an RIC man to set the short-tempered 'Ranger off again. Patrick Coughlin, who had been casting anxious glances at his friend, agreed. So they arrived at the Quinlan cottage in some style where Annie was delighted to welcome them with a special meal.

After supper, Michael Flynn dropped in to renew acquaintance with Patrick Coughlin and meet James Daly. Annie sent the children to bed, and retired herself shortly after to allow the men to talk in the kitchen. James Daly seemed relaxed and friendly, but both Jack and Patrick knew that he had something on his mind and were uneasily aware of what it was. As soon as Annie had gone to bed he brought up the subject that had been on the tip of his tongue all evening.

He looked directly at Michael. "I hear that you know some of the boys doing the job against the bloody RIC, Mick."

"Sure there's nobody at all in Ireland who doesn't know someone who is fighting for our freedom, Jim." Michael knew that it was a vague reply, but after what Jack Quinlan had done to help Kevin Ryan, he was determined not to put his old friend in an awkward position, by openly admitting that he was one of 'the boys'.

But Daly now had a head of steam and ploughed on: "Well I tell you this lads, I'm going to be joining them." He turned to Coughlin: "I mean it Pat, after what I've seen here at home I'm not going back to the bloody army. How can I go off out to India and do the same thing to the poor bloody Indians that we're doing here in Ireland. You can do the same, but I won't hold it against you if you don't."

"And what would you do without me you eejit?" said Coughlin, "sure you wouldn't last five minutes if I wasn't around to wipe your arse. But listen, Jim, we can't go AWOL here in Beaufort. After what happened today we'd only cause trouble for Jack, sure we're as good as being in his custody."

He knew that it would be useless to remind his fellow 'Ranger of the consequences of deserting and being caught, but he also knew that he would follow Daly in whatever his friend decided to do. And while the perplexities involved did not escape him, it seemed obvious that his comrade had made up his mind.

But surprisingly, Daly did stop to consider what Patrick had said. "You're right there Pat," he said, "we'll have to leave it until we're well away from Beaufort before we jump ship."

He turned again to Michael: "Tell me now Mick, sure there must be a whole lot of old British Tommies fighting for their own country now. And from what Jack was telling us about the shambles here a few nights ago I'd say that a few more good men would come in handy."

From his previous meetings with Patrick Coughlin, and from what he had heard about James Daly, Michael had known that this subject was bound to come up. Being pre-warned, he'd had time to think about his position and what he should tell the two 'Rangers. He had also tried to talk it over with Maureen, but she had not seemed very disposed to discuss it, and he put her reticence down to her dislike of British soldiers.

When he finally spoke, his words came as a surprise to Jack, and made him realise how much life had changed his easy going old schoolmate and made him into a man who thought deeply about things. And he wondered at how well informed Michael was on political matters:

"It's true, Jim," he said, "there are lots of ex-British soldiers serving with the IRA, and a grand job they're doing too. But they served their time and were de-mobbed after the war, like Jack here. But if you lads joined The Cause you'd be deserters, and that's a horse of a different colour. The British would have an entire army out after you and if they caught you, they might catch a whole flying column as well. And you'd get the blame for it. So the first thing you'd have to do is to convince the boys that you were real deserters and not Brit spies. But that's not the worst of it: The minute Michael Collins heard about you, and you can be sure that he would, he wouldn't let you go anywhere near any of the real fighting."

He let that sink in. "Why do you say that, Mick?" asked Coughlin.

"Look at it from his angle, Pat," said Michael, "what better propaganda tool could he be handed than British soldiers deserting to join The Cause? He'd have you paraded up and down the country as examples of what every Irishman should be doing. And I wouldn't mind betting that when things got too hot for you here he'd send you off to Eamonn de Valera to do the same thing in America. Sure it's a chance 'The Big Fella' would never be able to resist."

Even Daly, the man of action, had to accept that what Michael said was true, and had no real reply. "Jesus Christ!" he exclaimed in frustration, "sure isn't Ireland gone to the dogs altogether."

When he got home, Michael found Maureen waiting by the fire as usual. When she had made him a cup of tea he explained what had happened. He did not try to hold back the fact that what he had said to the two Connaught Rangers might well have persuaded them not to desert and join The Cause. He half expected her to be angry with him, but although she

229

listened to every word, he thought that for some time now she seemed not to have the same enthusiasm for The Cause as she once had.

She came to sit on the floor beside his chair. She looked up at him and smiled: "Aren't you the clever one Michael Flynn," she said, "and sure you'd make a grand politician. But sometimes you're as blind as a bat, and you can't see what's under your nose."

Then she told him that he was to become a father.

# Chapter 43

As he rose from his morning prayers he took a half turn to his right and looked out to the west beyond the wire to the hills of his native Afghanistan. Beyond them he caught glimpses of the rising sun touching the snow capped mountains of the Hindu Kush. Nearer to where he stood, as if inviting him to enter, he could see the gap in the mountains which marked the eastern entrance of the Khyber Pass.

The defeat of Turkey in the Great War had been met with dismay by the Muslim tribesmen of the Northwest Frontier Province of India and sparked off an increase in the lawlessness which had always been a feature of that turbulent outpost of the British Empire. In spite of the outcry following the massacre at Amritsar the previous April, the Rowlatt Act was still very much in force in India, and especially in the Frontier Province.

The prisoner standing by the wire had been picked up by Indian Colonial Government officials backed up by British soldiers and interned without trial in the camp near the city of Peshawar. He looked around at his fellow internees. Most of them were clad in the usual miscellaneous collections of ragged cotton and furs of their various tribes. He saw members of not only his own Pashtun (or Pathan) tribe but also Mashuds and Wazirs and men proudly representing most of the other warlike tribes who inhabited this vast frontier area. It struck him that there was something strange about his fellow frontiersmen this morning, and it took him a few minutes thought before realising what it was: none of them were armed. Men in this part of the world would never even dream of venturing forth without a weapon of some sort, and to be forced to do so was the ultimate humiliation. A hill tribesman would never be seen abroad without his rifle, be it an ancient muzzle loading jezail or a copy of a British Martini or Enfield. The British arms were mostly copied with amazing skill from stolen originals by native gunsmiths using the most rudimentary tools. Men from the towns and cities would carry at least a lethal curved dagger. The prisoner himself wore a Chitraly hat and shalwar kamees, clothes which marked him out as a man of higher rank and, unusually for the time and place, he rarely if ever bore arms.

On another day these tribesmen would have been sworn enemies, but today they were united in a common cause: hatred of the British backed authorities who had deprived them of their jealously guarded freedom.

The camp, which had obviously been built in anticipation of the Act becoming law, was almost filled to capacity. And the prisoner was aware that hundreds of other camps had been set up all over India; he had already been held in one in the nearby Punjab. Like his fellow prisoners he would have been classified as a 'terrorist'. But while he personally preached non-violence, his fellow tribesmen were merely continuing to follow the warlike traditions that had been a way of life in this belligerent borderland since Alexander the Great had passed through the Khyber Pass three centuries before the Birth of Christ. To them the British were just the latest addition to a long line of invaders, and were being met with the same aggressive resistance that had greeted all the others. All that internment would achieve would be to unite them against a common enemy. But it grieved him to think that there were also a few others in the camp, mostly merchants, who, unlike himself, were guilty of nothing more than being in the wrong place at the wrong time. Up to now they had been peaceful men and he was saddened to think that internment might easily serve to lead them down the road to violence. Although he took pride in being a man of peace, and the authorities knew full well that he was, he continually spoke out against British rule. He preached peaceful resistance, yet he was deemed to be a dangerous man guilty of sedition. He had, therefore, been singled out for internment.

His name was Abdul Ghaffer Khan. By profession he was a schoolteacher and by conviction he was a disciple of Mahatma Ghandi. In time, Ghaffer Khan would become one of the greatest practitioners of non-violent resistance to British rule in India. There was a determination in India to oppose the Rowlatt Act, which, he feared, for the present at least, could only lead to bloodshed.

*** 

The British Government responded to the situation in India in exactly the same way they were dealing with the problem in Ireland: they met force with force. Reinforcements sent out to defend the Empire included a battalion of Connaught Rangers. They left the army depot in Dover and arrived in India late in 1919, where they were posted to Jullundur and Solan in The Punjab. Old sweats like Privates Daly and Coughlin soon settled in and helped the new recruits find their feet. By Christmas they were ready to take up their duties.

In the hustle and bustle of the preparations for embarkation the fracas involving privates Daly and Coughlin in Killarney seemed to have been forgotten. They expected to be called before the battalion commander at some point during the voyage, but when this did not materialise, Coughlin suspected that the army and police in Killarney were just glad to get the affair over and done with and consequently had not submitted a report. The longer they waited without any developments the more convinced they became that this must be the case. But it was little consolation to James Daly. He had been profoundly affected by his arrest and as a result he developed an even deeper loathing for the RIC. He greedily devoured every scrap of information regarding the war in Ireland that he could get his hands on, and the more he learned the more his resentment about being sent out to India grew. He went through the motions and obeyed orders, but it was obvious that he was no longer the epitome of the professional soldier he had once been.

What worried Patrick Coughlin most was that his friend made no particular effort to hide his views on the situation in Ireland. He was prepared to talk long and loud to anyone prepared to listen and eventually some of his fellow soldiers did actually begin to listen. Coughlin knew that before long this would get Daly into serious trouble.

***

In Wareham, William Quinlan had finished his basic training and had begun a course of driver training. Being taught by the British army meant that he not only learned to drive but was also given a thorough grounding in the mechanics of motor transport. Whether coming to grips with the working of the internal combustion engine in the classroom, or putting the theory into practice on the roads of South Dorset, he took to it like a duck to water. He soon became proficient at driving the Peerless three-tonner and passed the course with flying colours.

There were times, however, when he missed home. As Christmas approached he worried about what kind of reception he would receive if he went back to Beaufort for the holiday. He knew that he would be welcomed by the family, but Jack had written to tell him of the treatment the two Connaught Rangers had received and warned him to be careful. It was not his own safety or reputation that worried him, joining the army had, he was certain, been the correct decision for him, but his family might well suffer as a result his coming home. He briefly considered volunteering for duty over the Christmas period thereby giving one of his friends the opportunity of spending the holiday with his family. But in the end he knew that his mother would prefer to see him even if it meant being subjected to pointed and even threatening remarks in the village, or after Mass on Sunday mornings. So he bit the bullet, asked for and received permission to wear civilian clothing, and went home on leave.

His journey was uneventful, and his welcome at the cottage everything he had expected. His mother was delighted to see him and set about preparing a very special Christmas.

"What about people like Mick Flynn, Jack, will they be wanting to have anything to do with me anymore." The brothers were walking along the riverbank; William could not resist seeing how they were looking after his favourite fishing spots.

"Ah sure there's no need to be worrying about Mick, Bill," said Jack. "He's well in with 'the boys' all right and I don't know what he is doing with them, but in spite of everything sure he's still the same decent Mick Flynn he always was."

This was borne out after Mass on Christmas morning when Michael and Maureen came across to greet William. William's mother had already told him that Michael and Maureen were about to start a family so congratulating them provided an excellent way of opening the conversation. Before leaving for home and Christmas dinner, Michael and William agreed to meet again the following day. As usual they walked by the river and talked frankly:

"How's Kevin doing now?" William had already heard from Jack about the ambush on the bridge and Michael had filled in some further details.

"He's grand thank God, he's back in Dublin and being well looked after. I don't know what Maureen would do if he'd been killed or taken, losing a second brother for The Cause would have taken away all the pleasure of expecting a baby."

"I thought she'd be mad at me for joining the army, but sure she never said a cross word about it."

Michael thought for a minute before answering. "She's changed a lot over the last year," he said. "Things will have to be different for me too. I'll have a family to think about so I won't be able to spend much time on other things, if you see what I mean."

"Jesus Mick, you're not thinking of giving up The Cause are you? I don't know what you're up to with 'the boys' but sure don't you know very well that they'll never let you get out."

"You're right there, Bill," said Michael. "And sure I'll never give up trying to make Ireland free. But between you and me, I have something in mind that might solve the problem for me, and I was hoping that you might do me a small favour."

Before the surprised William could answer, Michael added: "Sure it's nothing that could cause you any trouble Bill, all I'm asking is for you to put something in a letter to Jim. I don't like to ask Jack, it wouldn't be fair on him, but if you were to post it from England sure nobody else will know a thing about it."

William asked the obvious question and Michael explained as he handed over a sealed and addressed envelope: "The truth of it is that I want Jim to post this letter for me from inside America. If that was posted in the normal way from anywhere here in Ireland, or even in England, there's a danger that it would be opened. But if you put it in a letter to your brother nobody will take any notice."

William glanced at the address on the envelope. "Jesus! and what would you be doing writing to Eamonn de Valera, Mick?"

Michael explained what he had in mind and exhorted William to keep it to himself. "But you'll have to let Jim in on it. Do you think he'll do what I'm asking?"

William didn't hesitate. "Sure of course he will, Mick." Then he added: "I hope to God that it all works out for you."

Although theoretically on different sides in the war they parted as friends. In late 1919 this was still possible. But events would soon put an end to any lingering goodwill between the warring factions; events which would result in 1920 becoming known in Irish history as 'The Year of Terror'.

# Chapter 44

In November 1919, the Irish Committee of the British Cabinet recommended that Ireland should not be granted a republic, either north or south. Instead it would get two parliaments with limited powers, one in Dublin and one Belfast, linked under the Crown by a Council of Ireland. Even if accepted by parliament, this would be a long way short of the thirty-two county republic currently demanded by the Irish nationalists. In effect the Committee were making Sinn Fein an offer they couldn't possibly accept.

While moves, however lacking in substance, were being made to find a political solution, the government set about recruiting a special force to support the RIC in the bitter fight against the IRA. And there was no shortage of volunteers. There were plenty of ex-servicemen, survivors of the Great War who, for a variety of reasons, were only too willing to sign up for duty in Ireland. They had expected to come home to 'a land fit for heroes' but had been sadly let down, and instead they came home to a land of unemployment. They had either joined up, or had been conscripted, as very young men and now found that there was little call for men whose only work experience involved fighting. While in truth most had already had their fill of war, some volunteered simply out of economic necessity for the almost unheard of rate of ten shillings a day. But while initially some of these volunteers were accepted they were not exactly the kind of men the authorities were looking for; they had little use for men who might exhibit a reluctance to go back to war. Much different qualities were required. So most of the successful applicants came from among that class of men thrown up by every war: men who, after the fighting was over, could no longer settle down to a life of peace and quiet. They actually missed the danger of war and couldn't wait to get back the feeling of excitement engendered by it. These men, the organisers of the special force were convinced, would be much more likely to show the ruthless streak, and indeed the brutality, they felt the situation in Ireland demanded. In this they were not to be disappointed.

The new force began training, and because of a lack of both army and police uniforms' they were kitted out in a mixture on army khaki and police black. Because of this they were given the nickname 'Black and Tans', and as such would write an indelibly bloody chapter in Irish history.

Then, on January 15th 1920, local government elections were held under the authority of Dublin Castle – the seat of British power in Ireland. Although Sinn Fein still refused to sit in the House of Commons, they opted to take part in the election, and won 172 of the 206 seats contested. Most of the remaining seats went to the Unionists in the north.

One of the successful candidates in County Kerry was Michael Flynn.

\*\*\*

Having spent Christmas 1919 at home on the farm, Michael and Maureen went to Dublin to spend New Year with her family. A few weeks before they left, however, Michael approached his wife about the possibility of him standing as a Sinn Fein candidate.

Maureen, while clearly happy at the prospect of him standing, was more than a little mystified when Michael first broached the subject: "Where in the name of God did you get that notion from?" she asked.

Michael laughed: "Sure didn't you put the idea into my head yourself, love," he said, "when you told me that I'd make a grand politician. I don't know why Sinn Fein would want to be putting up candidates in an election organised by 'The Castle' but they are, and I'm thinking that I'd like to be a part of it."

He grew more serious: "You know yourself Maureen darlin' that for the last couple of years I've been looking for a way to do my best for Ireland. We know very well that I'm not cut out to be a soldier, and the more I see of what's going on in Ireland these days the more I think that working for Michael Collins isn't the right thing for me either."

"But didn't you do a grand thing helping your man de Valera to escape from jail over in England, and you can be very proud of yourself for that. So why wouldn't you want to do something like that again if they want to you?"

"Oh I'll do it again if I get the call," said Michael. "But the truth of it is that it's all getting a bit too complicated for me. Everyone knows that I'm mixed up in something for The Cause, but I can't say a word to them about it."

Maureen was slightly taken aback. "But sure you knew it would be like that when you started, Michael."

"True enough love, but it's getting very hard to look people like Jack Quinlan straight in the face, not to mention my own father. And another thing, any day now with all the talk going around in places like Devlin's, the RIC will start to look at me a bit harder. They're not all complete eejits you know."

They sat quietly for a short while. Then Michael took her hand. "It's like this, Maureen my love, what's bothering me the most is that I'll turn out to be exactly like the fella I killed that night at the bog. He spent all his time working all alone in the dark, and in the end even his own side didn't know what devilment he was up to. And if I don't watch out I'll finish up like him. What good will that do you and the baby?"

Michael didn't know it, but having political ambitions put him a lot closer to 'Mr Jameson' than he would have been happy about.

Maureen realised that the last reason given by her husband was the most compelling for Michael. Her old instinct prompted her to tell him not to worry about her, The Cause should come first. But the baby changed everything, she could no longer think only of herself, and she was delighted to know that Michael felt the same.

"I think that you're right, Michael," she said, "If you were to put yourself up for election everybody will know where you stand, and where they stand with you. And there's nothing surer but that someday," she added with a smile, "your son will be able to say that his father is *Taoiseach* of the Irish Republic. But anyway whether you get in or not, we'll all be very proud of you Michael."

Suddenly she sat up and smiled at him. "But didn't you forget something important, my love?"

He gave her a puzzled look: "And what would that be, darlin'?"

"You'll have to join Sinn Fein, you won't be able to stand if you're not a member of the party!"

***

In Dublin, once they had seen Maureen's family, Michael went to the IRA 'safe house' where Kevin was making good progress recovering from his wounds. When he explained what he had in mind, slightly to Michael's surprise knowing as he did his brother-in-law's opinion of politicians, Kevin was supportive.

"That's grand Mick," he said, "sure it'll be great for Maureen and the baby." The bond between brother and sister was stronger than even Michael had suspected.

In spite of his busy schedule, Michael Collins agreed to see Michael, and if he expected 'The Big Fella' to express any criticism of the way the operation in Beaufort had resulted in failure, he need not have worried.

"These things don't always go to plan," Collins said. "And in the end we did achieve our principal objective in that the RIC now have to expend even more resources protecting all those wealthy British landowners who choose to live in Ireland. Besides, we can always try again if we need to keep up the pressure. By the way, I understand that Kevin Ryan may well owe you his life."

"Ah sure I had a lot of help there," said Michael. He explained in detail the circumstances of Kevin's rescue, including the part played by Jack Quinlan.

"Is he the same man who vouched for the two British soldiers in Killarney?" asked Collins.

Michael had the distinct feeling that Collins knew a lot more about the incident, and about Jack Quinlan, than he was letting on. Instead of giving a straight answer he said: "I'd say that those two Connaught Rangers are real Irishmen in spite of the uniform they're wearing, the Brits are playing safe by sending them out to India."

He expected Collins to continue questioning him about the affair, but 'The Big Fella' only laughed. "All right Michael," he said, "I can see how people might think that you have the makings of a politician. I'll sponsor your membership of Sinn Fein and endorse your candidature for the election. Have you approached any other sponsors?"

"I wrote to Mr de Valera in America," said Michael. And, knowing Collins' obsession with security, he quickly outlined the precautions he had taken.

"I'm fairly sure that he'll back me," he added.

Collins frowned. "Oh I'm certain of it," he said, "politics seems to be Dev's mission in life these days."

When Michael made no comment, 'The Big Fella' went on: "But there's something you should know about Sinn Fein's involvement in this election, and I'm sure you know enough by now to keep this strictly to yourself."

When he had finished his explanation he asked: "Do you still want to go ahead?"

"Sure why wouldn't I?" said Michael. "What you just said clears up something that was bothering me."

When they got back to Beaufort they made a point of telling Michael's father what he planned to do.

Mr Flynn was obviously pleased. "I'm glad for you Michael," he said. "I think that you might have hit on something that you've been after for a long time now. Sure you won't have to be hiding things from us anymore, and God knows, your mother will be as proud as punch when I tell her. Sure won't she be telling everyone her son is a County Councillor."

"I'll have to get in first, Da," said Michael. "But if I do, I'll be spending a lot of time over in Tralee, and I won't be much help to you here at home."

His father gave him a sideways look: "Sure didn't we do well enough without you when you were in the prison camp. And when you were up in Dublin working on the docks," he added pointedly. "We'll manage all right, to be honest with you now that the war is over, there's not the same demand for Irish produce over there in England."

Michael received a letter from James Quinlan in New York with a note from Eamonn de Valera enclosed, and as result, he was able to set about preparing for the election.

Support from both Eamonn de Valera and Michael Collins immediately opened all the necessary doors to the local Sinn Fein party machine based in Tralee, and Michael was soon endorsed as an official candidate. He attended a meeting for all those standing for the party in County Kerry where a senior party official from Dublin explained the plans for the election campaign. Posters and leaflets were quickly produced and distributed and preparations proceeded smoothly. Michael's greatest worry, however, was the requirement for public speaking; he knew that he was not a proficient orator. He received some basic tuition and was given some pre-prepared speeches to practice with, but when he tried them out on Maureen she was not overly impressed.

"It's not right Michael," she said. "You're a whole lot better when you're talking about what you believe in, and what you can do for Ireland, in your own words. Sure there's no need at all for you to be reading someone else's ideas. Why don't we try that?"

He worked at it with Maureen and his parents and finally felt confident enough to address a crowd of electors after Mass in Beaufort on the following Sunday.

That he successfully got his point across was confirmed by Jack Quinlan: "Good man yourself Mick Flynn, sure you talked more sense in five minutes than all the other politicians in Ireland could put across in a day."

A much more confident Michael repeated his speech outside the cathedral in Killarney on the Sunday prior to the election.

The day of the election arrived and polling proceeded without incident. All of the Nationalist factions obviously supported Sinn Fein, and as the election was held under the auspices of Dublin Castle, there was no interference from the authorities. The contradiction of the RIC being obliged to provide protection for Sinn Fein candidates, all of them supporters, and some even active members of the IRA, was yet another perplexity associated with the Ireland of the day.

In the event Michael Flynn was elected virtually unopposed. Soon afterwards, as Michael Collins had said they would, Sinn Fein Councillors broke with 'The Castle' and began setting up alternative administrations under the authority of *The Dail*.

# Chapter 45

The first contingents of Black and Tans began arriving in Ireland in March 1920. Eventually there would be close to 8,000 stationed in the country, the vast majority of them in the south. In theory they were supposed to support the RIC, but from the very beginning they, in effect, acted as an independent force. Their primary task was to make Ireland 'hell for the rebels to live in' and they were given *carte blanche* in choosing their methods for achieving it.

As former soldiers they found the discipline to be much slacker that they had experienced on the Western Front and other theatres of war. Because of this and, due to the fact that they found it difficult to fight against the IRA guerrilla tactics, they turned on and set about terrorising local Irish communities. They were prepared to torture, take hostage and even indiscriminately shoot anyone even remotely suspected of helping the rebels. A favourite tactic was to use innocent civilians as human shields to deter IRA attacks. They burned homes, farms, shops and creameries in an attempt to wage an economic war, and in an attempt to force people to 'inform'.

One divisional commander wrote:

*"If a police barracks is burned or if the barracks already occupied is not suitable, then the best house in the locality is to be commandeered, the occupants thrown into the gutter. Let them die there? The more the merrier.*

*Should the order ("Hands Up") not be immediately obeyed, shoot and shoot with effect. If the persons approaching (a patrol) carry their hands in their pockets, or are in any way suspicious-looking, shoot them down. You may make mistakes occasionally and innocent people may be shot, but that cannot be helped, and you are bound to get the right parties some time. The more you shoot, the better I will like you, and I assure you no policeman will get into trouble for shooting any man."*

But the Black and Tans could in no way be described as 'policemen'. They were not members of the properly established police force, the Royal Irish Constabulary. They were best described as irregular mercenaries and the RIC they were in Ireland to assist often feared them almost as much as did the people they terrorised. One RIC sergeant described them as being 'both a plague and a Godsend, they brought help but frightened even those they had come to help'.

These tactics, designed to undermine Irish morale and erode support for the IRA, had the opposite effect. The worse things got, the stronger feelings grew against British rule.

Among their principal targets for intimidation were members of Sinn Fein and especially those elected to public office. Thomas McCurtain, Lord Mayor of Cork, was shot down in front of his family simply for being a popular local figure. In common with the other elected Sinn Fein councillors who had broken ties with 'The Castle', Michael Flynn was a victim of constant harassment. He was followed, stopped without the slightest cause, and on two occasions he was arrested on the pretence that his 'record' as an internee after the Easter Rising marked him out as a 'terrorist'. He was released by the RIC, not by the 'Tans, but not before being threatened that should he put one foot wrong in future he would not get off so lightly.

Michael was by now experienced enough to be able to cope with anything they threw at him, but he worried for his wife and unborn child.

As a senior member of staff on an estate owned by an important British government official, Jack Quinlan was not subjected to any such rough treatment, but he nonetheless did not for one minute like what he saw happening all around him. Unlike many others in jobs like his, who jealously guarded their positions, he was not opposed to the idea of Ireland being free of British rule; in fact, providing it could be achieved by peaceful means, he thought that it would be good for the country. This did not stem from any great sense of patriotism, but rather from the point of view that an independent Ireland was the only way of improving the daily lot of the majority of Irish people. And, more importantly in Jack's opinion, it might herald the end of the pre-war social conventions still entrenched in Ireland; conventions which had obliged him to go to war, and in peacetime had allowed him little or no leeway in choosing how he should earn his living. He could see the old social orders being gradually eroded throughout the rest of the United Kingdom but not in Ireland. Jack knew that he was materially better off than the majority of his peers, but he recognised that this was the result of circumstances largely beyond his control, and not through any great endeavour on his part. In this he envied his brothers, James and William, who had been free to choose their own paths through life.

In common with the vast majority of Irishmen, however, he abhorred the methods employed by the British authorities in the shape of the Black and Tans in their efforts to deny the Irish their dream of independence. As well as being morally indefensible, Jack felt that their brutal methods would provide the IRA with an excuse to follow suit in their efforts to achieve independence. Attitudes would continue to harden on both sides and any prospect of a peaceful solution would be pushed further and further away. By now well established in his position of 'steward' at Beaufort House, Jack felt confident enough to bring up the subject in conversation with his employer.

For a member of the British Establishment, and someone who had been the target of an IRA ambush, the Englishman was surprisingly sympathetic to Jack's views. 'His Lordship' was not of course, in favour of Irish independence, he could not, and would not, support any break-up of the Empire, but he too was appalled by the behaviour of the 'Tans and he agreed with Jack that they would only hinder the search for a peaceful solution to 'the Irish problem'.

"I fear, Quinlan, that if things go on as they are there will soon not be even a single Irishman who will want to settle the thing peacefully."

"Oh I think there will still be a few, sir," said Jack. "There's Michael Flynn here in Beaufort for a start. Mick's heart is set on seeing Ireland free, as he puts it, but sure he's dead against people being killed to get it."

'His Lordship' was sceptical. "Isn't he one of the Sinn Fein councillors who broke away from the legally constituted authorities? I fail to see how you can have much faith in him."

Jack took a deep breath, he knew he might be treading on dangerous ground appearing to contradict his employer, but he voiced his suspicion that it might have been Michael Flynn who had 'tipped his brother the wink' about the danger of the IRA ambush. He didn't think that he was putting Michael in any danger because the RIC would never accept the idea of a Sinn Fein man being an informer.

'His Lordship' exhibited some surprise but did not press the matter. "It seems that the situation in Ireland may be more complex than I thought," was his only comment.

In spite of everything that had happened, and even though he did not know exactly what the newly elected councillor had been involved in, Jack still liked and was friendly with Michael Flynn. In fact he admired Michael for standing for election and had voted for him. He knew what Michael was going through at the hands of the Black and Tans and sympathised with him.

It had become customary for the Flynns to visit the Quinlan cottage on Sunday afternoons after lunch. Annie welcomed the chance to have a chat with Maureen while Michael, who still liked to walk by the river, went for a stroll with Jack.

"I'm sorry to hear about the way things are being made hard for you since you got elected, Mick," said Jack. "Sure the RIC and these Black and Tans have no right to be picking on someone who was voted in by the people fair and square. Is there no chance at all of a peaceful ending to all this trouble?"

"I wish to God that I could see one Jack," Michael replied. "I thought there might be, that's why I stood for election, but I'm sorry to say the British Government have put an end to it by sending in the 'Tans. All that's happening now is that both sides are digging in their heels. More 'Tans are arriving every day, and on our side, hundreds of lads are waiting their chance to join the IRA and fight them."

Jack sighed. "Sure haven't I seen it all before," he said sadly, "young men full of what they think is patriotism, jumping at the chance to fight without having any real notion of what they're fighting for. I saw them dying in droves and without ever knowing exactly why."

Michael did not agree. "I know what happened in the war Jack, and I can see your point. But this isn't a bit like that. It was different in the war: those young men had no idea at all of what it was all about until they were sent overseas to fight in places most of them had never heard of. But here in Ireland, they can see with their own eyes what's going on all around them. They're joining up to fight for their homes and their families here in their own country. And sure who can blame them?"

They walked on in silence. Beaufort House came into view above the trees.

"I suppose your man up at the house there was glad to see the 'Tans arriving," said Michael.

"Now there's a queer thing, Mick," Jack replied. "Wasn't I thinking the same thing myself, but when I asked him about it sure he was as much against the 'Tans as everyone else. Oh he's dead set against an independent Ireland, he made no bones about that, but he's not too happy about the way his government is going about stopping it happening."

"Is that right, even after what happened on the bridge?"

"Right enough, Mick," said Jack. "I was as surprised as yourself about it. But I was thinking since then that the only hope for Ireland is for people like you and him to get together and thrash it out between you."

Michael laughed. "I'm sorry to say you're dreaming Jack. There's as much chance of that happening as there is for the King to have a pint of porter with the Pope."

"What about that fella de Valera you always used to be talking about? Maybe he'll fix things when he comes home from America."

Since joining Sinn Fein, and becoming part of the accepted party

244

machine, Michael had learned a lot more about what de Valera was doing in the United States. And he began to understand why Michael Collins seemed to have lost much of his enthusiastic support for the 'President of the Irish Republic'. Across the Atlantic, 'Dev' was increasing support for the republican cause among the large Irish/American lobby and raising awareness of the plight of the Irish in the country at large. But, particularly because of his enormous ego, he was making as many enemies as he was friends. He was raising a great deal of money but, much to the frustration of Collins and others fighting the bitter war at home, not all of it was being channelled directly into providing arms for the IRA. Dev was insisting on holding back large amounts for possible future contingencies and, to Collins' great annoyance, this money remained under de Valera's personal control.

Michael was not prepared to impart any of this, even to Jack Quinlan, so all he said was: "We'll have to wait and see about that, Jack."

\*\*\*

As they cycled home they were stopped by a heavily armed Black and Tan patrol in a Crossley tender. The patrol had obviously been watching them because the officer in charge demanded to know what they were doing snooping around Beaufort House.

"We have you now Mister Sinn Fein councillor. We'll teach the likes of you that it doesn't pay to spy on a member of the British Government."

Before he could say a word, Michael was dragged off his bicycle and roughly thrown into the open back of the tender.

Maureen was livid. All the old prejudices and hatreds came flooding back. She turned on the officer.

"You bastard! Is this how the brave British army treats innocent Irish people, you should be ashamed of yourself. Let my husband go this minute."

Although quite obviously heavily pregnant, she too was bundled into the tender. They were driven to the barracks in Killarney and thrown in the cells.

Later that night when the RIC duty sergeant went to check on them he found Maureen doubled up and groaning with pain. The sergeant knew that he should inform the senior Black and Tan on duty, but he had children of his own and knew that she was in labour. He had also seen enough of their attitude towards the Irish to be fearful of how they might deal with the situation, but involving a civilian doctor could be dangerous both for himself and the doctor if the 'Tans were alerted and decided to take a hand.

So he called the British army base instead. An army doctor was eventually found and examined Maureen. He immediately ordered that she be taken to the local hospital.

But it was too late. The doctors there managed to save the baby, but in spite of the best efforts of all the hospital staff, Maureen Flynn died in childbirth.

# Chapter 46

In early times Jullundur, now known as Jalandhar, in the Punjab, was the capital of a Hindu Kingdom. Even earlier, in the third century BC, the *Jullundur Doab,* a large fertile area around the city, marked the eastern extent of the conquests of Alexander the Great. There followed a succession of Mahommedan and Sikh rulers until the British annexed the Punjab in 1846 at the end of the First Sikh War. The military cantonments situated at the southeast corner of the modern city were built by the British and are still occupied by the Indian Army today. In June 1920 the cantonments were known as Wellington Barracks and housed B Company of the 1$^{st}$ Battalion of the Connaught Rangers. C Company, including privates James Daly and Patrick Coughlin, were stationed some twenty miles away in Solan.

Since the arrival of the Black and Tans in Ireland news of their brutal treatment of the Irish people had been filtering through in letters and newspapers to the Irish soldiers serving in India. Papers such as The Times carried stories of Black and Tan atrocities and the Daily News went so far as to call their behaviour 'organised savagery'. None of this was lost on the Connaught Rangers. Many men of the 1$^{st}$ Battalion had fought for Britain in the First World War, but as a result of the news from home, they were becoming increasingly concerned for their families, and like James Daly, disillusioned with serving The Crown. The thoughts long voiced by Daly were quickly spreading through the ranks.

***

In June, the midday temperature in Solan reached 100 degrees Fahrenheit, but like the hundreds of other Indian men, women and children demonstrating against the Rowlett Act, Abdul Ghaffer Khan showed no sign of being affected by the searing heat.

As the organiser of the peaceful protest he had positioned himself at the front of the crowd and, with them, he sat silently on the ground in the centre of the town, holding up the traffic and putting a stop to every kind of commerce. Indeed, the majority of Solan shopkeepers, stallholders and itinerate tradesmen were taking part in the demonstration. Showing the stoic patience of their race, they waited for the authorities to come and attempt to move them on; a task which the Indian police backed up by British troops would find frustratingly difficult to achieve.

The troops and police duly arrived and went through the by now tediously familiar ritual of trying to break up the 'mob'. The Indian police began by lashing the demonstrators with their bamboo canes, but to no avail, and it soon became obvious that stronger methods would be required. The officer in charge of the British troops ordered his men to fix bayonets. This brought no discernable reaction, so he gave the order for his men to bring their rifles to bear. The sound of the rifle bolts being worked caused a stir among the demonstrators but Ghaffer Khan called on them to remain calm. He was confident that, after the events at Amritsar, no British officer would give the order to fire on unarmed civilians no matter how severe the provocation. This, however, was a game the British officer had played before, and he achieved his first objective: he had identified the ringleader. It now remained for him to arrest this individual and, hopefully, the resolve of the others would gradually evaporate and the situation would become more manageable. He sent in a squad of six men to carry out the arrest.

Two of the soldiers grabbed Ghaffer Khan by the shoulders and hauled him to his feet while the rest of the squad stood guard around them threatening the Indians with fixed bayonets.

"Come on me bucko." The two soldiers dragged their captive out of the by now extremely restless crowd under the protection of their comrades' bayonets.

The crowd began to grow dangerously hostile and the British officer knew that he would need reinforcements to prevent a full scale riot breaking out. He did not know Ghaffer Khan but from the reaction of the crowd he realised that he had got his hands on an Indian agitator of some importance. He ordered the two men holding the captive to take their prisoner to the barracks in one of the army lorries, and lock him in the guardroom. He needed to get the Indian leader out of the way so that he could not cause any more mischief before the reinforcements arrived.

The two soldiers half dragged, half carried Ghaffer Khan to the lorry, heaved him into the back, clambered in after him and shouted to the driver to move off. Once they were under way the prisoner made a point of examining the badges worn by his captors.

"You are Irishmen," he said with a measure of disgust.

"That we are," said Patrick Coughlin, "but sure it's no business of yours."

"Ah but is," the prisoner spoke excellent English with only a slight Indian accent and was obviously an educated man.

"And how do you make that out?" asked James Daly.

"Because you are traitors to your country," the distaste in Ghaffer

Khan's tone was marked. "You serve your British masters here in India while those same British are putting your own people in Ireland to the sword. How can you complain about what the Black and Tans are doing in Ireland while you do exactly the same things here in my country?"

It was plain that this man was not only well educated, but extremely well informed. And he hadn't finished yet:

"I spit on you as treacherous dogs." The spittle splattered Daly's boots.

"Take it easy Jim!" Coughlin expected Daly to explode, but his friend seemed strangely subdued.

After a period of strained silence, an exasperated Daly finally exclaimed: "Jesus Christ Pat, hasn't he hit the nail on the head. Sure we have no right at all to be here."

He turned to Ghaffer Khan. "And we have no right to be holding you prisoner either. I'll tell you what we're going to do: I'm going to tell the driver to slow down and the minute he stops you jump out and run like a hare."

Under other circumstances the prisoner might have feared that he was being released only to be shot down while trying to escape. But he was a good judge of character and he had heard that there was some unrest among the Connaught Rangers; one of his reasons for organising the protest in Solan was to judge the strength of this unrest for himself. They were passing through a well cultivated part of the *Jullundur Doab*. Daly called out to the driver to stop the lorry. Ghaffer Khan jumped out and was soon lost in a patch of tall buffalo grass. As he ran off he could hear a chorus of shouts and curses behind him, but there were no rifle shots.

The identity of the demonstrators' leader was by now known to the authorities, and Daly and Coughlin were called before the Battalion Commander to explain the loss of such an important prisoner. The officer knew of Daly's reputation and the private's widely publicised views on the situation in Ireland, and was sceptical of the story that their captive had feigned sickness but had suddenly run off as soon as they stopped the lorry to examine him.

"Sure didn't the bugger make eejits out of the pair of us sir, and we couldn't shoot him because of standing orders."

The officer knew about the order not to fire on Indian 'natives' unless attacked. He was highly suspicious of the 'Rangers' story but could prove nothing. He did, however, decide that Private Daly would have to be watched.

# Chapter 47

The Black and Tan officer showed every sign of being in a black mood as he sat alone in a first class compartment of the night train from Killarney to Dublin. Under normal circumstances he would have thoroughly enjoyed the prospect of visiting the Irish capital, but this was different. This time he was not going there for a few days leave, but on a permanent posting. And worse still, it was a posting which did not involve the customary promotion. What he found really frustrating, however, was that he knew the posting was merely a convenient way getting him out of Killarney, and he was reasonably certain that the reason behind the move was not the result of any dereliction of duty on his part. On top of that he did not want to leave Killarney; in Killarney he had been in command. Like all Black and Tan local commanders, when it came to dealing with the rebellious Irish, he had complete freedom to follow his own agenda. He was the ultimate authority with the power to decide matters of life and death in the community. And he enjoyed exercising that authority. But in Dublin he would be subject to the orders of several officers senior to him and, even if the tactics for dealing with the Irish were exactly the same, they would not be carried out under his direct orders.

Because he was travelling alone by train, rather than in a lorry or tender full of heavily armed fellow 'Tans, he had been ordered to wear civilian clothing. This made him feel unusually inconspicuous: a fact which was brought home to him when the train stopped at Mallow Junction just after midnight. At Mallow travellers from Cork joined the train, and even at this time of night there were some people waiting to catch the last Dublin train of the day. One man boarded the first class carriage and moved up and down the corridor obviously looking for an empty compartment. Failing to find one to his liking he entered the compartment the officer had considered to be exclusively his. As the stranger entered, he gave the officer no more than a cursory nod, threw his mackintosh onto the luggage rack, sat down and unconcernedly opened a newspaper.

This would never have happened had the Black and Tan been in his distinctive uniform. Nobody would have dared to intrude on his privacy like this, and the fact that someone had, further blackened the officer's mood. He glowered at his fellow traveller, but when this failed to illicit the slightest reaction, he returned to resentfully reviewing the circumstances that had caused what he considered to be a fall from grace.

It had not been entirely his fault that he was being moved, of that he was sure, and what really rankled was the fact that he had not been given a plausible alternative explanation. In fact he had been given no explanation at all. A senior officer had simply arrived at the Killarney barracks and told him that he had been posted to Dublin with immediate effect. As this had happened soon after that bloody woman he had arrested in Beaufort had died in childbirth he could only surmise that it had something to do with her. But she was not the first woman to die in labour in Ireland and she certainly wouldn't be the last. These Irish believed in producing large families and it followed that many women would die in childbirth, whether they had been thrown into the cells or not. That stupid RIC sergeant should have called him immediately. Had his men known about it soon enough they could have quietly removed the woman from the cells and let her die quietly somewhere else. She would not be missed. Or they could have arranged things to make it like look like suicide. But with the bloody regular army involved there had been nothing he could do, even the Black and Tans could not argue with them.

And then there was her Sinn Fein husband, the rebel councillor. The orders to release him had come as a complete surprise. It was not as if he had been in court and found innocent; in the Ireland under Black and Tan rule he would have been deemed to be guilty and that should have been that. The only explanation that made any sense to the officer was that there had been some form of intervention at a very high level; so high that he was not considered senior enough to be enlightened as to who had interceded on the prisoner's behalf.

Another indication of the importance of whoever had been responsible for his removal from his post in Killarney was the attitude of the senior officer who had delivered the news. There had been no suggestion of a reprimand or any question of a fault being found with his conduct, and the senior officer had made no secret of the fact that he resented being obliged to reassign one of his officers. The Black and Tans, in carrying out their assigned duty considered that they were very much a law unto themselves. They were not accustomed to being dictated to by any other authority in Ireland. So the orders had clearly originated in London, and that was a disturbing thought.

The train sped through the night towards Dublin. He glanced across at his unwelcome travelling companion and found that the man had fallen asleep. It grated that anyone should have the nerve to even relax in his presence let alone fall asleep. But being out of uniform he was at a loss to know what to do about it. He resolved than when they arrived in Dublin he would make himself known to the police on duty at the station and have this arrogant Irishman followed. If it transpired that the man lived in Dublin he would be severely dealt with once the officer was back in uniform. He closed his eyes and tried to drop off himself but couldn't. His mind was far too occupied with his personal problems to permit him to sleep. He picked up the newspaper the sleeping man had dropped on the floor and was surprised to find that it was a copy of yesterday's London Times. He had browsed through several articles mostly covering the summer social season in England, before he spotted a headline alluding to 'Further atrocities in Ireland'. He read a few lines which proved to be highly critical of Black and Tan tactics and threw the paper down in disgust. How do these bloody people manage to get away with publishing such blatant lies? They should be made to come over here themselves and see how they liked being constantly attacked by an unseen enemy.

Dawn broke and the early morning sun lit up the city as the train slowed down through the Dublin suburbs. As this was the end of the line, all of the sleepy passengers began to stir and collect up their belongings in preparation for leaving the train.

The Black and Tan officer took his case down from the luggage rack and paid scant attention as the other occupant of the compartment stood and retrieved his coat from the rack. The officer sat down again. His travelling companion moved suddenly and when he officer looked up he found himself being threatened by an army issue revolver.

He started in shock but quickly regained his composure. Surprise was overtaken by anger, how dare this bloody Irishman point a gun at him, a Black and Tan officer. But the man was doing just that; he said nothing but the gun was rock-steady and he clearly meant business. The officer made to rise put was motioned back by a movement of the revolver. The train slowed to a crawl and people were moving in the corridor. The officer thought fast and came to the conclusion that his best chance of getting out of what he realised was a tight corner was to reveal his true identity.

"You would do well to put that gun away my friend," he said with as much menace as he could muster. "I'll have you know that I am a British officer, and you will never get away with this impertinence."

"Sure don't I know very well who you are, you murdering Black and Tan bastard. You killed my sister."

The train lurched to a stop. The officer tried to jump up and grab the gun. Kevin Ryan calmly shot him twice in the chest, dropped the gun, left the train and mingled with the crowd on the platform.

In the investigation which followed several descriptions of the gunman were offered, but none included the fact that the man had a pronounced limp.

# Chapter 48

By late June 1920 Private James Daly was not the only member of the Connaught Rangers to have grave misgivings about serving in India. As the news from home rapidly became worse, an increasing number of the private soldiers were coming to question why they were actively engaged in suppressing the independence movement in India while the Black and Tans were terrorising their own people at home. Things came to a head in Jullundur on July 28th 1920.

After the morning parade at Wellington Barracks, four men of A Company reported to the guardroom and informed the orderly sergeant that they were no longer prepared to serve as British soldiers. As long as the Black and Tans were allowed to terrorise their own country they could not continue to help suppress the independence movement in India. The sergeant decided to lock them in the cells while he sought out the Orderly Officer. Soon the entire company was ordered on parade and one man, Private Moran, asked permission to join the men in the guardroom. The Company Commander, Major Payne, tried but failed, to persuade him to rejoin the parade and when Moran refused he was taken to the cells. Twenty nine other men broke ranks and followed him, the guards on duty dropped their rifles and also joined them. B Company were out on the ranges and when they returned they heard the men in the guardroom singing Irish rebel songs. They stood to attention outside the guardroom and refused orders to return to their quarters. Colonel Deacon informed the men in the guardroom that they were committing mutiny and could face the death penalty. He had the reputation of the regiment at heart and was anxious to put an end to the protest, so he promised that if all the men returned to duty no disciplinary action would ensue. He could not, however, promise to do anything about the situation in Ireland. When it became obvious that he had failed to talk the men round he ordered the officers to leave the vicinity. The mutineers were released and went back to their barracks to plan their next move.

They elected seven men to form an action committee and act as spokesmen. Two men were sent into the town to purchase suitable materials, and from this they produced an Irish republican tricolour which they flew from the barrack flagpole in place of the Union Jack.

A further two men were sent to Solan to inform C Company of the mutiny. They were arrested, but not before they had passed the news to

James Daly. On June 30th Daly led about seventy men to their Commanding Officer and informed him that, in the name of Irish Freedom, they were no longer prepared to obey his orders. They too raised the tricolour. In an effort to prevent bloodshed, which he knew would only lead to the deaths of a large number of the mutineers, a Catholic chaplain, Father Baker, persuaded them to give up their rifles. Daly, however, insisted that they keep their bayonets. They settled down to wait for news from Jullundur.

On July 1st two battalions of British troops arrived at Jullundur and the mutineers there were arrested. In the 100 degree heat they were taken to a nearby hastily constructed detention camp and left in flimsy tents under heavy guard. They began to suffer badly from the heat. The regimental doctor made an official complaint, and when asked by the senior officers to retract he refused. Major Payne called out some of the men by name on the pretence of detailing them for fatigues, but the mutineers realised that the men named included all the members of their action committee and refused to move. The major, in a fit of anger, ordered the guards to raise their rifles and threatened to open fire on the mutineers. At that point another priest intervened. He stood before the 'Rangers and told Major Payne that he would have to shoot him first. Colonel Jackson was informed of the situation and ordered the mutineers back to their tents. There they remained for the next few days before being taken back to Wellington Barracks and locked in one of the huts. During the night some forty seven men, including all those thought to be the leaders of the protest, were returned to the makeshift camp. The tents had been removed and the mutineers were left under guard in the open without food and water. The regimental doctor again complained, but to no avail. After two days the forty-seven men in the camp were offered the chance to end their protest but refused, so they were taken back to the cells and kept away from the rest. Next morning the remaining mutineers, left without effective leadership, accepted the orders of Colonel Deacon and the mutiny at Jullundur was, to all intents and purposes, over. All but one man, who refused to give up and was put in the cells with the forty-seven men already there, were returned to their quarters without punishment.

In the meantime, however, a rumour reached Solan that the mutineers at Jullundur had been shot. James Daly led twenty-seven men armed with bayonets in a raid on the magazine to recover the arms they had given up earlier. They attacked the guards with bayonets and, for the first time in the mutiny blood was shed. During the struggle two men were killed and one was badly wounded. To prevent further bloodshed Father Baker again intervened and persuaded the mutineers to return to their barracks. By now the rest of the company had given up the protest and returned to duty, but

Daly and his men still held out. After two further days of stalemate a battalion of the Royal Sussex Rangers was sent in and overpowered them. The mutineers were taken in chains to join the forty-seven men from Jullundur in Dagshai prison.

In all there were seventy-six Connaught Rangers in the prison including James Daly and Patrick Coughlin. At the subsequent courts martial several death sentences were handed down, but only one was actually carried out. Private James Daly was executed by firing squad on November 2$^{nd}$ 1920.

# Chapter 49

Two days after he had shot the Black and Tan officer, Kevin Ryan travelled down to Beaufort with his mother for Maureen's funeral.

The number of mourners exceeded even the number of people who had helped to celebrate the wedding a mere twelve months before. The church was packed to overflowing for the Requiem Mass and funeral service. Michael sat in a front pew with his parents, Maureen's mother and Kevin. His week-old son slept in Mrs. Flynn's arms. The flickering of the candles, the pungent spicy smell of the incense, the sprinkles of holy water, the tinkle of the sanctuary bell, the solemn words of the priest and the responses of the altar servers all passed him by. He could not take his eyes off the simple coffin and he made no attempt to do so.

None of the mourners at the graveside made an effort to hold back their tears. Michael was aware that people were trying hard not to stare at him. But he knew that their sympathy was genuine and that most of them, particularly the men, experienced difficulty expressing it. And beneath the sympathy there was a deep-seated anger: people knew that Michael had not heard of his wife's death until he got home after the Black and Tans had reluctantly released him from prison. The authorities had not seen fit to inform him themselves while he was still locked up in the barracks.

After the funeral the parish descended en masse on the Flynn's farm. Unlike the previous occasion when they had gathered there, the mood was somber and there was no suggestion of gaiety. Michael gravely received the somewhat embarrassed but heartfelt handshakes from the men, and the tearful hugs and kisses of the women. On the outside he exhibited a calm dignity. Inside, anger, grief and bitterness fought to come to the surface but were manfully suppressed. Over the last two days and nights, and at the funeral, he had cried unashamedly, but gradually the tears dried up.

As soon as he felt that he had done what he felt his duty as chief mourner required, he sought out Kevin Ryan.

"I want to get hold of a gun Kevin, and you're the man to get it for me. And sure you know very well what I want it for."

"Sure of course I do," replied Kevin. "But you're too late Mick, the bastard who caused Maureen's death is already dead. Sure didn't I do for him myself, and I made sure that I made a damn good job of it."

Michael's first reaction to this news was to be extremely angry. "Jesus

Christ, Kevin, you had no right to do that! It was for me to settle up with the bastard."

He suddenly realised that people had heard the outburst and were watching with some curiosity, but he didn't care.

Kevin allowed him to calm down. "Sure that's what I said myself to 'The Big Fella' but he said that the bugger might be gone before you got out of the jail and we should take care of it for you. As soon as he said that, didn't I tell him that if he gave the job to anybody but me I'd shoot him as well."

"What right did Collins have to stick his nose into my business, and how did he know about what happened anyway?" Michael said testily.

"You know very well yourself Mick, that there's hardly anything going on in Ireland that Michael Collins doesn't know about," said Kevin. "And sure sometimes I think he knows about it before it happens. But the thing is, we didn't think that the 'Tans were going let you out once they had their hands on you, even after they killed poor Maureen, Lord have mercy on her."

Even in his state of grief this was something Michael had actually thought about. It was highly unusual for someone, especially a Sinn Fein councillor, to be released so easily by the Black and Tans, whatever the circumstances.

"Anyway," continued Kevin, "The Big Fella' was right. The bastard was being moved out of Killarney double quick, and I barely got to him in time."

"You're not telling me that Collins had a hand in getting me out of jail and having that 'Tan shifted?"

"Jesus no," said Kevin, "even he doesn't have that much power. But it's not the way the 'Tans normally do things, and he's sure that somebody important was behind it. I don't suppose you have any idea who it was?"

Being brought back into the world of the independence struggle cleared Michael's mind. He thought about what Kevin had said and a vague thought began to come to the surface.

"I think I might have an idea about that," he said, "but I'll have to check it out before I say any more. I'll let you and Collins in on it when I know a bit more. I'll be seeing him sometime soon."

"You'll be seeing him tomorrow Mick," said Kevin. "He wants you up in Dublin this minute."

When Michael began to protest Kevin cut him off. "Listen Mick, you can't stay here in Beaufort. The 'Tans are holding back until after the funeral, but they won't wait long before they're after you again, and this time they'll fix you for good. You're too easy to find here in Beaufort. And no matter who it was that spoke up for you before, the bastards won't let things lie after they lost one of their own."

Michael's anger rose up again. "I don't care, let them come, get me a gun and I'll settle things with a few of them before they get me."

Kevin pointed to Michael's mother holding the baby. "You can't think like that anymore Mick, you have a son to mind out for. You're coming up to Dublin with me tonight."

The words struck Michael like a hammer-blow. For the first time since hearing of Maureen's death, the fact that she had left him with a son sank in. He took the baby from Mrs Flynn's arms. He remembered hearing people say that the baby took after his mother, but in his confused state the remarks had not affected him. Now he could see for himself that, even at a mere week old, his son actually did look uncannily like Maureen. It brought back the tears.

Kevin went to speak to Michael's parents and told them that Michael was in grave danger and would have to leave Beaufort immediately. This time there was no question about the fact that the danger was very real. They were anxious to help and, while Mrs Flynn would certainly worry about her son, she was delighted at the prospect of looking after her grandson.

Before he did anything to prepare for his departure, Michael sought out Jack Quinlan and came straight to the point: "Did you go to your man up at the house, Jack, and was it him who told them to let me out of the jail?"

"I did so Mick," said Jack quietly. "I told him that you and your wife were arrested by the Black and Tans the minute you left here that Sunday, and that Maureen was expecting a baby at any minute. After that, all I know for sure is that His Lordship found out that the 'Tans were accusing you of spying on him and he was mad at them for not telling him about it."

Michael was far from satisfied. "There must be more to it than that Jack. Somebody spoke up for me or I'd still be in jail, and you and him are the only ones I can think of who would do it."

"Well I'd say for sure that you're right there Mick. Didn't I tell you before that he's not altogether happy about the way that the 'Tans are carrying on. I'd say that he used his influence somewhere, but one thing is certain, he'll never tell the likes of you and me about it. He can't be seen taking your side against the 'Tans."

Michael could understand that, and he had heard enough to be sure that he owed Jack Quinlan yet another debt of gratitude.

Some of the mourners left to attend to the ritual of the evening milking. As they were leaving, a Crossley tender loaded with Black and Tans drove slowly past and parked menacingly a few hundred yards up the narrow unpaved road. Kevin held a quick whispered conference with a few local men and they nodded. Mr Flynn and some men went across the road to bring in the cows for milking from the field on the far side. In the few minutes while the animals blocked the road a car drove into the farmyard. Michael and Kevin got in and the car sped off. There were shouts from the Black and Tans and the car was followed by a number of ineffective rifle shots. As soon as the road was clear of cows the enraged 'Tans burst into the yard, turned everybody out and lined them up in front of the barn. There then began an exhaustive and destructive search of the house and farm buildings. Suddenly there was a shout and a man on a bicycle shot out from behind the cowshed and cycled frantically off towards the Gap of Dunloe. By the time the Black and Tan officer had gathered up his men, loaded them into the tender, and ordered them to give chase, the man had a good head start. They followed the cyclist for some minutes gaining rapidly. But the officer, a replacement for the man Kevin Ryan had killed, was new to Ireland. He carelessly followed the fugitive through a small wood and foolishly led his men straight into an IRA ambush.

Later that evening they limped back into Killarney with one man dead and two others seriously wounded.

Michael and Kevin were not driven directly to Dublin. The car that had picked them up from the Flynn farm could not hope to reach the capital undetected as a description of it and its occupants would certainly soon be circulated. They were driven by a circuitous route to Killorglin where Kevin waited for his mother to join him the next day. Michael was taken on to Tralee and a train for Dublin.

***

Michael Collins' sorrow for Michael's loss was heartfelt, and he also expressed his sympathy for the Ryans. "That's makes two members of that good Irish family who have died for their country," he said sadly.

He changed the subject. "With everything that has been happening lately Michael, I don't suppose that you've heard the news from India."

When Michael said that he hadn't, Collins told him what he knew about the mutiny of the Connaught Rangers. He concluded his account by saying: "For obvious reasons the British are doing their best to cover the affair up, but the full story is beginning to come out. It appears that two of the mutineers are the men who were arrested in Killarney. In any case we will certainly be able to make capital out of it."

It was another demonstration of how well informed Collins was, but Michael was more concerned about whether Jack Quinlan had heard the news.

"I'll have to talk to someone I know about that when I get back to Beaufort," he said.

Collins grew serious. "You won't be going back to Beaufort for some time Michael. After what happened there, the only safe place for you is in America. By now you will be high on the Black and Tans wanted list and if they find you they will certainly shoot first and ask questions afterwards. Besides, we can't afford to hand them a coup by catching you. You'll do far more good for The Republic by being free over there than you ever could dead or in gaol here. In spite of my views on his methods, Eamonn de Valera is raising a great deal of sympathy for our cause among the Americans. Just think of what the reaction will be when they hear your story. They will see it a prime example of the kind of thing the Connaught Rangers were complaining about, and it will add credibility to the mutineers' actions. It may well also do those men some good because with any luck at all, the British will find it very difficult to justify treating them harshly."

Michael tried to protest but 'The Big Fella' cut him off: "This is not a request Michael. And in any case it's for the best. I'm not just thinking about The Cause here. It's best for you and your family too and certainly for your baby son. But, Please God, it won't be too long before you can come back to him."

It was time for Michael Flynn to become 'Father Flaherty' once again. Disguised as the priest, he travelled to Southampton and boarded a transatlantic liner bound for New York. The ship called at Queenstown in Cork. Immediately after they sailed he changed back into his own clothes and mingled with the Irish emigrants who had joined the ship there. As a priest he would almost certainly have been called on to perform some holy office on the voyage. He changed back again as they docked so the priest on the passenger list was seen to leave the ship. It also facilitated his entry into The United States: he was quickly processed through while the immigrants waited in line at Ellis Island. Michael was met by James Quinlan. After he had welcomed his old friend, James broke the news that there had been a price to pay for Michael's escape.

The Flynn farm had been burned as a reprisal by the Black and Tans. No one had been hurt but the house was badly damaged. Until it was made habitable again, Michael's mother and son were staying in the cottage with the Quinlans.

# Epilogue

## *New York City, November 1920*

*Michael Flynn sat in a bar in New York with James Quinlan and Pete Casey, James' old friend from his days at the munitions factory at Gretna and now a New York policeman. There had been an awkward moment earlier in the day when Michael was introduced to Pete's wife, Sara, the former security officer at Gretna. It was Sara who had suspected Maureen of being an Irish nationalist spy and had warned James that he was being hunted. But Sara was completely friendly and genuinely sympathetic for Michael's loss.*

*He had spent the last three months travelling across America with Eamonn de Valera speaking about his experiences, raising awareness of the plight of the Irish, and drumming up support for recognition of the fledgling Republic. To begin with, he felt less than comfortable talking about his internment and life in Ireland under British rule. He could describe the actions of the Black and Tans in general terms, but it took some time before he felt able to relate to anyone, de Valera included, the circumstances surrounding Maureen's death. Although he never mentioned the tragedy in his speech, there always seemed to be someone in the audience who had heard of the affair and who would ask a question. Eventually it dawned on Michael that de Valera was in the habit of 'planting' people in the audience to ask pre-prepared questions and at that point he felt that he had no choice but to bring the subject up himself. When he did, his feelings came to the surface and had the effect de Valera was hoping for.*

*In other ways he soon discovered that this was a much different de Valera from the man he had met in Lincoln prison. For one thing Michael was never allowed to mention to anyone his part in 'Dev's' escape from the British gaol. The man's enormous ego would not allow him to concede that he had been obliged to rely on outside help. It became clear to Michael that this ego was the principal reason behind de Valera's unfortunate habit of rubbing important people up the wrong way, and why Michael Collins became so frustrated at some of his leader's activities. At the beginning of his tour it was also made clear to Michael that he was very much a junior member of the Irish Republican delegation in America. But whatever his faults de Valera was the President of the Irish Republic, and in Michael's view, still his country's best chance of gaining its freedom.*

*James Quinlan was Michael's link with home. Letters to and from Beaufort were passed via James and, even if it caused delays, everyone concerned realised that it was a wise precaution. The last letter from home had included a photograph of his mother holding his infant son. The picture had been taken at the baby's christening. In Catholic Ireland it was the custom to have babies baptised within a few days of birth, and not knowing when or indeed if, he would be able to return home Michael had asked for the sacrament to be administered in his absence. Compared with his parent's wedding and his mother's funeral, Sean Flynn's baptism had been a quiet affair. He was christened Sean after Maureen's father.*

*"Sure he's a fine looking fella," said Pete Casey as Michael passed round the photograph.*

*"That he is," said James, "and for sure he takes after his mother, God rest her soul." Fearing that he had said something that might upset Michael he added: "I'm sorry Mick, sure I didn't mean to bring back any hard memories."*

*But Michael shook his head: "That's all right Jim; a few months ago it was hard for me to even hear her name. But now sure wouldn't I rather people spoke about Maureen out loud, than whispering it so that I can't hear them."*

*Pete had been the first of the trio to come to New York and on his arrival in he had searched out and found a bar that sold Guinness. He raised his glass. "Well here's to him anyway. And to yourself Mick, I suppose you'll be off around America again any minute trying to convert these heathen Yanks to Ireland's cause."*

*Michael gazed at the picture of his son. "No," he said. "Eamonn de Valera is going back to Ireland soon, and whatever anybody has to say about it, I'm going with him."*

*The rest I pass, one sentence I unsay. Had de Valera eaten Parnell's heart No loose-lipped demagogue had won the day, No civil rancor torn the land apart.*

*(W.B. Yeats from 'Parnell's Funeral')*

# Authors Notes and Acknowledgements

It is important to note that this book is a work of fiction albeit based on factual events in Irish history. Some of the fictional characters are based on members of my own family although, as in my previous book, the family name has been altered. Private James Daly and the major political figures apart, all of the other characters are fictional, and any resemblance to any person living or dead, is purely coincidental.

As ever, placing fictional characters into real historical events presents certain difficulties and requires the author to apply a little artistic licence, but I sincerely hope that I have not played fast and loose with Irish history. For example Eamonn de Valera did escape from Lincoln Prison, but there is no evidence of a priest, real or otherwise, being involved. It is said that he escaped using a key smuggled in to him in a cake. Michael Flynn and Kevin Ryan are purely fictional characters and to the best of my knowledge nobody bearing those names were ever associated with Michael Collins. I learned my Irish history at school, and from knowing and talking to people who had lived through the period covered in the book. As with the first book 'The Last Coachman'. Wherever I needed a reminder or confirmation, however, I turned to **Tim Pat Coogan's** excellent **'Ireland in the Twentieth Century'**.

I am again grateful to **Donald and Rachel Cameron** for allowing me to set the story in and around **Beaufort House**. Details can be found at: www.beaufortireland.com

Further information on life in the **Royal Tank Corps** is available from the **Tank Museum** website: www.tankmuseum.org

Thanks to the staff at **Olympia Publishers** for their help and assistance.

And last but by no means least a big thank you to my wife, **Shireen**, for her encouragement, help, and support.

**James Daly and the Connaught Rangers:**

Information on the regiment and in particular the mutiny is, perhaps understandably, sparse. After a trawl through several internet sites, however, I have put together what I believe to be a reasonably historically accurate account of their story. These sites include www.hubsites.com, www.answers.com, www.independent.co.uk, www.homepage.eircom.net, www.1914-1918.com.

I tried and failed to find any official accounts of the mutiny, but in any case I was more interested in the events leading up to it and the reasons behind it. Private **James Daly** who was deemed to be the ringleader is reputed to be the last man shot for mutiny in the British Army. There is no evidence that he ever served in Mesopotamia although the regiment certainly did and several hundred of its men lie buried there. My story of Daly being arrested in Ireland, and the supposition that Ghaffer Khan was involved in the mutiny are pure fiction.

Attempts are still being made to obtain a pardon for Private Daly.

## The Easter Rising

Easter 1916 is one of the most important, if not the most important date in Irish history. The armed rebellion known as The Easter Rising is often said to have been 'The Birth of the Irish Republic' and the repercussions are still felt today.

The Rising was planned by the Irish Republican Brotherhood Military Council led by, among others, Padraig Pearse, James Connolly, Thomas Clarke and Sean Mac Dermott. Originally planned to take place on Easter Sunday April 23rd, The Rising had to be postponed to Monday when a shipment of German arms arranged by Sir Roger Casement was intercepted by the British Royal Navy. There was also some confusion caused by Eoin MacNeill, leader of the Irish Volunteer Force, who was opposed to taking military action while Britain was still engaged in the First World War, and who issued a series of conflicting orders to The Volunteers. Initially many other Irishmen were opposed to military action in support of Independence; they felt that they should be supporting Britain in the war against Germany, but eventually those who saw 'England's difficulty as Ireland's opportunity' gathered enough support to mount The Rising.

Mainly confined to Dublin, where the insurgents took over and barricaded themselves in several prominent buildings including the General Post Office, The Rising lasted for some five days until the leaders surrendered to British forces. The actual military action failed, but Pearse and the others achieved their principal objective of a 'blood sacrifice'. Harsh British reprisals following the military defeat of the rebels served to drastically alter Irish attitudes towards British rule and support for independence increased dramatically. Today the executed leaders of The Rising are regarded as Irish martyrs.

## W. B. Yeats

*William Butler Yeats (1865-1939)* was a noted Irish poet and dramatist whose family probably came to Ireland from Yorkshire in the late seventeenth century. Yeats' father, John Butler Yeats, and his brothers were well known painters, but he preferred literature and was responsible for numerous plays and poems. His poetry was heavily influenced by the people around him, and he had a particular interest in Irish folklore. He wrote for an Irish audience and set out to create a unique Irish literature.

As a young man he met and fell in love with the Irish revolutionary Maude Gonne. Much of his poetry is dedicated to her and he proposed to her on three occasions but was rejected. In 1917 he married Georgie Hyde-Lees with whom he had two children. His wife was also a talented writer and collaborated in several of his later poems including *The Tower*. This proved to be his last poem and was inspired by the Norman stone tower called *Thoor Ballylee* near Goole Park in County Galway that he bought as a family home.

He became a Senator of the Irish Free State and chaired a committee that designed Irish coinage. He obtained honorary degrees from Queen's University College, Belfast and from University College, Dublin. He won a Nobel Prize for Literature and created the Irish Academy of Letters.

In later life he suffered from ill-health and spent his winters in Italy and in France. On 28<sup>th</sup> January 1939 he died at Roquebrune-Cap-Martin where he was buried. But in 1948 his body was exhumed and moved to Drumcliffe in County Sligo in accordance with his wishes to 'lie under Ben Bulben's Head in Drumcliff churchyard'.

His epitaph reads: *Cast a cold eye on life,on death. Horseman, pass by.*

The verses quoted in this book are taken from: W.B. Yeats, Selected Poetry, edited by A. Norman Jeffares (Pan Books Ltd. 1974)